THE BILLIONAIRE'S TRUST

ERIN SWANN

SWANN PUBLICATIONS

This book is a work of fiction. The characters, locals, businesses, and events portrayed in this book are fictitious. Any similarity to real persons, living or dead, businesses, events, or locals is coincidental and not intended by the author.

Cover image licensed from Shutterstock.com

Cover design by Swann Publications

Edited by Jessica Royer Ocken

ISBN-10 197391316X

ISBN-13 978-1973913160

The following story is intended for mature readers, it contains mature themes, strong language, and sexual situations. All characters are 18+ years of age, and all sexual acts are consensual.

Find out more at:

WWW.ERINSWANN.COM

Created with Vellum

ALSO BY ERIN SWANN

Chosen by the Billionaire - Available on Amazon

(Steven and Emma's story) The youngest of the Covington clan, he avoided the family business to become a rarity, an honest lawyer. He didn't suspect that pursuing her could destroy his career. She didn't know what trusting him could cost her.

Previously titled: The Youngest Billionaire

The Secret Billionaire – Available on Amazon, also in AUDIOBOOK

(Patrick and Elizabeth's story) Women naturally circled the flame of wealth and power, and his is brighter than most. Does she love him? Does she not? There's no way to know. When he stopped to help her, Liz mistook him for a carpenter. Maybe this time he'd know. Everything was perfect. Until the day she left.

The Billionaire's Hope - Available on Amazon

(Nick and Katie's story) They came from different worlds. She hadn't seen him since the day he broke her brother's nose. Her family retaliated by destroying his life. She never suspected where accepting a ride from him today would take her. They said they could do casual. They lied.

Previously titled: Protecting the Billionaire

Picked by the Billionaire – Available on Amazon

(Liam and Amy's story) A night she wouldn't forget. An offer she couldn't refuse. He alone could save her, and she held the key to his survival. If only they could pass the test together.

Saved by the Billionaire – Available on Amazon

(Ryan and Natalie's story) The FBI and the cartel were both after her for the same thing: information she didn't have. First, the FBI took everything, and then the cartel came for her. She trusted Ryan with her safety, but could she trust him with her heart?

Caught by the Billionaire – Available on Amazon

(Vincent and Ashley's story) Her undercover assignment was simple enough: nail the crooked billionaire. The surprise came when she opened the folder, and the target was her one-time high school sweetheart. What will happen when an unknown foe makes a move to checkmate?

The Driven Billionaire – Available on Amazon

(Zachary and Brittney's story) Rule number one: hands off your best friend's sister. With nowhere to turn when she returns from upstate, she accepts his offer of a room. Mutual attraction quickly blurs the rules. When she comes under attack, pulling her closer is the only way to keep her safe. But, the truth of why she left town in the first place will threaten to destroy them both.

Nailing the Billionaire – Available on Amazon

(Dennis and Jennifer's story) She knew he destroyed her family. Now she is close to finding the records that will bring him down. When a corporate shakeup forces her to work with him, anger and desire collide. Vengeance was supposed to be simple, swift, and sweet. It was none of those things.

Undercover Billionaire – Available on Amazon

(Adam and Kelly's story) Their wealthy families have been at war forever. When Kelly receives a chilling note, the FBI assigns Adam to protect her. Family histories and desire soon collide, causing old truths to be questioned. Keeping ahead of the threat won't be their only challenge.

Trapped with the Billionaire – Available on Amazon

(Josh and Nicole's story) Nicole returns from vacation to find her company has been sold to Josh's family. Being assigned to work for the new CEO is only the first of her problems. Competing visions of how to run things and mutual passion create a volatile mix. The reappearance of a killer from years ago soon threatens everything.

Saving Debbie – Available on Amazon

(Luke and Debbie's story) On the run from her family and the cops, Debbie finds the only person she can trust is Luke, the ex-con who patched up her injuries. Old lies haunt her, and the only way to unravel them is to talk with Josh, the boy who lived through the nightmare with her years ago.

Return to London – Available on Amazon

(Ethan and Rebecca's story) Rebecca looks forward to the most important case of her career. Until, she is paired with Ethan, the man she knew years ago. Mutual attraction and old secrets combine to complicate everything. What could have been a second chance results in an impossible choice.

The Rivals – Available on Amazon

(Charlie and Danielle's story) He was her first crush. That ended when their families had a falling out. Now, they are forced to work together on a complicated acquisition. Mutual attraction is complicated by distrust as things go wrong around them. A second chance turns into an impossible choice.

CHAPTER 1

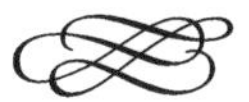

Bill

Monica had come back. The lavender scent she wore floated in the air as she leaned in. The din of the other customers receded for a moment when her warm tit brushed against my arm, intentionally for sure.

Her weapon of choice tonight was a sexy red dress cut even lower than the last one, showing cleavage deep enough to create its own gravity well, deep enough to get lost in.

She licked her lips. "I always know what I want," she said in a husky voice.

Two nights ago, when she had first appeared at the restaurant, she'd asked to speak to the owner to gripe about her scallopini and then flirted with me when I came over to hear her complaint. The dish had been prepared just the way it should've been, and it had been hard to focus on her words with her cleavage right over the plate. Was she a D or maybe a double-D? Who knows, but certainly more than a handful, and with nipples protruding through her tight black dress, it had been difficult to keep my eyes up. Distracting as hell.

In college, my fraternity brothers had kept up a running debate on whether more than a handful was wasted. Even though I'd attended an all-boys Catholic high school, my vote always surprised them. I was firmly on the *more is wasted* side. They generally favored the *more is the better* option, and Monica definitely had more.

Ever since I'd broken up with Cynthia last year, my mode of operation had been *C-E-D*: charm, enjoy, and discard—— though I wasn't into one-night stands. It took more than one night to truly enjoy a woman, to learn what pleasures she had to offer, and to show her the pleasures I could offer her. A week or two was good, but beyond that, it was time to move on.

However, the last few weeks had not allowed me the time to even get through C, much less to E with anyone. Too much work and too little play had made Bill grumpy…and horny.

Monica wore too much makeup for my taste, but she was certainly a willing candidate. My usual rule was to avoid entanglements with any of the guests at our restaurant, but she looked like she would do her best to be an *E*-ticket ride—something to distract me and allow for some exercise. Taking things in hand, so to speak, had been okay for a few days, but it didn't get the job done over the long haul.

Getting to the question of her place or mine took but a millisecond with Monica, and she managed to put her hand on my arm twice and my thigh three times on the short drive over. This girl was beyond eager.

Once we arrived, I turned the key and held the door to my condo open for her.

Once again, she managed to brush against my thigh as she passed. She sashayed over to the full-length window overlooking the city, swaying her hips seductively. No doubt this woman knew I was watching her, and she knew precisely what she was doing. What man could resist?

"This is so beautiful," she called from the window. "Look at that view."

I had become rather immune to the skyline. "Sure is, and it looks even better when the wind clears out the smog layer."

"I don't see how it could get any better. You're so lucky to see the city like this."

I opened the wine fridge and took out two bottles. "White or red?" I held up one of each.

She hesitated. "Red, so it won't matter if I spill on my dress." She giggled.

A real genius, this one, but that wouldn't matter when her clothes came off.

I carried over two glasses of the well-aged cabernet and motioned to the couch.

As soon as I sat, she kicked off her heels and drained her glass with one hand while the other found my thigh, inching up little by little. I was already getting hard.

Her left hand made its way to my crotch. "My, what do we have here?" she purred as she licked at my ear and rubbed her tit against me again.

I grew harder by the second. This vixen liked to take charge, but little did she know that would change in a few minutes. I got up and sipped more of my wine as I led her toward the bedroom.

Such a waste. I had opened a superb cabernet, but we had no time to enjoy it.

She put her glass down as we entered the bedroom. "Why don't you use the bathroom first, and I'll go second?"

"Just make yourself comfortable," I said as I rounded the corner into the master bath.

I could hear her unzipping her dress as I slid out of my jacket and brushed my teeth. When I returned, she was removing her lacy red bra, and she looked me up and down hungrily, finally focusing on the bulge in my pants.

"Ooh la la, am I going to have fun tonight," she announced.

Clad in only a pair of panties that read *ALL YOU CAN EAT* in black lettering, she traced her finger across my chest on her way to the bathroom, rubbing the tip of her tit against my arm yet again as she passed. It didn't look it, but it felt real.

Eager for her return, I picked her dress up off the floor, folded it, and placed it on the chair along with the bra.

Then I saw it.

She had placed her phone on the shelf up behind the chair and balanced it oddly on edge. I picked it up. It was recording video, and she had pointed it straight at the bed.

The fucking bitch.

Of course. This had been way too easy. She'd planned to set me up for blackmail. I killed the recording and turned off the phone, placing it right back where it had been. I clenched my jaw. After those panties, what a temptation she had become.

I fished out my phone and started the audio recorder to protect myself, placing it face down on my dresser.

Two can play this game.

I composed myself just as she rounded the corner, returning from the bathroom.

I handed her lacy red bra back to her. "Put this back on. You're moving a little too fast."

Her perky smile faded to a frown.

"Put it back on and let's do this right." I pointed to the kitchen. "Let me get the champagne."

A smile returned to her face. "Aren't you the charming one?"

I found a bottle of Moet, uncorked it, and returned from the kitchen with two glasses. I poured the champagne and handed her a glass.

"To fame and fortune." I lifted my glass to hers.

"To fame and fortune," she said with a devilish smirk.

She was hoping for a quick fortune in her future. After a sip, I traced across her thigh with my free hand and stood.

"Do you like caviar?"

She shivered at my touch. "Sure." Her eyes lit up.

I returned to the kitchen with a smirk of my own, grabbing a can of Beluga caviar from the fridge along with the cream cheese. I picked up her clutch from beside the couch as I got a box of water crackers and put six on a plate.

"What is taking so long? I'm getting lonely in here," she called from the bedroom.

"Doing caviar right takes a few minutes," I answered. I spread a bit of cream cheese on each of the crackers and placed them around the tin of caviar on the plate. A small spoon in the caviar finished the preparation as I located her driver's license in the clutch. Rather than *Monica,* she was Katya Droznik from Pasadena, and she had turned thirty-one last month. I replaced the license and carried the caviar toward the bedroom.

"I think you'll like this," I told her. "Fresh Beluga."

She was sitting up on the bed with a refilled glass of champagne. "Took you long enough," she pouted, patting the bed beside her. She had put her bra back on.

"Like I said, some things can't be hurried." I set the plate down on the nightstand and took up my glass. "Hold still." I dabbed my finger in the bubbly and traced a circle of champagne over the swell of her left breast. "Don't move."

She trembled and giggled.

I sniffed the champagne circle, taking in her scent as she blushed and giggled some more. "You smell delectable, but you need to hold still." I repeated the procedure with the other breast, getting another shiver from her. I licked the champagne off her breasts to even more giggles.

I took a cracker and dabbed caviar on top. "Do you like caviar?"

She smiled. "You bet, and I can think of something better to lick it off of than a silly cracker."

This one was full of the devil. "Well, Monica…" I said, raising my glass to hers for another toast. "To truth or consequences."

"Truth or consequences," she repeated with an amused look as we both sipped.

"Want the caviar, Monica?" I held the cracker up in front of her. "What's your last name?"

"It's sort of silly." Another giggle.

"Go ahead. Try me." *Will she go with truth or consequences?*

"Dempster, and don't laugh."

Consequences it is then. "Strike one." I pulled back the cracker and put it in my mouth, savoring the salty taste.

"What the hell?" she almost screamed. Her amused look was now more dumbfounded.

"I can tell when a woman is lying to me." I spooned caviar on another cracker. "Next chance, Monica. Where do you live?" I held the cracker up but pulled it back as she grabbed for it. "Now, now, hold still. Where do you live?"

Indecision clouded her eyes as she pondered her answer. "Santa Monica," she said with a quiver.

"Strike two." She had chosen consequences again. I slid the second cracker into my mouth.

Her demeanor was moving steadily toward angry as she gulped down more champagne. "Why'd you bring in that damn caviar if you're not going to give me any?" She painted a pout on her face and slid her hand up my thigh.

I brushed her hand away. "You need to follow the rules, Monica."

"I don't like these rules. I want to play." She reached for me again as I got off the bed.

I spooned caviar on the third cracker. "Monica?" This was going to be the killer question, the hardest for her. "How old are you?"

"You should be able to tell I'm not jail-bait," she spat, the anger surfacing again.

"How old, Monica?"

"Twenty-seven, if you must know." She looked like a frightened little girl trying to put one over on the teacher.

This time, I put the cracker back on the plate and laid the plate down. My aching cock was going to have to wait another day. I stood and grabbed her phone from the shelf. "Strike three."

I walked over and dropped her phone in my aquarium.

She shot up off the bed. "You fucking asshole. That's a new phone," she screamed.

I threw her dress at her. "Get the hell out of my house, thirty-one-year-old Katya from Pasadena."

The shock instantly turned her white. She slipped the dress over her head and shimmied into it.

"You can zip it up outside. Get the hell out," I shouted, pointing to the door.

Her face was priceless. She rushed to the aquarium.

"Those are lionfish in there. Their sting is deadly."

The color drained from her face. She hesitated as she peered into the tank.

"Put your hand in there and sign your own death warrant."

I was exaggerating. The sting hurt like hell and might kill a small child, but a grown woman would just be miserable for a few days. Very miserable.

She continued to gaze into the tank. I didn't think she could get any whiter, but she did.

"You fucker. Who keeps fish like that?" For a second, it appeared she might tempt fate.

"The kind you don't mess with. Now get the hell out." I grabbed her wrap, opened the door, and threw it into the hall. "Out!"

"Fuck you." She stopped trying to get her heels back on and scurried out the door as I swatted her on the ass. "Fucking asshole," she added as I slammed the door behind her.

"I may be an asshole, Katya, but I didn't fuck you."

CHAPTER 2

LAUREN

I WAS RUNNING LATE AGAIN. THE LINE AT STARBUCKS HAD BEEN longer than usual this morning. I held a grande, five-pump hazelnut, half-caf, soy latte, extra hot, with a dash of cinnamon for my boss in one hand as I juggled my purse and the marketing presentation I had worked on last night in the other.

As I rounded the corner into marketing, Marissa Bitz, my boss at Covington Industries, tapped her foot, waiting for me. She greeted me with her usual charm.

"You're late again, Zumwalt." She was only about three inches shorter than me, but all of us towered over her in the flats she wore to work——something about bad ankles that we didn't care to have explained to us.

Welcome to my world. This job offered the best pay in the city for somebody at my level, but the worst boss. She was a total bitch and lazy as hell, but it could have been worse. At least she didn't have BO, a pot belly, a receding hairline, and hit on me.

Thank God for small miracles.

Her Highness waited for me to deliver her coffee, eyeing me

over the ugly horn-rimmed glasses that made her look even older than her forty years.

"I'm sorry, Marissa. The new barista was a little slow today." We'd been told to call our boss by her first name. It was too easy for her last name to come out sounding like the *bitch* we all knew she was.

She took a sip of the latte I handed her. Her face curled into a sneer as she spat it into my trashcan. "This isn't right. How many times do I have to tell you five pumps, not four, and definitely not six?" Her face reddened. "Take this back right now and get it right."

She shoved the cup back at me, a splash of coffee landing on my blouse as I grabbed it before it hit the floor. Two weeks ago, I hadn't been fast enough, and I'd been the one blamed for the spill on the carpet outside my cubicle.

I bit my tongue briefly. "Right away, Marissa" came out of my mouth, while my brain said, *"get it yourself, bitch."* I had learned the hard way that she did this about once a week to exert power over us peons.

The first time she'd done it, I'd protested that I *had* gotten it right, and Mt. Vesuvius had nothing on the Marissa eruption that had ensued. I was not going down that road again today. Brandon needed me to keep this job.

Jimmy, the other newbie in the office, gave me a consoling look as I turned and headed back to the elevator on my assigned coffee run for the witch. Harold had been the most recent marketing grunt to graduate out of coffee runs, and he had confided in me that it went easier for him when he learned to bring back a venti on the return run instead of the original grande.

I will not be trained so easily.

She had such rotten taste in coffee. I always dumped the "bad" latte in the trash as I left the elevator and headed across the street for the second cup. I contemplated my revenge as the elevator passed the floors with a series of dings. I could swat a fly or two and add them to her coffee next time she sent me back like this, or maybe I'd add a worm.

The door opened, and I started out. I looked down at the cup, smirking to myself. Flies in her latte. That would serve the witch right.

I ran straight into him.

The lid was still on the coffee, so it didn't spill on his jacket or my blouse. But I lost my grip on the cup and jumped back instinctively. The collision with the floor was too much for the plastic-and-cardboard contraption and its contents splashed, getting both of our shoes. I was so caught up in my revenge fantasy, I hadn't been looking where I was going.

"I'm so sorry, miss," he said.

"No, it was my fault. I'm the one that wasn't looking." I still wasn't looking up.

I used the one napkin I'd been carrying to blot the coffee off my shoes and ankles. Gus, the security guy from the front desk, rushed over with some paper towels.

The guy I'd bumped in to handed me a handkerchief. "Here, use this." His voice was low and cool like a chocolate sundae.

I nearly melted when I stopped long enough to get a look at him: not a guy, a man, Adonis in the flesh. He had a chiseled jawline, short stubble, kissable lips——the lower one a little pouty, a crop of slightly windswept light brown hair, and wide linebacker shoulders, all covered in a blazer with no tie and the top few buttons of his shirt open, showing just a hint of chest hair. I lost my breath and all rational thought. Blue eyes, like warm tropical water, smiled back at me. A smile to die for. A smile to make your pants fall down, and dimples cute enough to cause instant paralysis.

He introduced himself as Bill.

I couldn't get my brain-to-mouth connection to work for shit with my few remaining functioning neurons.

"Lauren," I mumbled, trembling as I leaned over to concentrate on mopping up the witch's coffee before I made a bigger fool of myself.

When I looked back up, the elevator door was closing.

He was gone.

Shit.

I was a complete fucking dork. I didn't even get his whole name or what floor he worked on.

Gus and I finished the cleanup, and I realized Bill had disappeared without retrieving his handkerchief. As I walked across the street to Starbucks, I wondered how I could find out where Bill worked in the building? I would have to get his handkerchief back to him——after I cleaned it, of course.

What a fucking klutz.

Could I possibly have made a worse impression?

CHAPTER 3

Bill

I WAS RUNNING LATE FOR MY MEETING WITH DAD.

I should have stayed to help clean up that spill.

As the elevator passed the fourth floor, I hit the button for six and got off short of my destination. I caught the other elevator on the down trip, but when the door opened to the lobby, she was nowhere to be seen. I had missed her and made myself even later for the meeting I was dreading.

Back upstairs, I entered the office and my father rose to greet me with his usual firm handshake and pat on the shoulder. Maybe this wasn't what I thought. No sense jumping to conclusions too quickly.

"Sorry I'm late, Dad. I had a little mishap in the lobby."

"No problem, Bill. Did you get a chance to think over what we talked about on Monday?"

Wendell Covington deserved his reputation for being direct.

"Dad, I told you *no* last time I was here, and as I recall, I was clear that I didn't need to think it over."

Direct was also the best way to handle my father, but I was not always sure who was handling whom.

"Son, you know your destiny is with the company your grandfather and I built, and starting with the food division we're buying is a perfect way to get comfortable with the workings here. It's also a good fit with that restaurant you're tinkering with."

There it was in black and white: my restaurant could be extremely profitable, win awards, and get great write-ups, and it would still be too little to register with the great Wendell Covington. To him, I was just tinkering. But before long, I would surprise him with what I could accomplish. I just needed some time.

"Dad, for the hundredth time, I need to do things my way." He never saw my way as fitting with his way. "In time, I'll make my mark, and then I'll feel more comfortable joining you here."

"I wish you would see the value of joining the business now. Talk to your brother Liam. He's making a real difference here."

My stepbrother, Liam, had joined Dad straight out of college, but he was the round peg for the round hole, and I was the square peg at this point. Couldn't Dad see that this constant pressure was just pissing me off?

"Sure, I'll talk to him," I spat.

No danger that Liam would try to change my mind——he and I had always been close due to our similar ages.

"And Patrick is coming up to speed fast in London, but you're the oldest," Dad continued.

Like I needed to be reminded again that in this family, the eldest had extra responsibilities. Patrick was younger than Liam and older than Steven, and Dad always seemed to forget about my poor sister, Katie. It was like the English monarchy. Girls didn't count.

I felt envious of Katie, in a way. She didn't have an expectation to live up to, and she wasn't required to be a part of the family business. She and my youngest brother, Steven, had been "allowed" to pursue alternative career paths. Katie was an accountant, and Steven was finishing his law degree.

I changed the subject. "By the way, is Uncle Garth around? I have a quick finance question for him."

Not true, but it might get me out of here, and I needed to escape before I said something I would regret.

My father shifted in his seat and smiled. "Sorry, Bill. He's on a trip to Asia right now." Rising to shake my hand, he seemed to be giving up for now. "We have a dinner planned for Sunday. It would be great if you could join us."

I lied. "Sure thing, Dad. Love to."

The dinner would be fine, but this was his way of telling me he didn't think this discussion had come to the proper conclusion.

We shook hands, father, and son. We weren't that different. At least I came by my stubbornness honestly.

I closed the door on my way to Liam's office.

He hasn't won this round.

LATER THAT NIGHT, I FINALLY POURED MYSELF A DRINK AFTER THE dinner rush at the restaurant, which had been hectic as usual. I was ready to call it a night when my partner, Marco Cardinelli, came over to join me. Marco and I had been friends since high school, and as long as he didn't get too drunk, he was great to be around.

"So how did the meeting with your father go today?" Marco asked as he ordered a glass of Gold Label.

I had contented myself with Black Label tonight. "The same old thing. He wants to get me into the company and doesn't accept that I'm not ready yet."

Marco waited patiently for more detail, ever the good listener.

"And he wants me to join him for dinner on Sunday when Uncle Garth is back so they can both give me the hard sell." I scratched my head, done talking.

"So, you going?"

My belly tightened at the prospect. "To dinner, yes, but I'm not budging until we finish the project."

Marco seemed deep in thought for a moment. "Maybe you could start part-time and get him off your back. You'd still have time for this place and the project. You know I can do this place pretty much single-handed anyway."

"Not happening. The project comes first."

It was true that Marco was mostly ready to handle the restaurant by himself, but joining the family business had to be on my terms and my timing, not Dad's. He'd always taught me to stand up for what I believed in and not let others dissuade me from what I knew was right. Well, this time, his advice was going to work against him, because I knew what was right for me.

Marco raised his glass. "To the project."

"To the project," I agreed and took a good slug down the hatch, the burn of the scotch helping to steel my resolve.

I had been down this road with my father before, and it would take time to heal his hurt. But in the end, I was sure he would be proud of me. *He'll laugh at himself when this is all over.*

I was getting ready to leave again when Marco decided he wanted a recap of last night.

"So I see you survived that Monica chick without getting smothered by her knockers." He laughed at his own joke.

"We didn't get that far."

"She couldn't fucking keep her hands off you. What happened?" he asked, incredulous.

"Like I said, we didn't get that far."

"Earth to Bill. She was like the Energizer Bunny, all wound up. It looked like not even a serious fart storm was going to stop that chick."

I tempered my anger as I recalled last night. Marco always had my back, so telling him was the right move.

"That bitch was just angling to make a fucking sex tape to blackmail me."

Marco gasped. "You're kidding, right?" He put his drink down.

I took a deep breath, but that woman had really pissed me off. "No fucking way. She set her phone to record the whole thing. Fucking bitch. If you ever see her around here again, kick her ass straight to the street." I was even madder than I sounded, and I was proud of my restraint. "And her name ain't Monica."

Marco's eyes went wide for a moment. "Women. Can't trust 'em. So how the hell did you figure it out?"

Controlling my breathing, I felt a little calmer. "I found the phone before we started."

"Lucky, huh?"

"For sure. I turned it off, and then we played twenty questions. I checked her driver's license, and she'd even lied to me about her name."

"Well, duh! She didn't want you gunning for her while she was shaking you down."

I shook my head. "Anyway, I gave her three chances, and she lied every time, so I kicked her ass out and dumped the phone in with the lionfish. That totally pissed her off. Up until then, I think she still thought she could put one over on me. Did I mention she was a fucking bitch?"

Marco laughed. "A few times. So, like, what are you going to do to get back at her?"

I peered deep into my glass. "Nothing."

Marco slapped my back. "So what was shaping up to be a pretty good evening ended up clusterfucked."

I took another swig of my scotch. "Like you said, women suck." I raised my glass to his.

"Women sure do suck." Marco paused and then smirked. "And the good ones can suck-start a leaf blower." Once again, he laughed at his own joke.

"That's about the size of it." I wasn't into Marco's humor this evening.

"It's your family name, bro. The dollar signs short-circuit their brains, and it turns 'em all into gold-digging sluts, one way or another."

I raised my glass again. "Women suck," we said together.

I finished my drink and slapped Marco on the shoulder. "See ya tomorrow." I pushed back and added, "And the good ones can suck the chrome off a trailer hitch."

He was laughing again as I left. "Got that right."

CHAPTER 4

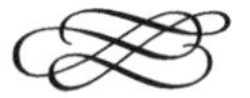

Lauren

I HAD THOUGHT ABOUT BILL FOR A WEEK NOW. I'D KEPT AN EYE OUT coming and going from work without catching a glimpse of my coffee-spill date.

If only I hadn't been such a klutz. I could still see his face, his hair, those shoulders, and those dimples——oh, those dimples. It would be too obvious to take a laptop down and spend a few mornings working in the lobby, but how else was I going to see him again? I'd even hung out by the window overlooking the street to see if I could find him. No such luck. I'd lost my chance.

On the way upstairs this morning, I finally asked Gus at the security desk who he was and learned that Bill was *William Covington,* of all people, the eldest son of our company's CEO. That put him way out of my league. I didn't even qualify for his universe.

So much for that fantasy.

A short time later, I was heading back downstairs. Another Monday, another trip for a second latte for the witch. I ordered the same coffee as always, resisting the temptation to add anything poisonous to the concoction. As bad as it tasted, I doubted Marissa would have noticed. I trudged back across the street to Covington. Coffee duty wasn't why I'd gotten my degree.

Brandon, you'd better appreciate what I'm going through for you.

Fat chance.

My brother, Brandon, never thought about anybody but himself. Self-indulgence is what led to his latest relapse and his accident. I had promised Mom I would take care of him, but the bills were drowning me. I pressed the *Up* button to the elevator and promised myself this would be Brandon's last chance.

I'd said that the last time too.

Just as the door to the elevator was about to close, an arm shot in to stop it, and *he* joined me in the empty car. Bill. Adonis with dimples in the flesh. And this time, I hadn't spilled anything on him. My gaze drifted over to the reflection in the chrome of the elevator door. I had spent too much time with Sandy, my crazy roommate. I was totally checking him out——particularly his crotch.

Careful, girl.

He hit the *Stop* button, and the elevator lurched to a standstill as I concentrated on not spilling the Starbucks cup. I could hear the light whisper of an overhead fan in the small space as he turned to me.

"You're the one who spills her coffee on strangers." He licked his lips. "What's your name again?"

His voice froze me in place. A tingle went through me and settled between my legs. His smile was so mesmerizing I had trouble with the simple question.

I finally got my brain engaged enough to blurt out, "Lauren." *It's getting hot in here.*

"Does Lauren have a last name?" He licked his lips again, the dimples getting deeper as his smile widened and his blue eyes bored into me.

My heart pounded, and the blood rushing in my ears made it hard to hear anything else.

"Zumwalt," I managed as my panties melted.

"Put down the coffee, Lauren Zumwalt. I wouldn't want you to spill it."

I set the cup in the corner, my knees so weak I was barely able to stand.

As I turned, he grabbed me by my waist and pulled me to him.

His touch scorched the skin under my blouse. My heart pounded so hard I thought it might escape my chest.

"Lauren Zumwalt, you are the most delectable creature I have seen all year," he whispered as he leaned down and kissed my neck.

His lips moved to claim mine. His tongue probed insistently, parting my lips. As our tongues dueled for position, one of his hands lifted from my waist and his thumb traced the underside of my breast through my blouse. My nipples hardened, anticipating his touch. The other hand gripped my ass, pulling me against his cock as he deepened the kiss.

I molded my body to his and pulled myself closer yet, squeezing against his hardness. My panties had grown damp. The musky scent of him, his hand clutching my ass, the sound of his breathing, the fiery touch of his thumb teasing my breast...

The chime sounded.

My fantasy evaporated, and the door opened on my floor.

Fantasizing about elevator sex? How lame is that?

The heat in my cheeks told me my blush must be visible from a mile away. Damn, all he had to do was stand next to me, and I went all high school. We'd never even been introduced.

Quite the gentleman, he motioned for me to exit as he held the door open.

I watched those wide shoulders and nice ass saunter toward our CEO's office. I licked my lips, walking toward marketing as I heard Judy, the CEO's assistant, greet the younger Covington.

Before I turned the corner, I glanced toward Judy's desk, and Bill looked over. I could've sworn he winked at me.

Or had I imagined that as well?

Marissa greeted my return with the same scowl as before. "Took you long enough. We have work to do."

Who was she kidding? Her version of *we* never included her doing anything beyond criticizing the rest of us in the department.

She took the coffee and sipped it. Seeming satisfied that I hadn't poisoned her, she turned and over her shoulder asked, "Did you finish the graphic for the airline handout?"

"Yes, Marissa. It's ready anytime you want to look it over."

I resisted the temptation to use her last name and piss her off. She had assigned me this project for the airline seat division at a quarter to five last night and expected it to be completed by this morning, even though she'd been out the door at five sharp, heading to some dinner or other that was too important for any of us to understand.

My student loans were massive, the rent in this city was expensive, and my brother's medical bills on top of it all meant I needed to keep this job for another year or two. My mom had sacrificed everything to get me the chance to go to school and get a good job. And then the cancer had taken her.

All I had to do was keep my head down, make the witch look better than she deserved——the easy part——and my mouth in check, which was the hard part.

I UNLOCKED THE DOOR TO MY APARTMENT TO THE ENTICING SMELL OF Thai food. Four unopened containers from Sandy's favorite restaurant sat on the kitchen counter.

"Sandy, I'm home."

I could never figure out how my roomie was always spot-on in guessing when I would get home from work. She must've had a spy at the company or ESP or something.

Sandra Targus came out of her room, her arms in the air, dancing to the music in her earbuds. Sandy always ordered out for Thai when she had something to celebrate. Her cat, Bandit, ran by and tagged me on his way to hide under the couch.

"What's worth Thai today?" I asked as she twirled around for the second time.

With her earbuds still in, she nearly yelled, "I got the next four Calvin Klein spreads under contract."

Sandy was a photographer and a fantastic one at that. Clients flew her around the country to do shoots on both coasts. She told people she did clothing layouts, but her real specialty was underwear——to the point that she hardly did anything else these days. She was her happiest when she'd booked another gig, and I'd never heard her complain about the travel or the hours.

It didn't matter whether the models were men or women, Sandy was your girl. The women felt more comfortable around her, and the guys? Well, let's just say part of her job was to dress slutty and talk dirty to get a "fuller shot," and for the gay ones, she had her assistant, Timmy, to charm them.

Sandy took the earbuds out, and steam erupted from the white paper containers as she opened them.

"So, girl, tell me what happened to make *you* so happy." She turned to grab plates from the cupboard.

I lied. "Nothing. Just another regular day." The last thing I needed right now was Sandy ribbing me about my crush on William Covington. I'd told her about colliding with him last week, and that's all she'd talked about for three days straight.

Her eyes narrowed as she pointed a pair of chopsticks at me. "Spill, girl. I can see it all over your face." She waited for an answer.

I didn't say a thing, but my warming cheeks were probably giving me away.

"Okay, you want me to guess." She placed her hands on her hips. "You know you're going to lose this. I have my bullshit detector turned up extra high. No way you're getting out of this without giving me the truth." Twirling her chopsticks, she giggled. "So, you made out with little Jimmy in the copy room."

"Ew, no way. At least not unless he grew six inches overnight. One down, nine to go." This would be fun. No way was she going to guess, and no way was I going to let it slip.

"So, it wasn't Jimmy in the copy room." She spooned out some massaman curry next to the rice as she pondered her next guess. "Then how about Harry in Accounting?"

"No way. He's, like, older than dirt. Two down, eight to go." I laughed.

"But he sure has a fat wallet."

There it was again. In Sandy's book, there were only two types of guys worth dating. They had to have a big wallet or a big *package*.

She added the Thai basil chicken to the plates and handed me mine. Then a smile came to her. She tapped her temple with her chopsticks. "I got it. You saw big-dick Billy Covington again today, didn't you?"

How did she know? I would have to ferret out the spy. I tried to keep a straight face, but it was no use, which is probably why I'd always lost to Johnny Cassidy at strip poker back in high school. No, he probably cheated, the little weasel.

Sandy shook her head. "Busted, girl. Spill. What happened? Did he ask you out?"

"No, we just rode up in the elevator together." I looked down at my curry and stirred it for a few seconds.

"And what else?"

"That's all."

"Is not."

This was so embarrassing. I didn't even want to share it with my best friend. "Well, I sort of had this daydream that he kissed me." I was blushing for sure now.

"Well, what are you waiting for? He's the real deal——big package and big wallet. Go for it before he finds someone else."

"He doesn't even know I exist." This sounded like a repeat of the conversation we'd had last time.

"And he won't, not until you get up the nerve to say hello."

"For the record, I'm not interested in the size of his *package*."

"Why not? I've seen pictures of him, and in my professional opinion, he's packin'."

"Really? You're going to compare him to those guys you shoot?"

"Of course not. He owns a restaurant, has a bazillionaire father, and obviously has a head on his shoulders filled with real gray matter. There's no comparison. The guys I deal with? The half who aren't gay can only count to fifty because that's the reps they do at the gym. And they struggle to remember their next chest-waxing appointment."

It wasn't nice, but I had to laugh.

"All I'm saying, girl, is go for it. Big-Dick Billy has the equipment that won't disappoint."

I sighed. "You can be so superficial."

"I do pretty pictures for a living. Superficial is my whole world."

~

IT HAD BEEN TWO WEEKS SINCE MY RIDE IN THE ELEVATOR WITH BILL. I had managed to make a lot of trips by Mr. Covington's office and the elevator on our floor, but to no avail. No more Bill sightings. He was just an occasional visitor to the building, after all.

I pulled into the parking lot. Kathy in Finance had set me up on this evening's blind date with Zack. She said he was a nice guy "that grows on you."

It was retro night at the Cineplex, and *Casablanca* was playing. The plan was a movie followed by Chinese just down the street. Zack turned out to be shorter than me by an inch, which wasn't a problem by itself, but he also showed up with a few drinks under his belt already and hair that needed a wash.

My second clue that this would be a long night came when he didn't get us tickets for *Casablanca*, the real classic. Zack's idea of a perfect first date was *Striptease*. I wasn't looking forward to spending two hours watching Demi Moore bounce around on the big screen mostly naked, but I told myself at least it was better than *Nightmare on Elm Street*, which was also playing. That one had given me nightmares for a month the first time I saw it.

Maybe the Chinese food would make up for it. He had raved about the place on the phone.

We walked to the restaurant after the movie, and my first impression was somewhere between underwhelming and *Danger, Keep Out.*

Kathy, you so owe me for this.

He ordered for us after I suggested he include Mongolian beef. He got two beers for himself to start. Our conversation was mostly normal, and I was just waiting for my safety call from Sandy to get me out of here.

After our food arrived, it started to get weird.

"The Illuminati are real, I'm tellin' ya," he began.

He was working on his third beer, and it was hard to hold back my laughter as he kept dropping the peas he tried to pick up with his chopsticks.

He gave up and reverted to a fork. "These shticks are bent," he said, looking at me for confirmation.

"Mine are fine," I assured him.

Kathy, what do you mean 'he grows on you'?

"They control every-ting."

Okay, no more beers for you, Zack.

"Like what, do they control the weather?" *Shit,* I forgot to install the filter between my brain and my mouth.

"Make ff-un all ya want. I'm tellin' ya, theys control lots a things. Aa-nn be careful what ya sez on the phone."

Where was Sandy's call? I needed my emergency escape call right now.

Bzzzt. Bzzzt. My phone vibrated to tell me a text had arrived. I had put it on silent so as to not interrupt this date, but that was no longer a concern.

"Just a moment. I have to check this."

"Whatever." Zack rolled his eyes like I was insulting the president or something. "Be-ez careful what ya say," he warned me.

It wasn't what I expected.

MARISSA: 911 Drop everything Call NOW

It wasn't Sandy, but it would have to do.

"Gotta go," I said cheerily. "The office needs me."

My boss enjoyed ruining an evening every couple weeks with some emergency I had to deal with. She constantly reminded me that shit flowed downhill to us on the lower rungs of the corporate ladder. But this time, I was relieved to hear from the Wicked Witch.

I shouldn't have, but I put a ten on the table as I stood. Life wasn't fair. I deserved hazard pay for putting up with this douchebag for three hours.

"Maay-bee Slaturday?" Zack looked at me with sad puppy-dog eyes.

"Maybe not." I left before I could say anything meaner.

On the way out, I mentioned to the waitress that they should call Zack a cab. Once outside, I dialed the Wicked Witch of the West.

She started right in on me. "What took you so long? Never mind, I don't want to hear it. Get to the office right now. We have an emergency."

"What's the emergency?" I asked.

Nothing but silence. She had hung up before I'd even said a word.

Right on cue, Sandy's call came in. "So, there's an emergency at work, and you need to get over there right away," she said.

"It's okay, Sandy, I just left him. What a loser. Tell you about it when I get home."

"No, girl, there's some meltdown emergency at your work. Your boss called here looking for you. And don't worry, I didn't say anything nasty to her."

I walked faster now. *What is so fucking important?*

CHAPTER 5

Lauren

Her call had been helpful in the moment, but truly, Marissa had such terrible timing. I should have been on my way home for my after-date autopsy with Sandy.

Usually, Marissa's 911 after-hours emergencies were nothing much. She was such a drama queen. She'd had me come in one night to change a comma to a semicolon in a press release.

Her car was actually in the lot when I arrived——hogging two parking spaces. *This must be three-alarm serious.* Normally, Marissa would just call in and instruct us over the speakerphone, snug in her Marina Del Ray condo.

When I got upstairs, I found her standing at Judy's desk instead of in marketing.

I had to stifle my laugh when I saw her. She hadn't gone to Stanford, but here she was trying to hold up Stanford sweatpants that were a size too large for her with an obviously broken drawstring.

"Mr. Covington was in a crash," she announced in a shaky voice. "I can't get a hold of anybody. We have to find out how to reach his family. Somebody needs to go to UCLA. They called me because my name was on one of the papers in his briefcase." She was babbling a mile a minute.

A chill enveloped me. "My God, is he okay?" I had never experienced Marissa like this. She was frantic, like a cat that had been thrown in the bathtub, clawing to escape.

"Would I be here if he was okay?" she shrieked. "He was in a car accident." She searched Judy's desk for something. "I'm sure he'll be fine. But somebody needs to tell the family."

"So, how can I help?"

To keep from telling Marissa what an ass she was, I needed to do something constructive.

She looked out over her horn-rimmed glasses. "We need to find the emergency contact list here somewhere, but I can't get the desk open." She pushed her stupid glasses back up on her nose.

"Have you called Judy? She should be able to help."

As she rifled through the items on top of Judy's desk, she screamed back at me, "I can't find the number anywhere." Her face was clouded with anger.

Logic was not Marissa's strong point, especially when she cranked up the volume. Her vocal cords were sucking up all the oxygen before it could reach her brain.

I took my phone out. "Okay, calm down. I have Judy's number in here."

Judy had been nice enough to give me her cell number in case I had to call and say I was going to, God forbid, be late. The news went over better with Marissa when Judy delivered it than if I did.

Marissa huffed and tapped her foot impatiently.

The sooner I got away from her bitchiness, the better. I dialed the number, and Judy answered.

"Judy, this is Lauren at work——"

Marissa grabbed the phone away from me and started in on Judy about why her desk was locked. From this end of the conversation, I gathered that even-tempered Judy was not happy with Marissa's ravings.

Brandon, you so owe me.

"I am not yelling," Marissa shouted into the phone at poor Judy. "Yeah…okay, you handle it then. Yeah. Yeah. She wants to talk to you." Marissa handed my phone back to me. "I'm going home. Call me later to let me know what's going on," she growled.

She hefted her purse and stomped off toward the elevator, tugging the waist of her oversized sweats up as she walked.

I put the phone to my ear. "Judy, this is Lauren Zumwalt."

"Is she gone yet?" Judy's voice was cool as a cucumber.

"Almost." After the elevator doors had closed, I said, "Now she is."

"Okay, Lauren, all I could understand from Marissa was that she got a call that Mr. Covington was in an accident. Do we know anything more?"

"No," I replied. "That's all she said, except that they took him to UCLA."

"Okay, do you have something to write with?"

I located a pen on her desk. "Yeah, go ahead."

"Wendell's brother-in-law, Garth, is in Asia today. His son Liam is in the air now on a flight to Europe to join Patrick. His daughter, Katherine, is in Atlanta, and his youngest son, Steven, is on the east coast at law school. I'll take care of them, but I'm in San Francisco tonight, so what I need you to do is to find his oldest son, Bill, there in L.A. and let him know."

That sounded easy enough——not the part about where all the family members were, but the part where I only had to locate one of them.

"Okay."

"He doesn't always answer his phone. You'll probably need to get him at his home on Wilshire." She gave me his phone numbers.

I read them back to her.

Then she gave me the address. "Please locate Bill and tell him where his father is. It would mean so much to Wendell to have Bill by his side."

"I'll find him."

"Thank you so much, Lauren, and if you have any problem with your boss, just let me know and I'll take care of it."

We hung up, and I dialed Bill's home phone. He didn't pick up. I left a message on the answering machine.

The cellphone was no better. Straight to voicemail. I left a message asking him to call me right away.

The only thing left to do was drive my shitty little Corolla over to the Covington mansion or palace or whatever and camp out on the stoop if he wasn't there. That was assuming the guard dogs didn't eat me or the cops in his part of town didn't haul my ass to jail for vagrancy.

THE NICE MAP LADY IN MY PHONE ANNOUNCED, "YOUR DESTINATION is ahead on the right." Large backlit numbers on a huge vertical stone announced the address, and a circular drive led up to the building. This was no house. This was a gigantic fucking tower.

I pulled up, and the doorman came around to greet me. *How rich do you have to be to have a twenty-four-hour doorman?* Sandy and I considered ourselves lucky to have a neighborhood mailman most days.

"May I help you, miss?"

"I'm here to see William Covington."

"And your name, miss?"

"Lauren Zumwalt." *What's with the twenty questions?* I headed for the door. "I need to know if he is here." The door was locked, of course. Can't have the rabble just wandering in off the street.

The doorman consulted a clipboard at his little podium and said, "Miss, you are not on the list."

"I'm from Covington Industries. There's been an accident, and I need to see him right now." I decided against stomping my foot.

"I'm sorry, miss, but you are not on the list," he repeated in his fake British accent. His name tag said *Oliver*.

Change of tack. I was not going to be stopped by a fucking doorman with a fake accent.

"I know I'm not on the damn list, Oliver," I shouted. "His father has been in an accident and is in the hospital dying, Oliver, and he didn't have the courtesy to call ahead and put me on the damn list, Oliver, so that I could come get his damn son, Oliver, who won't answer his damn phone, and take him to the damn hospital to see his dying father, Oliver."

I made up the part about dying, of course, hoping it wasn't true, but at least I got all of that out without swearing at the poor man.

That did the trick as Ollie buzzed open the door. "I'm sorry, miss. I didn't know. Yes, Mr. Covington is in residence. Unit 221 on the twenty-second floor."

The lobby was all stainless and chrome and enough polished marble to put the Capitol Building to shame. I hesitated at the elevator. I was going to meet fantasy Bill again. My stomach churned at the thought of being face to face with him in private. The elevator only had buttons up to twenty-two——obviously nothing but the very best if you were a Covington.

The doors opened on a wide hallway, with doors to only two units.

I steadied myself and knocked on 221. No response. I pushed the little ringer button thingy and heard a chime inside. No response, so I leaned on the button and pounded the door.

Finally, "Jussss a sec" came from behind the massive door.

When the door opened, there stood my dream man with a short satin bathrobe draped over his wide shoulders and tied loosely about his waist, open down to his navel, showing sculpted muscles and more than a hint of chest hair. He was in less than stellar condition. His eyes were more bloodshot than blue, and he steadied himself against the doorjamb. He seemed to register some recognition as he scanned my face and then the rest of me.

Just being near him had me tongue-tied again as heat rose in my cheeks. I pressed my thighs together to control my impulses.

"Wha you here for?" He looked at his wrist. "At?" The watch he expected to find wasn't there. "Whaa time tiiiss anyway?" He stood at the doorway, swaying slightly.

I finally found my voice. "William, there's been an accident."

He moved his free hand to his head and winced. "Huh?" He stepped aside slightly.

I pushed past him into the condo and started again after he closed the door. "William, your father was in an accident, and he's in the hospital."

The open great room had an entire glass wall overlooking the city. The kitchen alone looked bigger than my apartment. The floor was a warm oak, and the furniture was masculine——substantial with warm woods and dark leathers.

Instantly more awake, he grabbed for my arm, but he missed and braced himself on the wall instead. "Where izz hee?"

"UCLA Medical." I had barely gotten the words out when he staggered across the room to the couch, dropped the bathrobe, and picked up some slacks from the floor. He started putting them on, not wasting time with underwear, and fell over, unable to balance himself.

I should have turned around, but I froze, and he showed me the whole *package* as I stood there. My God, here I was in his condo, watching him get dressed with all the dangly parts on display. A warm fuzz engulfed my brain.

How am I ever going to get the image of his cock and that ass out of my head? Some things can't be unseen. And that back and those abs and those broad shoulders…

I gave myself a mental slap, but I didn't look away. I was trembling. He had barely mumbled to me. What would I do——how would I feel——if he actually talked to me like a man talks to a woman?

He stood and wobbled again, nearly falling over, as he buckled his belt and grabbed a shirt off the couch. He sat and worked his feet into a pair of loafers.

"Wher'ess my…?"

"What?" I asked.

He wasn't making a whole lot of sense. But perhaps it was just the hot guy haze in my brain from being close to him.

"Lezz go." He headed back my way, lurching toward a car key on the counter.

I grabbed up the key before he reached it. He was four or five martinis past his limit. "You're in no condition to drive. I'll take you there."

"Riiight," he stammered as he grabbed a jacket and some house keys from the counter, and we headed down the hall.

I was going to have to endure another elevator ride with him, and right after he had gotten naked in front of me. *Damn, it's hot in here.*

When the elevator opened, he said, "Afffer you, Lauren." He held the door open with his arm. Rushing to see his father in the hospital, ridiculously wasted, and still the ultimate gentleman.

As we passed the tenth floor, it hit me. I stopped avoiding him and looked straight at him. I heard Sandy in my head. *"You can do it, girl."*

"How do you know my name?" I blurted. It came out squeaky, but at least it was a complete sentence, and this time, I wasn't staring at his crotch. Much.

"Simmle, Misss Zumwalt. I asskd Yuudie."

That was the sum total of our conversation all the way to the car. As the floor numbers counted down, the temperature steadily rose. I tried to keep from looking at his reflection in the door, I really did. I called for Oliver's help when we reached the lobby.

Ollie helped Bill into the passenger side as I opened the squeaky door on the driver's side. No doubt, riding in my shitty little Corolla was going to be a whole new experience for him.

Bill

SHE STARTED DOWN THE ROAD AFTER OLIVER HELPED ME WITH MY seatbelt. *That wasn't humiliating.*

"My dad all right?" I managed to get out, concentrating on sounding out the words.

"Well, he was in an accident, but I hope so."

She was quiet as she drove me toward the hospital. The sweet jasmine scent of her perfume and her look in profile as she drove were even more attractive than the other day in the elevator. Something about this woman was insanely alluring, and not just because I had been drinking.

My head felt like a dozen little men with jackhammers were working inside.

"You work at Covington?" At least I got that out without slurring my words...I thought.

"Yes, I work in marketing," she replied, not taking her eyes off the road.

Why couldn't I come up with a better question than that? Of course she worked at the company.

I sound like a moron. What is wrong with me? Why is my brain not working?

"Right turn ahead," her phone announced.

Things were so foggy. I must have had way more to drink than I remembered.

I changed the subject. "What happened——in the accident?"

"I don't know. I'm sorry, all I know is that the police found some papers with Marissa's name——that's my boss——on them, and they tracked her down, and she tracked me down. I spoke to Judy, and she asked me to find you."

"Uh-huh."

"I just hope your father is all right." She smiled but kept her eyes on the road. Her smile seemed genuine, not the painted-on kind I was so used to getting.

"He a tufff ol' biiird." The fog on my brain had begun to lift a little.

One minute later we arrived at the hospital parking lot.

CHAPTER 6

Lauren

When we got to the hospital, I was able to confirm that Wendell Covington had been helicoptered in and was in surgery.

I'd meant it when I told Bill I thought his father was going to be okay, but the fact that they'd airlifted him in instead of using an ambulance was not a good sign.

The nurse at the desk refused to give us any more information. Her nametag said Jackie, but her demeanor said Nurse Ratched, and Bill didn't get anywhere trying to sweet-talk her. The alcohol on his breath and his slurred speech didn't help his cause.

Two hours later, I had gotten three cups of vending machine coffee into Bill and made three more attempts with Nurse Ratched, all to no avail. I could only tell Bill we didn't know anything yet.

Also, I was done sitting in the stuffy waiting room next to the lady with the cough from hell and a snoring fat guy who hadn't showered in a week or two or three. It was time for Plan B.

I found the admissions desk, got a map of the university, and checked. Sure enough, the buildings Judy had told me about were on there. I brought the map back up to Nurse Ratched's desk.

"Hi, Jackie, I hate to disturb you," I told her. "I know how hard your job is. My sister is an ER nurse at SF General."

Total lie, but Marketing 101: develop rapport.

Jackie's look softened.

"You see these three buildings here?"

She nodded. "Miss, I don't have time for——"

"They're the Covington buildings. His grandfather…" I pointed toward Bill in the waiting room. "…donated them to the university. I wouldn't want to be in your shoes tomorrow when the director finds out nobody would give him the time of day around here about his father."

I guessed there was a director of something or other here at the hospital who would motivate her.

My guess was right. Jackie thought for a second, then picked up the phone.

"Just a moment. Let me make a call."

"Thank you." I smiled and walked back to Bill. Mission accomplished.

A few minutes later, a Dr. Dalton arrived, and everything changed. I'd gotten their attention, and now Bill and I were VIPs.

Dr. Dalton led us upstairs to a private waiting room, which was like being in a little cocoon, separated from the real hospital.

As we entered, Bill asked for the about the fortieth time, "What happened?"

"I have some details for you, Mr. Covington," Dr. Dalton said.

Bill sank into the couch next to me. The time and the coffee were taking effect, and while he wasn't one-hundred-percent sober, he was getting better.

"The accident was a head-on collision. Your father was driving northbound when another driver crossed the center line and hit him. The other driver died at the scene, and your father was transported here by air-ambulance. He has a ruptured spleen, along with other injuries, and is hemorrhaging internally."

Bill hung his head. His eyes filled with tears. He didn't say a thing.

I put an arm around him.

Dr. Dalton continued. "He's still in surgery, and we have a top team on him. Dr. Ziegler is our best trauma specialist, and we called in Dr. Warner, who is possibly the best vascular surgeon in the country."

I kept my arm around Bill as he leaned in. I felt so sorry for him.

"I'll be back as soon as I have more information for you, Mr. Covington. Just dial 4101 if you need anything," the doctor said as he left.

Bill just sat there. A few minutes later, he searched his coat pockets. "I mussa left my phone at home."

"Well, you weren't exactly operating on all cylinders when we left." Damn, that sounded mean. The guy's father was in surgery, for God's sake.

He merely nodded.

"I'm sorry. I didn't mean that the way it sounded."

"Don't be, Lauren."

We sat in silence. This was a hell of a way to get introduced to the man of my dreams. In just a few weeks, I had gone from elevator stalker to being on a first-name basis with my arm around him. It had felt so natural to be here comforting him, waiting to hear about his father, and then I had to go and say something stupid.

And there was still that indelible image in my head of him naked in his condo. I had so much to tell Sandy.

Bill surprised me by getting up and hugging me——not a family kind of hug, but a long, tight, boyfriend kind of bear-hug. Really tight.

Hey, Bill? My boobs aren't that big to begin with. Let's not flatten 'em, okay?

What the hell? I hugged him back and then some as I melded my body to his. My head spun, and a mist settled over my brain. I closed my eyes and enjoyed his warmth, my breasts pressed hard into his muscular chest. It was an eternity before he released me.

"I hates to ask, but coulds you go back and get my phone?" he asked. "I gotts to call my brothers and my sister, and I dunno the numbers by heart."

The coffee seemed to be getting him more sober.

It took a second for me to get enough gray matter working to respond. "Will you be okay here alone?" I mentally crossed my fingers for a *no*.

"Yeah, nothing to do but wait. And one more thing..."

I waited.

His eyes were pained. "Theeere's a girl. I need her out." He looked down.

So he has a girlfriend.

That blew my Bill fantasy all to hell. I got up and opened the door, turning back. "And should I send your girlfriend over here to keep you company?"

Why do I have to be mean again?

"Sheee's not a girlfriend," he shot back.

"Got it, not your girlfriend. What's her name?"

His shoulders fell. The pain in his eyes amplified. "Dunno."

"You don't know her name?" This might be worse than her being a girlfriend. "So, how much do I pay her?"

Ouch. I had been up way too long. A minute ago, I'd been consoling him, and now I was insulting the hell out of him. His expression told me I had definitely crossed the line with that one.

What an idiot. Two years of enduring Marissa, and I have to go and lose my job by insulting the boss's son in the middle of the night.

"She's not a professional."

I yanked at my purse and left before I screwed this up even more.

A few minutes later, I pulled up in front of the Battlestar Covington to find Oliver still on duty.

"Back again, Miss Zumwalt?"

"Hi, Ollie, are you pulling an all-nighter?" I hoped this would be easier than the first time.

"Just filling in. I take the overtime when I can get it. I'm sorry to tell you that Mr. Covington has not returned."

"I know. I left him at the hospital. His father's still in surgery. I just need to pick up some things for him."

"I'm sorry, Miss Zumwalt…"

I interrupted him. "Not on the list. I get it." I pulled Bill's keys out of my pocket and jangled them. "Got the keys from Bill. I'm following his instructions." I hoped the use of Bill's first name would get Ollie's attention.

He looked relieved not to argue the list again as he buzzed me in.

"And Ollie, please call me Lauren."

That elicited a smile. "Yes, Miss Lauren."

At the condo, I had to try three keys before I found the right one. The phone wasn't in the kitchen. I went to the living room area and found a dress and bra on the floor… She was a busty girl, it seemed. I couldn't fill half of that thing. I picked up the clothes as I continued to the bedroom.

When I opened the door, there she was——sprawled out on the bed, only half covered by the sheets. Big boobs and quite a tan to go with her brunette hair. She couldn't have been much over nineteen.

I turned on the light. "Time to wake up. Gotta go," I said as loudly as I could without yelling.

She rolled over and buried her head into the pillow. "What the fuck?"

"Time to go," I repeated as I headed to the bathroom, looking for Bill's cellphone. I didn't care to spend any more time here with this Barbie than I had to.

Some muffled swearing into the pillow followed something I couldn't make out. She was fucking pissed.

Tough shit, Barbie.

I didn't find the phone in the bathroom either. I returned to the bedroom and finally located it plugged into a charging cord on the nightstand. I had to step around a used condom on the floor to get to it.

More information than I want right now.

I put the phone in my purse and yanked the covers off her.

"What the fuck? Where's Bill?" she said as she tried to yank the covers back.

He didn't know her name, but she knew his. Figures.

Her vocabulary wasn't impressing me. I threw the dress and bra at her. "Time to go, Barbie."

"It's Amy, and who the fuck are you?"

At least she knew more than three words, but so far, none of them were more than four letters long. "I'm the maid."

"What the fuck?"

Bill was pegging the douchemeter by sending me here to deal with this. "Time to get moving. Next time pick a guy that takes the time to learn your name."

"You're not the boss of me," she argued, but she did get off the bed and start looking around. "Bitch." She found her panties and struggled into them.

Wow. Where in the world did Bill pick up such a charmer? The mall? "Go home, and next time have more self-respect. You can do better than him. Try dating guys your own age."

"I'm not fuckin' Barbie, and I'm not leavin'."

Sure thing, Mall Barbie.

How the hell did I end up having to deal with this? I picked up the condo phone and dialed four random numbers. Just static on the line. "Hey, Oliver? Can you come up to 221 and escort Barbie here out of the building?" I paused a few seconds. "No, I don't think you'll need the stun gun, but bring it anyway."

That got her moving. She got her dress on without bothering with the bra and was out in a flash, throwing out a last *Fuck you, bitch!* for good measure.

"I'm doing you a favor," I yelled after her.

This crap was not in my job description.

Good thing there wasn't any traffic at this time of the morning because most of my brain was focused on Bill and Barbie. A used condom, and he didn't even know her name? What a super dickhead.

When I returned to the cocoon room upstairs at the hospital,

Dr. Dalton was removing rubber gloves, and Bill was in a chair holding a cotton ball to the inside of his elbow.

The doctor gathered up a dark vial of blood and the needle he had just removed from Bill's arm.

"I'll be in touch, Mr. Covington," he said as he left.

After the door had shut, I closed the distance to Bill's chair. I threw the phone into his lap and stared at him.

He looked back at me with a guarded smile.

"And that other item," I said as I composed myself.

Don't blow it, Lauren.

He raised a quizzical eyebrow. "Yeah?"

I couldn't help myself. "I might have screwed up your chances for a second date." I left and slammed the door behind me.

"Not interested," I heard through the closed door.

WHEN I WOKE UP THE NEXT MORNING, THERE WAS A NOTE FROM Sandy. She had left early for a morning shoot in San Diego. I had forgotten about that.

After getting ready, I pointed my crappy Corolla toward the hospital instead of work. I needed to tell Bill I was sorry for being such a bitch last night.

As I opened the door to the cocoon room, he was pacing.

"Any news?"

A broad smile took over his face as he looked up and saw me. That was a good sign. Then it disappeared.

"He's out of surgery and in critical condition. They let me visit him for a few minutes. They may operate again any moment now."

I didn't know what to say. "I'm so sorry, Bill."

The lack of sleep showed in his face, but most of all, he looked forlorn. "Can you stay a little while?"

Anything for you, Bill.

"Sure. Why don't you sit down?"

I took his hand and led him over to the couch. He said he

hadn't eaten yet, so I dialed 4101 and asked for some breakfast. It appeared quickly, and there wasn't a Jell-O in sight.

I needed to get this out. "I'm really sorry for the way I acted last night."

He frowned, or was that just surprise?

"No need, Lauren." He put a hand on my arm. His lips turned up in a smile and his soft blue eyes warmed mine.

His touch scorched my skin through the fabric, and the room got instantly warmer. Just that one touch sent me through the roof. My heart raced. I was falling for the douchebag Mall Barbie troll.

He pulled his hand back. "You just said what needed to be said. I appreciate that."

We ate in silence. They must have had a special kitchen for VIPs or doctors or something because it didn't taste like any hospital food I remembered.

Dr. Dalton entered and offered Bill a piece of paper. "The lab results. It's as I suspected. We can talk about it later."

Bill put the paper in his pocket after a brief glance.

I didn't pry. It wasn't my place to get involved in his dad's care. I hung out with Bill for another hour before he sent me off, insisting I should go to work and let them know what was happening.

"And please thank Judy for reaching Uncle Garth for me," he said as I was leaving the cocoon room.

When I reached my floor at work and the elevator doors opened, I headed toward Judy to give her Bill's message. I didn't make it.

The witch intercepted me, her face turning redder by the second. "Come here, Zumwalt," she commanded.

I followed her to the marketing area. She exploded before I could fill her in on Mr. Covington's situation.

"You are late. Where the hell have you been? And where is my latte?" Her face had turned a shade of red that was a nine on the

Marissa scale. "Never mind, it's too late for that. I will not tolerate you being late again. Do you hear me?" Her hysterics generated stares from people nearby.

"I went to the hospital," I replied sheepishly. *The CEO is in critical condition, and all you can think about is your fucking coffee?*

Good thing my brain-mouth filter was working properly this morning, or I would've been out of a job in less than a minute.

Her hands balled into fists. "You were supposed to call me last night!"

I had forgotten. *Big fucking deal.* "I thought it was too late by the time we got to the hospital." *Fuck you, Marissa.*

"We don't pay you to think, Zumwalt. When I say call, that means call. Is that clear?"

"Yes, Marissa."

Her eyes turned to tiny slits. "And just who is *we*?"

"Bill and I... I mean, Mr. Covington's son."

Her eyes widened, and her nostrils flared. "What the hell were you doing that for? Let *me* handle Mr. Covington's family."

Trying to explain anything to her at this point would be a waste of time and brain cells. I looked down at the floor, half expecting to get slapped. The slap did not come.

"Get back to work on the aircraft-seating materials. I marked them up for you."

It was half an hour before I could slip away and deliver Bill's message to Judy.

This job sucks.

~

Bill

It was late afternoon. Dad had been in surgery again since noon when Dalton came in with another doctor dressed in scrubs. The looks on their faces told me what they were about to say.

"I'm sorry, Mr. Covington. Your father passed away in

surgery," the scrubs doctor said. "We did all we could, but the injuries were just too severe."

That knocked the wind out of me. I felt faint. I settled into a chair, my head in my hands. This was so unfair. He had always taken care of himself. He should have lived to a ripe old age and had the chance to retire and enjoy himself. Instead, he worked almost every day and then a drunk driver took it all from him.

I was mad at myself. The last time Dad and I had talked, I was angry with him, and he knew it. Why did I have to leave it that way? I could have tried to meet him halfway and patch things up.

I had such a grand plan to make him proud of me without having to bend completely to his will, and now I had no time to show him what I could do.

After taking a few minutes to compose myself, I dialed Uncle Garth. It would be early morning in Asia, and hopefully, his phone would be on.

"William." His voice came through with just a bit of static. "What do we know?"

I could barely force the words out. "Dad didn't make it."

"I am so sorry. I know this is a shock. What can I do for you?"

The man had just lost his brother-in-law, and he was concerned about me.

"I'm already scheduled on a flight back today," he continued. "Let me handle the arrangements. Okay?"

"Thanks, Uncle Garth. You know what makes it extra hard? The last time I saw him…" I sobbed. "He wanted me to join the company, and I turned him down again, but I wasn't very nice about it." I sobbed again. "So, the last time we talked, he knew I was angry with him, and I never got a chance to apologize."

"I know he knew your heart, William," Garth said after a moment. Then we talked over an hour about Dad and his sayings. It helped to talk it out. Finally Garth said, "Another thing, William. You are going to have to take over the CEO position."

Talk about something out of left field. The news hit me like a ton of bricks.

"You're the CFO," I told him. "You should take over. I don't know anything about the company."

He took a loud breath over the phone. "It is not up to me. It has to be a Covington. My sister married your father, but I am not a Covington. Your grandfather put the majority of the voting shares of the company in the family trust. And the trust documents specifically say that you are next in line. That's all there is to it."

It was just like the monarchy again.

"No thanks. I'm not doing it. It's not right. It should be you or Liam or Patrick."

"You do not have a choice. I did not make the rules. Your grandfather did. The trust makes you the CEO. Period." He paused. "You can not avoid it. And if you refuse to show up and do the job, how many customers do you think are going to stick with us with an absentee CEO?"

"There has to be a way around the trust."

"I am afraid not. I have looked." He paused. "William, listen to me. With your father gone, there is nothing you or I can do about it. You need to step up. You are now the patriarch of the family, whether you want to be or not, so stop complaining. You need to grow up. Like it or not, you are now the patriarch of the family, and with that comes responsibility."

Uncle Garth certainly had a way of putting me in my place when he wanted to.

"And you should call your brothers and sister."

After wishing him a safe flight home, I called Judy. I passed on the bad news about Dad and the worse news about me. I told her I would come by the office tomorrow, and I was now the CEO.

Uncle Garth was right. I didn't have a choice. And I had more calls to make. Telling the family was my responsibility.

CHAPTER 7

LAUREN

WHEN JUDY CALLED ME OVER, THE AFTERNOON APPEARED ABOUT TO turn even worse than the morning.

Her hair was up in her usual neat twist, her suit the very definition of professional office attire, but she dabbed tears forming in the corners of her eyes as she told me Mr. Covington had died. She stifled a sob.

I felt so sorry for poor Bill. I could already tell he wasn't the kind to admit it, but he needed someone, and I wanted to be that someone. I wanted to find him and just be with him, but that wasn't going to happen with Marissa around.

Then Judy rolled out the surprise. She told me Bill was coming in tomorrow to take over as CEO. My afternoon brightened.

"Mr. Covington asked me to tell you," she continued. "He said he would tell everybody else tomorrow when he comes in."

So Bill had confided in only Judy and me…

I had accomplished all I needed to for today, but I couldn't leave early because the Wicked Witch wouldn't get on her broom until five. So I made my weekly call to check on Brandon. Everything was going fine, the woman on the phone said. Rehab took time.

~

WHEN I GOT HOME, SANDY WAS THERE WAITING FOR THE ZACK-DATE download. That seemed so long ago, but I started there and delayed telling her about Bill and his father. Sandy agreed that it was super gross for Zack to show up tipsy and then pick a T&A movie for a first date.

"Then, we get to the Chinese restaurant, and it was terrible. Hot, grungy, and the food was so bad the cockroaches didn't want it."

She giggled. "Go on, girl."

"He starts sucking down more beers. He got so drunk he couldn't speak straight, and he starts telling me the Illuminati are after him."

We spent an hour eating the Chinese Sandy had brought home and comparing Zack to some of my other recent losers. It was close, but we agreed he beat out "bad breath Bobby" for the worst first date of the year so far.

When I couldn't hold back anymore, I told her about last night with Bill, starting with going over to Battlestar Covington and meeting my new favorite doorman, Oliver.

"You're kicking ass and taking names." Sandy nodded approvingly. "Good for you."

Then I recounted the naked dressing scene in the condo.

"Full frontal of big-dick Bill? Wow, that's hot for a first date, girl."

"It was not a date," I complained. "I was taking him to the hospital."

"So, you drove the bazillionaire in your shit bucket of a car. Did he get a tetanus shot at the hospital?"

"I'm guessing he'd never been in anything the size of a Corolla before. So, then they ignored us for a while until they figured out his granddad had built part of the place." I left out my part in their illumination.

"So is that when they started bringing out the caviar and shit?" she asked.

"No, they just stopped treating us like mushrooms." I suppressed a grin——this was one of the good parts. "Then Bill asks me to go back to get his phone from his condo, and get this..." I paused, letting her anticipation build. "Get rid of a girl."

Sandy gasped. "No way."

She laughed for a long time when I told her about Barbie and how I'd gotten rid of her.

"So, I don't get it. This guy is a pervert that fucks little girls without even catching their names, and you still like him? And you went back to see him again this morning?"

It didn't sound so good when she put it that way.

"You didn't see him," I told her. "He was really hurting. I can tell he's a good guy inside."

Am I saying this to convince her or me?

"Well, look. Go jump his bones, fuck his lights out, and then forget about him. You're gonna get hurt otherwise."

Sometimes Sandy was wrong, and I hoped that this was one of those times.

"And don't forget the ring hold," she continued. "Just squeeze the base of his cock real tight with your thumb and one finger, like a cock ring. It gets 'em every time."

Just what I needed, more dating advice from Sandy. I punched up an old episode of *The Bachelor*. I had to figure out what to do about Bill.

After two episodes and a glass of wine each, Sandy was ready to call it a night. And I had made my decision.

I went to my room, pulled out my phone, and dialed.

Bill answered quickly. "Hi, Lauren. I was hoping you'd call."

His voice was like a balm to my soul. Sandy had it wrong.

We talked for two hours. He told me about his conversation with his uncle——how they had talked about his childhood, how his uncle said times like this were trying, but that crisis revealed character, and it was time for Bill to step up and show what he was made of.

I just listened and asked a few questions. This was what he needed to start to heal. This was the Bill I wanted to get to know. His voice was soothing. His descriptions of people and events were kind. This was my Bill, the bear-hug Bill, the one I guessed he kept hidden most of the time.

He had wanted me to call.

CHAPTER 8

Bill

As the elevator chimed on the top floor of the Covington building, the dread I had felt earlier began to dissipate. Judy was at her desk and greeted me warmly.

But my dad's office seemed incredibly large and empty without him behind the desk. The mementos on the wall brought back memories I thought I had gotten control of before I started in this morning.

In my head, I heard him say, "*You can do this,*" as he'd said so many times before——my first at bat in Little League, the time I'd had to retake my driving test, when he'd sent me into that giant hall to take the SAT.

I turned back to Judy. "Let's get started. Do you have an organization chart I could look at?"

She had anticipated this and had it ready.

"Okay, let's get the direct reports into the conference room at nine. And see if you can set up an all-hands meeting in the cafeteria at nine thirty."

"I'll take care of it." Judy left the office, and I followed her out.

"Where's the closest Starbucks around here?" I had spent as little time as possible in this part of town the past few years.

"What would you like me to get you?" she asked.

"No, I'll get it. I need the exercise anyway."

I brisk-walked my way out of the building, and when I stepped into the Starbucks down the block, there she was, four people ahead of me in line. I would've recognized that golden blond hair anywhere. I waved when she turned in my direction after ordering.

She came over to join me in line.

"Get your coffee here every morning, Lauren?"

Her smile was infectious. "Like clockwork. It's one of my duties, and I can get yours, too, if you'd like."

Ever the considerate one, she might make me disagree with Marco next time he said all women sucked.

"No thanks."

Her smile dimmed. She looked toward the end of the counter. Her order wasn't ready yet.

I admired her ass as discreetly as I could when she looked away. She had the body of a goddess——perfect tits and lots of curves in all the right places.

"I like to get my own."

The smile returned, and her gorgeous blue eyes softened. "I guess we'll bump into one another on occasion then, now that you've got a new job around here." She combed her hair behind her ear with her finger.

She had the admirable habit of holding her chin up and not always looking at the ground.

It was all I could do to keep from asking to meet her here every morning. "Yeah, and I have the first-day jitters to go with it." I was next to order. "Venti mocha, dark roast, extra shot, please."

She touched my arm and said gently, "You'll do fine. Just do everything Judy tells you."

A tingle went up my arm where she'd touched me and traveled

straight to my twitching cock. I adjusted the binder I was carrying to hide the growing bulge behind my zipper.

"Good advice."

The guy at the end of the counter announced, "Five-pump, grande hazelnut, soy, half-caf latte, extra-hot with cinnamon," and Lauren moved to get it.

"You surprise me. I didn't peg you for a foo-foo coffee girl."

"This isn't for me. It's for my boss. I get mine from the coffee pot in the breakroom."

"That's considerate of you."

She brushed her hair behind her ear again. "Just one of my daily responsibilities, and I didn't hear you ordering straight coffee either."

This woman had spunk. "Chocoholic——one of my many vices, and I need a big one because somebody kept me up late last night on the phone."

She returned a knowing smile, and we walked back to the building together. She answered a few of my questions about work.

I continued to hold my binder where it would shield my arousal from prying eyes on the walk back. I would have to apologize for the other night as soon as I got the chance.

I watched her perfect ass as I held the elevator door for her, and I wondered what her tits would feel like in my hands as the floors went by.

She smiled at me as the door opened on our floor, and we parted ways with her still unaware of my lurid thoughts.

Once in my office, I took a few minutes behind my desk to calm myself. No way was I walking around my new work in this state. Something about that woman made me lose my usual control. It had to be Dad's death. This hadn't happened to me before. Women were my thing, but I never let them get to me——not since that bitch Jane in college.

The department-head meeting went well, and gave me a chance to meet the foo-foo coffee lady, Marissa Bitz, Lauren's boss.

Later I would have to set her straight on my views about sending employees to do personal errands. I asked them to reassemble at ten thirty to give me a status update.

Although I was nervous about the bigger all-hands meeting, I got through it without embarrassing myself too badly. Mr. Burnwood, my public speaking professor, would have been proud.

Then I was back with the department heads for my third meeting of the day, which was the status meeting I had requested. By the end of it, my head was spinning. Trying to get a handle on everything was going to be harder than I'd thought. This was decidedly *not* a part-time job.

I saw Lauren walk by a few times in the afternoon. Each time, I lost track of my thoughts and my eyes followed her like a compass follows the north pole, watching her tits bounce as she moved. Each time, I wanted to grab her and apologize for the other night, and each time, I didn't.

That was not like me. I was the king of compartmentalization. I could always focus totally on one thing at a time——this block of time for work, this time block for working out, that time block for enjoying a woman. When I was at work, I focused totally on work, regardless of the number of boobs in the room. When I was with a woman, I was completely focused on her, her words, her desires, her pleasure——and my pleasure, of course.

I had never allowed myself to be distracted like this before. Something about Lauren had knocked my world off kilter.

A real woman.

I WOKE UP LATE THE NEXT MORNING, AND EVEN THOUGH I HAD CUT down on my workout, I was still a little late getting into the office. Lauren remained on my mind, but I hadn't called last night, and neither had she.

"Hey, big brother," I heard Liam say as I approached Judy's desk. My stepbrother called me that even though he was only three months younger than I was.

"Hey, shorty. How was the flight?"

At six foot one, Liam was no shrimp, but I had two inches on him and never let him forget it. If we hadn't been in polite company, his usual retort was "Not short where it counts."

"How does a twelve-hour flight one row ahead of a screaming baby sound?" He took a sip of his coffee as he followed me into my office. "Now that you're the big cheese, Patrick and I think we should get a corporate jet or two for these trips. You know the Rosenbergs have three."

"Not happening, little brother."

Dad had always been against extravagant perks like that. He said when the managers allowed themselves excessive perks compared to the rest of the company, they lost touch. And more importantly, it gave everyone else the impression that wasting money was okay.

Uncle Garth walked in through the still-open door. "Good morning, boys. Are you ready?"

"Ready for what?" I asked.

"The finance meeting. I put it on your schedule late yesterday."

"Judy," I called. "How do I tell what's on my schedule?"

Judy came in and showed me how to pull up my calendar on the computer.

"Sorry, guys, not up to speed yet." I motioned for them to sit around the table in Dad's, correction, *my* office.

"I have brought the latest financials." Uncle Garth handed me and Liam a dozen sheets. "Things are going to be tight through the end of the quarter, but if the Benson transaction stays on schedule, we will be fine."

That sounded ominous. "Slower, please," I said. "First, what is a Benson transaction, and what do you mean *if*?"

Uncle Garth nodded. "Your father loaded the company down with significant debt in the past few years, and the food division we just bought is almost a financial bridge too far. With the slow-down in the economy and an election coming up, the projections have become progressively worse."

Now this was sounding terrible. "So what does a Benson transaction have to do with anything?"

Garth cleared his throat. "Your father arranged for an infusion of cash from Benson Corp. that is scheduled to close this quarter, and we just need to make sure that your father's death does not affect it."

"And if it does?" I asked.

Liam spoke up. "Then we're toast. Like, Chapter Eleven toast. Kaput. Broke. Done."

A chill moved through me. I looked at Uncle Garth. "Is that right?"

His face contorted. "Not exactly, but close. It will be tight, and I have been working on some contingency plans."

"What kind of plans?"

"Layoffs mostly, and closing the aircraft and paint divisions."

Liam looked Uncle Garth in the eye. "There is another alternative."

"Your father was vehemently against that," Garth interjected.

"Just a minute, Uncle Garth." I turned toward Liam again. "What's your alternative?"

"We could refinance through the Four Corners Hedge Fund."

This sounded very contorted. I was going to need a second cup of coffee to follow this, but my stomach was in no mood.

"And why was Dad against that?" I asked.

Garth's face grew red as he leaned forward and answered angrily. "Because it means giving up control of the company and basically selling an option to them with no way to get it back. So later, Covington becomes the Covington division of the Four Corners empire," he spat.

I could tell he viewed the Four Corners empire as fondly as the Evil Empire in *Star Wars*. I needed these two to calm down.

"So, let me make sure I understand." I looked at each of them. "My father flew too close to the flame, and if we don't get financing from Benson, the alternatives are bad and worse."

Uncle Garth nodded. "That is about the size of it. Your father has been friends with Lloyd Benson since they went to graduate school together. He assured us the Benson deal was in the bag. But his passing… Well, it changes things."

All I had to do was convince him I was my father's son.

I got this.

CHAPTER 9

Lauren

The conference room was packed. Bill had started a few days ago, but I hadn't seen him since that morning at Starbucks, except in passing. He'd called this meeting to go over action items for the transition from his father to himself. Each of the department heads was there, along with some of the worker bees like Karen, Herbert, and me from our department.

I made sure I didn't follow Marissa into the room, so it was a little less obvious when I didn't sit next to her. Karen took the seat on one side of the witch, and poor Herbert ended up on the other side. I took a seat next to Bill's stepbrother, Liam Quigley. I had been in a few meetings with him before. He was a nice guy, just a bit reserved.

I had prepared a set of slides on what we needed to do for the aircraft seating and brake equipment divisions from the marketing perspective. I had worked on it most of the night. Karen had the easier projects of the food and appliance divisions, and her work looked good to me. We didn't expect any problems there. Things were stable.

A few different departments presented ahead of us, and Bill asked questions that were quite insightful, given his lack of exposure to the company. He was going to be a good boss——different from his father, but quite good to work for.

I caught him looking in my direction more than once.

Down, girl, he hasn't called...probably too busy with Barbie.

Bill looked at his agenda and called for food to present next.

Liam's assistant came in and slipped him a note just before Karen started. He opened it right in front of me. It read *Your mother called. Call back ASAP.*

All I knew about Liam's mother was that she was the late Mr. Covington's second wife, and Liam was her child from her first marriage.

When Mr. Covington's marriage to her had ended in divorce, the words *not amicable* had been a gross understatement, Judy once told me. The ex got a big settlement and became persona non grata here at the company. Judy had instructions from Mr. Covington that if his ex-wife ever called, she was to read from a note card he had dictated a long time ago. She'd showed it to me once, and it basically said *fuck off and don't ever call again,* just in more polite language. Judy told me Mr. Covington had once threatened to fire an assistant who took a call from the ex-Mrs. Covington. Yet he seemed to get along with Liam just fine.

Liam folded the note and put it in his pocket.

Karen's presentation went smoothly, as we'd expected. When Bill called for the brake equipment division, I started to get up, but Marissa quickly went to the projector and began giving my presentation——the one I had slaved over all night while she was tucked into her cozy condo. She then proceeded to do my aircraft interior presentation as well.

I slumped into my seat. *How could she?* She hadn't done any of the work. She prattled on as I contemplated a scratch in the table in front of me.

Bill seemed pleased with the material when she finished.

She had impressed the new boss.

With my work! The bitch.

~

When I got home, Sandy was already there, taking care of her cat.

"So did you get any time with BD today?" she asked, waggling her eyebrows.

It was my fault. I had talked about Bill every day since the accident. I put my purse down and collapsed on the couch.

"He's been pretty busy learning things."

"Is that why you look so beaten?" She had her special bullshit-detector smirk on.

I didn't want to unload. "You know that project I worked on until late last night? Well, I was supposed to present it today, and Bill was there."

She sat up expectantly. "Yeah, and what happened?"

"That bitch Marissa took over and presented it like she'd done it all. I was the only one at the meeting that didn't present anything. She made it look like she'd only brought me along to carry her slides."

"That's why I don't have a boss." Sandy pointed her finger at me. "And you just sat there and took her fucking shit, right?"

I shrugged. "Yeah. Pathetic, huh?"

"Way past time for a new job, girl." She picked up the comb off the coffee table and went to work on Bandit. The cat purred loudly.

We had this conversation every couple of weeks.

I threw up my hands. "But I can't. You know that. I can't pay them back the moving allowance. I spent the whole thing on my brother's bills. I just have to stick it out another six months till that expires."

"I say fuck 'em. Make them sue you for the money."

Sandy worked freelance, and she just didn't get it. It wasn't that easy.

"Yeah, like somebody's going to hire me in this economy, with no recommendation, no other experience, and my previous employer suing me."

Sandy was still combing Bandit, and the apartment was quiet except for the cat's purring.

"Okay, you choose," she said after a moment. "Moping around here with Ben & Jerry's or margarita time at the Bucket?"

I knew we were out of Chocolate Chip Cookie Dough, so I voted for drinks. The Rusty Bucket was a short walk, and it was Sandy's usual solution to a bad day. It worked, mostly.

She headed for her room. "Get changed."

I was too tired to change. "I'm good."

"Not like that, you're not. I don't want to have to pay tonight, and you're not leaving early just cuz some guy spills beer on your nice work clothes. I'm wise to you, girl."

Busted again.

I changed into skinny jeans with cowboy boots and an Anaheim Angels T-shirt.

"Now you're cooking, girl. Lose the bra, pour a little water on your chest, and we won't even have to buy the first drink."

I laughed. This one was tamer than some of her other suggestions. "How come you never volunteer yourself for the wet T-shirt?"

"'Cause I'm bigger than you. I don't need a wet tee to get their attention."

She had a point there. Sandy had boobs that turned heads, and she wasn't bashful about undoing an extra button or two.

My cell rang. "It's probably work," I said as I prepared to have Marissa screw up my evening again.

"Fuck 'em," she said, trying to grab the phone away.

She had the right idea. "Fuck 'em." I turned the phone off and left it on the table.

~

Bill

. . .

THE STATUS MEETING THIS AFTERNOON HAD GONE WELL. I WAS GETTING an appreciation for how complicated the many divisions of the company were. The presentations were very well done, for the most part, thoughtful and concise. Lauren had been there, but oddly, she had not spoken a word.

I so wanted to talk with her, but I didn't seek her out after the meeting. I had kept my distance, as hard as it was.

After most of the employees had left for the day, I picked up the phone on my desk. I hesitated, then dialed Lauren's extension. There was no answer. It went to voicemail, and I hung up without leaving a message. *Fuck.*

Marco had agreed to handle the restaurant while I got things settled at the company, and he was already waiting when I got to the bar he had picked for tonight's meeting. We tended to not go to the same place twice in the same week. "You haven't been by the project lately."

"Not enough time yet. Can you handle it for me while I get things under control at my dad's company?" I waved to the bartender.

"So what's it like to be a master-of-the-fucking-universe, capitalist?"

"Harder than I thought, and a lot more paperwork and meetings than I'd like," I replied. The bartender came over, and I ordered. "My dad's company has grown, and it's a lot more complicated than I realized."

"What's so complicated? You make something for X, and you sell it for Y. You make sure Y is bigger than X, and everything is cool."

"It's more than that."

"Like what?"

I lowered my voice. "My dad took on way too much debt, and it's like a bomb about to go off."

I shouldn't have been embarrassed about telling Marco this. He was my business partner and best friend, but I had kept him insulated from the insanity of being a Covington.

"So use the cash flow and pay down the debt. Isn't that what they taught you in college?"

I took a swig of my beer. "We don't have the time for that."

"I can introduce you to one of my loan shark buddies," he offered.

I had to laugh at that. "I think that's how Dad got into this predicament in the first place."

Marco took a sip of his drink. He had opted for the hard stuff instead of a beer. I was the lightweight tonight.

We spent the next half hour talking about restaurant stuff and ordering more drinks. We switched to margaritas by the pitcher to go with the chips and salsa the bar had.

Some girls had come by earlier, and Marco sent them off politely, telling them we were waiting for our dates. It turned out our dates tonight were margarita-filled glasses. This was buddies' night: getting wasted together and forgetting our troubles. No chicks allowed.

"Your dad wasn't fucking stupid," Marco said after a pause. "So he musta had a plan to deal with the debt. Just figure it out and do it."

"Yup, his plan was to get an investment from one of his college buddies. So, I'm gonna do that. I have a meeting set up next week."

"What's got you so spooked then? They'll fuckin' love you. No problem."

I didn't know why, but I lowered my voice again. "It's my Uncle Garth. He's worried, and he's the coolest operator ever. If he's worried, there must be a good fucking reason."

"Time to get Plan B ready," Marco said, refilling his glass.

He was right about that. I needed to have a Plan B ready.

I had Ubered over here, so I filled my glass and ordered another pitcher.

What the hell was my Plan B? Another margarita was the first step.

~

LAUREN

SANDY AND I DIDN'T BRING PURSES TO THE BAR, BECAUSE TONIGHT WAS about not paying after the first drink, and that might require a dance or two.

Our usual spot at the end of the bar was open when we arrived. We liked to watch the dance floor from our seats and handicap the crowd. This spot gave us a view of any approaching guys as well.

We were regulars, so the bartender hustled over and set two napkins on the wood. Neither of us had eaten, so Sandy ordered nachos and a Tom Collins, and I got a rum and Coke.

The crowd was light. A few couples were out on the floor, and most of them were already blitzed. I started in on the nachos, trying not to spill on myself before I'd even had anything to drink.

I pointed to a pair of girls on the near side of the dance floor. "That looks like a younger version of us." The girls were drunk and grinding up against their guys, no inhibitions at all.

Sandy leaned over. "They just have a head start. We'll look like that in about two hours," she said, sucking down more of her drink. "And we still look way better than that."

I started on my drink and scooped another chip in the cheese. The music was loud, and I was drifting away, thinking about my night with Bill. He was so damn hot and irresistible. I wished he would walk in now and sit down with us. I wanted to introduce him to Sandy so she could see the Bill I saw. But then Barbie came to mind. Maybe that was all I needed to know about Bill.

I was still vacillating between the huggable Bill and the despicable Bill when they came up behind us.

"Can we buy you two another drink?" the tall one asked. He was better looking than his short sidekick.

I didn't need to think before answering. "I'm good, thanks."

A light kick to the shins woke me up. I was violating Sandy's game plan.

I downed the rest of my glass. "Now I could use another," I said, laughing.

Since I'd only had two nachos for dinner so far, downing the whole drink was not a good plan. But I had to make it up to Sandy.

The guys were good sports about it. The short one sat beside me, and the taller, better-looking one took up station on the other side of Sandy. Just my luck. They were older than we were and wore expensive suits. They could have used quite a bit more time at the gym, or more likely, they needed to start using the gym. The short one's paunch made him look even shorter than he was. At least I got a chance to follow my drink with more food when they added wings to the order.

After some small talk and more than a few glances down Sandy's shirt, the tall one suggested a dance, and we both agreed.

When we returned to our seats, they bought another round of drinks and some poppers and hung out for a while. They said they were on a business trip from Chicago. The short one told me he was in finance, and the tall one was in sales. Their answers were becoming less and less important as the night wore on.

When Sandy had had enough of them, she lied and intimated that we were gay. After that, it wasn't long before the guys excused themselves to the restroom.

"What'd you do that for?" I complained. "I was just about to get another drink."

"There's other fish in the sea."

The Slut Sisters arrived just then and took a table off to the side. We had seen them operate before. They always came in together and almost never left alone. Usually, they went with some older rich-looking guy.

When the guys got back from the bathroom, they took a table rather than join us again and ordered a pair of beers. It didn't take long for the Slut Sisters to lock in their targeting radar. They headed over to their table, the younger one leading the way.

"Do you think they know what they're in for?" Sandy asked.

"Not a chance in hell," I replied. "Which one do you think they'll pick?"

"No idea, but this should be fun to watch."

They weren't actually sisters, at least we didn't think so, but they always came in together and left together. What the two guys didn't know was that one of them was headed for disappointment. The Slut Sisters always left with only one guy. And that guy would have a shit-eating grin on his face because he was about to be double-teamed.

We didn't know, but Sandy thought it likely the guy woke up the next day with a lighter wallet, too.

I was sucking down the last of my drink when another pair of guys came at us from across the room. So, we got another round after all. The tall one was Todd, and he sat next to Sandy. Chuck was left with me. Why did I always get the shorter ones?

They were pretty sauced already, and Chuck started getting a little too touchy-feely for my taste. I had removed his hand from my thigh, and now he had his arm around my waist. He also should have brought breath mints.

Sandy was getting much the same treatment from Todd. She didn't look happy. Although it wasn't all that late, she stood and announced, "It's pumpkin time."

Time for us to go. No more free drinks tonight.

As I stood up, Chuck grabbed my arm and said, "You're not leaving yet." He made it sound like a statement, not a question.

"It's our bedtime," I told him.

Bad idea.

That was not the right phrase for these guys. The douchebag comeback was inevitable.

"We can help you with that," Chuck said with a chuckle.

In your dreams, Chuckie.

I gave him the evil eye. "No, thanks." My response was much more polite than I felt as I wrested my arm away.

"What? I'm not good enough for you 'cause I don't wear a suit?"

It's not the suit, dude. It's the way you smell.

I was pissed. I got up in his face. "No, Chuck, it's your breath." I turned to walk away.

That's when he grabbed me again and jerked me back to the bar.

Bad move, asshole.

I grabbed his drink off the bar, threw it in his face, and brought my knee up into his balls.

"Bitch!" He doubled over. My knee had done the trick, and he let go of my arm.

Todd backed away, his eyes wide as we made our escape.

CHAPTER 10

Bill

It had been another long day——and not just because of my night at the bar with Marco yesterday. Most everyone had left by the time I finished my call to Singapore. I put the letter Dad had written me away, after reading it for the millionth time. His memorial service had been last week, and I still couldn't come to grips with him being gone.

I had used the company town car this morning, so I called our driver, Jason. He assured me he would be outside by the time I got downstairs. I had no idea how he did it, being on call all the time. I made a point of trying to give him as much notice as possible when I needed him, but this evening, it had just been one thing after another.

I thought about Lauren as I rode the elevator down. I had hoped she would call again, but she hadn't. I still wanted to invite her to lunch for helping me that night at the hospital, but the one time I had run into her in a private setting at work, she'd been somewhat colder than glacial. She'd asked me if I got a second date with "Barbie."

I probably needed to let her cool down before approaching her again, because I didn't want to screw it up. Next week for sure. I just needed to figure her out. For some reason, she was more of an enigma than any woman I had known.

With any other woman, I would have treated it like baseball. If I struck out, who cared? There was always the next pitch, the next girl. But I didn't want the next girl.

Then when I opened the door to the street, I found her there, waiting, twenty feet away.

"You working late too?" I asked.

I'd startled her. She turned around, and a smile of recognition grew on her face.

"No rest for the wicked. What's your excuse?" She didn't approach. She looked away down the street again.

Jason had parked right in front of the door. I passed him by and walked over to her. "I don't have a boss to tell me when I can go home."

"Neither do I," she countered with a smile. "Mine is always telling me when I can't."

She was not a happy employee today.

I chuckled. "I'll have to do something about that."

"Yeah, like write a memo or something?"

This woman certainly had an attitude on her. "Something like that. By the way, if you were just here on the street waiting for me, I'm honored."

Her face flushed. Her lips pursed, then a slight grin appeared ——my first good reaction from her since my father died.

"No way, Casanova. That engine light thingy in my car lit up yesterday, and they said it wouldn't be ready till tomorrow morning. So I'm splurging on a taxi tonight."

More sarcasm. The Casanova comment hurt, but I guess I'd earned it based on our previous encounters.

"Could I offer you a lift?" I pointed toward Jason in the town car. "Your chariot awaits."

She stood her ground. "You take limos everywhere?" She turned and looked down the street again.

Always that attitude. "Please just say yes, and I can show you the difference between a limo and a town car."

She looked back up the street. With still no taxis in sight, she relented. "Thank you, Mr. Covington. I haven't seen a cab in ten minutes."

"Just one thing," I said. "You have to call me Bill."

"Deal."

I placed a hand at the small of her back and guided her toward the car. She didn't resist. A tingle ran up my arm. I should have approached her earlier. This felt so right. *Why did I wait so long?*

She scooted across the seat to the far side, keeping distance between us. She combed her hair behind her ear with her finger, highlighting her striking neck. Her earrings were simple hoops with just the right dangle. I couldn't help but stare.

She caught me looking longer than I should have. "Something you want to say, Mr. Covington?"

"Bill," I reminded her. "Could I interest you in a bite to eat?" It was worth a try.

"I don't think it's a good idea for me to go out with you."

That was not encouraging. "Lauren, it's not a date, just a bite to eat to thank you for helping me," I said.

"Dinner is still a date, Mr. Covington. No thanks."

"Bill."

"No thanks, Bill."

The return to Mr. Covington was not encouraging, but *no thanks* was better than a flat *no*. "Please, and not dinner… How about just appetizers and you pick the place?" I could sense I was getting closer to a *yes*.

She cocked an eyebrow. "Is this a condition of the ride?" Her lips curled just slightly. Her words said *maybe*, but her eyes said yes.

"Absolutely not. Just tell Jason where you want to go."

She thought for a moment, eyeing me cautiously.

I put on my best puppy dog face, and it looked like I might get to a *yes*. Why did this woman get under my skin?

She hesitated. "Jason, do you know the Rusty Bucket?"

"Yes, ma'am," he said, looking into the rearview mirror.

Lauren looked at me. "I'm not going unless you get him to stop calling me ma'am."

Jason corrected himself. "Yes, Miss Lauren. Anything you say."

My heart skipped a beat. This was a *yes*.

The tension in her jaw relaxed. Her lips turned up as a hint of a smile emerged, and her eyes appraised me. "This is not a date."

"Absolutely not," I agreed.

Success.

~

JASON WAITED WHILE LAUREN AND I WENT INTO THE RUSTY BUCKET.

She picked a table near the bar. "Sandy, that's my roommate, and I come here when we want to hang out. The drinks are cheap, and they don't skimp on the appetizers." Her face was radiant, and her blond hair reflected the hanging lights in this place. She tore her napkin in little strips.

"What do you recommend?" I asked, unsure how to start this conversation.

It didn't make sense. I was never tongue-tied with women. I had to concentrate on not bouncing my nervous knee.

She ordered a nacho plate and a chardonnay for each of us.

The place had a dance floor, pool tables, a bar, and a section of tables. The walls were covered in old wooden planks like the side of a hundred-year-old barn, with antique farm and carpentry items up on the walls. An old-style jukebox sat against the wall next to the dance floor. A nice-looking place, and it was probably hopping on the weekends.

"It suits you," I said, motioning to the room. I grabbed a chip and loaded it up. I tried to avoid staring at her cleavage.

Her brow arched. "How so?" She continued to fidget with her napkin, not looking directly at me.

"It looks like an honest, no-nonsense kind of place, not pretentious. What you see is what you get. Just like you."

A blush rose from her chest to her cheeks. "Why, thank you."

Her blush had drawn my attention to her tits. Her blouse was open a respectable-for-work amount. A thin gold chain around her neck supported a small, gold heart-shaped pendant above her cleavage. My pulse quickened. I wanted to be that pendant, listening to her heartbeat. My dick swelled as I imagined unbuttoning her blouse farther, like down to her navel. I wanted to feel and kiss those tits. I sipped my wine as I consciously shifted my glance more appropriately higher.

Her warm eyes greeted mine with a knowing twinkle.

"One thing you'll learn about me, I'm honest," I told her, looking into her eyes, the soft blue of tropical water.

Her smile brightened, and her head tilted a little to the side as she fingered the stem of her wine glass. "What makes you think I want to learn about you?" She took a sip. She eyed me over the rim of her glass as she appraised my reaction.

She was toying with me. That was more progress.

"Maybe you don't just yet, but I would like to learn more about Lauren Zumwalt, and I can only do that if I can convince you to spend some more time with me."

Her eyes brightened as she contemplated how to answer that.

Her grin told me she liked the idea. She was just apprehensive for some reason.

"Not tonight," I added.

She giggled. "Of course not." She sipped some more of her wine and loaded up a chip.

"But when you're ready." We had finished less than half the nachos, and she was right. They were good.

She touched my hand with hers. The touch was more electric than it should have been. It was just my hand, after all.

"Since you're all about honesty tonight, maybe you could tell me about Barbie," she said.

Where did that question come from? I was so focused on her touch that I went blank.

"Who?" I couldn't recall a Barbie. Then it occurred to me who she meant.

"The girl whose name you didn't know," she explained, "the one I ruined your second date with."

This was going to shit pretty quickly. "Oh, her. Was that her name?" I was fucking this up. "It's not what you think."

She dropped her smile. "What mall did you pick her up at, anyway?"

Where is all the anger coming from? "What are you talking about?"

"She looked like she was just out of high school, for God's sake." Her nostrils flared. She was really testy now.

I put my glass down. "Do you really want to know what happened?" I stared straight into her eyes.

After all, what happened that night wasn't my fault.

She stood up and put the strap of her purse on her shoulder. "Not really." She turned and left.

All the air rushed out of my lungs. This had started so well. How had I fucked it up so royally?

CHAPTER 11

LAUREN

"IT'S NOT WHAT IT LOOKED LIKE," BILL CALLED FROM BEHIND ME.

Is he running after me?

"Lauren, she drugged me."

What a lame thing to say. I turned to face the jerk. "What the hell kind of excuse is that?"

He reached for my hand as he jogged up.

I pulled it away.

He looked into my eyes with an intensity that froze me in place. "She approached me at a bar. I had two scotch and waters and got so drunk I could barely walk."

"Sure. So being drunk is your excuse?"

"She took me home in a cab. I don't remember anything about what happened before you knocked on my door."

I gritted my teeth. "Maybe the used condom on the floor spells it out for you?"

He grabbed for my hand again and held it tightly. I couldn't pull it away this time.

"I don't get falling-down drunk on two scotches. She drugged me." His eyes were piercing and sincere. His hand was warm. He loosened his grip.

"So you're going with she drugged you, and that's your story?"

"I told you I was honest, and that's the truth, so help me God. The doctor at the hospital that night took a blood sample because I was so disoriented."

I blinked. This was so off-the-wall batshit crazy that it didn't make any sense. "So, now you're going with she was a crazed teenage psycho out to take advantage of a grown man like you?"

"I've got the tests to prove it. The lucky part is her plan failed. She left her phone, which I found when I got back to the condo. She had pictures of me——*us*. It's the second time in a fucking month that's happened. She planned to blackmail me or sell them to the tabloids or something." He spat the words out with fury in his voice.

I looked at him, unable to sense any deceit. Either he was telling the truth or he was the best bullshitter I had ever met. I gave him my evil stare——the stare that would wear the bullshitters down and lead to a smirk that would give them away.

He didn't smirk. He didn't fidget. He didn't blink.

"That's why I was so out of it that night," he said.

"You're really sticking with she drugged you?" I continued my stare.

He pulled papers out of his jacket pocket. "You want to check the results Dr. Dalton gave me that night?" He shoved them at me.

I *had* seen the doctor take some blood from him. I'd thought the test was about his father.

I took the sheets from him. If this was a ruse, he would crack as I read the papers. I opened them and watched his expression.

His face told me the story. He was relieved to have me look at them. He was telling the truth.

I had taken him for a mall-trolling deviant, and I had been wrong. The poor man had been targeted by the teenage equivalent of the Slut Sisters.

"Being rich sucks, huh?" I snorted.

I should have given him the benefit of the doubt and listened at the table. *Now who's the ass?*

He returned the papers to his pocket. "You have no idea."

I felt so ashamed to have prejudged him.

We started walking, and he took my hand again, gently this time.

"How far to your place?" He smiled at me.

I had gone from spilling coffee on this man and fantasizing about elevator sex to being convinced he was a pervert, and accusing him of it, to now holding hands as he walked me home. What a turnaround.

"Just two blocks."

"Please don't tell anyone what I told you tonight."

His eyes pleaded with me. He was hurt as well as angry about what had happened to him.

"Your secret is safe with me." We walked in silence, hand in hand like teenagers.

My apartment building wasn't much, but it was home. He followed me up the stairs to the second floor, and we stopped outside my door. I put my hand in my purse to fish out my keys, but I couldn't end things like this. I dropped my purse, and I put my arms around him. I rested my head against his chest.

He hesitated, then put his arms around me and pulled me close.

I listened to his breathing and his heartbeat. "I'm sorry I jumped to the wrong conclusion," I said softly.

He rubbed my back. "No worries, Lauren." He gave me a squeeze. "This was a very good not-date. I had a good time."

"Me too." I looked up into the passion in his eyes and brought my lips up to his. I speared my hands through his hair, pulling him near.

A heartbeat later, his mouth claimed mine as his tongue parted my lips. His hair smelled woodsy, like a pine forest. He pulled me closer. I felt the hardness of his arousal against my belly just before my panties melted from the heat.

One hand moved down to grasp my ass, and the other drifted

up to caress the side of my breast. A rush of heat washed over me. This was even better than my fantasy. Liquid heat pooled between my thighs. He pushed me against the wall as I strained to pull myself higher.

Our tongues jousted for position as I feasted on him, inhaling his scent, weaving my fingers through his hair, and feeling the hardness of his cock against me. All logical thought stopped. This was chemistry and passion I hadn't experienced before. I melded my body to his. I needed more——more contact, more touching, more feeling, more tasting, more *him*.

He pulled his mouth away and sucked on my lower lip, giving himself enough room to palm my breast. My nipples pebbled as he teased my breasts, tracing his fingers over the swell of my cleavage and leaving a trail of tingles as he cupped and massaged my breast over my blouse. He moved his thumb back and forth over my hardened nipple and kissed my neck down to my collarbone.

This was unreal. I whimpered. His touch was soft and exhilarating at the same time. I was lost in his lips and his hands. I arched my hips and rubbed against his cock, getting a moan out of him.

He took my earlobe in his mouth and sucked on it before he blew into my ear, sending any remaining rational thoughts through my head and out the other side.

This was getting too intense too quickly. My brain was misfiring. I had to stop. I pulled back and kissed him gently on the lips.

"Bill," I said.

He loosened his grip on me but continued to trace circles over my breast with his thumb. Circles of heat and longing followed his touch. I ached for more. I wanted to invite him in so badly, but instead I did the hardest thing I have ever done.

"Goodnight, Bill." I let go of him.

He released me, but his eyes were still hot with lust.

I picked up my purse, located my keys, and unlocked the door.

Why didn't I just invite him in? Because I'm the stupidest girl on the planet. The absolute stupidest. Dumber than a rock.

"How about a real date next time?" he asked before I opened the door.

I tried to act cool. "Maybe lunch next week."

I opened my door. My brain said *play hard to get,* but the dampness in my panties and the ache in my breasts argued otherwise. I almost grabbed his hand to pull him inside. Almost.

"Lunch then. Goodnight, Lauren. I had a good time." He turned and walked down the hallway toward the stairs.

I was such an idiot. "Bill," I called.

He turned, and longing filled his eyes.

"I had a really good time too," I said.

Then I chickened out, waved goodbye, and went into my apartment. *Alone.*

Did I fuck this up?

I closed the door and leaned back against it. At least we had agreed on a date, though only a lunch date. *A date.* Wow, I was flushed, and my heart was racing.

Sandy emerged from the kitchen and looked me over. "What the hell happened to you? You win the lottery or something?"

"He kissed me," I blurted.

"Guys do that sometimes." She opened the fridge. "We agreed Zack was a double loser, so who did Kate set you up with this time, girl?"

I smiled. "Bill."

"You mean BD Bill? You fucking with me?"

I pried myself away from the door, dropped my purse on the counter, and sank into the couch. "Nope."

"So spill. What happened? Girl, I want all the X-rated details." Sandy joined me on the couch.

"He drove me to the Bucket."

She pulled her knees up to her chest. "How does a rich dude like BD know about the Bucket?"

"I suggested it."

Sandy's eyes went wide. "Are you fucking losing it? When a bazillionaire takes you out, you go to someplace expensive like Melisse. You don't fucking waste your date on the Bucket."

"It wasn't a date," I corrected her.

Sandy almost doubled over, laughing. "Listen to yourself. You two go out, you catch some food or drink, then you kiss. On what fucking planet is that not a date?"

She had a point. "Okay, so it was sort of a date."

"You are so screwed up, girl. I told you to jump his bones and then forget him. Instead, you're doing the opposite. You're getting a crush on the guy."

"Am not," I argued.

Sandy was not going to let this go. "Are too, and you're not even getting laid. It's all ass backwards."

She could be so annoying when she was right.

THE NEXT MORNING, I WAS STILL REPLAYING SCENES FROM LAST NIGHT'S *Bachelor* episode in my head. I had barely put down the Wicked Witch's latte when she tasted it and threw it in the trash.

"Five pumps, not four. Can't you get anything right, Zumwalt?"

"I ordered five pumps."

Me and my big mouth. Talking back to Marissa was always a mistake. No more mental *Bachelor* reruns for me.

The eruption was immediate. "You think I can't tell the difference?" she yelled. "Go get another one, and get it right this time."

They were probably recording this event on the seismograph at Berkeley.

Get your own, bitch! I didn't say it, but I came close, and the look on Karen's face told me she would have cheered if I had.

I was now down to five months and nineteen days before Freedom From Marissa Day. I walked back to Starbucks, mentally calculating the number of work days involved. If only I didn't have to worry about Brandon. Math complete, I moved on to my other favorite mental activity.

Bill hadn't called me. He had only talked to me in passing since our not-date kiss last week, and so far, there'd been no mention of lunch. Maybe Sandy was right. She'd pegged him as the type who was always charming the nearest woman out of her pants and moving on. He probably preferred girls who dropped their drawers on the first date anyway. Was it stupid to wonder if he still wanted to have lunch?

He had disappeared a few afternoons last week and come back to work a little sweaty and disheveled. I'd asked Judy where he went, but she said she didn't know.

Maybe he had some hot after-lunch rendezvous with a Barbie type. No, my Bill wouldn't do that to me. Would he?

But he wasn't really *my* Bill. We had shared a mind-blowing kiss——at least I thought it was mind-blowing——but if he felt the same way, wouldn't he have called?

This mental ping-pong was not getting me anywhere. He'd said he wanted to go out, hadn't he? I was pretty sure I hadn't imagined that.

When I got back upstairs, Marissa wasn't waiting for her stupid latte. She was glued to her computer, clicking between sites.

"Oh my God," was all she said, three times in a row. I set down the cup.

I went back to my desk, happy to not interact with her.

Karen came over with wide eyes. "You have to see this," she said in a cringe-worthy tone as she leaned over and typed an address into my browser.

It was a tabloid site, and there at the top of the page was Bill with a buxom blonde. I started reading. Bill had been in a car accident with her, and she was not just any blonde, but Kourtney Belzarian, of celebrity-sex-tape fame. They'd been out drinking, and he'd crashed the car. The headline read *Can Kourtney hold on to Two-a-Month Bill?* The article recounted how last summer he'd earned the nickname by dating six different actresses over the course of a few months.

How could he?

This explained why lunch was off. Sandy was right. Men were assholes. I needed to cool off before I did something super stupid. I still had five months and nineteen days here, and Brandon was counting on me.

How could I have been so gullible? I had even believed his lie about Mall Barbie. Had sex-tape Kourtney drugged him too?

The lying sack of shit.

CHAPTER 12

Bill

The dinner last night at the Belzarians' had gone well until Kourtney had driven me down the hill. She hadn't paid attention to the road——"*watching for paparazzi,*" she'd told me.

It wasn't a bad accident, but the tree had pushed the fender in against the wheel, and the car needed a tow.

I'd switched places with her after the airbags deflated because I knew I would pass the breathalyzer, and she might not.

The cops had arrived and called a tow for us. They got out the breathalyzer for me.

Then it started. The paparazzi had come out of nowhere. What asswipes.

This morning, I'd woken up with a sore neck and some bruises. I'd skipped my workout but still got to the office late. The problems began as soon as I arrived.

Judy had a stack of messages for me, and Uncle Garth was waiting by my door.

He followed me in, closing the door after him. "William, this will be a problem."

I was in no mood for a lecture, especially when the accident wasn't my fault. "I'm fine, thank you. How are you this morning?" I replied tersely.

That slowed him down. "Sorry. Are you okay?" The concern on his face was genuine.

"Just a sore neck and a few bruises. Thanks for asking." I sat and motioned for him to take a seat as well. "Before you start, I was not the one driving. Now, what were you saying?"

"You were just the passenger?"

"That's what I fucking said, isn't it?"

A semblance of a smile replaced the grimace on my uncle's face. "Good, then we can go out and correct the news people and get you off the hook."

"We're not doing that," I insisted.

"Why not? Right now you look reckless and out of control."

I leaned forward. "Kourtney is a good friend of mine. She has a prior DUI. If she'd failed the breathalyzer, it could mean jail time. So we switched places before the cops came."

Garth thought for a moment. "William, we have to get ahead of this. It is all over the internet, and the bad publicity could torpedo the Benson deal." He shifted in his chair. He seemed truly worried.

I was the CEO, wasn't I? So it was my turn to give orders.

"Thanks for the heads-up, Uncle Garth. You just babysit the deal and make it happen. I'll meet with them and butter 'em up, but I'm not throwing Kourtney under the bus." I picked up my stack of messages. "Now I have some calls to make."

Uncle Garth left the office. He was not a happy camper, but that was his problem. He'd been the one to insist I had to be the CEO.

After I had gotten through the top half of the stack, I walked to the break room for some coffee.

There she was, just the person I needed right now. The room was empty except for Lauren with her back to me. Her beautiful blond hair cascaded over her shoulders, and she shifted her hips as she poured a cup of coffee from the carafe. Oh, those hips were killing me. Fucking irresistible was the only way to describe her from this angle.

"There you are," I said. "How about tomorrow for lunch?"

She stiffened.

Not a good sign.

She didn't look up. When she finished pouring, she turned and fixed me with an icy glare. "Have a good time last night?"

Fuck me.

I should have asked her earlier. "Lauren, it's not what it looks like." I approached her.

She raised her hand to stop my advance. "You say that a lot. I don't want to hear it." She put her head down and started around me. "How could you?" She walked out.

How could I what?

I let her go.

How much shittier can today get?

I LEFT WORK EARLIER THAN NORMAL AND WENT HOME INSTEAD OF TO the restaurant. The soreness from the accident was getting worse, and I was bushed. After a microwave dinner and a glass of red to wash down a handful of Advil, it was time to tell Lauren the truth about last night. I couldn't stand to have her mad at me. I picked up the phone and dialed her number. She didn't answer. Probably out with her roommate, or out on a date.

That last thought hurt.

Less than five minutes later, and into my second glass of wine, I rushed to my phone as it rang.

Damn. It was Uncle Garth, not Lauren.

I answered.

"William, I have Liam with us on a conference call."

"Okay."

"I have bad news," Garth began. "The Bensons are pulling out. They just called to say that they have reconsidered the investment and are not ready to move forward right now based on the changes in our situation."

This was not what I needed to hear. "How much more time do you think they need?"

"William, their position is that they might reconsider in six months or so, and we do not have that kind of time," Garth replied.

Liam interjected. "Bill, Lloyd Benson was investing because of Dad, and they just think you're too much of an unknown at this point."

Now the seatbelt bruises had to compete with a sudden headache. "I can meet with them tomorrow and every day after that until I get them back on board." I took another swig of wine.

There was a pause on the line before Garth spoke again. "William, that will not do it quickly enough. We are going to have to execute a Plan B. I am calling to urge you to start the cutbacks right away."

Liam interrupted. "Or we could start the ball rolling with Four Corners."

"That is why Liam is on the call," Garth said. "I disagree, but he deserves to be heard."

"Liam," I said, "why do you keep suggesting selling to Four Corners?"

"I've seen Uncle Garth's projections, and they're not pretty," he said. "I think it could get much worse than he anticipates. If we get Four Corners on board now, we can bridge the time until the avionics division becomes cash positive. If we don't, and we can't get past the current liquidity crisis, then the company goes completely down the tubes, and in Chapter Eleven, we all get wiped out. I think it's just playing it safe to get something from Four Corners while we can. Otherwise, everybody in the family——you, me, Patrick, Katie, Steven, *everybody*——gets wiped out. With Four Corners, we get something. With bankruptcy, we get nothing."

"So you don't think we can make it through the rough patch with Uncle Garth's approach?" I asked.

"I think the chances are slim to none," Liam responded. "I saw what happened to the McCullens when their suppliers heard they had a cash crunch. The deliveries stopped, the shit hit the fan, and they went Chapter Eleven in two months. That's the kind of unpredictable downside Uncle Garth can't project."

He had a point there. The McCullen firm had seemed in fine shape, until one day it just wasn't. And it had not turned out well for them, that's for sure.

"Thanks for calling, guys, but I'm not going to decide on something like this tonight."

"Bill, the worst thing right now is delay," Garth said.

I was not going to be rushed. "Call a department-head meeting tomorrow morning. I would like to get some more input on this."

Liam spoke again. "I'm not sure it's wise to involve that many people. We need to keep something like this under wraps. If the word gets out, it could sink us."

That sounded just plain wrong to me. "This is their company and their jobs too, isn't it? I want their input. Let's say nine thirty."

After a few more attempts to get me to whittle down the meeting, they gave up, and we ended the call.

This had been a really shitty twenty-four hours. Car accident, followed by Lauren snubbing me, followed by this call. I could end up being the Covington to oversee the demise of the company my grandfather and my father had spent two generations building. In just a few weeks, everything had blown up.

I poured another glass of wine. The whole world was turning to fucking shit, and the one person I wanted to talk to about it wouldn't answer her phone.

WHEN I WALKED INTO THE CONFERENCE ROOM AT NINE THIRTY THE next morning, the group was assembled, but they had not yet been told the topic of the meeting.

"Everybody here?" I asked Garth.

"All but one," he said. "Marketing is not here. Ms. Bitz is across town and not expected back until eleven."

I could solve that one. "We can't have them excluded, so invite Lauren Zumwalt in to cover for her, please."

Lauren arrived, and I started the meeting. "I wanted all the department heads here this morning for two reasons," I began. "First, I want you all to know the current situation at the company. And second, I don't want to decide among the alternatives without your input, because all of you know so much more about Covington than I do right now, and we all have a stake in this."

The room was so quiet you could have heard an ant fart.

"When my father recently purchased the food division, he took on a significant amount of debt in the transaction. His plan was to get an investment from the Benson Group to take care of the increased debt after the purchase, and that was scheduled for this quarter. Last evening, we were told they no longer wish to go forward. The debt is so large that without that investment, we have a big problem."

That shook the crowd. Several jaws dropped.

"Garth, would you fill them in on some of the options for dealing with this?"

Uncle Garth went on for some time, and it was evident on the faces around the table that the cuts he was suggesting would be painful. Everyone looked scared, as if they had just been diagnosed with cancer.

"Thank you, Garth. Now, those are not the only options. Liam, could you please explain your alternative?"

Liam did so, but the group seemed no more pleased with the idea of selling a stake to the Four Corners Hedge Fund than they had been with Garth's draconian cuts. No doubt they'd read the magazines and knew the Four Corners' reputation as well as I did.

Around the table, they looked like deer in the headlights, stunned——or maybe appalled was a better description. Liam was concerned about his net worth. They were concerned about their jobs, and feeding their families.

When Liam finished, I opened the floor for some discussion. Several of them had questions about Garth's alternatives, most of which he handled with ease. He had spent considerable time on this. None of his answers did anything to cheer the group.

Several people expressed apprehension about Liam's Four Corners alternative.

Garth was explaining something about debt payments when I heard *"You are the problem"* in a hushed tone.

I was pretty sure Lauren had said it, leaning toward Herbert. She'd meant to share this with her neighbor, not the group.

"What was that, Miss Zumwalt? Could you repeat that, please?"

She slumped in her chair and looked down at the table. "Nothing."

"No, out with it," I insisted. "We need to discuss all the options." I stared at her. "Should I repeat it for you?"

She returned my gaze in a very determined manner. She spoke in a quiet voice. "I said *you* are the problem."

A hushed quiet enveloped the room.

"But I meant you're a *marketing* problem," she added.

Several people moved back slightly from the table, as if they wanted to get as far away from her as possible—not to mention the bomb she'd just lit the fuse on.

"Please explain," I said calmly.

My response seemed to embolden her. "With your father at the helm, we would have been fine. The problem is that you are not him, and you have not been able to do what he could do. You have also done things he would *not* do, such as get caught in a compromising situation that ends up in the tabloids."

I caught only a slight quaver in her voice. She certainly didn't pull any punches. It hurt to acknowledge that she was absolutely right on the tabloid part. I waited for her to continue.

The room was deathly quiet. The group seemed to be waiting for me to unleash a thunderbolt and make Lauren disappear in a puff of smoke.

The paparazzi had gotten it all wrong, but only I knew that. "The news reports were wrong. It wasn't how it looked," I said. I shouldn't have even said that much.

"It doesn't matter what really happened," she continued. "The perception is the reality we have to deal with."

What could I say to that? My stomach sank. I was the problem, all right. If Dad were still here, we wouldn't be in this predicament.

"Any other comments?" I asked half-heartedly.

The group was quiet, seeming stunned by her direct assault on me and likely still expecting the thunderbolt. Nobody came to her defense. Garth looked oddly pleased.

She was the only one willing to be honest in the whole group.

And in her opinion, I was a dickhead or worse.

CHAPTER 13

Lauren

I nearly died when Bill heard my comment. For a moment, it looked like I might not have to count down my remaining five-plus months at this job.

After the meeting, I wandered back to my desk.

What did I just do?

How quickly could they fire somebody, anyway? Or would I merely be one of the first of the layoffs that were evidently just over the horizon? *Ten thousand people,* his uncle had mentioned we might need to let go. That was ten thousand lives affected. Many more, once you figured in the families.

Why couldn't he keep it in his pants? And Kourtney Belzarian? Sure, she wasn't jailbait like Barbie, but he was probably going to need some heavy-duty shots. Was he going to insist that she'd drugged him too? Or was he going to star in her third sex tape?

Marissa returned just before lunch. Not long after that, Bill called her into his office with his brother Liam and his uncle, the CFO. I heard them say they were going to explain the meeting to her.

Afterward, when she rounded the corner into marketing, she looked madder than a cat thrown in a lake. She escorted me into one of the small conference rooms.

"How could you take my spot at the table?" she yelled.

"I didn't volunteer. They told me to go."

She pointed her finger at me as I backed up. "Then you should have had the good sense to keep your mouth shut. Insulting Mr. Covington? How could you?" She paced back and forth, mumbling to herself. "Get out of my sight."

I left the room while Marissa went back to her office, still mumbling. This morning had started off so normally. How had it all gone to shit?

~

Bill

When I returned to my office, I leaned back in my chair, scanning the ceiling. It didn't have any answers for me. I closed my eyes to think.

I had Judy hold my calls until Ms. Bitz from marketing returned and we brought her up to speed. Needless to say by lunchtime, things still didn't feel any better.

"You are the problem." I could still hear Lauren's words clear as day, and they were just as clearly correct, despite her boss's outrage about them.

I could not allow two generations of Covington work to go down the toilet. There had to be a solution.

I closed my eyes again, but the problem didn't get any easier. We had a debt and cash-flow problem. Was there any way to fix the cash-flow problem? Yes, and that path led in the direction of Uncle Garth's cuts. The company could recover, given enough time, but Liam was right that suppliers could be fickle and the situation could worsen in an instant, so we needed a bigger cushion than Uncle Garth had projected.

Accountants viewed everything as precise, numerical, and predictable, but events didn't behave that way. Like the weather, things were always changing.

Neither Garth nor Liam held out any hope of resurrecting the Benson financing, so that path led nowhere unless I had a time machine to undo last night's encounter with the tree.

Nobody had mentioned that we might find a suitor other than the Bensons or Four Corners.

That was what we needed——an alternative somewhere in between the two——but time was limited.

I was the problem, she had said, but then she'd added a caveat, *"a marketing problem."* I had the urge to hear more of her tormenting words. There was thought behind what she had said, not malice.

I got up, called Jason, put on my coat, and launched myself in Lauren's direction.

LAUREN

MY PHONE RANG. IT WAS SANDY, SOBBING.

"Hey, girl, Bandit is getting worse. I got a vet appointment for him at twelve thirty. Could you please take him for me? They said he needs to go in today or it could get really bad."

Bandit had thrown up all night and was clearly very sick when I had left for work.

"I have to be in Pasadena in an hour," she continued. "Please? And they said to bring some of his throw up, so I got it bagged for you."

"Sure thing. Which vet?" I wrote down the address and ended the call.

As I gathered up my purse, Marissa blocked my way. *What does the witch want now?*

She glared at me. "Where are you going? You have to stay here until I get back and wait for a call from the Robertson Group."

What now? "I can't today. I have an errand to run."

"No, you don't. You're staying here. If you want to go, leave your resignation letter on your way out."

The witch turned her broom toward the elevator and flew away.

This morning, I'd thought I could survive the next five and a half months. Now, I wasn't sure. I had to stay, *and* I had to take Bandit to the vet. That little cat meant the world to Sandy. I couldn't let her down. I blinked back tears.

I looked up the phone number for the vet and called. If I got there any later than one, they said they had no idea how long I would have to wait, or if they could fit him in at all. And yes, based on Sandy's description of his symptoms, the cat needed to be seen right away.

They recommended another vet. I couldn't hold back the tears anymore. The second vet didn't answer the phone the first time I tried. When I tried again, I got put on hold. Why was everything going wrong?

"Lauren?" It was Bill.

Why did he have to see me like this? I dabbed at the tears with a tissue and looked up. "Yes?"

He took the seat next to my desk. He probed me with soft eyes. "What's the problem?"

The nice Bill was back.

I paused. "I have to take my roommate's cat to the vet, but my boss told me I have to stay here to wait for a phone call, and I don't know if I can find another vet to take him to in time." I managed to get the words out with only two sobs.

Why can't I just lie to him and make him go away?

"Well, I can't have my most important employee in such a predicament, now can I?" Bill stood up and looked around.

"Jerry, got a minute?"

Jerry came over. "Yes, sir, Mr. Covington."

Bill put a hand on Jerry's shoulder. "Jerry, could you please cover Miss Zumwalt's phone until we get back? It could be a while, but I'd sure appreciate it."

Marissa was going to have a cow.

"Sure thing," Jerry responded.

"Thanks, Jerry." He motioned for me to get up. "Miss Zumwalt, we're going to the vet."

I told Jerry about the call Marissa expected, grabbed my purse, and Bill and I took the elevator to the street. Jason was waiting with the town car.

We got to my apartment quickly in light traffic. As we entered the hallway outside my door, a tingle ran up my spine. I couldn't help but recall the kiss Bill and I had shared right here. But that was before his date with Kourtney, the sex-tape goddess.

"This is the place, isn't it?" Bill asked.

Was he thinking about it too? Yes, this was the place where we'd kissed, but I doubted that was his question. I opened the door and stepped inside. It took a few minutes to locate Bandit. He was hiding under the couch. He didn't even try to run when I found him. I loaded him into the carrier, grabbed the gross plastic bag Sandy had left on the counter, and we were on our way.

"Why do you call him Bandit?"

The real story was that he'd stolen Sandy's heart when she first saw him, but we had a better one now.

"Because every time you come in, he ambushes you like a bandit. You can never tell where he might be hiding, then he races out, tags you, and runs back."

We got to the vet on time, and Bill insisted on accompanying me into the exam room.

After a short wait the vet, Dr. Amati, came in. "So, this is our patient, Bandit?" She petted his head and ran her hand down his back.

"Yes, Sandra Targus should have called this morning with his symptoms."

She checked the sheet on her clipboard. "So he got out last night, is that right?"

"Yes," I answered.

She took out a thermometer to check his temperature and examined the plastic bag of cat barf I had brought with me. "You have lilies in the garden?"

"We don't have a garden, but there are lilies in the courtyard."

She continued the exam for a few more minutes. She looked closer at the bag of cat barf again. Her face was unreadable.

"Based on what he looks like now, I think we got to him in time. This looks to me like lily poisoning, and the regurgitated material seems to confirm it. The plant can be extremely toxic to cats."

I gasped. "Those flowers? I had no idea." I might have been the one that left the door open last night. I shuddered at the thought.

The doctor continued. "Most people don't. He will need to stay with us for two or three days to get IV fluids, but it looks early enough. I think he'll be just fine when we're done with him."

Bill put his arm around me. His warmth was comforting. He tightened his hold.

What if I hadn't gotten here in time? Sandy would be devastated if she lost Bandit, and it would've been all my fault.

Leaving the exam room, I stopped him, the nice Bill. "Thank you so much. Sandy would just die if something happened to that cat."

Bill was quiet as we walked to the car. As he opened the door for me, he asked, "Would you say you are in my debt?"

What a loaded question. There had to be a catch. "No, I would say we're even."

That threw him. His eyebrows arched. "How do you figure that? Didn't I just save Bandit?"

I slid inside the car and smiled. "And I took care of Barbie for you." I pulled the door shut.

He rounded the car and entered the other side. His face told me I had scored points.

"Well, if it's even, I insist that you join me for lunch. I'm famished."

"I have to get back. As it is, my boss is going to throw a fit or fire me, or both."

His smile was wide and warm. "Let me handle that."

He did have a point; I owed him for saving Bandit. I didn't really have a choice. The CEO wanted to have lunch. *What am I supposed to say?*

CHAPTER 14

LAUREN

JASON DROVE US TO THE RESTAURANT BILL HAD PICKED, CARDINELLI'S in Westwood. I hadn't heard of it before, probably because it looked way out of my price range. And who has time to go to fancy restaurants, anyway?

The main room was spacious, with tall ceilings. Large windows to the courtyard lit the room with warm sunlight. Completing the scene were white tablecloths, plush decor, and older waiters with matching vests and trousers——no college part-timers or aspiring actresses slinging burgers and beer here.

I shouldn't have been surprised that a rich kid like Bill would eat at a place only other spoiled rich people could afford.

We were shown to a table next to the window with a view up the hill toward UCLA.

Bill ordered a bottle of wine, and he did it in Italian. They'd probably had a class in that sort of thing at his prep school.

I opened the menu. Naturally, it would require a degree in a foreign language to read. I could figure out that they had some types of pizza at lunch, and I found a *Ravioli Alla Lucana*, whatever that was, but the rest of it might as well have been in Russian.

"I don't read Italian," I complained. "I can't find the spaghetti and meatballs anywhere."

Bill smiled and stifled a chuckle. "I assure you it's all very good, and if you have your heart set on spaghetti and meatballs, I'm sure the chef can oblige." His dimples were on full display, but his eyes showed the predator I knew lurked just beneath the charm.

"Since you abducted me, why don't you order for both of us?" I needed to get out of here without making a complete fool of myself.

That succeeded in getting not quite a chuckle, closer to a giggle. I studied his face as he ordered *Insalata Di Spinaci* and *Petto Di Pollo Al Peperoncino*.

I loved the way his dimples danced around when he spoke. His voice, melodious but firm, sent waves of heat through me. He had a small scar on the left side of his chin. His eyes were warm and full of life. Predator be damned, I could probably look past that if only he weren't the douchebag that was at the root of ten thousand soon-to-be-announced pink slips.

"Well, do you?" he asked.

Do I what? I had totally missed the question, absorbed in his dancing dimples and my disdain for his trust-fund lifestyle.

How could he be so nonchalant? We had just heard this morning that more people than live in some small towns were going to lose their jobs and not be able to pay their rent or mortgage or whatever. Here he was, ordering expensive Italian food while those people——probably me among them——weren't going to be able to afford McDonald's for lunch.

I stretched the truth, a little beyond the breaking point. "I'm sorry, I was just thinking about poor Bandit. What did you say?"

I could have sworn he licked his lips. "I said I forgot to ask if you like Italian."

"Sure, who doesn't? I have microwave pizza pockets at least once a week."

That merited a laugh from Bill.

He wouldn't be laughing if he needed his job to make ends meet.

"You're a very funny girl when you put your mind to it, Lauren Zumwalt."

"I'm just trying to distract my abductor so I can make a run for it later."

Sort of a lie. I liked being here with him. I just didn't like the damage he had caused. He was still a douche——make that super douche.

"It's not working." He glanced around the room as if checking for something.

The waiter brought a salad for each of us, calling Bill "Mr. C" as he set them down and ground a bit of fresh pepper on each one.

He must eat here a lot if they know his name. Escape was the furthest thing from my mind right now. I knew it, and I think he suspected it as well. We sipped our water in silence, like fighters sizing each other up.

After the waiter left, Bill continued. "It just makes you more interesting and has me paying even more attention." He stabbed a piece of spinach and lifted it slowly to his mouth. "And the last thing I want right now is for you to escape."

"Wouldn't you rather be having lunch with Kourtney?"

He was trying to be nice. Why did I go and screw up the good vibe?

"Wow, that hurts. Kourtney Belzarian is just a good friend." He rubbed the back of his neck.

With a snap, the filter between my emotions and my mouth just stopped working. "Like, a good enough friend to get drunk with, but not good enough to make a sex tape with?"

All of my pent-up anger from this morning spewed forth. He had his trust fund and his perfect little life and not a care in the world except what harlot he was going to fuck tonight, regardless of what happened to the company. The rest of us peons were living paycheck to paycheck, and what would happen to us when he screwed up the company and ten thousand jobs went poof? We'd be the ones trying to afford rent and food on our unemployment checks——to say nothing of my poor fucked-up little brother.

He put down his glass. "What is your problem? We're friends from high school. Where is all this anger coming from, anyway?"

I put down my fork. My leg trembled. "While you don't care about crashing a car or two, you put the rest of us at risk. Do you have any——"

"Any what?" he asked in a huff.

"Any idea how many people's livelihoods you put in jeopardy because you can't keep it in your pants? You go about your cozy little trust-fund life without a care in the frigging world while the rest of us mere employees might be about to lose our jobs." Tears pricked my eyes. "And our families will pay the price."

His face darkened for a moment. "Would you like to know the real story? Or would you be more comfortable believing that crap you just spouted so you can be mad at me for no good reason, just because my family is rich?"

I wiped my eyes. "I have plenty of good reasons——start with about ten thousand employees who are going to lose their jobs." I dabbed the napkin to my face again.

He sat stoically.

"All so you could party with the high priestess of the sex-tape industry."

He sighed. "So perception really is all that matters to you? My question still stands; do you want to know the truth or not?" His eyes hardened.

"Go ahead. Enlighten me." *If you dare, asshole.*

"I never dated her. Not once. Like I said, I know Kourtney from way back in high school, and I asked her to get me a meeting with her father to discuss financing for a project I'm working on." He took a sip of water. "We took her car to her father's place in the hills and had the dinner meeting. She was driving me back when we had the accident."

"You mean *you* were driving," I corrected. I hadn't just looked at the headlines. I'd read the whole story. It had said he was cited for excessive speed or some such thing.

He pointed his fork at me. "Like I said, she was driving. I switched places with her before the cops got there because she had been drinking, and I hadn't. If she had failed the breathalyzer, it would have meant jail time for her. So I told them I was driving. She's a good friend, and I couldn't let her go to jail."

This was a lot to process. "So you were just rescuing the damsel in distress?"

"Like I said, she's a friend, and where I come from…" He glared at me before continuing. "Friends help friends."

I glared at him. The same thing was true where I grew up. "It just looked like…"

He loosened and then removed his tie. He then started unbuttoning his shirt, staring at me the whole time and seeming oblivious to the impropriety of undressing in the middle of a fancy restaurant. Finally he pulled open his shirt to reveal a dark diagonal bruise.

"From the seatbelt," he explained.

The bruise ran from his right shoulder down across his chest.

"The passenger's side seat belt."

I shrank in my chair.

He quickly buttoned his shirt back up, still glaring at me.

I didn't know how to continue. Could I be a bigger asshat? I had questioned his honesty twice now and been wrong both times.

"Forget it." He took a sip of water. "And you can't repeat a word of what I told you," he added, pointing his knife at me.

I slumped in my chair. I needed to change the topic for sure. Luckily, the waiter returned with our main course.

It turned out to be the most delicious chicken dish ever. Compared to this, the previous Italian food I had eaten was like cooked cardboard with ketchup on top.

"This is delicious," I repeated for the third time a few minutes later, just watching him eat, drinking in his presence.

He put down his fork. "I wanted to talk to you about what you said at the meeting."

Fuck, I was going to get fired after all. I didn't respond. Maybe this is how the rich fire people: buy them a nice meal, then *wham!*, off with their heads.

He looked over at me, finding my eyes. "I thought about what you said, and I want your opinion on how to fix the problem."

Sure, you do. You just want me to say something insulting so you feel good when you fire me. "I don't see what else I can say." That was a safe non-response, right?

"Yes, you do. You're in marketing, so if this is——rather, if *I* am ——a marketing problem, how do we fix it? Do I need to resign?"

I read his face for a moment. His gaze was questioning, not malevolent.

"My God, no."

He was serious. He actually wanted advice. *My advice.*

"Then what?" He took another forkful of his meal as he waited for me.

"This is a marketing problem. Marketing is all about perception, all about customer needs and customer desires."

If he wasn't serious, this was where I was going to get fired for sure, but I needed to go all-in.

"I heard you say basically that the Benson Group thinks the company is worse off with William Covington than it was with Wendell Covington. So from a marketing perspective, we need to determine their needs and desires. Then we sell you——" It was my turn to point my fork at him. "——as the correct Covington to meet those needs and desires. Last night's tabloid episode is clearly not the way to go, so you change what you need to change, and we sell them the new-and-improved William Covington."

"Go on."

If he wanted to fire me, he already had enough ammunition. "We heard about cutting staff and operations this morning, but those options presuppose that there's no way to resurrect the financing with the Bensons or to get similar financing elsewhere. I would suggest that you re-engage with the Bensons, and we sell them on the new-and-improved William Covington, thereby making the cuts unnecessary." I took a sip of water.

"And save ten thousand jobs or so?"

"That's the payoff. If it works, it helps a lot of people."

I had just treated this whole thing like a college case-study exercise, and half the time, the professors who explained their solutions were talking out of their asses. They never had any idea whether their ideas would work——and neither did I——but it sounded good when I was saying it.

"Why not try?" I continued. "Your uncle and your brother just want to give up. If this doesn't work, you lose a little time and your uncle can just cross off ten thousand and write in eleven thousand and implement his plan."

"I like your logic, Lauren." Bill nodded thoughtfully. "New and improved——I like that, sort of like laundry detergent. Instead of the new-and-improved Tide, the new-and-improved me." He smiled broadly.

Then he switched the conversation to talking about high school.

Five minutes ago, I had accused him of being the world's worst scumbag, and now he was regaling me with stories of growing up with his friend Marco as if nothing had ever happened. How gracious could a guy be? Me and my big fucking mouth.

As he went on, I flashed back to that first night at his condo, and my eyes undressed him. I imagined the bulging biceps under his shirt; the tufts of hair on his broad chest, hidden behind the buttons; the powerful legs under the table; and that nice, tight ass ——then that huge cock Sandy insisted he had. He had the rugged good looks to put Sandy's pretty-boy models to shame, and he was rich to boot.

He looked up to catch me staring, and a wolfish smile crossed his lips. His storytelling stopped, and we ate for a few minutes in relative silence.

"William, daaaahling." The voice came from across the room where a platinum blonde sauntered in our direction with way too much hip sway. If she worked it any harder, she was going to dislocate something.

Bill's smile vanished. He looked over and watched the exaggerated bouncing of her boobs as she approached.

She was a big-chested size four poured into a tight blue satin size-two dress with a plunging neckline and a slit up the side right to her hip, all balanced on red four-inch stilettos. She was about my height, but with perfect waves in her hair, and her nails even matched her shoes——or it could have been the other way around.

"William, what a surprise to see you. How have you been, you rascal?"

Miss Broadchest ignored me and placed her perfectly manicured red talons on his shoulder, stroking it ever so lightly.

Bill ignored the hand. "Hi, Cynthia. I'd like you to meet my good friend, Lauren."

Good friend? Where had that come from? Just this morning, I was insulter-in-chief. I smiled. I didn't know what his game was, but I could play along.

Miss Broadchest gave me a disdainful look cold enough to produce frostbite. "Charmed."

She turned right back to Bill. Even the good friend comment hadn't gotten her hand off him. She turned the smile up another notch.

"William, are you coming to the museum fundraiser this year?" Her tone was so syrupy sweet I expected a swarm of bees to descend upon her. "I hear the items in the silent auction are just to die for."

"I don't think so, Cyn."

That didn't dim the artificial smile one bit. "Well, I'll be looking for you." She disengaged her claws from my new good friend and walked away, working her hips for all they were worth.

The check arrived with Bill's eyes still glued to Miss Broadchest's ass as she shimmied away.

I could see he had a type. Between Barbie and Miss Broadchest here, it was clear that Bill was a tit man, and he liked them a D-cup or bigger.

"Will there be anything else, Mr. C?" the waiter asked.

"No thanks, Vinny. We're good," Bill replied as he took out his wallet.

"She looks determined," I noted. "You may not get out of that invitation with a simple no."

He frowned. "I'm not kidding. I went with her last year, and once is enough."

"And she is...?" I inquired.

He pulled out two crisp hundred-dollar bills and laid them on the table.

This place must've been even more expensive than I thought, and that was more Benjamins than I had ever owned.

He contemplated his answer for a moment. "A miner of rare metals."

I took another sip from my water glass. "And that is rich-people speak for what, exactly?"

He pursed his lips. "A gold digger, just like all the others."

I spat out some of my water with the laugh I couldn't control. "Like I said, rich-people speak. Why not use words ordinary earthlings can understand?"

"I just think it sounds less insulting my way."

"And what do you mean, *all the others*?"

Bill wiped his mouth with his napkin and checked his watch. "I have to head back to the office. Care to join me?" He got up from the table, obviously not intending to answer my question.

I slid back my chair. "How else would I get back? You've got the wheels."

He guided me to the door with his hand at the small of my back, and once again his touch scorched my skin. I meant to ask him something else, but my mind went blank. I focused completely on the feel of his touch.

As we reached the door, I finally recalled my question. "You must eat here often."

He held the front door open for me.

As we exited, the valet opened the door of an SL Mercedes for Miss Broadchest. The car was a godawful pink color——custom, naturally. The Germans probably had a law against colors like that. She waved at Bill as she saw us.

Bill gave a half-hearted wave back. "I do," he answered. "I own the place——or rather, my partner and I own it."

I had started to envision she of the red talons getting pulled over on the autobahn for an illegal paint color when Bill's statement snapped me back to reality.

"Naturally. All you rich kids must own restaurants." I regretted it as soon as the words came out.

He was silent as we waited for the car. "You really have a bias against people with money, don't you?"

I was mortified because he was right. That had been a really mean thing to say.

"I'm sorry. That was uncalled for. So how did you get into the restaurant business?"

Jason pulled up the car and we got in.

"It just seems pretty far removed from the things Covington does," I added.

"Like I told you, I've known Marco Cardinelli since high school. We were in the same fraternity in college. Anyway, it was his dream to start a restaurant. I thought we would be good at it, and it sounded like fun. I had the money, so we went into business together. After college, the last thing I wanted to do was go to work for my father, so that place…" He waved his hand back toward the eatery. "…is my sanctuary, my escape from Covington. Marco specializes in the preparation side, and I specialize in the procurement side, working with the growers. It wasn't up to my father's standards, but at least I'm not a surf bum."

So high-school Marco was the same Marco who owned the restaurant with him… Interesting. Bill knew how to have long-term relationships——with men, at least.

The town car wended its way back toward the normalcy of the Covington building.

"So if you own the restaurant, why'd you leave two hundred for the check? Don't you get to eat for free?"

"I could, but that wouldn't be fair to the staff. In addition to salary and tips, we have a profit-sharing plan for all the employees, so if I take up a table without paying, it takes money out of the pockets of everyone on that shift. The lunch was only sixty. The extra was a tip for Vinny. He has a new baby at home."

That floored me. This guy cared about his wait staff. And who the hell puts in a profit-sharing plan at a restaurant? I sat silently for the rest of the trip, contemplating what I had learned. The Bill Covington I'd just had lunch with was not anything like the picture I'd had of him this morning——or for part of lunch, for that matter.

I had been careful to only have a few sips of wine at lunch, but still, the elevator ride alone with him up to our floor was intoxicating. He kept his hand on my back the whole way up, not pulling me closer but keeping contact just the same. It acted like a primitive jamming device, keeping my brain waves from operating properly. This time, I didn't need to fantasize because he was holding me for real… Okay, not really holding, more like touching, but why be nitpicky?

Then the chime sounded, and the ride was over.

He said something about getting coffee, I think. His brain-wave-jamming touch got in the way. He went left, and I shuffled off to the right.

I rounded the corner into marketing.

And there she was, with eyes as black as death.

Marissa started right out in full witch mode at a million decibels. "Where have you been? I told you to stay here, and when I get back, I find you've left!"

Her face was beet red, beyond a ten on the Marissa scale, and the veins at her temples were pulsing. It looked like she was on the verge of a stroke.

"What part of *stay here* didn't you understand?" If anything, her volume was rising, broadcasting her venom to the entire floor.

"Mr——"

She cut me off right there. "HR. Now." She pointed behind me, toward the elevator. "I'm putting a written reprimand in your file, at the very least."

Marissa then marched past me and around the corner toward the elevator I had just left.

Life as I knew it had ended. Five months had just become impossible. *What am I going to do about Brandon's drug treatment?*

Seeing no way out of it, I followed Marissa sheepishly. When I turned the corner, I found Bill standing right in front of her. He had his hand on his chin as if pondering something.

He lifted his finger just as Marissa started to say something. "Ms. Bitz, I heard what you just said to Miss Zumwalt, and it seems to me that she's causing you a lot of aggravation. Is that true?"

What the what? Asshat.

Marissa seemed confused. Her anger temporarily in idle mode, she nodded. She dialed her voice down out of loudspeaker range. "I'm on the way right now——"

Bill lifted his hand to stop her. "No need. I can fix that."

Marissa froze in place.

"Actually, you go down to HR…" He hesitated thoughtfully. "…before I count to five, and you tell them today is your last day."

The eruption began again. "You can't do that! She——" Marissa was about to boil over.

"Yes, I can, and I just did," Bill said calmly. "ONE," he announced.

The entire floor was deathly quiet.

Marissa's face dropped. Things like this didn't happen in her world. Up was down and down was up. She was lost, unable to grasp this new reality.

"I fixed it so she won't aggravate you anymore, Ms. Bitz," Bill said firmly. "TWO."

"B–but…she…"

Marissa had become a babbling mess. The blood drained from her face.

"One more word, Ms. Bitz, and you can forget a severance package. THREE."

Horror flashed in her eyes. She scurried to her office without another syllable. She located her purse.

"FOUR."

She almost bowled poor Jimmy over in her rush to the elevator.

The floor remained quiet as people looked around, not quite sure what they had witnessed. If somebody had applauded, everybody would have joined in, but nobody was that sure of themselves.

Bill turned around and returned to his office without so much as a look my way.

Stunned didn't even begin to describe how I felt. Five and a half months felt doable once again.

CHAPTER 15

Bill

When Lauren had told me she worked for Marissa Bitz that first night at the hospital, I couldn't remember whether she was the nice manager on that floor or the one with the terrible reputation. I hadn't spent enough time at Dad's company yet to know. I had asked Liam later, and he'd confirmed that Ms. Bitz was the one with the turnover problem.

Although Lauren had hinted at it before, this afternoon, Ms. Bitz had *shown* me her true colors when she yelled at Lauren loudly enough for the entire floor to hear. It was hard to stay around the corner and listen——my first instinct was to stop her and protect Lauren——but I had to hear it through to the end. How had my father overlooked such an obvious morale problem? It's not like she was subtle.

Directly after telling Ms. Bitz to resign, I went to my office, called down to HR, and told them I expected her off the premises in a half hour or less and to call me when it was done.

Finished with that, I opened the door. "Judy, would you please ask Miss Zumwalt, Sarah from HR, and my brother Liam to come in? And you join us too, please."

Judy rounded up the other three and joined us in the office a few minutes later.

Lauren looked more nervous than she had at lunch. She kept her eyes down, not meeting mine.

"That was exciting." Liam couldn't contain his satisfaction. "They'll have plenty to talk about at happy hour tonight."

I leaned against the side of my desk. "Lauren, it seems there's now an opening in your department. I would like you to take over Ms. Bitz's job and figure out who to promote or hire for your old position."

Lauren looked up at me, but sat in stunned silence.

"Sarah, I would like you to work up an appropriate compensation package for Miss Zumwalt."

Sarah smiled at Lauren. "Yes sir, right away."

I moved on to my brother. "Liam, I would like you to inform the other departments of the changes and tell them they are to take their marketing issues directly to Miss Zumwalt."

He nodded his assent.

"Lauren, we're going to need all hands on deck for Operation Tide, and I would like you to chair the first meeting. How long do you need to get ready?"

Her answer was immediate. "We just need a day for research and brainstorming. We'll be ready the day after tomorrow." Confidence bloomed on her face.

I didn't expect such an aggressive schedule, but I nodded. The sooner the better. "I'll have Judy arrange the room and invite the others."

Liam spoke up. "I missed something. What is Operation Tide?"

"Didn't we say this morning that the company needed to rehabilitate my image and create a new-and-improved me? I rather prefer Operation Tide to Operation Rehabilitate."

Liam nodded and chuckled.

"Judy, please get Lauren situated in Ms. Bitz's office and arrange for new keys and an upgraded access card, please."

As the rest of the group filed out, Lauren lingered.

"Why did you do that?" she asked as she closed the door after the others had gone.

"Do what?"

"Promote me over Karen. She's been here a lot longer than I have."

I motioned for her to sit down, which she did. Her lips quivered.

"Because you are clearly the one for the job." I sat behind the desk. "You size up a situation rapidly, you have good judgment, you act quickly, you get things done, and you're not afraid to speak the truth. Don't sell yourself short, Lauren."

She looked down at the desk and blushed. The blush showed in her cleavage, and I tried not to stare at her tits. The corners of her mouth turned up in a growing smile. She brushed her hair back.

"You can't possibly know that about me after only a few days."

"Sure I can." I waited for her eyes to meet mine before continuing. "You sized up the situation with what's-her-name Barbie that first night and dealt with it. You were the only one with the balls to tell me I was the root of the company's recent problems. Nobody else would. And you articulated a strategy to deal with our most pressing problem. Who else had the insight for that? Certainly not anyone in that meeting this morning. You have all the attributes of a good manager."

She smiled. She deserved the compliments, and it felt good to see the joy they brought her.

"Meet with your new team, and spend tomorrow working up a plan."

Her blush diminished, and the grin grew. "You know I may have more unkind things to say about you. Are you ready for that?" Her eyes twinkled.

She stood, taking a confident but not aggressive stance. This was the girl——the confident, brash one. *My girl.* She might not know it yet, but she was definitely going to be *my girl.*

My dick took notice as I absorbed *all* of the woman standing in front of me. Her tits pushed against her blouse. I tried to guess what color panties she wore today and how easy or hard it would be to get into them. I didn't get up from behind my desk for fear she would notice the bulge in my pants.

I had never met anybody quite like her. I didn't know how to tell her I was looking forward to lots of long conversations with her…over lunch, over dinner, over the desk, over a couch, and maybe even over my lap——or better yet, me over her.

"I look forward to it," was all I said.

After she left, I called Sarah to make sure HR took proper care of *my girl* financially.

THAT EVENING MARCO AND I MET FOR DINNER BACK AT THE restaurant. Good thing I liked Marco's menu.

We had a habit of eating dinner at Cardinelli's at least once a week so we could see the place from a customer's point of view. We always told the staff to treat us as guests and that we were not available for consultation on any restaurant business for the evening. This gave us time to discuss our other project and review new ideas without constant interruptions.

We spent the meal reviewing the downtown project before the talk turned to my lunch with Lauren and the events that had followed at the office.

"So she's fucking yelling her head off at Lauren. Completely unprofessional bitch. She says she's going to take her down to HR to write her up, and she comes around the corner and bumps right into me."

Marco's eyes were wide. He didn't get much exposure to employee drama at the restaurant. "And?"

"So I fired her on the spot and got her the hell out of the building."

"No shit?"

I took another sip of my iced tea. I was going downtown soon, and I didn't want to drink before that.

I nodded. "It felt so right. Judy told me afterward that the whole floor had felt like cheering. I can't understand why Dad kept her around this long."

"Maybe she had pictures or something," Marco offered.

"Maybe something like that. I'll have to ask Uncle Garth. He must know."

Marco finished off the last bit of his pasta. "So, what are you going to do about your problem?" A wicked smile appeared.

"What problem?"

"It's so fucking obvious. *Her*."

"What the fuck are you talking about?"

"This Lauren chick. She's the only girl you talk about since you met her, and the last time we had lunch, you didn't even notice the two hotties giving you the eye at the next table. You're off your game, man. Bet you haven't gotten laid since you met her."

I had to think for a moment. He was right. I hadn't noticed any women in particular the last few times we'd gotten together. But I wasn't going to confirm his observation that I was currently a member of the Blue Balls Club.

"So, why aren't you movin' on this Lauren chick?" he pressed.

"She's different. I can't put my finger on it, but she's a challenge. And she's my employee. I need to go slow. I like talking to her. She's like a breath of fresh air."

"This is what I'm talking about. Listen to yourself. The Bill I know doesn't waste time talking. He's too busy unzipping things."

"Fuck you, Marco. My dad just died, and I got put in charge of the company, and I'm a little over my head with all that." I pushed away from the table. "Gotta go. I'm late as it is."

Marco waved me away. "Just remember, women suck. And the good ones——"

I finished his sentence for him. "Can suck a golf ball through a garden hose. Yeah, I know."

Marco laughed, as he always did at those one-liners. "You got it. Now go put some of those fancy rich-guy moves on this chick and get her out of your system."

I ignored him as I made my way out the door.

~

Lauren

I closed the door of my apartment behind me as I put my purse on the table by the door and took off my coat. *What a day*. Right now, I needed a glass of wine and thirty minutes on the couch with *Judge Judy* to unwind. For once, the cat didn't ambush me as I walked in.

Then I remembered why. With all of this afternoon's excitement at work, I had forgotten about Bandit.

"Any news on how Bandit is doing?" I called.

Sandy came out of her bedroom. "Yeah, they said he was really sick, but in a few days, I can get him back, and he should be okay. Thanks again so much for taking him."

"That's good. When I took him in, they said it looked like lily poisoning, of all things."

"No shit? I didn't even know that was a thing. I'm just so glad you got him to the vet in time. I really owe you."

I didn't have the heart to tell her I wouldn't have been in time if it hadn't been for Bill.

She spotted my grin. "You got that look again, girl. Did you get to spill hot coffee on your boss or something?"

So much had happened today that I didn't know where to start.

Sandy plopped down on the couch and pulled her knees up. "Get right to the juicy part."

I found the open bottle of chardonnay in the fridge and unscrewed the cap. "Well, I have good news and better news." I poured a glass for myself. "Want any?" I held up the bottle.

Sandy nodded. "Sure, I'll take a glass. So is the good news that you survived another day as the tiny cog in the gigantic Covington corporate machine?"

I handed Sandy her glass and collapsed at the other end of the couch. "The good news is that my boss got fired today." I fist-pumped the air.

Sandy gave me a high-five. "That qualifies as fucking great news! So how do you top that?"

I took a gulp of my wine, making her wait. "The better news is that I got promoted to her job."

"You're shittin' me! That's way better than awesome. This calls for a celebration." Sandy raised her glass in a mock toast. "But first, give me all the wicked details. Did they pour a bucket of water on the witch and melt her ass?"

"It was after we got back from lunch."

"Who's *we*?"

"Bill and me." I still couldn't call him *Mr. Covington*.

"You had lunch with BD? Well, why didn't you lead with that? So you got the trifecta today. You had a second date with BD——"

"It wasn't a date," I complained.

She raised a questioning eyebrow. "Did you pay for your lunch?"

Sandy had a knack for asking trick questions. I flushed. "Well, no, but——"

"No escaping it then. It's a date for sure when you don't pay. So let's see…lunch with BD, the Wicked Witch of the West gets her ass melted, and you get promoted. How much more awesome can a day get, girl? *And* you saved Bandit."

She tuned the DVR to *Judge Judy*. "Hey, did you hold out for a good raise?"

I grabbed the remote and paused the DVR. "You won't believe it. You know that twenty-four-month payback period on the relocation money I've been counting down? Well, it turns out twelve months is the normal time. That bitch Marissa told HR to double it."

"She's a fuckin' sicko."

"So that got erased, and I got a twenty-K promotion bonus and a thirty-five-percent raise. Can you fuckin' believe it?"

"Sweet, girl, this deserves Thai. Twice." Sandy gave me another high-five before picking up her phone to order.

I restarted *Judge Judy*, and we watched three episodes over Thai before I felt relaxed enough to get on my computer and start work. I didn't have any more wine.

I had to research everything about Lloyd Benson and figure out how we could repackage Bill and Covington Industries to be the opportunity he couldn't pass up.

After a while, I started to worry I'd talked myself into a promotion I didn't deserve.

But about two in the morning, I saw an opportunity.

CHAPTER 16

BILL

I DOUBLED THE LENGTH OF MY RUN THIS MORNING AND CUT OUT MY visit to the gym. Putting one foot in front of the other, it should have been easier to clear my mind, but I couldn't stop thinking about Lauren.

It was going to be a long day. I had a lot to learn, and the entire company was counting on me, but my mind was on her instead.

Liam and Garth were both waiting for me when I got to the office. Liam was not his usual cheery self.

"Are you guys going to be double-teaming me every morning?" I asked.

Liam shook his head. "No way. I avoid a meeting with Uncle Garth whenever I can. He puts me to sleep with all of his numbers."

Garth chuckled. "At least I have facts to back up my slides. All you have are pretty colors."

"You can borrow my crayons anytime. Science has proven that colors help the audience retain more information," Liam replied.

I opened the door to my office. "I'll be inside when you two are done debating presentation techniques."

Liam jumped in front of Uncle Garth and closed the door behind us. "I have a quick item." He paused and stood behind a chair as I rounded my desk. "I need to go out of town for a while."

"What's up?"

"You remember Roberta?"

"Sure. I always thought she made a mistake when she left. You two were good for each other."

Roberta had been Liam's girlfriend for the last two years of college, and he'd been heartbroken when she left to pursue a career as a journalist at the *Boston Globe*. He had intended to propose to her, but she'd told him she was leaving before he got up the nerve. If he had been smarter about it, she would be my sister-in-law now.

"She called, and she's not well. I need to go see her," he said, his eyes downcast.

"Sure, take whatever time you need. She's almost family, and family always comes first."

"Thanks, big brother." Liam left without another word, but his posture said it all. He still had a thing for Roberta, and her call had upset him.

Garth entered as Liam exited and closed the door. He moved to the chair and took a seat.

"Got a minute?" he asked.

It must be serious. He was normally the kind to ask first and sit second.

"Sure."

Garth leaned forward. "I wanted to talk about the outcome of yesterday's meeting." He fidgeted with the pen he held.

"Yes?" I waited.

"I am concerned that by embarking on this effort to resurrect the Benson financing, we are delaying the tough choices, and if it does not work, we may not have the time to put the proper actions in place early enough to avoid the devil's bargain with the Four Corners group."

"And what do you suggest?"

"I think we need to start on the cutbacks right away, or we will have no negotiating leeway with Four Corners. I know Liam wants to engage with them right away, but I think that is foolish."

"Just a moment. Let's be clear. I know Liam is set on selling the company, but that's happening over my dead body. I've met Lloyd Benson before, and I think I can talk with him and do the original deal that he and Dad negotiated——or maybe sweeten it a little. It's my job to pass the company on to the next generation in better shape than I found it, and the way to do that is getting the Benson investment."

"Okay, William. I just have to give you all the options I can."

"What I need is a Plan B and Plan C that don't involve Four Corners. If we have to pare it down to a window-washing business and grow it again from there, that's what we'll do."

"I will leave the Bensons to you, then, and be working on Plan B." He moved to leave the room.

"Don't forget Plan C," I added as he left.

I opened my drawer and took out the letter to read one more time. I had found it on my second day here, but I hadn't shown it to anyone.

Dear Bill,

If you're reading this, it's because I have gone on to a better place and you are now in charge of Covington Enterprises. I have groomed you to become the head of the company, and more importantly, the head of the family. I know you will excel at both.

You can trust your Uncle Garth and your brothers Liam, Patrick, and Steven to assist you, but the burden is yours alone as the eldest. Your one charge is to leave the family, the company, and the community better off than when you started. Let that principle guide you, and you shall accomplish great things and do so with a clear conscience. Do good to others and good will come to you is what the good book teaches us.

I have included your grandfather's Navy Cross medal. When he gave it to me, he told me he didn't deserve it because he wasn't trying to be brave. All he did was follow his gut and do the right thing.

Remember that houses and businesses can be rebuilt, but a reputation cannot. Once lost, it is gone forever. Trust your gut and do the right thing. That will serve you well.

Love,

Dad

Of course, he had neglected to mention my sister, Katie as if girls had nothing to contribute.

I put the letter and the medal back in the desk drawer. Selling the company, as Liam suggested, was not an option.

I will make you proud, Dad. I promise.

I didn't see Lauren all day. She and her new team were huddled in one of the conference rooms. They'd closed the shades so I couldn't get a peek at what they were up to. I was going to have to wait like everybody else.

THE OPERATION TIDE MEETING STARTED ON TIME THE NEXT MORNING with more marketing faces around the table than I was expecting.

"Okay, Miss Zumwalt, this is your show," I told her. "How do we start this brainstorming?"

"I have made some notes on how we could restructure the deal to make it more attractive to the Bensons without giving away the store," Uncle Garth interjected. He rose and turned toward the projector with a few slides in his hand.

Lauren smiled. "Thank you, but marketing has a few things to start with."

Garth sat back down.

Lauren looked around the room. "Instead of brainstorming from scratch, I think we have a fair amount of data to share with you already that gives us several good starting points. Karen, why don't you run us through these?"

"We've done a lot of research on the Benson Family, Lloyd

Benson in particular, and the companies under him," Karen began. "What we have here are the Bensons' key motivators and interests." She put up a slide. "Ken, why don't you tell us about this one?"

I didn't recognize the man she introduced as Ken. Must've been a new hire.

"The primary motivators here are charity and giving," he began. "I have listed here the top ten charities and causes that they give to or participate in."

The list was impressive. The Bensons contributed to the local food bank, food kitchens, the breast cancer run, housing charities——including for battered women, and Habitat for Humanity.

"This one provides particular insight." He pointed to Habitat for Humanity. "They don't just open their checkbooks. They take up hammers and help with the construction, including Lloyd Benson himself. We've confirmed that he spends two days each quarter at the building sites."

"Do we know when the next building day is?" Lauren asked.

"Not exactly, but it has been almost two months since he was there, and the next house Habitat will be working on is scheduled to begin soon, so maybe that one," Ken answered.

Lauren looked at me. "If you don't know how to use a hammer, you'd better learn by next week."

I nodded. She was certainly taking charge. "You came up with all of this since yesterday?"

Lauren nodded. "This is not all. Julie, what else?"

Julie had another slide. "By categorizing the charities and giving levels, we can see that food for the poor is, by far, their biggest priority. The regional food bank and soup kitchens, for lack of a better term, receive their biggest donations."

Lauren looked around the group. "How big a list do we have?"

After totaling the responses, the report came to twenty-one.

"I'd like the sorted list on my desk this afternoon," Lauren told them. "Karen, what else do we have?"

"Jimmy, you're up."

A kid who looked young enough to get carded at any of the

local bars moved to the projector. Jimmy had sandy blond hair that he had to keep brushing out of his eyes as he leaned over the projector. His slides included lists of articles and interviews of and by Lloyd and the other Bensons.

"We're not quite done analyzing all of these. A few are videos that we have to get from the news sources, and we won't have those until tomorrow. But we do have enough to say religion is not a factor." Jimmy shuffled.

"Spit it out, Jimmy," Lauren insisted.

"Lloyd Benson is a bit old-fashioned." He avoided eye contact with me.

So that's why he was nervous. I was not a good fit for old-fashioned.

"Anything else?" Lauren asked.

"They're also big into family get-togethers——holiday parties, barbecues, and the like."

"Are outsiders ever invited?" The question came from Karen.

"Yes and no. Some of them are hosted fundraisers, and those are a definite yes. As for the others, we don't know yet for sure."

Lauren made some notes. "Any coming up soon that we know about?"

"The museum fundraiser is next on the list, as far as I can tell," Jimmy responded.

Oh shit. I'd had an awful time at that last year with Cynthia, and I was not about to repeat it.

"The last thing on the list then, Karen."

Karen put up another slide. "This is our current list of news and media contacts."

The list was extensive.

"We still need to parcel this out so we have someone responsible for each person, but we should be able to get good coverage if we pick the appropriate outlets carefully."

I thought about raising my hand to ask my question but didn't. How silly would that be?

"What coverage?" I asked.

Lauren answered for Karen. "News and media coverage for the

new-and-improved you. We need the Bensons to be aware of the new you. The news coverage is so they can't miss it."

"And how does what I do become newsworthy?"

"Just leave that to us," Lauren answered with a knowing look. "Now, the first item on the agenda for change is that Lloyd Benson dislikes formality, so from now on, you are Bill Covington, not William Covington. Judy is already changing the nameplate on your office door and getting you new business cards."

She brushed her hair behind her ear, the ear I wanted to whisper into later.

This was a lot to take in. And Lauren had coordinated this effort in just a day. What a dynamo. I smirked to myself. Did this level of intensity carry over to the bedroom? I played my little game again and guessed basic black for today as her bra color.

Lauren rose and opened the door to the conference room. "Just one more thing."

Jason entered and stood by the door, smiling.

"Jason is taking you and Jimmy on your first outing. You're serving lunch at the soup kitchen today, and Jimmy has arranged for the press coverage. Just remember to smile and look like you're happy to be there."

"Now?"

She wore a mischievous grin. "You don't want to be late. And come see me for a debriefing when you get back."

"Yes, Miss Zumwalt. Whatever you say."

"Remember, we like informality here. It's Lauren."

That's my girl.

I stood and looked around the room. "Before I go, I want to say how impressed I am by what all of you have accomplished. Thank you."

The group was full of appreciative smiles, though Lauren was already busy assigning press contacts to each of her team.

Poor Uncle Garth didn't get a chance with his slides.

CHAPTER 17

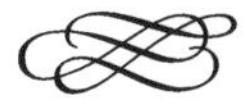

LAUREN

BILL AND JIMMY CAME BACK UP THE ELEVATOR IN THE EARLY afternoon. Bill had a small stain on his shirt.

I pointed to the smudge. "You should have worn an apron."

"I did. I was just in a hurry and got careless," he responded.

I looked at Jimmy. "Did *The Times* show up?"

"You bet, and it will be a great piece. They said we should see it on Sunday." Jimmy pointed to Bill. "You didn't tell me they knew him at the kitchen, or I would have been prepared with the history."

Jimmy had lost me. "What history?"

Jimmy looked back and forth between Bill and me. "I thought you knew that Mr. Covington——"

"Bill," I corrected him.

Bill wore a shit-eating grin that told me I'd been had somehow.

"Well, Bill has been giving food to the kitchen for years and volunteering one Monday a month. So they all knew him there. I thought that's why you sent us."

My mouth hit the floor.

Bill's shit-eating grin grew. He had totally surprised me again.

"Why didn't you tell me?" I asked him. I hoped steam wasn't coming out of my ears.

"You didn't ask," he said matter-of-factly.

I couldn't leave it like that. "So tell me now. What's the deal?"

"As Jimmy said, Marco and I don't like the amount of food waste restaurants generate, so at the end of the day, the kitchen staff packages up what we have left——both prepared foods and raw ingredients we won't need for the next day——and they're refrigerated overnight. The next morning, on our way to get the day's fresh ingredients, we drop the extra by the kitchen for them to reheat and use. That way, everybody wins. We don't throw away edible food, and the people who use the kitchen get some good leftovers."

I was blown away. Who was this guy? The spoiled rich kid who dabbled in restaurants instead of holding down a regular job, the playboy pervert who trolled the malls for young girls to seduce, or the man I'd just heard about who paid his staff to save leftover food for the soup kitchen and volunteered there to serve it himself?

"Did *The Times* get all this background?" I asked Jimmy.

"No, I didn't know this stuff, so I wasn't prepared with everything they wanted. We're going to circle back with them this afternoon with more details and set up a restaurant visit for some pictures, if that's okay?"

Bill patted Jimmy on the back. "Just let me know the timing, bud, and I'll set it up for you."

Bill cocked a brow at me. "So I take it this kitchen visit is not all you have planned for me?"

"No, just the first step in your public rehabilitation."

Bill smiled. "It was fun. Jimmy is great. And I have to say again that I was very impressed by you and your group this morning. You should be proud of them."

Heat rose in my cheeks. This boss gave compliments, something I hadn't experienced before. "Thanks. I'll pass that along."

Jimmy beamed as he turned and hustled back to his desk.

I followed Bill toward his office. I tried so hard not to watch his ass, but I failed. My heart accelerated.

"We need to schedule some time to go over your personal history…so I can build an appropriate bio," I called.

He stopped and turned to face me in the middle of the floor. "So you want to spend one-on-one time with me? Is that right?"

His eyes took on a predatory tinge. I could feel the animal magnetism radiating from him.

I felt like a schoolgirl. "Yes, I'd like…" My nipples hardened, and my breasts felt suddenly swollen.

My body reacted as if we were standing alone naked instead of fully clothed at work. I relived the naked scene at his condo in my mind as my face flushed and my brain stopped working.

"Good, how about eight o'clock tonight back at the Rusty Bucket? I'd like to spend time with you as well."

I nodded, and in full schoolgirl mode, I continued to check out his ass as he walked away.

Nice ass to go with a nice guy.

~

THAT EVENING WAS THE THIRD DAY OF NO BANDIT ATTACK UPON entering the apartment. I missed that little troublemaker.

Sandy had already started on her evening wine. "We didn't get a chance to celebrate your promotion again yesterday with you glued to that laptop of yours," she called from the couch. "How 'bout we go see how many shots we can down in a few hours at the Bucket?"

I checked the fridge——nothing very interesting. "No, I need something to eat first, and I can't drink tonight. I have a meeting."

I opened the freezer, looking for something remotely resembling food. A spaghetti and meatballs Lean Cuisine looked the closest to an actual dinner.

"Girl, did you take some sobriety oath with the new job or something?"

"No, I have to meet my new boss after dinner."

Sandy thought for a moment, looking intently at her wineglass like it was a crystal ball.

"Didn't the Wicked Witch work for the CEO?" She jumped off the couch. "My God, you're going to go meet BD again, aren't you?"

It did sound good when she said it.

"Yeah, we have to get started on this new project." And I wanted to see him alone, for a change.

"Let me get this straight; you're going back to the office tonight to meet up with Big-Dick Bill after everybody else has gone home?"

"Well, not exactly."

"So spill, girl. What are you holding back?"

"He's meeting me at the Bucket at eight."

"So, another not-date date?"

Busted again. "I don't know." I so hoped it was.

"Then I'm going with." She finished her glass of wine. "I want to meet BD and size him up for myself."

I almost told her to keep her hands off my boyfriend. "First I need to veg out on some *Judge Judy* to unwind."

We watched two episodes before changing for the Bucket. I chose ripped jeans and a UCLA sweatshirt with flats. I did my mascara and touched up my eyeshadow. No perfume tonight.

Sandy was more aggressive. She came out of her room with a short skirt, a tight top, and heels.

"You can't go on a date looking like that," she told me.

"It's not a date."

"Bullshit, now fix that outfit."

I was not going to win this argument. I changed into skinny jeans with cowboy boots and a western shirt with mother-of-pearl snaps.

The Rusty Bucket was moderately crowded for a weeknight. Sandy found us a spot near the pool tables and went to get some appetizers. That girl was constantly hungry. She returned with a plate of potato skins and two beers.

We had just started on the skins when Sandy's phone rang. It was work, and by the time she hung up, she was pissed.

"I have to go fix what some Photoshop idiot messed up. Tell BD I said hi."

In an instant, she was off, and I was all alone with an entire plate of potato skins and two beers staring at me.

I turned down an offer of a game of pool from one of the regulars and an offer to dance from another.

Then, I saw him——smelly Chuck from the other night. Tall Todd was with him. I had no desire to make their acquaintance again. I ducked away from the table and skipped off to the ladies' room. I didn't think they'd seen me. It was already eight twenty. Where was Bill?

I texted him. No answer. After five minutes of hiding in the bathroom, I ventured out. Chuck and Todd were nowhere to be seen. I walked back to my table to get my coat on the way out.

"Hey, pretty lady. We meet again." It was Smelly Chuck, grinning ear to ear, coming up behind me.

"Still not interested," I said as I grabbed my coat.

Todd appeared, blocking my escape to the door as Chuck grabbed my arm.

"I think we should all sit down and finish the skins you got here," he said.

He shoved me down into the chair and sat in the one next to me, still holding my arm in a vise grip. Todd sat on the other side. Chuck leaned closer. If anything, his breath had gotten worse.

I glared at him. "Like I said, not interested."

Storm clouds gathered in his eyes as he squeezed my arm tighter.

CHAPTER 18

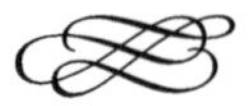

Lauren

Bill appeared behind Chuck. "Sorry I'm late. Marco was talking my ear off."

I let out a breath. My knight in shining armor had arrived.

Chuck turned toward Bill. "Buzz off."

Exactly the educated response I expected from this ignoramus.

Bill stepped around the seated Chuck and placed his hand on my shoulder. "I wasn't talking to you. I was talking to the lady here."

Chuck was not taking the hint. "I said buzz off, suit."

Todd rose from his chair. He was big, even taller than Bill.

Bill gave him a wary eye. "Time to go now," he said, patting my shoulder.

Chuck let go of my arm, stood, and shoved his finger into Bill's chest. "Maybe you don't understand English. She's with us, and you're the one leavin'."

Bill smiled. "You touch me one more time, and you will definitely regret it."

"Big words from a suit." Chuck shoved his finger into Bill again.

Bill's movements were a blur. He grabbed Chuck's finger, bent it back, and twisted Chuck's arm over and around. With a scream of pain, Chuck landed face-first in the plate of potato skins with his arm twisted up in the air behind him.

Todd came to Chuck's rescue with a fist Bill deflected with his free hand.

Bill turned and kicked Todd in the midsection so hard he went flying back. He landed in the center of the pool table behind him.

I escaped my seat to get away from the fracas.

Bill leaned over the struggling Chuck. "If I ever catch you near my girl again, I'll break this finger off and feed it to you. Do you understand me?" He poured one of the beers on Chuck's head.

Did I hear him say *my girl*? That sounded so right. I smiled.

Chuck just grunted, trying to twist free. Todd rolled off the pool table he'd landed on.

Bill poured some more beer on Chuck. "I didn't hear you." He twisted the arm up higher.

Chuck screamed in pain. "I got it. I got it," he sputtered.

Bill relaxed the pressure on his arm, jerked Chuck's wallet out of his pocket with his free hand, and threw it to me. "Check his ID. I want his name."

I found the license. "Charles Dinkus," I read out loud.

Todd had gotten off the table but was holding his midsection. He didn't take another run at Bill. Poor Chuck was on his own in this fight.

Bill leaned close to Chuck's face. "And Charles, if my girl here so much as sees you across the street, I'm going to find you and break both your arms." He twisted the arm up a little higher.

Chuck whimpered, his eyes bulging with fear.

Bill let Chuck go and kicked him in the ass, sending him sprawling onto the floor.

After a moment the two slunk out, Todd hunched over, holding his stomach, and Chuck cradling his injured hand.

The surrounding crowd slowly dispersed, except for one of the pool players.

"Those two deserved it," he said before returning to his game.

As if nothing had happened, Bill said, "What do you say we switch tables? This one is a little messy."

That was an understatement.

We found an empty table. Bill ordered nachos and more beers.

I was still trying to process what had just happened. My heart raced from the excitement. My palms were sweaty. My boss kicked serious ass. My knight in shining armor didn't need a sword. He'd just beaten the smelly dragon to a pulp with his bare hands.

I had witnessed bar fights here at the Bucket and other places, but nothing like what Bill had just done to those two idiots.

"Did they teach barroom fighting at prep school or what?" I was still shaking.

Bill took a swig of his beer. "My father insisted that we learn self-defense. He was afraid members of the family might become targets at some point. Our instructor was a retired Seal——a good guy to have on your side in an argument. Sure glad I remembered some of what he taught us."

He grabbed a chip. "The Master Chief had a saying. 'You never start a fight, but if you get in one, you finish it.'" He ate the chip. "And nobody lays a hand on *my girl*." The gleam in his eye was seductive.

Instinctively, I wanted to object to the term *my girl*, but I controlled myself before I said anything stupid. I actually liked it. This whole rescue scene had warmed me inside. I had never been rescued before.

"What was that asshole's problem, anyway?"

I giggled at the memory. "A few nights ago, he wouldn't take no for an answer, and I gave him a knee in the balls."

Bill chuckled, then grimaced. "Remind me not to get on your bad side." He sipped some beer. "I don't think he'll be back." He winked at me.

"I hope not." The understatement of the night. My stomach was doing somersaults sitting this close to Bill.

His gaze caressed me top to bottom. "I didn't get a chance to tell you how lovely you look this evening."

My heart pounded. The heat in my cheeks felt like a three-alarm fire. Holy shit, this was a date after all.

"Thank you, Sir Knight."

That was lame, but my hormones were winning the battle over my gray matter. I reached for a nacho to stuff into my mouth.

Bill raised his beer with a warm smile. "I'm glad you agreed to meet me." That same magnetism I'd felt this afternoon emanated from him. His eyes were warm but penetrating.

"So am I." Another lame statement. *Get it together, girl.* I grabbed another two chips.

"I would like to talk a little more about this project without a crowd around."

Me too. I nodded, my mouth full of nachos.

"This place is a little noisy." He was right about that.

Was my date turning into a business meeting again? I tried to hustle the chips down my throat.

"We could go to my place," I offered almost intelligibly with a mouth full of nachos. *Please say yes.* I wanted the hugging and kissing Bill back, not just the boss Bill.

"Sounds good." He stood and offered me his hand. It was warm and comforting.

My insides churned with anticipation as we left the bar. He opened the door to the street for me. We turned toward my place, and he placed his arm around my waist, pulling me into him. Tingling erupted under his touch. I moved my hand around behind him and held him tight.

"How's the cat doing?" he asked.

"Better. Still at the vet. We might get him back tomorrow."

I couldn't come up with anything else normal to say, so we continued walking in silence. We got to my building.

"This is it."

"I remember."

Of course you do. My speech generator was still stuck in lame mode. He released me as we went up the stairs. In a few seconds, we were in the hallway outside my door.

He pulled me around to face him. "The other thing I remember is…this is where we first kissed."

First means there's at least a second, right?

"How about more kissing and less talking?" I said.

That was the first intelligent thing I'd come up with.

He pulled me close and placed his lips on mine. I opened myself to him. His tongue was sweet with a nacho aftertaste. He squeezed me tighter as one hand moved down to cup my ass. My breasts pillowed against his muscular chest. The hardness of his cock was undeniable as he pressed against me.

I was soaking wet. The blood rushing in my ears drowned out all other sounds. His hair smelled like outdoors in the woods as he pulled me tighter and tighter into his signature bear hug, momentarily lifting me off my feet.

I was flying. This was even better than the first time.

"Is this better?" he whispered into my ear as he nibbled on my earlobe. His stubble was scratchy against my neck.

My next-door neighbor's door opened. Her mangy little excuse for a dog emerged before Mrs. Hiddlestone waddled out.

Bill and I disentangled ourselves before she looked up.

I fished out my keys and opened the apartment door. We were inside in a flash.

"Would you like some wine?" I asked.

"Sure, but I doubt it will taste as good as you."

"Keep it up, big guy. Flattery becomes you." He was sure lighting my fire.

He followed me to the fridge. As I opened the door to check for the wine Sandy had opened earlier, he wrapped his hands around my waist and pulled me back into him.

He whispered into my ear, "And you smell delicious as well." One of his hands cupped my breast as his thumb rubbed over it.

Screw the wine. I turned toward his embrace, wrapped my hands behind his neck, and pulled him down to me. The third kiss was just as good as the second. His thumb rubbed along the side of my breast and up to my nipple.

He nibbled on my ear. "I think we can skip the wine." He lifted me, and I wrapped my legs around him as he carried me over to the couch.

I started on the buttons of his shirt as he settled me on the couch next to him. As I got the third of his buttons undone, he undid the snaps on my shirt and slid his thumb inside my bra, playing with my hardened nipple. With him cupping my breast with one hand and holding the back of my neck with the other as he kissed me, I couldn't see what I was doing. I was having trouble with his next button.

He slid his hand around to unhook my bra. Circling my nipple with his fingers and then taking it between his thumb and forefinger, he twisted gently, sending shivers through me. I moaned. I wanted more. I needed more.

I finally had success with the buttons and was able to run my hands over his chest, through the tufts of hair, over the hard pecs and solid abs, and around to his muscled back. I slipped his shirt off his shoulders and shed mine as well.

He pulled my bra free. "I guessed right," he said as he kissed my neck.

"Guessed what?"

He kissed down to my collarbone. "Your bra color——I guessed black today," he said before venturing farther down to my breasts, licking around my nipples and blowing on the wet skin, sending shivers to my core as I ran my fingers through his hair and kneaded his shoulders.

He sucked on one nipple and then the other, massaging my breasts.

Gentle bites had me arching my back and thrusting my chest forward. He then put one leg between mine and came up to kiss my mouth again as his hand settled over my crotch and massaged me through my jeans. I moved my hand down to stroke his cock, but he stopped me and placed my hand over his back as he worked on my belt buckle and then my zipper.

His hand slid inside my panties, and a finger gently parted my wet lips and slid into my core, sending a surge of electricity through my body. He pulled the finger out and up my folds, bringing lubrication to my clit, circling it round and round.

He did this again and again, bringing my wetness up to my clit, circling, teasing, rubbing, and stroking. Every touch of my engorged nub sent tingles to all my nerve endings. I arched my hips toward him to get more pressure.

He didn't push my hand away as I moved to the bulge of his hardened cock for the second time.

He let out a low groan as I rubbed him through his jeans. I pulled at his belt and got it loose enough to slide my hand inside and squeeze his massive member as he rolled to the side to give me room. His breathing was heavier now. I didn't have much room to work, but I pulled and squeezed, receiving groans of appreciation.

I whimpered as he kissed and sucked on my nipples. He continued to push all my buttons. I climbed closer and closer to the edge as he slid one and then a second finger inside me and played my tiny bud like an instrument with his thumb.

I squeezed his cock tightly just below the crown and worked my hand up and down, trying to return some of the attention he lavished on me.

His panting became more rapid.

"I'm close. I'm really close," I whimpered. My eyelids clamped shut as I neared the edge of my release.

Keys jangled outside the door.

My God, Sandy was home. We jerked up and grabbed for our shirts as I stuffed my bra under the couch.

A key slipped into the lock and released the deadbolt. Sandy came through the door and headed for the fridge, at first not seeing us.

I lay on the couch as I struggled into my shirt. This was so embarrassing.

Bill was on the floor beside the couch, out of view for the moment.

"You're home early," I said as I got my shirt snapped.

Sandy looked over. Her eyes said it all. "Busy, I see." She smirked.

I hadn't gotten my belt buckled and I was braless, but I was covered up.

Bill stood. "I'm Bill. You must be Bandit's owner."

Sandy's eyes raked his entire length, pausing at his crotch, checking him out in her underwear-photographer way as she put her coat down.

"Glad to meet you, BD. Lauren can't stop talking about you."

"BD?" Bill asked.

Before Sandy could say anything, I blurted out, "Big Dog."

Bill started for the door. "Lauren, I have to run. I think we can finish going over the program at work tomorrow."

"Sure, see you then." I waved a goodbye as Bill left. I was mortified.

After the door closed, Sandy started to crack up. "Going over the program? Really? You two were playing doctor on the couch. If you wanted privacy, you should have used the bedroom."

I was silent.

"Not a date, my ass, girl," she added.

She was right about that.

"Okay, now that he's gone, you can tell me all the dirty details." She flopped down on the couch, waiting.

I told her about Bill's beatdown of Chuck and Todd.

She alternated between laughter and wide-eyed amazement.

I didn't give her the details beyond that Bill and I had kissed. She could put together the rest.

And she was right. If we had moved into the bedroom and closed the door, there would've been no interruption.

I couldn't get to sleep, still thinking about how the night might have progressed. I even imagined Bill stroking himself and thinking about me. Guys did that a lot, didn't they? My mother had once told me eight out of ten guys would admit to masturbating, and the other two were liars.

He was jerking off thinking about me. That was a hot image. My fingers slid down to part my folds as I imagined he would do.

~

AT WORK THE NEXT MORNING, I LEARNED JIMMY HAD GONE TO BILL'S restaurant last night with a photographer. They'd gotten great shots of the cooks packing up leftovers for delivery to the soup kitchen, and good interview material for the upcoming article. This morning, Jimmy had confirmed a few things with Bill and was doing a data dump with *The Times*.

This would be one hell of an article. Take that, all you other CEOs of billion-dollar companies. *And I bet my boss can beat up your boss too.*

Last night had been quite the roller coaster——being cornered by Chuck and having my boss beat him up, followed by getting hot and heavy back at my place, only to be interrupted by Sandy? I was playing it back in my head, getting wet as I considered once again how it might have progressed, when Bill rounded the corner.

I managed to jerk myself to attention in time. "Got a sec?" I asked as I pointed to the closest conference room.

Once inside, I closed the door behind me. Now I was tongue-tied.

He started. "I had a very nice time last night."

I wasn't sure how to broach the subject. "I was sorry to see you leave."

His smile was entrancing, and I was already flustered. "The price you pay with a roommate, I guess," he said.

"Just go for it, girl" would have been Sandy's advice. "I was wondering how we're going to handle this at work."

He advanced toward me. "I really don't think I should handle you at work, do you?"

I giggled, and I must have turned a bright red. "You know what I mean. Are we going to be discreet about this or are we going to tell people?" I waited.

I should have suggested discreet. What an idiot. I didn't want people to know. People would think this had started before the promotion, and my credibility would be shot.

Bill shrugged. "My dad thought a no-dating policy was out of place in a family company. Why should the owner's family be the only ones with relationships within the company? It's up to you, I guess. There shouldn't be a stigma, but if you're uncomfortable, I can be as secretive as anybody."

His gaze fixed me in place as he moved closer, placing one arm on each side of my shoulders, trapping me against the door.

My heart raced. I was getting mushy brain again just being this close to him. "I think discreet is best for now," I managed without tripping over my tongue.

"Got it. New rule: no displays of affection. Mum's the word." He pushed closer, brushing against my breasts, his lips just inches from mine.

I grew wetter as his magnetism enveloped me again. Maybe I should have, but I couldn't resist the pull this man had on me. I leaned forward to press my breasts just slightly harder into him, my nipples trying to pierce the fabric between us.

He licked his lips and put a finger to mine. "I think we'd best meet with other people in the room when we can. I don't think I can control myself when we're alone." He kissed me on the forehead. His hardening cock pressed against me and proved his words.

Heat raced through my veins. I lowered my hand and traced my fingers over the outline of his cock.

He moaned lightly as he breathed into my ear. "You're making this difficult."

"Don't you mean hard?" I asked. I pushed him back a few inches. "You'd better get out of here before I rip your clothes off and break our new rule."

"Promises, promises," he said as he backed away.

We kept apart for the rest of the day, but as I was beginning to think about going home, my phone dinged with a text.

BIG DOG: Meet 4 dinner? I know a killer Italian restaurant

ME: Do they have spaghetti and meatballs?

BIG DOG: No - how about 6:30?

ME: C u there

I WORKED A LITTLE LATE AND DROVE STRAIGHT TO CARDINELLI'S. IT was Thursday night, so parking was easy.

Bill was waiting for me inside the door. He had changed out of his suit, now sporting slacks and a blazer. We were ushered to the same table we had used at lunch the other day, though tonight it was set for three.

Bill graciously held out my chair. I couldn't remember when a date had last treated me so chivalrously, if ever.

He took his seat and ordered a bottle of wine——in Italian, of course. The words sounded melodious as he spoke, even after he switched to English.

"I have to say, you look radiant this evening."

I smiled. "I haven't changed since you saw me at work."

"With our new rule, I couldn't tell you how beautiful you looked at work, but I was thinking it."

"Well, thank you, Sir Knight."

"I think I like BD better," he said. "Big Dog——it has a nice ring to it."

Ya think? You should try on Sandy's real meaning and see how you like that.

The wine arrived, and Bill approved it before ordering for both of us again. The dimples were back, and the waning light coming in the window played on his hair.

I watched his lips as he spoke, wondering how they would taste if I jumped across the table to kiss him right now. Sandy would have done it, but I didn't have the nerve. I flashed back to the night I'd found him at his condo after his father's accident. Was he going commando now? I pictured him shirtless——broad shoulders, defined pecs, and muscular arms, all topped by those kissable lips.

I needed to taste his lips again. Soon.

"Well?" he asked.

Oh shit, I had been daydreaming again. "I'm sorry, what?"

"I said, are you up for a surprise this evening?"

"Why not? You seem to always be surprising me." I didn't ask if the surprise was clothing-optional or not.

"Just how do I surprise you?" he asked.

I couldn't think of a nice way tell him he'd surprised me by being a much nicer guy than I'd expected. "Oh, you just do."

The salad arrived, rescuing me from a more complete answer.

After a minute of munching silently, he said, "Lauren, I think we need a second rule."

Where did that come from? "And what would that be, Sir Knight?"

He smiled at me in full dimple mode. "We need to be completely honest with one another." He speared more of his salad, a twinkle in his eye.

"That's a good rule." *Honesty is always the best policy, isn't it?*

"Then tell me how I've been surprising you." His gaze probed my reaction.

Oh shit. "Well, I knew you had this restaurant, but it surprised me that you went out of your way to get food to the soup kitchen." I hoped we could stop here.

"I got that one. What else?"

Maybe I could get out of this with humor and flattery?

"You're a really good kisser."

"Stop stalling." Now his demeanor was more demanding than questioning.

"Okay, that first night when I got Barbie out of your apartment for you…" *How can I put this?* "I didn't think you were a very nice person."

"So your prejudice against people with money led you to believe the worst of me?"

I stared at my water glass. "Sort of," I admitted.

His eyes were entrancing when I looked back up. "Lauren, I have wanted to date you since that first night." He reached over to touch my hand. "You and only you."

My face flushed. "Surely you jest, Sir Knight."

"Remember our new rule number two. I'm serious."

His gaze was penetrating. "Next time your first instinct is to think I'm a dickhead because I'm rich, just remember you're my girl, and I care for you, so take a breath and don't jump to conclusions. Things are not always what they seem."

The main course arrived. But my mind still lingered over how quickly everything had changed.

Only me?

CHAPTER 19

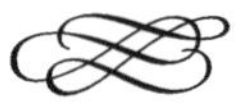

LAUREN

OLLIE HAD ACKNOWLEDGED ME WITH A KNOWING WAVE AS WE CROSSED the lobby. I pinched myself to make sure I wasn't dreaming. Bill and I were in the elevator to his condo. Sandy had interrupted us last night because I was stupid, but that wasn't happening tonight.

The elevator door opened on the twenty-second floor of Battlestar Covington. Bill unlocked his door and pulled me in.

My heart raced. Just ahead of me was the couch where I had seen Bill naked, dangly parts and all, that first night. I got goose-flesh just remembering it. He had looked so perfect, yet he'd been so vulnerable.

Bill put down his keys, exactly where they'd been on the counter that night.

"White or red?" he asked, opening a wine refrigerator in the kitchen. His movements looked fluid, as if in slow motion.

"I'll stick with white."

I couldn't resist visually undressing him from across the room. I sat down on the couch, taking in the enormity of his place. It had struck me as large that first night, but now it seemed big enough to merit its own zip code. The view from the full-length windows was straight out of a movie, looking out over the Los Angeles basin onto a sea of twinkling lights.

He handed me my wine, and we both sipped as he scanned me, moving away from my eyes and slowly down my neck to my chest.

His grin widened. "Red. I'm guessing red tonight."

I kicked off my shoes. "Wouldn't you like to know?"

"Am I right?" He removed his shoes as well.

"I'm not telling."

I was giddy with anticipation.

Bill put his glass down on the end table, and I did the same.

"Truth or dare?" he asked.

I could never get this game right.

"Truth," I replied. I guessed I could handle any question he came up with.

"Did you diddle yourself after I left last night?" His lips turned up in a wicked grin.

I was not prepared for that. I hesitated. "A lady doesn't discuss such things."

"You chose truth, so answer the question." His voice was stern.

I guess I didn't always have to be a lady. "Yes."

"Were you thinking of me?"

I didn't answer. "You got your question. Now it's my turn. Truth or dare, big guy?"

"Truth." The grin remained.

I turned the tables on him. "Did you jerk off thinking of me last night?"

"No," he said instantly.

I was disappointed. Mom was wrong. My face must have fallen a mile.

"I was thinking about *us,*" he clarified.

That brightened my spirits and made me so hot I was afraid my clothes would ignite. "No trick answers——that's not fair."

He laughed. "You have to be more careful with your questions."

"I was, but you didn't answer truthfully. If you thought about *us*, you were thinking about me. You lose a turn."

"I do not," he interrupted. "Truth or dare?"

"Truth," I said reluctantly.

"When was the first time you thought about getting naked with me and doing wicked, enjoyable things?"

This man had a knack for embarrassing questions, but that was the point of the game, after all.

"The first time we rode up in the elevator at Covington." There, I'd said it. I'd admitted to stalking him before I had even met him.

"Truth or dare?" I asked.

His brows raised, and his eyes filled with lust. "Dare."

I was hot and tingly all over. It had taken all of my self-control not to jump him when he admitted to jerking off last night. That was so hot. I was done.

"Take me to bed."

He pounced. His mouth claimed mine as we became a tangle of arms and legs. He was heavy on top of me as he laced his arms around me. He rolled off the couch and onto the floor, carrying me on top of him.

I ran my hands through his hair as the kiss grew in intensity. I relished his every breath, his moans as I rubbed his cock with my thigh.

He moved to kiss my neck, and at the same time, he undid my bra through my top with one quick motion.

"I said to bed, big guy," I moved my hand down between us, looking for his belt.

"I lost it after you said 'take me'," he answered, moving to lick my earlobe and blow into my ear.

I found his belt and gave it a tug, but it didn't budge.

He rolled over to his side, rose, and lifted me off the floor like I was a feather.

I giggled in his arms, draping mine around his neck to hold on, feeling his power as he took me into the bedroom and laid me on a bed much bigger than my own.

He stood over me and quickly removed his shirt.

I struggled out of mine. His shoulders were so broad, his muscles so defined, he would definitely fit in at one of Sandy's shoots. I licked my lips.

He knelt over me and removed my cami. He straddled me, pinning my thighs to the bed as he looked down with ravenous eyes. He pulled my bra loose and freed it from my arms. His face lit up as his eyes caressed my chest, first one breast, then the other.

My nipples pebbled in anticipation of his touch as he cupped my breasts and worked the tender tips with his thumbs.

His touch was sizzling as he pushed my breasts together to lick and blow on them. I tensed my legs, trying to control the spasms that shot to my core as he traced his fingers up and down my sides and over my breasts and stomach.

I pulled and scratched at his back as he devoured my breasts. My pussy throbbed every time he blew on my wet nipples. I moved my hands to his belt and worked the hook, finally freeing it as he moved up to focus on my collarbone, sending an eruption of shivers down my shoulders and arms.

I pulled at his zipper to release the monster I knew was inside.

He yanked my hand away as he shifted up to undo my pants. He pulled them down and urged me to lift my butt.

I kicked myself loose of them as he stroked me through my wet underwear, sending shockwaves through me with each touch.

He lay beside me and slid his hand inside my panties. A finger found its way through my curls and down my slick folds, teasing my entrance. His fingertip entered me and pulled more wetness to my clit, circling it first one way, then the other, teasing me as I arched my hips up for more pressure. His fingers pressed and flicked my swollen nub as I came closer and closer, moaning at his every touch, trying to grind against him.

I pulled on his shoulders and brought his chest to mine as he kissed my shoulder and worked his way across my collarbone and up my neck, teasing me with his tongue while his fingers continued to work their magic on my clit.

"I need you inside me," I breathed into his ear between moans of pleasure.

I tried again to free his cock, but he pushed my hand away and returned to teasing my clit and entering me with his finger, followed by a second finger as he stretched me.

He pulled my panties off and pushed my legs apart. He moved down between them to focus on my pussy. I had never had a man in this position before. And I hadn't showered since this morning. I cringed as he licked his lips, looking at me. He licked from my entrance up to my eager bud and flicked his tongue inside me. Then he went around and over my clit again.

I was unprepared for these sensations. Waves of rapture crashed through me as he worked me in an ever-increasing tempo, with a finger inside stroking my G-spot.

"You taste so good," he mumbled as my legs squeezed around his head.

I arched my hips into his mouth and threaded my fingers through his hair, pulling him into me. I had no idea it could be like this.

The waves came faster and faster, taking me up and over the edge until I saw stars behind my closed eyes as my pussy clenched down on his finger and I screamed out his name.

The spasms eventually slowed and stopped as I came down off the cliff, exhausted, relaxed, and content. My God, *the tongue magician*.

Bill looked up from between my legs with a smile to kill for. He wiped his mouth on the sheet.

"I think you're ready now." He leaned over and retrieved a condom from the nightstand drawer. He pulled off his pants and boxer briefs. His massive cock finally sprang loose.

He was huge in all dimensions. I had seen him that first night, and he had been impressive, but he hadn't been aroused. Now his engorged cock gave new meaning to the phrase "hung like a horse." I didn't have much experience, but he qualified as having a full package in any girl's book.

He tore open the packet with his teeth and offered me the condom.

"You want to help with this?" He knelt on the bed, his cock in front of me.

I sat up, grabbed his shaft, and kissed the tip. It had a slightly salty taste. I rolled the latex down slowly, little by little, toying with him, stroking as I went. I worried I wouldn't be able to fit him. He was going to split me open.

Finished, I lay down as he positioned himself at my entrance. I gasped as he guided the tip of his cock in.

He moved slowly, in a little and out, and in a little farther.

"You're so fucking tight." He groaned with a huge smile that told me that was a good thing. He pulled out when I winced as he went in farther.

"No, don't stop. I can do this. I want you so bad," I pleaded.

He pulled me up and kissed me. "Let's do this differently." He lay down and pulled me over on top of him.

I had only been on top once before. I shifted around and straddled him, positioning myself over his cock.

He guided my hips down to meet his tip so he just entered me.

"Take your time." His hands left my hips to find my breasts, lifting them, squeezing them, and jiggling them.

I lowered myself slowly, little by little, onto him. A bit of pain and then it subsided. I rose and came back down a little farther. I had a goal. I wanted him inside me, all of him. I wanted to take the whole cock and ride it——ride it hard and make him come and me come, but not just from his fingers and his tongue.

I was going to learn to be a sex machine and ride him so hard he'd lose himself completely. "Fuck his lights out," as Sandy had put it.

He kneaded my breasts and pinched my nipples lightly, sending jolts through me as I moved up and down, taking more of him.

"Baby, you have the greatest tits."

"And you have the biggest cock." I was almost there, and it was getting easier to take more as I rotated my hips forward and back and up and down. I leaned over, offering him my breasts.

He pulled them toward his mouth, sucking and kissing.

I pulled up to the tip and squeezed his shaft with my hand, stroking my wetness down his length. I was rewarded with a gentle moan, so I continued holding the base of his cock tightly as I lowered myself. This would have been much easier if he were smaller, but I didn't want smaller. I wanted him, all of him. I pulled my hand away, and with one final push, lowered myself to the root.

He pushed his hips up to meet me.

I had done it. I rocked my hips forward and back, grinding myself against him, then raising and lowering, slowly at first, then faster as he moved his hands to my hips to guide me. The pangs of pain were replaced by hot rushes of pleasure as he guided me up and down.

His expression was pure bliss mixed with dogged determination as he thrust into me, and I ground against him, finding our rhythm together. He pulled me down with one hand as he brought his other thumb to my clit. The waves overtook me again as he stroked and his cock filled me.

The crescendo came rapidly, and the waves broke over me, bringing my second orgasm of the night——this one more mind-blowing than the first. Lights flashed in my eyes as I constricted around him.

He thrust hard several more times and pushed my hips down as he pushed in as deeply as he could. He went stiff and groaned out my name as my pussy spasmed around him, milking him dry.

Exhausted, I leaned forward and rested my chest on his. His heart was pounding, his breathing short and rapid as I felt his cock pulse inside me.

His breaths slowly returned to normal, and finally he shifted me off of him and went to the bathroom. He had disposed of the condom when he returned with a warm washcloth for me.

I knew from reading *Cosmo* that some girls could have multiple orgasms, but I had never experienced that until tonight.

I fell asleep quickly on Bill's shoulder, contented and fulfilled. My man, BD, the *pussy whisperer*.

CHAPTER 20

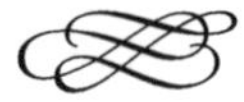

LAUREN

I ROLLED OVER. BILL'S SIDE OF THE BED WAS EMPTY. MUFFLED SOUNDS came through the door, so I found my panties on the floor and climbed into them, adding his button-down shirt with only the bottom two buttons done. Isn't that what they did in the movies? Then I changed my mind and ditched the panties. Let him wonder. I put a condom from the drawer in the shirt pocket just in case.

As I approached the door, I noticed two phones in the bottom of his aquarium——both iPhones with colorful, girly cases.

I stepped into the hallway, and my mouth watered as the scents of coffee and bacon hit me. A few steps and I could see Bill busy in the kitchen, wearing a satin bathrobe. Who would have thought? The rich kid cooks.

Light streamed in the windows with the city laid out before us. The wind had blown much of the smog out, and the morning air was clear.

His face lit up as he noticed me. "Good morning, SP. I didn't want to wake you. You looked so peaceful." He held up a mug. "I've got your coffee ready, and the rest of breakfast is just about done." He flipped an omelet in the pan, and he'd already put bacon on the plates he'd laid out.

He put down the spatula as I reached him and his eyes met mine. He grabbed me in one of his signature bear hugs, lifting me off my feet. He offered me an *I've been waiting all morning* kiss.

His lips were soft and sweet. The taste of coffee entered my mouth as our tongues reacquainted themselves. The scent of bacon in the air, the firm grasp of his arms, and the warmth of his chest against mine made everything perfect. I ran a hand through his hair, the other behind his neck, keeping him close and not coming up for air until he finally set me down.

"That's my kind of breakfast." I pinched his ass through the bathrobe as I scooted by.

"Keep that up, and we're both going to be late for work." I looked back. His eyes were on the bottom hem of the shirt I wore as an ultra-short minidress.

I leaned over the dining table, repositioning the silverware, and the shirt hiked up. "Can I help?"

"No thanks. I'm used to doing my own cooking." He turned the omelet in the frying pan. "I didn't know what you liked, so I put everything in it."

"Sounds good." I set the napkins on the table as he finished. Then I put my shoulders back and unbuttoned another button of the shirt. "Who puts their old phones in a fish tank?"

His eyes showed he was losing his self-restraint. A definite tit man.

"Those aren't mine." He turned back to the stove.

"I guessed that much." My hands soaked in the warmth of the coffee mug as I waited for a better explanation.

"Remember I told you that girl you called Barbie was the second girl in a month to try to get pictures of me? Well, hers is one of those phones, and the other is from the girl before her who tried to record a sex tape without my knowing."

"No way."

"Like you said, it sucks to be rich. So those phones are a reminder that evil forces are at work out there."

He was right, wealth and fame sometimes came with a price. I looked down and watched the people on the street moving about on their way to work. *Work.*

"Oh shit," I exclaimed. "My car is still at the restaurant."

He scooped the omelet out of the pan onto a plate. "Don't worry. I'll drive you to your place and still get you in on time." He set the plates on the counter.

That wouldn't work. "What if someone sees us drive in together?" I paced around the kitchen island.

Bill watched, a bemused look on his face. "So what? It's not a problem."

Of course he would think it wasn't a problem. He's not the one they would think slept his way to the top.

"They'll think I got the promotion because I've been sleeping with you."

"Then we'll walk in separately. Simple as that. You'll just have to wipe that *I just got laid* smile off your face and stop staring at my ass when I walk by."

"I do not stare."

"You do too. So, you want me to tell them, then?"

"No!"

"Then don't get your panties in a twist."

"I'm not, and who says I'm wearing any?" I swatted his ass as I walked past him to the table. When I looked back, his eyes had turned predatory.

He lunged for me. "You're naughty," he said as he spun me around and hoisted me over his shoulder.

I shrieked as he carried me to the couch and placed me on the edge. He ripped open the shirt I'd put on. The fastened button popped off and slid across the floor. He pushed my legs apart, standing between them. His eyes feasted on my body.

"You are the most beautiful creature I've ever seen." He dropped the robe that had been tented over his bulging cock.

His words flowed over me with a warmth I could never have imagined. I stayed still, my pussy aching for him, my nipples pebbled at the raw power of his physique and the view of his twitching cock as he licked his lips, his eyes shifting between my breasts and my open pussy. I considered leaning forward to lick him.

He went down on his knees in front of me as he placed himself between my legs and slid two fingers up and down my slick folds.

"Tell me what you want, naughty girl," he demanded.

I laced the fingers of one hand through his hair. My pussy ached to have him, but the shy girl in me could only say, "This is a good start."

He pulled my hand away and removed his fingers from my pussy.

"Tell me what you want, naughty girl," he demanded.

I tried to grab his hair again, but he swiped my hand away. I pulled the condom out of the shirt pocket and offered it to him.

He didn't take it. He didn't say a word. His breathing was heavy as his eyes bore down on me. He didn't return to touching me.

I sat up and grabbed his cock. I needed him inside me so badly. "I want you to take me," I said breathlessly.

"You have to be clear, naughty girl."

I pulled on his cock. "I want you to fuck me again."

With that, he backed away and sheathed himself with the condom. He pulled me up off the couch and walked me to the table. He cleared the tabletop with one swipe of his arm. The silverware clattered loudly to the floor.

I was going to get my wish. He pushed me over, forcing my chest down on the table.

The wooden tabletop felt cold against the heat of my breasts as I spread my legs apart, my arms sprawled on the wood.

He positioned himself behind me and grabbed my arms, pulling them behind me. He grasped them together at the small of my back and held them immobile while pushing me against the table.

He positioned his cock at my pussy and teased me, running it up and down my slippery folds, rubbing the tip over my sensitive bud. I was so wet.

"You were naughty, so you don't get what you want."

What the hell?

I tried to squirm loose, but he had my wrists in a vise grip, forcing my chest down and my hips up against the edge of the table.

"You have to do what I say. You're going to have to come for me first before you can have what you want, naughty girl." He gave me a quick spank on the ass with his free hand.

It stung. I squirmed, but he held me in place. He held the tip of his cock against my clit and rubbed it forward and back, increasing the pressure and shifting back and forth between the tip of his cock and his fingers. The touches were electric as he worked my swollen nub to a frenzy, pushing my chest into the table so I couldn't move, holding my wrists so I couldn't reach him, and teasing and rubbing and stroking my clit as the explosion built within me.

He pushed his thumb inside me as he continued touching my clit with his fingertips and cock. I couldn't hold back as the shocks overwhelmed me, and I shouted out his name, my core clenching on his thumb over and over as my legs and my breathing spasmed with my pussy.

I needed him. I ached to have him fill me.

As I came down off the high, completely spent, he released my wrists. He pulled my hips back, and in one movement, he entered me. He was huge. I was still not accustomed to the size of him, but my orgasm had made me so wet that he slid in easily.

He started to thrust. The slap of flesh against flesh grew louder as he pulled out and rammed home again and again, grunting each time. The animal in him took me, claiming me as his mate. Each thrust was harder than the last, and he gripped my hips and pulled me against him as he rammed into me.

"More, more," I groaned as he thrust harder, filling me to the end, painfully at first, but then waves of pleasure overwhelmed me to blot out any memory of the pain.

He slid an arm around my front and found my clit. The combination of his thrusting and his fingers brought me quickly right back up the cliff and over again as the surges of pleasure crashed over me for the second time.

My core clamped around his massive member as he thrust harder and growled my name, going stiff and pushing my hips against him as he stayed deep. His cock pulsed inside me several more times as he collapsed on my back, pressing me more intensely into the wood, his breathing heavy in my ear.

I was wonderfully exhausted. Bill had claimed me in the most primal way. I was his, and he was mine. More than a trifecta of pleasure, I had come four times since last night, exceeding my previous *monthly* total.

He took care of the condom and put his robe back on. I didn't bother to button the shirt, which hung open to tease him. He retrieved our plates from the counter. Our breakfast had gotten cold, but it was still the most delicious thing I had eaten in forever, sitting across from my man with the grin I knew I had put on his face.

We showered quickly and we were only a little late into work after stopping at my place for a change of clothes and some makeup. By the time we arrived, I couldn't have cared less if anyone saw us drive in together. I had to concentrate on walking normally. I was more than a little sore from all of our "exercise."

Sometimes being naughty is nice.

CHAPTER 21

Bill

I WAS ONLY AT THE SUSHI RESTAURANT BECAUSE KOURTNEY'S FATHER had picked it for another discussion about his possible investment in my farm project. He had seemed genuinely interested.

Our meeting now concluded, I exited the restaurant and turned right.

There they were, directly across the street.

Chester Dunlevy and Sheila——Liam's mother and my ex-stepmother——were seated outside the Starbucks, talking. Dunlevy's face had been on the cover of *Forbes* last year, along with the headline "Chainsaw Chet's Latest Massacre." He'd racked up over fifty thousand layoffs at one of his most recent corporate conquests, and the article had made it clear why he was both feared and despised.

I stepped behind a parked van. I could see them through the windshield, though it was doubtful they could see or recognize me.

Sheila had been Dad's second wife, and she was Liam's and Steven's mother——Liam from a previous marriage. In the years she and Dad had been married, I had never been comfortable calling her my mother. She had alternated between doting on me when Dad was around and ignoring me when he wasn't. It was creepy. The only person she treated worse than me was my sister, Katie.

After the divorce, Sheila hadn't wanted to take Liam or Steven, so they'd both stayed with us. She was too busy chasing a Greek shipping tycoon to be carting kids around, so Liam had grown up as my younger brother.

I'd never thought of him as a stepbrother. Although we had different biological fathers, we were both Dad's sons. Sheila had not been a part of either of our lives since that day she left, and none of us had any desire to change that. The woman was poison.

Dunlevy was one of the principals at the Four Corners Group Liam had suggested we sell to. More often than not, Chainsaw Chet got quick results, but at what cost to the employees and long-term morale within the company? Long-term prospects did not concern him. He never stayed around long term.

What business could Sheila possibly have with him? She was currently married to a man who owned half of Sweden or something like that. Dunlevy was well off, but she was way out of his league.

Five minutes later, they were still talking, so I hustled off.

Back at the office, I sought out Uncle Garth. When I found him, I closed the door behind me.

"Did you know Sheila was in town?"

"No, but it is a free country. As long as I do not have to talk to her, she can go wherever she pleases."

My feelings were less kind. "I just saw her at lunch in Santa Monica." I wasn't sure how to broach this. "She was with Chester Dunlevy of Four Corners."

Garth's eyes darkened. "Any idea what they were talking about?"

"No, I was across the street, but this was not a chance meeting. I left after five minutes, and they were still going strong."

After a few moments, Garth responded. "William, let me look into this and get back to you when I figure it out. I do not like the sound of it, though. Sheila is not to be taken lightly. She lacks the votes to force us to do anything with Four Corners we do not want to do, but how did she even know they were talking to us?"

I stood. The Earth was definitely off axis somehow. I'd already had enough of Sheila to last a lifetime.

That woman made my skin crawl. Everything she said or did carried an ulterior motive.

~

Lauren

Around mid-morning, I made my weekly call to check in on Brandon, and the response was the one I got every week: Progress was good. It was frustrating that they never gave me any more detail, but that's the way it had been at the previous treatment facility as well. Dependency took time to overcome, and I guess no news was good news.

After lunch, I returned from the cafeteria with Judy's Chinese chicken salad. She'd had to stay at her desk and wait for some important phone call.

"Miss Powell on line one for you, Mr. Covington," she called into Bill's office as I walked up.

"Thanks, Judy." Bill's voice came out of the office as she put her receiver down.

I could hear Bill speaking as he closed the door. "Hi, Cyn, sure. Lunch would be great…"

Judy cocked an eyebrow.

"Who is Miss Powell?" I whispered as I put down the salad and napkins I had brought her.

I hint of a smile came over Judy's face before she answered in a hushed voice. "Miss Powell and Mr. Covington were engaged, but they broke it off last year. And none too soon for his father. Wendell was never fond of her. He even suspected William had proposed to her just to spite him."

"Is her name Cynthia, mid-twenties, about five-six with platinum blond hair and big assets?"

Judy giggled. "Sounds like you've had the pleasure."

"Yup," I replied curtly.

So *Cyn Powell* was the red-taloned Miss Broadchest with the gaudy pink Mercedes. Was Cynthia's call the important one Judy had to stay at her desk to wait for? Why did Bill want to meet with her?

Judy giggled again. "Well, you know, to some men what's below the shoulders counts more than what's above." She held her hands out in front of her, mimicking big boobs.

"The story of my life," I replied.

My Bill wasn't that superficial, was he? But Judy was right. I had seen it often enough going out with Sandy. She got a lot more stares than I did, and the men didn't start out looking at her face.

One thing Sandy had taught me, though, was that men often underestimated the intelligence of a chesty woman, and she could use that to her advantage. Most men thought a big brain and big boobs were mutually exclusive, and it went double for blondes.

I hoped Bill hadn't underestimated the cunning of Miss Broadchest.

I returned to marketing, surreptitiously looking down at my blouse. *There's not a lot to work with, but maybe a push-up bra tomorrow, and my black pencil skirt.*

~

Bill

Uncle Garth wore a sour expression as he stood at my door. He entered and closed it behind him. Not a good sign.

"I have some bad news," he said.

"Did Benson cancel the meeting again?"

"No, that is still on." He placed a folder on my desk. "The initial report on your ex-stepmother."

The folder contained several pages with timelines and quite a few photos of Sheila around town.

"Where did this all come from?"

"I told you I would look into it. We have some superb investigators on retainer for the company. This stuff is from them. Sheila does not look to be getting ready to leave town. She has met two more times with Four Corners since you came to see me, and also with two big banks."

"So what do you make of this?"

"Cannot tell yet, but whatever she is working on is big. Sheila does not do small, and neither do those banks."

"And how does this affect us?"

"Normally it would not, because she has no leverage here, but did you know she has had several calls with Liam?"

That can't be true. "Liam? No way. He hates her guts. He has a restraining order against her."

Garth's brows shot up. "Is that so? I did not know that."

"He didn't want anyone to know," I explained. "So I set him up with an attorney to get it done quietly."

He nodded. "Anyway, my investigators have contacts who were able to access Sheila's cell records, and she has talked to him three times recently, but this one here…"

He sifted through the papers to find a list of phone numbers and times, pointing to the second highlighted line on the page. That was Liam's cell number, all right.

"This one was while she was in the Four Corners building." He shifted back to the timeline page, pointing out the window of the timeline that showed her inside the Wilshire office of Four Corners.

This didn't make any sense. Why would Liam be talking to her without telling me?

"My investigators will keep their research going until you tell me you want to stop. Here is the sign-in information for a Dropbox account they will keep updated with the latest photos and progress reports." He handed me a slip of paper that I folded and slid into my wallet.

The combination of Four Corners and Sheila was bad enough,

but what was Liam's connection to this? Could he want to force a vote on the Four Corners deal and be soliciting his mother's votes? Or was it Dunlevy enlisting Sheila's help? We didn't have any way to know yet.

I closed the folder. "Okay, let's keep this going for now, and keep me up to date."

CHAPTER 22

Bill

Liam returned from his trip to Boston two days after Garth brought me the disturbing report from his detectives. Liam found me just after I returned from my soup kitchen duty.

"Hey, Shorty, how's Roberta?" I asked.

He motioned to the small conference room nearby. "Can we talk for a moment?"

His lack of reaction to my ribbing was a bad sign.

"Sure." I followed him into the room. Now would be as good a time as any to ask him about the calls with his mother.

He closed the door. "I wanted you to be the first to know. I married Roberta."

I grabbed him and pulled him in for a hug. That was certainly not what I had expected to hear.

"That's great. You sure don't waste any time fixing your mistakes, do you?" I slapped him on the back.

He stepped back. His eyes were watery. "It would be a lot easier if I hadn't screwed it up in the first place."

The sullen look on his face scared me. He should've been the happiest guy on the planet right now. It had torn him apart when Roberta left.

"So why the long face?"

He looked down. "Bill, she's very sick."

I waited for him to say more.

"She might need a liver transplant." He shook his head.

Things were going from surprising to terrible in a hurry.

"I had no idea it was this serious," I told him. "I'm so sorry to hear that. Is there anything I can do to help?"

"She couldn't get onto the transplant wait list without insurance to cover it. So now she's covered on my plan, and we can also get her into an experimental program."

My brother had finally landed the girl of his dreams, but these were not the circumstances any of us would have wished for.

Liam continued. "I'm just back to sign the paperwork in HR and let you know I need to take some of my vacation to help her through this."

"Sure, whatever you need. I'm so sorry. Roberta's a really great lady. Family comes first, so take all the time you need." I had no idea how to support him beyond this without more information.

Liam sniffled. "She is unbelievably upbeat about the whole thing. I don't know that I could hold it together the way she has. I want to help her through this, and she'll come out here when she's better. She says she's done with the east coast." He wiped his cheek.

"Anything I can do for you two, just let me know." I gave him another hug and handed him my handkerchief.

He dabbed at his tears. "Could you tell Uncle Garth for me? He wasn't in his office when I walked by. I don't have much time before my flight back to Boston."

"Sure, I'll let him know. Take care, little brother, and remember to call once in a while."

Liam headed back to the elevator.

What had just happened?

I couldn't ask him about the calls with his mother after what he'd told me.

But not knowing what Sheila was up to was going to drive me nuts.

My little brother Liam was married. I hadn't seen that coming, but sooner or later, one of our generation had to tie the knot.

~

TWO DAYS LATER, UNCLE GARTH CLOSED THE DOOR BEHIND HIM AS HE entered my office. He carried a tattered expanding folder in one hand and his UCLA Bruins coffee mug in the other, and he sat in front of me with a deep crease in his brow.

"William, I have a problem I need to discuss with you."

"I hope it's not next quarter's capital plan again." I had told him twice now that I wouldn't address that until we made more progress on the investment front.

He shook his head. "No, it is more serious than that."

This was not good. I couldn't imagine a problem Uncle Garth couldn't tackle on his own. He usually brought me his plan for approval after he'd already figured out the solution he considered most appropriate.

He opened the expanding file and pulled out a tattered document, placing it in front of me. The title along the top read *The Covington Industries Family Trust.*

I knew this existed, but I had never read it.

Garth cleared his throat.

What was he waiting for?

"Yes?" I asked.

"As you know, the family trust holds the controlling interest in Series A of the common stock. This is to make sure the company stays in the hands of family members."

"Yes, I know that. What's the point?"

He paused, seeming to search for his next words. "Your grandfather designed it such that the oldest male heir would run the company, which is why you are in that seat instead of me, because I am your relative by marriage, not blood."

"Uncle Garth, you are as much my family as anyone. If you think——"

"That is not the issue here. I am not suggesting that anyone other than you occupy this office. Quite the contrary."

"Well, what's the problem then?"

"I have reread the documents, and I had the family attorneys review them as well. The problem is Liam."

Now I was lost. "How is Liam a problem?"

He cleared his throat. "The papers were drafted by your grandfather in a different era than today. It seems that the correct interpretation of these today is that as the Conservator of the trust, I will have to vote the family stock for Liam as CEO at the next annual meeting."

"How can that be? I love Liam like a brother, but he's not a Covington by blood either, and he's younger than I am."

Garth wiped sweat from his brow. "The period-correct interpretation of the document is that he became eligible when your father married his mother."

"So? Stepbrother or not, I'm still the oldest of the five of us."

"Now we get to the real problem. This document says that in the event the oldest is not married, the running of the company will fall to the oldest *married* male sibling, if there is one."

Now I understood. Liam had just married Roberta. As it stood, Liam would take over, and given his recent state of mind, he would sell the company to Four Corners, and that would be the end. There would be no company to pass to future generations of Covingtons.

"Is there any way around this?"

"No, not yet, as far as I know."

We talked through the possibilities for a few more minutes but didn't come up with anything new. Then suddenly Uncle Garth turned to me with a smirk.

"There is always Cynthia Powell. Marrying her would solve the problem."

As Garth left my office, I could only think about how Dad had placed his faith in me to pass the family business on to the next generation in better shape than I'd found it. Right now, that looked like an impossible task. And my uncle truly thought me marrying Cynthia was our way out. I scrubbed my hands over my face.

Later, after a short meeting with Sarah from HR that I had set up yesterday, I picked up my cellphone and scrolled down to Cynthia's number. I couldn't bring myself to dial it.

CHAPTER 23

Bill

Today had sucked. A stiff drink, or perhaps several, lay in my future as I closed the door to my condo behind me.

I looked out over the city lights. How had it come to this in such a short time? The family business had survived and thrived for two generations, and just as it was handed to me, it was all coming to an end. *Fuck.* If I didn't get married before the annual meeting in a few months, Liam would sell the company to Four Corners, and that would be the end of it. I would fail in my commitment to Dad.

I poured myself half a glass of scotch and started to sip. *I have all night to get drunk.* Then, I put down the glass and punched up Marco's number.

Wednesday was his normal night to be in the kitchen instead of taking care of guests out on the restaurant floor. He liked to see firsthand what challenges the kitchen staff faced rather than hear it secondhand from the chef. He answered quickly.

"Hey, you got time for dinner?" I asked. "I need to talk."

Marco agreed, and we set to meet down the street from Cardinelli's at a small steak place with quiet booths in the back.

Marco was my ultimate sounding board, the one constant in my life. He'd been with me in high school, through college, and beyond.

Half an hour later, he joined me in the back of the restaurant. After we'd ordered, Marco got straight to the point.

"So what's bothering you? The last time you wanted to have dinner on a Wednesday, you wanted to talk about breaking it off with Cynthia. So I'm guessing this has to do with a woman."

Shit. Marco knew me.

"I got some bad news today." *Where do I start?*

He sat back, waiting silently and drinking his wine.

I had already drained half my glass.

"I had a visit from Uncle Garth today, and it turns out that as it stands now, he's going to have to put Liam in charge of the company at the annual meeting."

"So it's not about a woman." Marco took another drink. "That's not so bad. You didn't want to work at your dad's company anyway."

"But Liam is dead set on selling, and that will be the end of Covington Industries."

"Oh yeah, and you promised your dad to keep the company in the family and improve it for the next batch of little Covingtons down the line. So why is your uncle going to put Liam in charge? You said he didn't want to sell the company either."

I drank the rest of my wine and raised the empty glass toward the waitress.

"The family trust has voting control of the company, not me or him."

The waitress arrived with another glass, and I handed her my empty.

"A clause in the family trust forces him to vote the trust for the oldest married son."

Marco completed my sentence for me. "And Liam just got married, and you're not."

I gulped down most of the second glass and raised it again for the waitress to see. "Yup."

"You're screwed. As I see it, your dad fucked this whole thing up."

"The fuck he did."

"He went and loaded the company up with debt and didn't fix this trust document. Then he goes and gets himself killed and gives you this pile of shit to deal with, and you have no way out. That's a big-time fuck-up."

"Like he did this on purpose?" I spat.

Marco shrugged. "You're up shit creek without a paddle. No way out." He laughed.

I should have gone slower with the wine. It finally hit me—classic Marco. He told me I had no options, forcing me to disagree with him and logically lay out the possible alternatives.

"There is a way out of this," I told him.

"Let's hear it, Sherlock. I say you're screwed."

Asshat. He could see the possibility as clear as day, but he insisted I say it first.

"Uncle Garth suggested I marry Cynthia." There, I did.

Marco took a bite of his bread and just looked at me.

I waited him out and was saved when the waitress brought our salads.

Marco broke the silence. "You said she suggested going to the museum fundraiser together again."

"She did, but..."

How did I state the obvious? Cynthia was destined to be somebody's trophy wife, the perfect eye candy to take to social events, and she was okay in bed. But deep down, I knew she was a gold digger like my stepmother, just nicer about it.

"I'm not ready to get married and make the same mistake my dad did."

Marco took a bite of salad. "You mean your stepmom?"

"Yeah, I don't want to go through all that. Cynthia is like a copy of her, just not as devious."

"Well, that sounds like something to put in the plus column." He had nearly finished his salad.

I pushed mine away after a few bites.

Marco took another sip of wine. He was still less than halfway done with his, and I was on my third.

"You know there are steps you could take," he said.

"Yeah."

"Write a good prenup so you don't get taken to the cleaners in a few years."

"I thought of that. But as soon as I tell her we have to get married before the meeting, she's going to smell blood in the water."

"Then approach her with it as a business proposition. Make a deal. She gets what she wants, and you get what you need to keep the company in the family. Then when you get the company straightened out, you part ways."

My gut tightened. "But I would have to live with her the whole time, and I saw what it did to my dad after he figured out Sheila was just after the money."

Marco shrugged. "Just bang her every night and get over it."

"Easy for you to say."

"You'd have to give up on Lauren, of course."

That came out of left field.

"What?" The scotch and the wine had slowed down my thought processes, and Marco had me just where he wanted me.

"You haven't so much as looked at another woman since your dad died and you met this Lauren girl."

"Yeah, well, I've had a lot on my plate."

"When we walked in here, there were two hotties up front. Tell me what they looked like and which one had the bigger tits."

"Were not."

"Were too, and the old Bill would *not* have passed by them without noticing. The same thing happened the other night at dinner. You didn't even glance at the redhead making eyes at us."

He had a point. I hadn't noticed the women the way I used to since Dad died.

I sighed. "I just met the girl."

"You look just like you did when you were head over heels for that girl, Jane, in college——till the Hawaii fiasco, at least."

It still hurt to remember Jane Asher. I had dated her for almost all of my sophomore year at college. Then she went to Hawaii for summer school at U of H. I flew in to surprise her with a visit and found out she'd fallen for some surfer hunk she'd met on the beach down by the Royal Hawaiian. I'd about died when she'd suggested we could still be friends. She said I was nice. *Nice*. I'd felt like such a fucking doormat. I left the next day.

"Look, you got it bad over this Lauren girl. I can tell."

I finished my third glass and held it up for a refill.

"Okay, let's take a little test. Tell me the worst thing about her," he said.

I thought for a moment and came up blank. I shook my head.

"Well, tell me some good things about her then."

I found this easier. "She isn't afraid to speak her mind and tell me what I need to hear instead of what I want to hear."

"And?"

"She takes charge at work, and she's smart as a whip. Her coworkers like her and respect her."

"Does she like to be on top, or on the bottom?"

"What?" He wasn't making any sense now.

He laughed so hard he almost choked. "Don't you see it? With any other girl, you would know the answer to that question before you knew any of this other shit——if you would know it at all."

He was right. I had relegated all the other women in my life to casual acquaintances and sexual playthings. I had tried to get beyond that with Cynthia, but not successfully.

"But I just met the girl," I repeated.

"Look, just reverse the order. Marry her, then get to know her better. Do a prenup, and don't get her pregnant. If it works, great. If after a year or two it isn't working, you can get out of it and still be better off than you would have been with Cynthia. Cynthia ought to be your second choice, or if you don't like that, there's always Russia."

"Russia?"

"Yeah, there are plenty of chicks over there who will marry you sight unseen to get a visa to the US. You could get married by the weekend, I bet," he said with a laugh.

"You can be an ass." I meant that in the best way.

I had just met her, but Lauren instead of Cynthia. The real solution was obvious.

CHAPTER 24

Bill

The next morning I entered the conference room about a minute early. All the participants were there, save Uncle Garth, who strode in about twenty seconds later. The Operation Tide meetings, as we called them, had become fairly routine. Lauren would go around the table with her people, getting updates on the PR progress and dealing with any issues.

They invariably gave me some appearance or task to perform that would rehabilitate me and help the company's public image. The soup kitchen lunches had increased to every week, and that was easy. I had volunteered for fundraising drives. I had cut the ribbon on a new homeless shelter the company had donated items to. I volunteered at the pet rescue.

That woman was full of ideas.

Lauren started this meeting with her usual inquiries of her people and congratulated them on the press we were receiving. I had to admit, it impressed the hell out of me. Then she got to Karen, who had two large shopping bags beside her.

"Karen, do we have all the items Bill needs?"

"Sure do," she said with a wry smile directed at me.

"What items?" I asked.

I had been watching Lauren's face, the way her eyes danced as she talked, and I must have missed what had been said.

"Karen, why don't you show him? With his upbringing, he may not be familiar with things like these."

That got a round of laughs from the room. Evidently everybody else in the room was in on the joke.

I'm a big boy. I can take it.

Karen rose and pulled the first item from one of her bags and announced, "Safety glasses."

She slid them in my direction to a round of *ooh*s and *aah*s.

This didn't sound good.

"Leather work gloves. I got you deerskin. The guy at Home Depot said they were the best." She slid those over as well. "You should check that they fit in case I need to trade them in."

I put my hand in one to check the size. "No problem," I announced.

Out of the other bag, she pulled a pair of brown boots. "Steel-toed work boots. Judy gave me your size."

Jimmy walked them around the table to me.

"I'll try them on later, if that's okay."

"Sunscreen," she said as she pulled the next item out of the bag, followed by "hammer." A large claw hammer appeared.

She continued. "Lunch box." It was a green workman's lunch box, thermos and all, with *STANLEY* written on the side.

"And to round out the ensemble, hat." It turned out to be a baseball cap with the Home Depot logo on it.

I smiled as I modeled it for the group.

"And the end-of-the-day items?" Lauren asked with a mischievous smile.

"For the end of the day," Karen said. She fished into the bag one more time and pulled out two bottles of white wine.

"Only two?" I asked.

Even Uncle Garth was laughing at this point.

But she wasn't done yet. "And last but not least…" She pulled two more items from the seemingly bottomless bags. "Ben-Gay and Advil for sore muscles."

That brought down the house.

When they quieted down I asked, "Why not just a good bottle of scotch?"

Lauren looked at me. "You remember that Lloyd Benson likes to volunteer at Habitat for Humanity? We've arranged for you to be at the same build site as him three weeks from now."

"I look forward to it." I turned to point the safety glasses in my hand toward Uncle Garth. "Maybe a department head or two should join me. What do you think?" I asked as I rotated to point squarely at Lauren. *Two can play this game.*

"Jimmy and I were planning on being there. That's why there are two bottles of wine," she answered.

She was certainly full of surprises.

"I'll pass on this one," Garth said.

Lauren had even more surprises in store for me. "The next item is the museum fundraiser gala, which is happening the weekend after this one. We know this is an important event for the Benson family, so we got tickets for you and your date, and Karen will go along with her husband. It would be an excellent opportunity for you to strengthen your connections to the entire family."

I squirmed in my chair. The museum fundraiser. I'd forgotten they'd mentioned it at the first meeting. I wasn't sure what to say.

"As I recall, you already have somebody who would like to go with you," Lauren said with a grin. "Didn't Miss Powell ask you to join her?"

Garth sat up in his chair at the mention of Cynthia's name.

"Cynthia Powell?" he asked. "She would make an excellent companion for the gala. She goes every year, and I think she also knows one of the younger Bensons quite well."

He was way too excited about this. It was sounding more and more like my uncle had set a trap for me. He'd been by my office already this morning to prod me on proposing to Cynthia.

"I'll be glad to go," I said with as much of a smile as I could muster.

As if I had a choice at this point.

"It would be a great place to get a few moments with the man in charge and pitch him on the company investment——if Miss Powell and his son can introduce you," Lauren added.

Ambushed.

CHAPTER 25

Lauren

It was Sunday afternoon, and Bill had promised me a non-standard dinner date. He warned me to dress casually in something I didn't mind getting dirty. Intrigued, I had no clue what his plans might be. Perhaps a crab feast. That was always a messy affair.

He knocked at precisely four, as he'd said he would. I saw Jason from the window. The town car was waiting below.

I opened the door and greeted him with a kiss as he entered. His smell was different from his usual aftershave…muskier.

I licked at his ear as I whispered, "Right on time, as always."

He gave me a signature Bill bear hug, lifting me off my feet. I would never get tired of that. I had to adjust my bra after.

Sandy clicked off the DVR. "Hey there, BD. Good to see you again."

That girl was trying to get me in trouble. Sooner or later, she was going to let slip her interpretation of *BD*.

"Hey, if you guys want, I can leave for a while. Just text me when y'all are done." She winked. "And take all the time you want, BD. Girls like that."

Bill didn't take the bait. He just smiled.

"I think we have to go," I blurted.

I had to get Bill away from Sandy before she embarrassed me even more. I gave him a nudge toward the door, but he didn't move.

"Sandy, Lauren tells me you're a professional photographer," he said instead. "You have any shoots coming up locally?"

This was going to get embarrassing if I didn't get us out the door soon.

"Yeah, this Tuesday is the next one," Sandy replied, smiling.

Bill held me tightly by the waist. "Perhaps Lauren and I could stop by. I'd love to see how a professional like you works."

Not a good idea. I shoved him toward the door. "Too bad this one is a closed set, right, Sandy?" I shot her the most evil stare I could muster without Bill catching on.

She nodded. "I think you're right. Sorry, BD. Tuesday is a closed set. Maybe another time. Ya never know, you might want to try your hand at modeling."

"Thanks for the offer, but I don't think I'm cut out for that," Bill said.

Sandy would not let this go. "Oh, I think you've got what it takes." She smiled broadly.

Bill loosened his grip on me. "Maybe next time then. SP and I need to get going, or we'll be late."

I grabbed my purse on the way to the door.

"Good talking to you, Sandy," Bill called as we left.

As we went downstairs, I asked, "And what is with *SP*, anyway?"

Bill opened the car door for me. "You guys have initials for me, so I thought it only fair that I have some for my girl."

I slid into the backseat. "Are you going to tell me what it means?"

"Later."

The door closed, and he went around to get in the other side. I would have to wait him out, but the "my girl" comment felt good.

On the ride south, he refused to let on where we were going, and Jason was no help either.

Bill took my hand. "Lauren, I think it would be fun if you came with me to the gala next week."

That floored me. "We've been over this. We can't have the people at work knowing about our relationship."

"Promise me you'll take Cynthia." I hated the idea of her claws on my Bill, but she would be helpful in getting access to Lloyd Benson, and I couldn't stand the humiliation of everyone thinking I'd slept my way into my current job. How would I ever convince them otherwise?

"Maybe in a few months," I added. *But that still might be too soon.*

Now off the freeway, we drove down Beach Boulevard. As we passed IHOP and McDonald's, I pointed to each, and Bill just shook his head. The wax museum was coming up on our left, and Bill shook his head again. Jason stopped in front of a building with coats of arms and pictures of knights on horseback on the outside. This was the place.

"Milady, welcome to your castle," Bill said. "You will love it, I promise."

Medieval Times, it said on the building. Bill had tickets for the five o'clock seating. He tucked me into his side as we walked in and waded through the line for pictures. Bill paid for the print, which he pocketed.

They had a torture chamber museum, which I suggested we skip, and we found our seats on the far side of the arena. The king and queen of the castle invited all the guests to join the evening meal. We were seated around a giant oval dirt riding arena in rows facing the center. The dinner was served by dozens of well-endowed wenches with corsets that made their boobs pop out the tops of their low-cut bodices. They always seemed to lean forward in front of the men to give them a better look. Very entertaining to watch.

I soon found out why Bill had told me to be prepared to get dirty. They served the food Medieval-style, which meant on wooden plates with no utensils. So we made a game of feeding each other chicken, bread, and corn on the cob with our fingers and sipping tomato bisque soup from the bowl without a spoon. We were laughing so much it was hard to finish eating. After licking my fingers relatively clean, I wiped them on Bill's jeans.

As the wenches cleared the dinner and brought the ale, the show began. We were in the blue area, and so we rooted for the Blue Knight to win the competition. On horseback, the knights jousted, followed by a lance-accuracy competition and then sword fighting on foot. The people in the front rows got lots of dirt thrown up at them by the horses as they galloped past. I loved the falcon demonstration. Our knight put forth a valiant effort but didn't win.

Bill and I had kept our hands on or around each other the entire time. He had ogled our wench a little too obviously—— clearly to get a rise out of me, and I answered him with a jab in the ribs. I grasped his thigh several times, moving my hand just close enough to his crotch to tease him, and he retaliated by putting his arm around me, tickling and stroking the side of my breast.

I was sorry to see the evening end.

Bill held me tightly all the way out as I leaned my head on his shoulder. My side tingled where his hand rested. Like magic, Jason appeared outside to pick us up.

Once back in the car, Bill settled his arm around me. "How did you like the surprise evening, SP?"

What does SP stand for?

I kissed him on the neck. It was so warm and comfortable here with him.

"The show was amazing. Nobody has ever taken me to something so exciting. This sure beats a movie date. You're the best, BD."

This left the dates I'd had in college in the dust, particularly the time Sam took me to a football game and got so drunk and rowdy with his frat buddies that one of the other girls and I left at halftime.

"Do you take all the girls on this date?"

His eyes narrowed, and I looked away.

Fuck! Why do I always have to screw it up and say something stupid? I mean, I do want to know, but…

His eyes were entrancing when I looked back over. "Lauren, like I told you, I have wanted to date you since that first night."

The arm around me pulled me closer, but I had to look away, suddenly shy.

"I'm serious." He pulled a necklace out of his pocket and placed it in my hand. It had a small medallion on it.

"For me?" I felt like a middle school girl on a first date.

"My grandfather gave this Saint Christopher necklace to my grandmother when he started courting her. I want you to wear it."

The heat in my cheeks became unbearable.

His gaze was penetrating. "I won't embarrass you by telling anybody at work, but wear this, knowing you're my girl. My only girl. I promise."

I teared up, and fingered the medallion gingerly, then fastened the chain around my neck.

He had called me his girl, and tonight, he had surprised me again by giving me something that had special significance to him. I had so completely misjudged him. The dipshit who trolled the malls for young bimbos had been transformed into my knight in shining armor, my protector, and now my real boyfriend. My chest tightened at the thought.

I leaned over, and we became a tangle of arms and legs as I gave him the kiss he deserved. The kiss that sealed this commitment of ours. I was his, and he was mine.

"Get back over there and fasten your seatbelt," he said after a while. "You're too precious to me to take chances."

Reluctantly, I gave him one last kiss before doing as he asked.

His precious girlfriend, his one and only. I could get used to that.

I was so tired from cheering for our knight that I dozed off in the car, leaning against Bill's warmth.

He woke me as Jason pulled up outside my building. We walked up to my door, and he pulled me in for one of those long, tongue-dueling kisses of his. He hugged me tightly with his hand behind my ass, squeezing so hard I was sure he was going to leave a handprint.

I hoped Sandy had gone to bed. Bill's hard cock pressed against me, asking for more. I unlocked the door after he finally came up for air, and I pulled him toward it, but he resisted.

"I have to go," he said. "See you in the morning."

Another quick kiss, and he was gone down the hallway as I leaned against the door.

How come I can't catch a break here?

I turned the key and opened the door as Bill reached the stairs. The room was dark. I closed the door behind me and headed for the kitchen, but before I got to the light switch, I tripped.

"Shit," I yelled as I crashed to the floor.

I fumbled for the light switch as Sandy emerged from her room. I had tripped over a pile of red boxes stacked on the floor.

"Yeah, those came while you were gone," Sandy said.

The knee I had landed on hurt. I rubbed it. "Fuck, you could have moved 'em out of the way."

"They looked important, so I didn't want you to miss 'em, girl."

My name was printed on top in elegant calligraphy. My knee became less important. I opened the box hastily. Inside was a formal black dress neatly folded in tissue paper. It was my size, assuming I went easy on the burritos this week. The tag read *Versace of Beverly Hills*. I couldn't believe it.

"Holy shit, Sandy, this is a couple-thousand-dollar dress."

I held it up for her to see. It looked like a Hollywood red carpet dress.

Sandy was now completely awake and scooted right over to me.

"Who brought this stuff?" I screamed.

"Look, I just live here. They're for you, Little Miss Hot Shit. So I didn't mess with 'em."

Under the dress were a clutch and a Jimmy Choo shoe box, also in my size. I opened the box and found matching heels to die for.

Sandy pulled a black lace thong from the box. "And you get color-coordinated underwear, assuming you plan on wearing any with that dress."

I grabbed them from her. La Perla. It was Christmas time. An envelope lay on the bottom of the box. The card read, *I won't go to the Museum gala unless you come along* —— BD, and included a ticket to the fundraiser.

"BD has a hard-on for you, girl, and he likes to pick out your underwear. My kind of man."

"Well, he has good taste."

"What's this museum gala anyway?"

"Just another charity event we scheduled for him."

"Cool, and he's takin' you."

That deflated me completely. "No, he's going with his ex-fiancée, that Cynthia bitch I told you about."

"But the card says he's inviting you."

"She's his date. He knows that."

"Look, you're the one he took out today. You're the one he's picking out panties for, not Little Miss No-Manners. You're the one he's playin' doctor with."

"I guess," I said meekly. "But she's his date."

"Unless maybe he likes threesomes." Sandy snickered.

"Yuck." To change the subject, I moved on to the next box, which had a different marking on it. It was Sandy's full legal name.

"This one's for you, *Sandra,*" I said, shoving it in her direction.

"You shittin' me?" she said. She tore open the box after she determined it did have her name on it.

It was Christmas, all right, but how had Bill known Sandy's full name? I'd never told him.

Her box had a blue Tom Ford dress and matching heels with a silver clutch, as well as two tickets to the gala——but no thong.

"I guess I have to supply my own underwear," Sandy noted. "Or it's a hint that I shouldn't wear any."

"Get your mind out of the gutter, roomie. This is a dignified affair. And careful who you bring to this."

"Like they're going to have some kind of test at the door?"

"Yeah, no nose rings, no eyebrow piercings, and easy on the tats. And one more thing——he needs an IQ bigger than his jacket size."

"So you want handsome, clean cut, and smart. Hmm, that's a pretty tall order. That rules out most of the guys I work with."

There were three more boxes, two for me and one for Sandy. I couldn't wait to see what they held.

My second had another dress, clutch, stilettos, and a thong for me; this time a red dress from Dolce & Gabbana and shoes from Christian Louboutin. Even the thong was designer, Carine Gilson, and naturally, red to match.

Sandy went nuts. "Red is *so* your color. I'd pick this one over the black any day."

Sandy's second box was a long canary yellow dress from Vera Wang, a gold clutch, and heels, once again without underwear, which Sandy made note of again.

My third box was no disappointment either. The one-shoulder dress was from Christian Dior, complete with shoes and a clutch, but no panties this time. Holding up the dress, I could see why. It had a sheer panel on one side all the way down, wide enough to show some side boob and make it obvious you had left your undies at home. Fat chance I was ever going to wear that. I was down to two choices.

Naturally, Sandy thought the third one was the most appropriate.

"Now that's a kick-ass dress, girl. BD must have had a blast picking that one out for you. Bet you anything he had more than one of the salesgirls model it for him before he bought it."

I giggled at the picture in my mind of Bill putting the entire sales staff through that.

"Lauren, this is it. You'll knock 'em dead, and it will be fun watching all the guys there drool when they see you from the side." She laughed. "Add a little temporary tat on the edge of your boob, and it'll drive them crazy."

I had to laugh. Sandy could come up with the most outrageous things.

"Hey, what is that?" she asked, pointing at my new necklace.

I touched the medallion and tried to control the smile that overcame me. "Bill gave it to me. It was his grandmother's."

"Looks like BD has way more than a crush on you." She hugged me quickly and looked straight into my eyes. "Seriously, you better be puttin' out, and don't you dare let this one get away."

When I settled myself down, I called Bill's cell. No answer, so I pulled down his condo number and dialed it. No answer again. I was going to have to wait until tomorrow to talk to him.

Unless.

As I drove over to the Covington condo in the sky again, all the things I wanted to say ran through my head. I couldn't figure out where to start. He was just the best. First, the enchanting dinner date at Medieval Times and now, these dresses.

But then something dawned on me. I was being too pushy.

I turned around and headed back to my apartment. This was his surprise for me, and I needed to let it play out the way he had planned it, not muck it up by being my normal pushy self.

Still, the anticipation of talking to Bill about the dresses kept me from getting to sleep forever.

CHAPTER 26

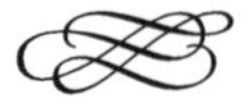

Lauren

I stumbled out into the kitchen in the morning to start up the coffee machine and get some caffeine into my system. Pieces of wrapping paper and fragments of boxes were still strewn about. I hadn't been dreaming.

Bill had sent over dresses and shoes for Sandy and me while he and I were eating dinner with our fingers and watching sword fights at the castle. I hadn't suspected a thing.

Just as I put some bread in the toaster, Sandy emerged from her room, rubbing the sleep out of her eyes. "You got back late last night, girl." She wagged a finger at me. "I hope you gave BD the ride of his life after all those expensive presents." She laughed.

"Thanks for the dating advice," I said.

She grinned like a Cheshire cat. I was not going to get into a long conversation about what men were good for and what they weren't.

"Looks like you didn't get much sleep. Let's hear all the details." She plopped down on the couch, pulling her knees up to her chin.

My toast popped up, and I grabbed a knife to butter it. "You can't just live vicariously through me, you know."

She was right about the lack of sleep. But I didn't want to tell her I chickened out about going to see Bill.

I desperately needed to change the subject. "Don't you have photo finishing to do today?"

"Yeah, but if I do anything before those two marketing boneheads get there, I'll just have to redo it. And they don't get in very early." Now she was getting wound up. "Those two think their degrees make them experts, but between the two of 'em, they don't have the common sense of a squirrel." She laughed at her own joke. "They think a color wheel is a plate used with Mexican food."

I sprinkled cinnamon on my buttered toast and went to get showered. Sandy continued talking to herself, coming up with more and more derogatory ways to describe the two guys she had to work with today.

I traced the medallion Bill had given me and climbed into the shower.

He'd called me his.

~

WHEN I GOT INTO THE OFFICE, BILL WAS NOT AROUND. JUDY SAID HE'D called to say he would be late, and I asked her to get me a minute with him when he arrived.

Shortly after that, Karen rushed into my new office and closed the door. "Judy just told me that Mr. Covington——"

"Bill," I corrected her.

"Okay, the boss said I should go out and buy whatever I thought was appropriate for this Saturday's fundraiser at the museum and submit an expense report. Is that right?"

I nodded. "The party is an important part of what we're doing with the boss. So splurge. He wouldn't have had Judy tell you that if he didn't mean it."

After a busy morning, Bill found me in the cafeteria at

lunchtime as I was slurping down my cream of broccoli soup. He joined me with a slice of meatloaf and a bowl of chili on his tray.

"Slumming today?" I mumbled as he pulled out his chair.

"I'm here for the company." He eyed me hungrily. "Mostly."

I smiled.

He grabbed the ketchup, poured a small bit on his meatloaf, and spread it with his knife. He spooned half his chili on top and started eating the concoction.

"Do you always play with your food?" I asked.

"I figured since Liam and I liked chili dogs so much when we were younger, why not try chili meatloaf?"

Funny he should mention his stepbrother. "Speaking of Liam, I haven't seen him around lately. Did you fire him?"

"No, nothing like that. He got married on his recent trip to Boston, to Roberta, a lovely girl, and he's out east spending time with her."

That blew me away. The office grapevine must have a serious defect. How could the boss's stepbrother get married, and nobody knew before or after?

"Married. Good for him. I thought all you Covingtons were confirmed bachelors."

Keep your cool, girl. It's just another day at the office.

"Not at all. We're just picky. He's been after this girl for a long time. He just screwed it up by letting her leave the first time."

"Which one of your brothers do you expect to go next?"

I probably shouldn't have asked such an intimate question here in the cafeteria.

"I think…I might be next," he said. His eyes bored into me, and his smile grew.

I looked down, embarrassed by the possible implication. I took a few more spoonfuls of soup in silence.

He can't mean it.

"I tried to call you last night to thank you, but you didn't pick up," I said, changing the subject.

"Sorry. I turned off my phone. I had a business call, and then I crashed."

"Yeah, I was tired too."

Curiosity killed the cat, and it was about to kill me too.

"And do you have a minute to talk about yesterday?"

He reached across the table to take my hand. "Sure," he said.

I stood and took my tray to turn in the dishes.

He stood with his even though he hadn't finished his meatloaf yet. He followed me into the hallway.

I turned in to the small conference room before the elevators, and he joined me, closing the door.

"Are you wearing it?" he asked.

"Yes." My blouse today was buttoned high enough that nobody could see the necklace around my neck.

"Remember what it means."

"I will."

"And before you start anything we can't finish in this room..." he growled as he backed me toward the door. His eyes bored into me. "I meant every word I said yesterday."

His words were slow and firm, his eyes penetrating. His voice ignited my panties.

I threw my arms around him and pulled myself close, my face planted in his chest. I held him tightly as he caressed my back and ran his fingers through my hair.

I moved my hand down and stroked his cock through his pants. It sprang to life immediately. "I started to come over last night because I wanted to thank you with more than words, but I chickened out."

He squeezed me tightly before releasing me.

"No need," he replied. The reaction my hand got from his cock was conflicting with his words. "The pleasure was all mine, milady. I hoped you would enjoy the Medieval Times experience as much as I enjoyed taking you there."

I continued to stroke his pants. "It was great, Sir Knight, but I also wanted to thank you for the boxes."

He looked truly puzzled. "What boxes?" he moaned as he kissed my neck. My hand was having the desired effect.

I needed to stop breaking all of our rules. I pulled my hand away. "Are we really going to play this game? The boxes you had delivered to my apartment while we were out."

His face reddened. "Oh shit," he mumbled. "You weren't supposed to get those until tonight. I wanted it to be a surprise."

So he *hadn't* expected to hear from me again last night. The delivery date got messed up.

"Well, we sure were surprised. What were you thinking?"

"I thought that if going to the gala was a good idea, we should buy a whole table. So Judy took care of that, and I invited Garth and his wife, and I thought we could fill out the table with you and Sandy and her date."

I kept my voice down. "We agreed that Cynthia was your date."

"I promise you she and I will be there, but since I'm supposed to hang out with old man Benson, I need my marketing guru there too." He kissed my forehead. "Just in case." He smiled.

"Okay, I'll go, but I can't accept the dresses. They're way too expensive."

I took the high road, secretly hoping he would argue and overrule me because there was no way I could buy anything so gorgeous on my own.

"Nonsense, milady. Any of the three will look spectacular on you." He leaned into me. "I have a favorite, if you want me to pick." He grinned. "And I need you looking your best. As you said, Saturday night is an opportunity to impress the Bensons."

No way you're getting me into that sheer one. "But three dresses?"

"I thought you would enjoy having a choice," he said.

"I'll return the ones I don't use then."

His smile turned to a frown. "I don't know what your family taught you, Miss Zumwalt, but where I come from, returning a gift is considered an insult."

Then he smiled with such innocence that I couldn't bear to keep arguing with him.

I tried to look humble as I chalked up my win. We parted in opposite directions.

As I walked back to my office, I kept seeing the look on Bill's face in my head——the way he'd looked at me across the table when he'd said *he* might be the next one getting married.

How crazy would that be?

He was the total package...unlike any other guy I'd ever dated ——hell, unlike any guy I'd ever met. And now that I thought about it, *Mrs. Covington* sounded good. Damned good.

I walked by a conference room and saw my reflection in the glass.

Get a grip, girl. You're way ahead of yourself.

~

Bill

At the condo after a long day, I opened the wine fridge and pulled out a zinfandel. I had to figure out how to approach this weekend and the two things I had to accomplish at the gala.

The meeting with Benson could be tricky, but I thought I could handle it with Cynthia's help. She was more than agreeable, but I'd known her long enough to know that things were not always as they seemed. Everything could be on track and going smoothly until she decided that there was a change of plans that served her interests better.

I was most worried about how things were going to unfold with Lauren. So much depended on her. Had I done enough to prepare myself?

After a few sips of wine, it was clear to me that the answer to that question didn't matter. Most importantly, I hadn't done enough to prepare Lauren. I hadn't done anywhere near enough to have her understand the depth of my feelings for her, and I was running out of time. *I can't waste this evening.*

I picked up the phone and dialed her number. She answered right away.

"Are you up for an evening at the Bucket?" I asked. "I have an undeniable urge for two things, and one of them is nachos at the Bucket."

"And what's the other?"

"Why, your company, of course, milady." She might think I was laying it on thick, but I was as sincere as ever.

"It's sort of late. After your fight last time, they might not let you back in."

"They'd better. After buying those dresses, it's all I can afford."

That made her laugh. "Meet you there in half an hour."

I relaxed. The verbal sparring and easy banter with her felt good, but I needed *her* to feel good about being with me.

Like Marco said, I got this.

WHEN I PUSHED OPEN THE DOOR TO THE RUSTY BUCKET, I SAW Lauren at the far end of the bar, probably her preferred seat. Sandy had come along. Not what I preferred.

Deal with it, dude. You got this.

Sandy jumped up, throwing her arms around me. "You are the best, BD." She planted a big kiss on my cheek. Luckily, she wasn't wearing lipstick. "If you get tired of Little Miss Prim-and-Proper here, I'm available."

"Thanks for the offer," I said. "But I'm spoken for." I kissed Lauren and took the seat next to her.

Lauren smiled. "So, what's on the menu tonight?" she asked.

"Why, you, of course," Sandy interjected.

I tried not to smile, but those were my thoughts exactly.

Lauren hit her on the shoulder and started to blush. "Grow up, or I'm going to have to send you home."

We ordered nachos and a pitcher of margaritas and moved from the bar to a table. Sandy was getting pretty sauced by the second round of drinks. She was quite a tease and had a sexual-innuendo comeback for almost anything that was said.

I could see why Lauren liked her. She was what my dad would

have called a *barrel of laughs*——never a dull moment with her. And she insisted on calling me BD, not once using my name.

Lauren began hinting that she might want to head home. I hoped that meant she wanted to be alone with me.

"Sandy, do you have a date for the gala yet?" I asked.

"Still working on it."

"Hurry up. It's going to be a very special night. You won't want to miss it.

Sandy poked me in the arm. "So, BD, tell me, was it a hint?"

"Was what a hint?" I had been watching Lauren's eyes and hadn't caught Sandy's drift.

"The thing you left out of my boxes."

After my third margarita, I wasn't following her question. "What did I leave out?"

"You didn't give me any panties," she said in a loud voice. The people at the next table looked over.

I must have turned beet red, but I didn't let it stop me. "Sandy, I almost forgot to ask——how's your pussy?"

That got a total wide-eyed response from the next table.

Sandy laughed. "A little lonely, but my cat's just fine," she responded loudly enough to keep the neighboring table informed.

Before I could get myself in any deeper, Lauren grabbed my hand and yanked me up. "I wanna dance."

Saved from Sandy, I eagerly followed Lauren to the dance floor. It was slow music, and as I held her, she melted into me and pulled me close, pressing her breasts into my chest.

"I'm sorry. Sandy gets a little rowdy when she drinks."

"I like her. She's fun."

Lauren was warm against my chest. Her hair smelled of strawberries. "Are you wearing my necklace?"

"Always."

"It's okay to let people at work see it."

As we rocked back and forth, she made a point of rubbing her leg against my crotch. "I'm not going to have a choice. I'm running out of things with a high neckline."

"Good, I can't bear to keep it a secret much longer."

She looked up at me. "You sure?"

I kissed her forehead. "Trust me. It'll be fine."

She swayed in my arms for another song. "I trust you."

"Would milady like to come back to my castle?" I whispered into her ear.

Lauren lifted up on her toes. "Take me home, big guy," she whispered as she pinched my butt.

I bit her ear gently. "I'm going to fuck you till you can't walk if you keep that up."

"A threat?"

"A promise," I told her as I dragged her off the dance floor.

Lauren retrieved her coat and said something to her roommate.

"Good seein' ya, BD," Sandy called as we left to catch an Uber outside.

CHAPTER 27

Lauren

Bill kept his arm around me as we sat in the back of the Uber, teasing the side of my breast with his fingertips. He kissed and blew into my ear, making me shudder. It was a good thing he hadn't driven tonight. He was playfully over the limit.

I retaliated by running my hand up the inside of his thigh, right up to the bulge in his pants. We kept up this teasing all the way to Battlestar Covington. I was wet and hot and tingly all over, anticipating what awaited me upstairs.

Bill held the door open for me as we walked into his condo in the sky. I would never get used to this spectacular, panoramic city view. I set my purse down and walked toward the window.

Bill turned the lights on low. "Stop right there."

Stunned, I stopped and turned to face him.

He eyed me hungrily. "Take off your shirt. Right there."

I slowly pulled my tee off, not sure of his plan, but as long as it involved getting naked, I was all for it.

"Now the bra." His voice was stern, commanding. "And dance for me."

I undid the hooks behind me and very slowly slipped off one strap, then the other, holding my arms to my sides to keep it from slipping off. If he wanted a strip tease, that's what he was going to get. I started to dance in place as I lowered one cup and then the other and dropped the bra. I squeezed my breasts together and licked my lips as I continued to move.

His eyes were ravenous, and he couldn't stand still as he adjusted the bulge in his pants.

I kicked off my sandals, not needing to be told what to do next. I turned around and slowly slipped my jeans over my hips, rotating them as I did. I slipped them down all the way as I turned to face him again. I hoped he was getting as turned on by this as I was. I needed him to touch me. I needed him to kiss me. I needed him to fuck me.

His smile said *yes*, and his eyes said *hell yes*.

I bent over to reach my knees and slid my hands up my inner thighs as I rose back up. I slid my fingers over my panties, up to my belly button, and down again inside my panties, fingering myself. *Super wet.*

He tore off his shirt quickly, but he didn't move toward me. I was going to have to finish this before he would give me his touch, his fingers, his hands, his lips, his cock, all of him.

I danced some more and slid my panties down a few inches, just below my pussy, and pivoted away from him. I spread my legs, leaned over, and blew him a kiss from between my knees.

He was losing it as he struggled out of his shoes and pants, practically panting with lust.

I turned his direction again and slid the underwear all the way down, kicking it off, still dancing to the imaginary music.

"Turn around and walk to the window," he commanded.

I did as he said, continuing my dance as I went.

He turned up the lights when I reached the window.

My God, he was going to display me to the world. I stopped dancing and spun away from the window.

He reached me in a few strides. "Turn around."

I stood still, so hot, so wet, so at his mercy, but not wanting to face the window naked like this.

He twisted me around and placed my hands against the cold glass. He pushed me toward it. He urged my legs apart and brought his hand around in front of me, finding my slippery folds.

His touch was like a million volts of electricity as he teased my clit and my opening, pressing me against the glass for the whole world to see. I had waited so long for his touch, anticipating it, longing for it, needing it.

With my breasts pressed against the glass, he nipped at my ear. "Scared?" he asked.

"They can see us." A non-answer, but yes, I was scared and turned on at the same time.

"Only if they know where to look."

I'd read in *Cosmo* that men liked it when a woman talked dirty.

Why not? "Shut up and fuck me already."

He surprised me by entering me suddenly with his fingers, then retreating and playing over my swollen clit. He continued to nibble on my ear, kiss my neck, and generally drive me crazy, brushing his chest against my back.

He pulled my hips back and ran his cock up and down my pussy, past my entrance and over my hypersensitive bud, guiding himself with his fingers, which took turns with his cock, teasing the tiny bundle of nerves.

I angled my hips every time he brought his cock forward, trying for more friction, more pressure, needing more.

"Take me," I pleaded.

He pulled away and used his teeth to tear the condom package.

I stayed against the window without his urging as he sheathed himself. I needed him so badly I didn't care if anyone saw. The danger was exciting——like public sex, but not really in public, not knowing if anyone beyond the glass was a witness to this or not. We were just shadows against the window, after all.

He returned to me.

I put my hand down, stuck my hips back, and guided him into

my heat. I had been waiting so long. I felt a burst of pleasure as he finally began to slip inside. I needed him to fuck me silly.

He seemed hesitant at first, moving in slow, subtle movements.

"You're unfuckingbelievable, so fucking wet, so fucking tight." He groaned as I took him in.

I was so slippery he slid in easily, his girth slowly stretching me wider, without pain this time, just the sheer pleasure of him inside me where he belonged. His cock was mine now.

His hand returned to my aroused bud as his thrusts went deeper, and I arched my hips into him. His other hand came around to my breast, and I pushed away from the glass to give him access. He fondled and squeezed and teased me as I took him in all the way, and he increased his tempo. He pinched my nipple, releasing a split-second shot of pain that shot sparks straight to my clit.

His breathing came faster. He moaned, his release approaching, as I rocked against him, taking him in again and again.

The waves started to wash over me as I screamed from the hot, liquid pleasure of him. My orgasm had built so quickly that it surprised me as it crashed over me. Tremors had me clenching around his cock; they shook my legs and took away my breath.

He released my breast, took my hips with both hands, and pounded out his own release moments later.

Panting, my face against the glass, I looked down to the street. A solitary figure stood motionless on the sidewalk. Was he looking up? I couldn't tell. I didn't care anymore.

Bill drove me home the next morning before work. He had woken me for two more sessions before breakfast. Sleep had not been a high priority. True to his word, he had fucked me so hard, I had to be careful how I walked to the breakfast table.

CHAPTER 28

Lauren

Sandy had outdone herself. Her date for the museum gala, Ramon, was a real-life electrical engineer with two patents to his name who moonlighted as a model. She'd been ready for half an hour, gabbing with Ramon while I flitted around the apartment finishing up, when the stretch limo pulled up outside.

Judy had told me Bill would arrange for a limo to pick the three of us up. But when the doorbell rang ten minutes before the appointed hour, I wasn't ready. Sandy answered the door as I ducked into the bathroom for my final preparations.

"BD is here," she shouted from the other room.

What the hell is he doing here? We were supposed to meet him at the museum.

"Be out in a minute." I hurried to finish my makeup with trembling fingers as I heard Sandy introducing her date. After a final mirror check, I climbed into the silver-studded Jimmy Choo pumps that went with the black Versace dress I had picked from the three Bill had sent over.

I opened my bedroom door, and he took my breath away. "What are you doing here?" I blurted.

Why did I say the stupidest things when he was around?

He filled out his black tuxedo perfectly. The bright blue cummerbund accentuated his trim waist, offsetting his broad shoulders with a blue bowtie to match his eyes. And his hair was perfectly in place, for a change.

"You look stunning, milady. I think you'll have all the men at this shindig drooling the minute you step through the door."

Butterflies filled my stomach as the compliment warmed my heart. "Why, such nice lies you tell, Sir Knight."

"I'm here to claim the honor of seeing you safely to this affair, milady."

Who talks like that these days?

"But before we go, tonight is a very special night, and I have a little something for you."

He held out a small box the same color as the ones the dresses had come in.

Sandy panted with excitement as I tore into it. The inner box said *Tiffany*. My heart stopped as I opened it to find a pair of diamond solitaire earrings that must have been more than two karats each.

"Holy crap, BD," Sandy squeaked. "Those are worth more than my car."

Now that was saying something, because Sandy drove a Lexus.

I held one up to my ear. "How do they look?" Everyone was smiling. Even Ramon seemed impressed.

"Like they belong on you," Bill said as I grabbed him and hugged as hard as I could.

How much more wonderful could this man be?

On the drive over, Bill filled us in on what to expect at the fundraiser, but that still didn't prepare me for what awaited us as the driver dropped us off. Entering the museum was like stepping into a fairytale. Bill guided me, with an arm around my waist, past the colorful bunting, multiple ice sculptures, and tall floral arrangements at every entrance.

Waiters in white waistcoats floated across the marble floor carrying silver platters of champagne and hors d'oeuvres. How could anyone be prepared for the explosion of opulence around us, so removed from the gritty streets outside?

Bill checked the seating chart for our table.

"Seen your date yet?" I asked as Bill snagged champagne glasses for us from a passing waiter. We were on our way to the silent auction tables at the rear.

"Oh, yeah, she's here, all right," he said as he scanned the room.

The auction tables seemed to stretch on forever, filled with expensive items for people to bid on. Bill put his name down on a week for two in Maui with a ridiculously high bid. I was sure he intended to win it——no messing around for rich-kid Bill. I couldn't have afforded to bid on anything I'd seen except a pretty picnic basket filled with wine, cheese, and crackers.

"William, daaaahling."

I recognized the mating call of the Red-Taloned Rare Metal Miner. Miss Broadchest had appeared.

I elbowed Bill. "Your date has arrived."

I moved to escape, but he held me tightly to his side. I stopped resisting. I would have to endure another introduction to her sooner or later, anyway.

Cynthia Powell shuffled toward us from two tables over. Tonight she wore a turquoise gown with heels to match. Her hair was up instead of down, showcasing a necklace encrusted with dozens of diamonds and rubies. She'd done her nails in blue——to match her shoes again.

Bill couldn't have missed her plunging neckline, which exposed a generous amount of braless cleavage. She bounced and jiggled as she shuffled in our direction. His eyes weren't on the necklace.

She gave an extra jiggle as she stopped in front of us. "Dashing as ever, William."

Not so much as a glance in my direction. *Bitch.*

She leaned forward to embrace Bill.

"Cyn, I would like to introduce my date this evening, Lauren Zumwalt."

Promoted like that from coworker to date? Bill had lost his mind. *She* was supposed to be his date. I couldn't breathe.

"A pleasure to meet you, Lauren." Her extended hand said *welcome,* but her cool visage said *Keep your hands off him, bitch.* Scant seconds later she called, "Timothy, you stud." She pointed her cleavage at her next target and bounced away.

After she was out of earshot, I turned to my newly appointed date. "And just what was that all about? You're losing it if you think I'm your date. You promised me *she* was your date so she could connect you with Vincent and Lloyd Benson. Are you trying to screw this up?"

The Cheshire Cat grin was back. "Cool down, SP. It's under control. I'll go over to talk with them after dinner. And I never promised she would be my date. I just promised she would be here."

I felt lightheaded. "The people at the company… It's too early." This was crazy.

"Trust me, right now, it's between you, me, and Cynthia, and she won't tell a soul."

Fat chance of that. "So I'm a stealth date? How is everybody going to think she's with you?"

His gaze warmed me. "I got it covered, SP. You'll see. Everything will turn out fine."

I gave up. There was nothing left to do but damage control.

"So give. What does *SP* stand for?"

"Just a term of endearment, like *BD*." The corners of his mouth turned up. "You never did tell me what *that* stood for."

"Yes, I did. Let's go find our table."

"It's number fourteen on the other side." He walked with me, his hand perched gently at the small of my back. He leaned close. "My question still stands."

"Big dog, like the boss. You're the big boss."

"Funny, Sandy implied it might be something more exotic."

I looked to the right, turning my face away, hoping he wouldn't catch my smile.

"There she is." I pointed to Sandy and Ramon. "Let's go ask her."

That shut him up as he kept us on course for the table.

~

Bill

THE DINNER WAS FUN——NOT THAT THE ASSEMBLY-LINE CHICKEN WAS anything to rave about, but tonight, it was edible. I sat next to Cynthia, but I couldn't stop staring at Lauren and wondering how my plans for the rest of the evening would work out. But first, Cyn and I needed to get that chat with the Bensons.

I excused myself. Lauren showed me she crossed fingers as Cynthia and I left the table.

The Bensons had a table on the far side of the room. As we wended our way there, I glimpsed Sheila between us and our destination. What the hell was my ex-stepmother doing here? She was sitting with a group I didn't recognize. She didn't seem to have seen me yet, so I guided Cynthia toward the outside of the room to avoid going by her. No way was I going to let her ruin tonight for me.

Cyn told me she had already talked to Vincent Benson this evening. When we got close, he noticed us and whispered to his father, who waved us over.

Lloyd Benson looked like Colonel Sanders without the white suit. He had thinning white hair with a mustache and goatee, a generous midriff, a cane, and horn-rimmed glasses.

He took my hand. "I am very sorry for your loss, son. Your dad was a good man, and a good friend."

"Thank you, sir. We all miss him terribly."

"How are you holding up with all of the sudden responsibility?"

"Just fine, sir." *That is, if I can get you to reconsider investing.* "Although, it is quite a change from running the restaurant." *Saying that was a mistake.*

"I'm sure you'll do fine. Just give it time."

That did not bode well.

"I expected you to come looking for me tonight when I saw *Covington* on the seating chart."

"Yes, sir, I wanted to talk for a bit about revisiting your investment."

"Billy, I notice you've been in the paper a few times since taking over for your old man."

I hoped he meant that as a positive thing. "I guess the Covington CEO is more newsworthy than a mere restaurant owner."

"Perhaps. You know, when I agreed to invest, I was helping out an old friend and someone I had known forever. I'm just not sure you and he are cut from the same cloth, so to speak.

"Perhaps, though, you just need a little seasoning, as it were, a little time to get your bearings in the business." He placed his hand on my shoulder.

I didn't have a good response to that. How could I convince him I was up to the task? I tried to keep my eyes from showing my disappointment. He had already made up his mind.

"God knows it took your father more than a few years to develop his style, but after he did, there was no problem he couldn't solve."

So…solving problems might be his test of my mettle.

"There might be one…" He scratched his chin and leaned in closer, lowering his voice. "There is one way I might consider making a quick investment."

Finally, here it was. He wanted to make a deal. He just needed to have the pot sweetened. The old man had been playing us by acting coy when we were vulnerable.

"Yes, sir?"

He turned a bit to his right and motioned to his friends

standing around near their table. "You see the blond girl on Vincent's left?"

"Yes."

She was tall with a refined nose and long hair cascading over tan shoulders in a strapless full-length gold gown——a little younger than me, with slender hips. Quite stunning.

"Her name is Serena. What do you think of her?"

Odd question, but Lloyd Benson was from another generation, after all. "She seems a lovely girl."

Serena waved discreetly as she saw us looking in her direction. Benson waved back.

"Serena's my daughter." He paused as he moved closer, his brows furrowed. "She's looking for the right man to settle down with."

My God, the old codger expected me to marry his daughter. My legs weakened. This might've been the way business was done a few hundred years ago, but no way in hell was I getting roped into this. I felt woozy.

"She's quite pretty, sir." That was no lie. "But right now, I'm spoken for." I had to get out of this without insulting him.

"Gotcha, Billy." He chuckled. "You should have seen your face." He burst out in laughter. "I just couldn't resist. Your old man and me, we were always pulling each other's legs."

The blood finally returned to my face. "I thought for a minute…"

"Just jokin', Billy." He slapped me on the back. "Life's not worth livin' if you can't laugh a little."

He might be old, but Lauren had been right that being too serious was not his style.

"I see you're with that Powell girl again?" he remarked. "She's quite a looker."

"No, sir, she's all Vincent's. I have someone much more down to earth."

A sly smile came to his lips. "Good choice, son."

No doubt Lloyd Benson was wise enough to size up Cynthia, and he probably had his hands full keeping Vincent out of her clutches. We exchanged a few more pleasantries, and we went our separate ways.

The silent auction's results were about to be announced as I slunk back to the table.

I'd failed at my first mission tonight.

I can't fail at the second.

CHAPTER 29

LAUREN

THE LONG FACE AND SLUMPED SHOULDERS BILL PRESENTED AS HE walked back from the Benson table did not portend good news. He pulled out his chair slowly and sat next to me. Miss Broadchest was not with him.

"So, he looked like he was having a good time. Did you get a chance to ask about reconsidering the investment?"

The despair in his eyes spoke volumes. "He thinks I'm too new in the job to trust."

I felt sorry for Bill. He was trying so hard, and the predicament the company was in wasn't his fault. His father was the one who had flown too close to the flame.

"Well, doesn't he understand that this is a problem your father, his friend, created?"

"We didn't get into that." He rested his elbows on the table and set his chin on his hands.

"Maybe we just have to wait for him to see more of the new William Covington in the paper."

He looked at me with pained eyes. "He saw them. He just

doesn't care. It's the *new* part he doesn't like. He thinks I'm too new in the job. There's no way to fix that problem, except time."

I moved behind him and started to rub his shoulders. "He'll come around, you'll see. He cares too much about the community to ignore all the good you're doing."

"Well, at this point, I don't seem to have any choice but to wait."

The speakers came to life as the emcee called people back to their tables for the results of the silent auction.

The announcer started off at the top of the list, going in numerical order down the donations. As each winning bid was called out, the winners went up to the front to collect their envelopes and prepare to write their checks.

Bill and I followed along in the little booklet he'd picked up that listed all the auction items.

Bill had donated a weekend at a bed-and-breakfast in Napa, and it had gone to an elderly couple a few minutes earlier. The announcer was getting close to the vacation week Bill had bid on when he crossed his fingers and put his arm around me.

The announcer reached Bill's item. "And item number ninety-seven, round-trip first-class airfare and a weeklong stay at the Westin Ka'anapali on the beautiful Hawaiian island of Maui, donated by Mr. and Mrs. Forrest. The winner is William Covington. Come on up, Mr. Covington."

Bill kissed me and jogged up to the stage with childlike enthusiasm. He beamed ear to ear, waving his prize ticket as he returned to the table.

"Now all you have to do is pay for it on the way out," Garth reminded him.

"If you need a plus one, I'm available," Sandy offered.

She loved going to Hawaii whenever she got a chance. I had never been there, but her descriptions of the clear, warm water and wind blowing through the palm trees had always captivated me.

Bill ignored her. He was busy scanning the resort brochure and showing it to me.

The announcer continued as I daydreamed about Hawaii. He

finally completed the last item in the booklet, and none too soon. I needed a bathroom break. Bill's knee nudged mine. A broad smile grew on his face.

"And we have a very special last-minute addition that is not in your booklets," the speaker continued. "Item number one hundred and eight is a special mystery box donated by an anonymous party."

Bill squeezed my hand lightly, and I squeezed his back.

"The winner of this final item is Miss Lauren..." He stopped to squint at the paper. "...Zumwalt. I hope I'm pronouncing that correctly."

What the hell? I must be hallucinating again. I hadn't even bid on the wine and cheese basket.

"Miss Zumwalt, come on up and claim your prize."

Bill rose and escorted me to the stage.

I was in a daze. "This is a mistake. I didn't bid on anything. What will they do when I can't pay for it?"

Bill's guilty grin told the story. The rat had bid on it for me while I wasn't watching.

"No worries, SP. I took care of it."

The applause sounded louder as I got closer to the stage. The announcer was clapping enthusiastically, holding the microphone, which amplified the sound through the speakers at the front.

The emcee handed me a small gray box with a gorgeous red ribbon around it. I took it and retreated toward our table.

"Aren't you going to open it?" Bill's voice came over the loudspeakers. He'd taken the microphone from the announcer.

I stopped. The room closed in. Everyone was looking at me. *What an idiot.* I had no idea how these auctions were supposed to operate. All eyes in the room were on the dork from the poor side of town who didn't have the slightest idea how to behave at an event like this. The blood rushed in my ears.

I fumbled to untangle the ribbon holding the box closed. Inside was another small black box. I put the gray outer box down on an empty chair beside me. The older man nearby smiled expectantly.

I looked nervously at Bill and then the box, unsure what to do.

I opened the small black box and looked inside it.

OH MY GOD!

"Lauren Marie Zumwalt, will you do me the honor of becoming my wife?" Bill's voice came over the speakers again.

My God, he *had* meant it that day in the cafeteria.

I looked back at the box, then up at Bill, microphone in hand, waiting for my answer. The room was deathly quiet.

My heart pounded, and the instant tears in my eyes made it impossible to see any more than his outline. The box contained a ring, a diamond ring, the kind I'd dreamed of as a little girl——the ring every little girl dreams of. He had dated Hollywood starlets, a news anchor, and a tennis star, but he was proposing to me.

Bill lowered to a knee. "Lauren, will you please marry me?"

I couldn't stop sobbing. "Yes," I managed.

Sudden applause broke the silence in the room. I ran to him.

He dropped the microphone as he swept me off my feet, and his mouth mashed to mine in a passionate kiss that went on and on. The crowd was thunderous. His embrace nearly crushed my ribs, and I gave him back the same with all of my strength.

As he set me down, he yelled over the noise, "I've known you were the one for me since the first time we met."

The announcer rescued the box from my unsteady hand. Bill took it and slipped the ring onto my finger as a throng of well-wishers pressed around us. I couldn't keep track of all the people who came by to congratulate us.

Finally, the crowd thinned, and I was able to find Sandy, who seemed nearly as shocked as I was. From what she told me, this had been a complete surprise to everyone. Not even Bill's uncle knew he'd had this planned.

I listened as Lloyd Benson took Bill aside. "Billy, I think I may have underestimated you," he said. "Perhaps we should talk again in a week or two about that possible investment. That is, if you're not too busy with your new fiancée, extending the family tree if you know what I mean."

That dirty old man.

Later, an older, diamond-encrusted brunette woman offered me her hand. "It is so nice to meet you, dear. Let me congratulate you on your engagement to my son. I'm William's mother, Sheila Lindroth."

She wore what could have been the most expensive jewelry in the room, and that was saying something.

"It was so sad, what happened to his father." She dabbed a tissue to her eye where there was no tear. She instantly switched subjects. "We must get together for lunch. I have some suggestions for your wedding."

"Well, thank you for that offer." What was I supposed to say? Bill and his father obviously had no fondness for this woman, but I had just met her.

"I'll call you, then," she said. "I think lunch would be a splendid idea. I could tell you such stories about William."

Then she was off in the blink of an eye. Bill was still talking with old man Benson and didn't seem to have noticed that his ex-stepmother had been here.

As the throngs dissipated, Bill found me again. "Old man Benson is up for a meeting."

I'd heard. I gave him the congratulatory kiss he deserved. "I knew you could do it."

AT THE END OF THE EVENING, JASON DROVE US BACK TO BILL'S CONDO while the original limo took the others back to my apartment. I carried my heels as we passed the ever-present Oliver in the lobby.

Bill eyed me ravenously during the elevator ride with his arm around my shoulders. The heat of his body kept the chill away—that and the extra champagne we'd both had at the end of the night to celebrate. Neither of us was very steady right now.

I kept him upright on the way to his door, and he had trouble with the key. The lights of the city glittered in the full-length window, a fitting end to a magical evening.

I dropped my expensive pumps on the floor as I grasped his neck and pulled him down for my version of an engagement kiss.

As soon as he grabbed my ass the way he always did, I jumped up to wrap my legs around him, but the long dress prevented it, and we almost fell over. I ended up back on the ground on my tiptoes, giggling against his chest as we wobbled together. I could see it now——trying to explain at the hospital how I'd broken my tailbone on his marble floor.

He disentangled himself and led me to the bedroom and his palace-sized bed. He spun me around to unzip me. He had a little trouble with the clasp, but he got it done. I shimmied out of the dress and kicked it aside before turning to stand in front of him in just panties.

He stepped back, and his eyes ravished the length of me. "Did I tell you how beautiful you look tonight?"

"Just seven times." I had counted.

"Well, this looks even better." His eyes were as devilish as his grin was intoxicating.

I started on his shirt as he undid his cufflinks. "You, sir, are over the legal limit."

"I'm not driving."

"Exactly. Tonight, I'm driving this bus." I pushed him back until he fell onto the bed. "And the passenger has to obey the driver."

His eyes lit up.

I undid the cummerbund and his pants as he struggled out of his shirt and tie.

He lay on the bed naked with his stiff cock hovering over his abdomen.

I climbed on the bed and leaned over to blow on the tip of his engorged member, giving it a quick lick. It bounced upward at the attention, so I licked the length of him, from his balls to the tip, which resulted in a moan of satisfaction. I didn't have much experience at this.

I was probably one of the only girls in my high school to graduate without having given a guy a real blow job, and I hadn't had much more experience since. Bill had been so good to me in bed, so attentive, always giving me an orgasm before he fucked me--

except for a few times that I'd suggested we have a quickie over the table or the back of the sofa.

Tonight was his turn to be the center of attention.

I climbed over him and rubbed my pussy over his length, still in my panties. I did this over and over as I leaned toward him to give him access to my breasts.

He lavished them with attention.

Then I pulled my panties aside and slid my folds over his length. I was so wet from the friction. I moved down his legs, grasped his cock, and pulled it up to my mouth. I spread the bead of precum around the crown and sucked in the salty tip.

I stroked my tongue against his cock as I moved down farther. No way I was getting the whole thing in, but I took as much as I could and moved up and down on it, sucking and slurping and licking. I looked up to see his eyes close and hear slight moans of pleasure.

He laced his fingers in my hair as he guided my head up and down, careful not to push me to take more than I could handle.

I worked the shaft with both hands, twisting and pulling in rhythm with my mouth. I cupped his balls gently, then fondled them and pulled lightly on the sac. I moved back to two hands on his shaft.

All the while, he moaned and encouraged me. He began to tense as he encouraged me to go faster.

I stopped.

The look of disbelief in his eyes was priceless.

I waited a moment, then pulled off my panties and moved up to straddle him. I guided his tip to my entrance and started down on him very slowly. Then as I moved back up, I tried to tense my core around him. He had told me my being tight on him was the ultimate turn-on, so I did all I could to be as tight as possible.

I smiled down at him. I was in charge, and he was at my mercy. I had the power tonight. I started again and then stopped, watching as I controlled his every emotion.

It was empowering to manage his pleasure, giving it to him little by little. I moved down on him all the way to the root. I let his hands guide me for a moment as I leaned forward to kiss him. I kept up the pace until he tensed again. Then I slowed down to prolong it.

The problem was I was losing the ability to control myself. As I rode him, the sensations grew, and my pleasure could not be ignored. My brain grew fuzzy, and my desire took over as I rode him faster and harder. The test would be whether I could hold off long enough to give him his release before I lost my mind.

When I'd started this, I'd been sure I could hold off. Now it wasn't so clear. I lifted myself and grasped the base of his cock tightly with Sandy's recommended ring hold. I rode him harder.

He tensed beneath me and pulled me down hard against him as he arched upward. He screamed out my name as he lifted into me.

I had won, but just barely. As he relaxed into the bed, I ground forward against my clit.

Sensing what I wanted, he moved his thumb to rub my clit on the down strokes, and in a few more rapid thrusts, I lost myself in the waves of pleasure that engulfed me as my core clamped down on his still-pulsing cock and I collapsed onto his chest.

It was several minutes before either of us moved.

He stroked my hair. "That was fantastic. You can drive any time you want." He chuckled.

I rolled over beside him. A trickle of wetness ended up on my thigh. In our drunkenness, we'd skipped the protection.

"We forgot the condom, but it's okay," I told him. "I'm on the pill."

"No worries, little one. I'm clean."

"Me too." I nestled into his shoulder. Without the latex between us, the sensations had been even better. The big problem now was making sure I didn't have to sleep on the wet spot.

"I need to tell you about the family trust," he said into my hair.

His skin was warm under my cheek. "Not now. I just want to snuggle." The slowing beat of his heart in my ear soothed me like the beat of the drum of love. The evening had been perfect and all I wanted was to revel in the feel of him, of us, while sleep beckoned.

CHAPTER 30

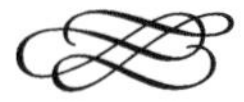

LAUREN

IT HAD BEEN A WEEK AND A HALF SINCE THE PROPOSAL, AND I STILL couldn't believe it. I was going to be Mrs. William Covington. Everything was happening so fast. Bill wanted to get married by the end of the month, so Sandy was helping to plan the wedding——just a small affair with some family and friends.

We settled on the Queen Mary in Long Beach Harbor for the ceremony. Bill thought it would be perfect, given the lifelong voyage we were embarking upon with each other. How romantic was that?

Bill had been disappearing from time to time in the afternoons these last few weeks——some kind of off-site meetings he wouldn't discuss. Then this afternoon he did it again, and when I asked him where he was going, he blew me off. Not cool.

CHAPTER 31

Bill

I HAD SCHEDULED SEVERAL MEETINGS TO GO OVER OUR PROJECT THESE last few weeks, always in a booth at the bar of a hotel near the downtown site. The bar was nearly deserted at this time of day, and the hotel was the kind my father would have called a *no-tell motel,* where perhaps some of the rooms were for rent by the hour. But I knew we wouldn't be bothered by anybody or recognized here. I always turned off my phone so the office couldn't interrupt us.

Marco, Paul, and Juan were waiting at the table when I arrived, and Marilyn came in just after I did.

The team was making incredible progress, and I couldn't wait to see what they had for me today.

"Paul, how are we looking on the enhanced temperature control?"

"The numbers are better by thirty percent on the two pods where we added insulation last month, so we'll incorporate that change into the production plans for about half the modules. The crops for the other half will be fine the way they are."

"What about standardizing, so we don't have to build two types of pods?" I asked him.

"That's the plan. We've designed the extra insulation so it's a simple add-on to the interior. It can be a field modification if the customers choose, and it's easy to do."

"Does it affect the capacity?"

"Just two inches per side. Should have no real effect."

"Great job."

"Marilyn, what about the cash flow?" I asked.

Marilyn Coombs may have looked like a busty airhead, but she had a Wharton MBA in finance and was acting as our CFO for the time being.

"It's fine for right now," she reported. "The burn rate is still less than a million per month, but that changes as soon as we go into pre-production. I've got leases ready to go on two manufacturing sites, and Paul and I have lined up good rates with about eighty percent of the suppliers."

As usual, the team was well-prepared and ahead of schedule. My little stealth project was taking on a lot more significance. It had originally been a mental diversion for me and a way to help our restaurant, but now it looked like it would be great in its own right.

"Since Paul and Juan are ahead of plan, we're going to need to move up the funding," Marilyn said. "Have you heard back from Belzarian yet?"

I shook my head. "Not yet."

So now *I* might become the limiting factor. I had planned to get bridge financing from my father, but with Covington's current situation, that no longer made sense. So I had shifted to pursuing other avenues for the money, and Belzarian seemed the most promising.

As usual, I kept the meeting short, and we disbanded in less than an hour. Marco stuck around after the others had gone.

"Something's bothering you," he said. "What's up?"

I stretched my shoulders and took a deep breath. "It's just nerves about this Benson meeting."

"So the master of the fucking universe is human." Marco chuckled. "Take a breath. You've got this. You're going to get married, you're going to impress the hell out of this Benson dude, you're going to save the company for the next generation of little Covingtons, the sun will shine, and you will go off on a well-deserved honeymoon to Tahiti or wherever." He slapped me on the back. "You've got this."

We left as the first of the dinner crowd trickled in. I turned on my phone, and it repaid me with a ding. Two voicemails, one from Lauren and the other from Kourtney.

What could possibly go wrong?

When I reached the car, I dialed Lauren first. No answer. Kourtney, however, picked up right away. Her father wanted to meet this evening, and when James Belzarian called, you came. That was especially true in my case, as I desperately wanted his investment in the farm project.

As I drove, I went through all the recent developments in my head, all the progress we had made in the last few weeks.

They buzzed me through at the gate, and I stopped in front of the main house in the massive Belzarian compound. Their horse barn was the size of my father's house.

Kourtney opened the door and rushed to hug me. It had only been a little while since the accident, and she still had a bit of a limp. "You were so gallant the other night, Billy. You saved me. I don't think I could have survived the night without you."

Ever the drama queen.

"Just trying to help. It's those damned paparazzi that should be jailed."

She screwed up her face with disgust. "There ought to be a law."

I walked with her down the main hallway. "There sure should."

She stopped outside the library. "Daddy is waiting."

I gave her a kiss on the cheek and opened the door, allowing her to enter first. I knew the drill. James Belzarian's office was beyond the library. A member of his security team was always posted outside his door. I handed the burly guard——Drago, I think his name was——my cellphone and raised my arms as he scanned me with a metal detector.

Belzarian didn't allow electronic devices inside his office. He was paranoid in that regard. Since I had been a friend of the family for years, I didn't get the physical patdown strangers endured.

Kourtney took a seat. "I'll stay out here while you two talk."

Drago held the office door open, and I walked in as James Belzarian came around his desk to shake my hand.

"Kourtney told me what you did for her the other night, William, and I wanted to extend my heartfelt thanks." He pumped my hand. "It's not often that boys of your generation act with such gallantry."

So that's where Kourtney had picked up the word *gallant*. It hadn't struck me as a normal part of her lexicon. He eventually stopped pumping my hand and directed me to sit as he returned to his overstuffed chair behind the massive carved desk.

"I just did what I thought was right."

"You know this desk is an exact replica of the Resolute Desk that sits in the Oval Office?"

"It looks magnificent, sir." It fit the man's ego.

"It reminds me of the bravery and ideals of the men who founded this great country, and what you did for my daughter is in keeping with that bravery."

He was laying it on pretty thick.

He paused. "I've gone over your proposal at some length."

This sounded encouraging. "Perhaps I could add a little regarding our recent progress?"

When he nodded, I recounted our latest data and test results. I had brought some of our revised projections with me, which I spread out on the desk as I explained them.

He didn't interrupt as I went through everything I could think of that he might want to know.

When I finished, he looked at the documents in silence. Then he said, "William, I like the idea behind your project."

Oh shit. Here comes the *but*. All that buttering up, all that talk of the desk was just because he felt bad for telling me *no* right after I saved his daughter from jail.

I should have known better than to think he would see the potential in this project.

"But I'm not sure you've designed enough profit potential for me to get involved," he said.

That was the whole point. Making an insane profit was not the purpose——it was growing food and providing jobs.

"Sir, I'm not sure what you're saying. Do you have some specific suggestions you think we should incorporate?"

I had to try to save this deal. So much depended on it.

"I think you need more professional management for this project."

"Do you have particular people in mind, sir?"

"You offered me a thirty-percent stake for eighty million. I'd be willing to put in one hundred million..." He rubbed his chin. "For a seventy-percent stake."

The arrogant ass wanted to steal my baby. I clenched my teeth and tightened my grip on the arms of my chair before I stood. I offered him my hand over his copy of the Oval Office desk.

"Well, thank you for your time, sir, but no thank you. Goodnight."

We shook goodbye, and I left before I said anything I might regret.

Kourtney handed me my phone as I stomped through the library. "You got a call, but they didn't leave a name. It was a girl."

Judy was probably wondering when I was getting back to the office. I pounded the steering wheel as I climbed into my car and sped away. The office wasn't my destination. The bar was.

~

LAUREN

. . .

THE SMELL OF DAY-OLD PIZZA GREETED ME AS I OPENED THE DOOR TO my apartment. Sandy was a lot of fun, but fastidious she was not. I made it all of four steps inside before Bandit made a run at me and nearly tripped me in the partial darkness. I turned on the kitchen light, opened my purse, and fished out my Advil bottle. This headache called for three instead of my normal two.

I poured a glass from the open bottle of chardonnay in the fridge and downed my pills with it. Bill hadn't answered his phone, and he hadn't returned my call. I plopped onto the couch, waiting for Sandy. I needed someone to talk to, but not anyone at work.

After an hour of feeling sorry for myself, Sandy opened the door. I was in the fetal position on the couch.

"Hey, girl, what's up? Somebody take your reserved parking space at work or something?"

She knew we didn't have reserved parking spaces.

I wiped my nose. "Bill's hiding something from me." The words came out a whisper.

"Okay, I'm guessing it has something to do with BD, but you're gonna need to speak up." She came over and sat next to me on the couch. "Is it nachos-and-margaritas bad? We could go over to the Bucket and get you good and tanked."

"No."

"Well, spill, girl. What did BD do now?"

Her use of *BD* made me giggle. He did have a big dick, after all.

"Don't call him that."

Sandy laughed. "So, what?"

"It's just that he won't tell me where he's going when he disappears."

"Maybe he's sneakin' off to see a shrink or something. Guys can get sensitive about the weirdest shit."

I hadn't thought of that. I snorted.

"Look, just put on your big girl panties and make him talk to you. If he still won't level with you, I'll give him a good kick in the soft parts. Either way, you can have great make-up sex after the argument."

She was right. I went into the bathroom to fix my face. I wasn't doing this without looking my best.

"Text me if you need me to come over and kick the shit out of him," Sandy called as I left.

CHAPTER 32

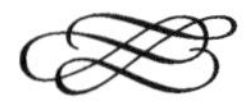

Lauren

Bill's gaze bored deep into my eyes. "Believe me, I couldn't tell you."

I wanted to believe him. "Why not?"

His eyes narrowed. The corners of his mouth turned up. "Because you would want to put it in the papers, and we can't chance that."

He wasn't making any sense. "What?"

He laughed. "On this, your first instinct would be the wrong one. I need to keep this under wraps. Nobody at the company can know."

"You don't trust me?" I asked.

He laughed. "I swear, it's not at all what you think. You're going to love it. I just didn't want you to have the added pressure of having to keep this secret. You have your hands full as it is."

That wasn't going to fly today. "I need to know."

He sighed. "Okay, remember I told you Marco and I were working on a side project? It's something we call CFP."

I dredged my memory and came up with a time he'd told me

Marco was working on something, but I'd just thought it had to do with the restaurant. My brain was going a mile a minute but getting nowhere fast.

"CFP stands for City Farm Pods," he continued. "Let me show you the project. Then you'll understand. What if I told you it had to do with one of the things you care the most about?"

That perked me up. His dimples were on full display with a rakish grin.

"And that would be what?" I asked.

"Let me explain when we get there."

Jason drove us downtown in silence. I was still mad that Bill thought he couldn't trust me. The buildings thinned to older warehouses and empty lots. The streets were dark, with only some of the street lamps working. We passed merely the occasional car or pedestrian.

Jason turned into an empty lot with a security fence and leaned out to enter a code that made the gate open.

The fence was topped with nasty razor wire. I had a bad feeling about this.

"Are you taking me to your dungeon?" I asked Bill, only half kidding.

He smiled. "I know this isn't the best part of town, but that's an important part of what we're doing here."

Jason turned to drive into a side entrance of the warehouse. The roll-up door closed behind us. The building was well-lit and filled with dozens of shipping containers stacked three high. Sets of stairs led up to the stacked units. A few workers in green overalls walked around the open space, and one or two were visible inside some of the containers. A blue-green glow emanated from inside the few open containers.

Bill opened the door, and we climbed out of the town car. Two of the green-overall guys walked over to meet us. Bill introduced them as Juan Ramirez, his chief agronomist, and Paul Weller, his chief engineer. He introduced me as his fiancée and didn't add that I was the paranoid psycho type.

After the introductions, Bill led me toward a nearby container.

I pulled at his sleeve and whispered, "What is this place?"

"My pet project. This is CFP, and the thing everybody is going to be talking about when we come out with it."

Sure thing. Most people I knew couldn't care less about container warehouses.

As we approached the container, Juan handed us each a pair of tinted safety glasses before opening the door. Bill escorted me into that same odd glow. The inside had racks of plants, floor to ceiling.

"This is what we call our Farm Pod," Bill explained. "Each container can grow the equivalent of an acre's worth of produce. This one is full of green peppers." He pointed to a string of lights hanging down between racks of plants. "We grow them semi-hydroponically and give them loads of growing light with these strings of LEDs, which make sure the lower ones get as much light as the upper ones. The entire operation is organic because the bugs can't get into the containers, so we don't need insecticides."

His eyes twinkled, and he scarcely stopped to breathe. He was obviously excited about this.

"And, because we control the temperature, the watering, and the light, we can grow all year round, and faster than if they were planted outdoors in a perfect environment. And, because we can stack these containers up to eight high, we can fit a huge number on a small lot in the middle of the city. We don't need acres of space."

"I see," was all I said, taking in the enormity of this. Sandy had been wrong; Bill wasn't seeing a shrink. He was a mad scientist hiding his new invention. My chest tightened with pride.

"Paul here has engineered the systems to be self-regulating, requiring almost no staff except the picking and planting crew. And since each container always has plants of different ages, we can pick year-round. The racks even exchange positions and move vertically so the picker doesn't have to lean over or reach up to harvest the crop. Juan has been perfecting the water and nutrient flows and is close to determining the optimal light colors for each of the crops."

"Colors?" I asked. He was going too fast for me to understand everything.

"It turns out different crops grow better with a slightly different light mix," Juan explained.

"The biggest nutritional problem for inner-city dwellers is insufficient access to fresh fruits and vegetables," Bill continued. "Our plan is to place these pods in cities and give neighborhoods access to fresh produce year-round."

"In addition, this will provide jobs for inner-city youth and others," Paul added. "Because it will be downtown and the hours are flexible, they can walk or take the bus to our locations."

"This looks expensive," I said. "How are you going to compete with the big farms?"

"That's not the idea. This is all about dealing with nutrition and unemployment in cities. Look, most people don't understand that the farmer gets almost nothing for his crop. Most of the money goes to the middlemen and transportation, the trucking companies. By locating these Farm Pods in the middle of the city, we provide jobs for people, and at the same time we get fresh food in their local stores at better prices by eliminating the distributor and not having to truck the produce hundreds or thousands of miles. This is about giving back to the community in the inner cities, where it's needed the most." His voice grew ever more passionate. He was wound up like an old-time preacher.

This was all so overwhelming. "How long have you been at this?" I asked, trying to formulate a question above the sixth-grade level.

"Marco and I started a bit over two years ago, but these two and rest of the crew here in the cave have been doing all the hard work, getting us from concept to reality. Most of our produce at the restaurant already comes from here." He was positively beaming with pride. "I told you you'd like it."

The team showed me through several more containers growing different crops, some with slightly different lighting, as Juan had explained. Everywhere I looked, there were mounds of fresh vegetables growing on the racks. Bill was a farming genius. This would make great press for Covington.

"This is great. When can I get *The Times* down here to do a story?"

Bill stopped in his tracks. "This is what I told you. Absolutely not." His visage was stern and uncompromising.

I turned around. "Why not? I see this as a big winner for your image. This is the kind of thing we need."

"That's exactly why I didn't tell you. No publicity. Not yet. Juan and Paul are still perfecting a few things, and we need to roll this out nationwide when we're ready. Innovation like this often runs into opposition from entrenched interests. The wholesalers are going to hate us, and the best way to get around that is to launch in lots of cities simultaneously before the opposition has time to react and do something like create zoning roadblocks we can't get around."

We needed this. He needed this. Ten thousand people at Covington needed this. "But Covington needs the kind of publicity this could generate."

Bill placed a hand on my shoulder. "Patience. This will work out. I knew you'd like it."

He picked me up in one of his signature bear hugs and topped it with a kiss.

"Hey, get a room, guys," Paul said after a moment.

I remembered Sandy's expected outcome for this conversation: wild make-up sex. I was already wet. Bill had no idea what he was in for.

"It looks like I've been naughty again," I whispered in his ear. "I thought you were hiding something you were ashamed of."

He swatted me lightly on the ass. "I'm going to have to punish you then." He winked. "When we get home."

And punish me, he did.

I ended up tied spread-eagle on his bed. He retrieved a can of whipped cream from the fridge and squirted it all over me, starting with my breasts and moving down my stomach to my thighs and in between, licking it off little by little and putting more on as I lay there unable to touch him. Every lick was pleasant torture. He drew it out and had me panting for his touch.

When he finally untied me, I was begging him to fuck me. I wanted him inside me so badly. He took me from behind, doggy style, pounding into me with animal intensity. The slapping of flesh as he rammed into me was probably loud enough to wake the neighbors on the floor below. We came together as he reached his climax with a ferocious yell.

The sheets were going to need to be changed after the mixture of whipped cream, sweat, and sex. But for now we were both exhausted. I fell asleep spooned against him with his hand holding my breast. I had to sleep on the wet spot, a small price to pay.

The next morning, he woke me, and I notched a fourgasm.

How have I gotten so lucky?

~

THAT DAY I MET SANDY FOR LUNCH AT ONE OF HER FAVORITE THAI places, but I beat her there, so I went ahead and found a table.

"You look well-laid, girl," she announced way too loudly for my taste as she came up and took a seat.

I could feel the flush in my cheeks. I had to get this girl to tone it down when we were in public.

"Shush——just 'cuz you're not getting any."

"That's what you think. Just why do you think I got back late from yesterday's shoot?" She winked.

That sounded like Sandy, all right. I took a sip from my water glass. "You're so bad."

"So I'm guessing BD is living up to his name?"

She had no idea. "That he is." We both laughed.

"So spill, girl. You got yourself all wound up for no reason, right?"

"I can't take you anywhere," I scolded her. "It turns out he's been working on this really cool secret project that… Let's just say it will help a lot of people.

"If you say it's cool, that's good enough for me. I trust you." Sandy raised her water glass. "Here's to BD and saving the fucking world."

CHAPTER 33

Bill

I gazed out the window as the car made its way to the Benson Headquarters in Century City. It was time for the meeting we'd agreed to at the museum gala. Lauren sat next to me, and Uncle Garth was in front with Jason.

I looked over at Lauren. Her face was serene despite the pressure of the situation. A smile came over me as I thought back over the two hectic weeks since I'd proposed to her at the museum fundraiser. She had such an enthusiasm for life, and she didn't let anything stand in her way.

When she was challenged at work by some of the department heads, she stood up to them and said exactly what was on her mind, just as she had with me those first days. She was a breath of fresh air, a woman without an agenda.

She placed her hand on mine and squeezed. That was about as much of a public display of affection as she allowed herself in the work environment, even though we were engaged now.

Benson would have his son, the COO, his CFO, and his head of marketing with him, and he'd suggested I bring along a comparable set of people.

I was hopeful as we pulled up to the building. I just hoped my fiancée wouldn't see me crash and burn, because nothing was in the bag.

"Are you recovered from yesterday, son?" Lloyd asked as we entered his conference room, which reeked of old money. "The first few times out, you can get a little sore swinging a hammer all day."

I'd seen him at our Habitat for Humanity outing yesterday. He was right about the shoulder.

I stretched the truth a little. "I'm fine, thanks."

His handshake was as strong as a twenty year old's. "Hope to see you out there again."

"You can count on it," I replied.

The elder Benson took his seat at the end of the long, polished table and introduced his son Dennis, the COO; Matt Williams, his CFO; and his younger son Vincent, their VP of Marketing.

After we exchanged business cards, Lloyd began the proceedings.

"Glad you all could make it. Now, I don't cotton to long meetings, so let's keep this as brief as possible."

I waited to be sure he'd finished before responding. "We're here today to show you that Covington now is the same Covington you planned to invest in."

His demeanor didn't change one iota. There was no way to read him.

"Well, let's get to it, then," he said. "The day's a wastin'."

Garth started his presentation. I had to agree with Liam's earlier observation——Garth's slides could use some color. The other side was losing interest as he droned on.

"Uncle Garth, just a moment, if you please," I interrupted. "Mr. Benson, when did you and Dad start talking about the investment, and when did you first agree to go ahead?"

I'd caught him by surprise. He didn't seem ready for this change in the script.

"I'm not sure." He scratched his chin. "I agreed about four months ago, but we must have started... Let's see... Matt, when do you think it was?"

Their CFO, Matt, checked his notes. "The first visit was about six months ago, and you signed off about three months ago."

Those dates would work fine for me. "Okay, Uncle Garth just went over our projections for this quarter a few minutes ago, and I have here..."

I pulled the two quarterly folders out of the portfolio I had brought along just in case.

"I pulled these out of Dad's desk this morning." Garth looked puzzled. "They're the same forecasts Uncle Garth has been showing you for this current quarter. I think if we have Uncle Garth put these up next to the current ones, Matt, you'll be able to tell Lloyd pretty quickly how they compare and if we're in better or worse shape than when you originally decided to go ahead."

"And you didn't alter these at all?" Matt asked.

"Not in the least; they have my father's original chicken scratches all over them. Lloyd, you and Garth must recognize the handwriting."

Garth put up the first slide.

"He always did write like a girl," Lloyd said with a chuckle.

Garth put up the slides, one by one, as he and Matt stood by the screen, pointing to sets of numbers and talking in financial techno-speak, agreeing with one another as the rest of us waited.

Matt turned to face his boss. "I would agree that it looks like things are no worse off than when we first looked at doing this, Lloyd."

The elder Benson looked up at the screen for a moment. "Vincent, what do you think of these?"

The younger Benson squirmed in his seat. "I think maybe we should go offline for a few minutes to discuss it." He couldn't hold eye contact with his father and looked down at his papers.

"Dennis, do you see any holes in this?"

The COO didn't flinch one bit, but he did dodge the question.

"I don't see how this changes anything. I'm with Vincent. We ought to huddle to discuss it."

"Then let's do that." Lloyd Benson looked to me for a moment. "Billy, we'll just go next door. Won't be long."

Garth was the first to speak after they left the room. "Well, that's not a good sign. It's pretty clear Dennis is opposed, and Vincent doesn't want to stick his neck out. If they were leaning toward no before, I don't think we've changed anything."

The lump in my stomach got heavier. I'd had such high hopes coming into this that Lloyd Benson had changed his mind.

"He could have just blown me off with a simple phone call," I said. "Why the dog and pony show then?"

"He might see it as the gentlemanly way to do business——give you one last chance to change his mind," Garth responded. "Lloyd is an old-school kind of..."

Lauren interrupted, "Then that's what we need to do." She put her hand on my shoulder. "You need to show him CFP."

Puzzlement showed in Uncle Garth's eyes. "And just what is CFP?"

"Bill's secret project," Lauren responded. "If Garth is right, then——"

"What do you mean, secret?" Garth interrupted. He was clearly upset that I might have kept something important from him.

"Bill, it's the big change, the thing you can bring into the discussion to change their..." Lauren stopped mid-sentence as the door opened and the Benson group returned to their seats around the massive table.

From Lloyd Benson's demeanor, it was clear this was not going to be good news.

"Billy, as I told you earlier, I respected your father very much, but making an investment of this magnitude without getting a chance to really know you is a risk I'm just not willing to take at this time."

I did my best to keep my shoulders up, but my stomach was not in it.

"I see. Well, thank you very much for your time, Lloyd.

Perhaps at a later date then." I knew as soon as I said it that a later date was not an option. We had to have the cash sooner, not later.

"Mr. Benson," Lauren addressed the old man. "I would like to show you something about Mr. Covington that will answer any questions you have about the kind of man you're dealing with."

"Young lady, I know you're the marketing whiz kid, but I don't need any more bullshit, and we all know you've been seeding the newspapers with all of these articles and putting on a charm campaign. You marketing types are always saying perception is reality. I'm not buying it. Like I said, time will tell me what kind of man I'm dealing with." He sat forward. "I've made enough money in my life that now I have the luxury of only having to deal with the people I want to deal with."

Lauren was not deterred. "Do you think this city and our country would be better off if there were more job opportunities in the inner cities, ones people wouldn't need a car to get to?"

She stared daggers at the old man. *That's my girl.*

Lloyd Benson seemed taken aback. His shoulders softened. "Yes, that's clear, but I don't see what that has to do with today's agenda."

She continued the attack. This was my Lauren. She wasn't about to back down.

"Do you think our city and the country would be better off if inner-city residents had better access to affordable, healthy, organic produce?" She stared at him intently, waiting for an answer.

Dennis squirmed. He and Vincent were not about to get into the middle of this.

Old man Benson looked at her squarely. "Sure, but a once-a-week visit by Billy to the soup kitchen is not going to fix that."

"I agree," she countered. "And that's why you should come with us right now to see a project Mr. Covington has been working on for the last two years that will accomplish both of those goals in a very big way. And this is not marketing bullshit. I think it's right up your alley."

Benson contemplated her for a moment.

"It's your choice," she said with a shrug.

Nobody spoke to old man Benson that way, but my Lauren did.

She rose from her chair to leave. "Do you really care about inner-city nutrition and unemployment? Because this is going to make the biggest change in those areas we've seen in a decade or two."

I went to join her, and Uncle Garth got the message and gathered his papers as well. The younger Bensons had slack jaws, not knowing what to make of my outspoken fiancée. We turned to go.

"Billy." It was Lloyd Benson. "I like her. She's got spunk. I told you she was a good choice. Sure, I'll come along. I need a little fresh air, anyway." He rose.

"It's Bill," I replied.

~

THAT EVENING, LAUREN SAT ACROSS FROM ME AT THE RUSTY BUCKET. All I saw as I looked into her eyes was love and a happy future. We'd been meeting here a lot since our engagement. She thought my restaurant was too stuffy, and I had to agree. Here we could share a plate of skins and beers and relax. I would get her up to dance when the music was slow so I could hold her and relish the way she felt swaying in my arms, smelling the strawberry in her hair, and feeling her breasts pressed up against me.

The Bucket was also rather convenient to walk back to her place. She resisted spending too much time at my condo and refused to move in with me before the wedding. She said it wasn't something a lady would do.

Right now, I didn't want a lady.

She'd put me off twice in the past two weeks when I'd started to bring up the family trust, but it couldn't wait forever.

"Santa Catalina, this weekend," I said into her ear during a dance. "Just you and me." It would provide the time and the privacy for the conversation that would only get more awkward if we put it off.

She looked up. "I can't. Sandy is taking me shoe shopping."

"It's important."

She relented with a nod. "Okay." I breathed in a lungful of her, wondering how I'd ever gotten so lucky.

"Well, do you?" she asked a half-hour later back at the table.

I had missed the question, lost in my reverie.

"If you're going to play hard to get, I'll dance with somebody else," she said.

"No way, woman. I'm ready." I shot up and took her hand.

She held me loosely, nestling her head against my chest. "What were you thinking about back there? It looked like you were lost."

I pulled her close and leaned into her ear. "I was thinking about how happy I am, and I was thinking I'm the luckiest man alive to have you."

She giggled. "If you keep flattering me like that, I may have to take you home and spank you."

I pinched her ass. "Promises, promises."

"Go on, tell me more."

I combed my fingers through her hair. "Your idea to show old man Benson the Farm Pod project was spot on, and that's why we have the financing lined up now."

Lloyd Benson had been won over by the Farm Pods project and now wanted to know if he could invest in that as well as Covington. The deal was back on, and it wouldn't have happened without my girl, my fiancée, my Lauren.

"So, you saved ten thousand jobs. That's a pretty cool thing."

"Go on," she said as we swayed. Her thigh kept rubbing against my cock, and I knew that was no accident.

My dick was swelling from all the attention, making it hard to concentrate.

"The only thing that would make it better is if you'd move in with me."

We had been over this before, and I knew the answer before she spoke it.

"You know I can't do that. I promised my mother."

"I won't ask again; we should always keep our promises."

She pulled herself up to whisper to me. "But you can take me to bed, big guy. And I mean *take me*."

I didn't need any more encouragement. I led her off the dance floor, we gathered up our things, I left a tip on the table, and we walked to her place.

Lauren unlocked the door, and we found a blissfully empty place. No Sandy. As soon as I closed Lauren's bedroom door behind us, she flicked off the light and was on me, kissing me with abandon, pulling my head down.

I snaked my arms around her, and she hopped up to wrap her legs around me. I supported her ass and pushed her back against the door. The strawberry smell in her hair tickled my nostrils as our tongues sought one another. She tasted like potato skins and sour cream with a double side of sex. She was more aggressive than usual, pulling me to her passionately. We couldn't get enough of each other.

I carried her over to the bed, and we fell into it with her legs still wrapped around me.

I had my perfect woman, and I wasn't ever letting her go.

CHAPTER 34

Lauren

The woman was persistent. The note on my desk said Mrs. Lindroth had called for the third time and was hoping we could have lunch today. I couldn't duck her forever. Bill didn't think it was a good idea, but I'd committed myself at the gala.

I dialed the number on the slip, and an assistant named Brita answered. Brita told me Mrs. Lindroth had made twelve o'clock reservations for us at Hamasaku, her treat, and asked if I would need a car to pick me up.

"No thanks, Brita."

Ugh, I would have to eat raw fish for lunch. Maybe I should get some Taco Bell on the way over just in case.

As I prepared myself, I took time to Google Sheila Lindroth. I found some society gossip——she was currently married to a Swedish Internet mogul, her fifth marriage, his second. She seemed to be a serial marriage artist, always finding a richer husband than the last. No wonder she thought she could give me wedding suggestions. An image search showed her always wearing about a hundred pounds of diamonds and whatnot. And every picture had a different hair color.

The recent images indicated she was getting a little long in the tooth to keep competing as a trophy wife. Sooner or later, Botox and plastic surgery wouldn't cut it anymore, and Mrs. Lindroth would have to develop a new gig.

I got to the restaurant a little late, even though I'd skipped visiting Taco Bell. Sheila was sitting alone in the corner, no Brita. I guess expensive lunches with the boss weren't part of Brita's package. A burly blond guy stood oddly against the wall nearby, scanning the room. He eyed me as I approached and moved to block my path.

"She's fine, Magnus. I'm expecting Miss Zumwalt," Sheila said, and Magnus slid back to his post by the wall.

Upper crust—private security to keep the riffraff at bay? But Magnus didn't rate a meal today either.

I forced a smile. "Mrs. Lindroth."

Her eyes were dull. Her smile didn't look forced, but a woman who had acquired five husbands was probably good at faking a lot more than a smile. A hint of Chanel No. 5 wafted in the air, and her face was framed by hair that was more chestnut than the brunette I remembered from the museum party. Her jewelry had changed from the gala but was no less impressive.

"Lauren, I'm so glad you could come, and please call me Sheila." She picked up the menu. "I hear the sashimi here is just to die for." Her crow's feet were more pronounced than in the pictures on the internet. She fingered an empty martini glass in front of her. "Will you join me in a martini?"

I wasn't sure what to make of this woman. "Iced tea will be fine." I had a meeting after lunch.

She waved over the waiter, who brought waters. She curtly instructed him to get me some iced tea and her another dry martini. Apparently, she couldn't be bothered to be nice to the help.

I was grateful that the menu had some cooked food on it. I ordered the skirt steak. She ordered five different kinds of sushi or sashimi——I could never keep them straight, and who wants to eat raw octopus and eel, anyway?

As we ate, she told me a few stories of her son Liam. She didn't once mention Bill or Bill's father, Wendell, or even Steven, the son she had abandoned as a baby.

I picked at my steak in silence as Sheila pushed the seafood around on her plate and ordered another martini. She made a point of implying that she knew the king of Sweden and the French president, as though I cared.

What a pretentious windbag.

She was off next week to Paris, blah, blah, and Rome, blah, blah, and Monaco, blah, blah, blah.

She hadn't once asked about our wedding plans. I didn't have much time before my afternoon advertising meeting.

"Sheila, thank you so much for lunch, but I have to be going."

Her eyes flashed angrily. "Nonsense, we have yet to talk about your wedding."

She took a sip from what was now her third martini. This woman could hold her liquor.

Her nose lifted into the air like a dog sniffing a scent. "I thought William's proposal was quite sensational but a bit ostentatious."

I didn't tell her I thought it was perfect. I did tell her Bill and I planned to have the wedding on the Queen Mary.

She was completely uninterested. "Splendid, dear. Now, how long will you need to stay married? And I can't wait to hear about the prenup."

"I beg your pardon?"

She must be over her martini limit after all.

We had done a prenup, which I barely read. I considered it to be par for the course with rich kids like Bill, but what kind of evil snake plans for a divorce before the wedding?

"Dear, I know all about the family trust. My son Liam is married now, and if William wants to stay the CEO, he's going to have to get married before the annual meeting. That's where you come in. I trust you two have discussed it and the prenup will adequately compensate you for your services, so to speak."

What the hell was she talking about?

"Since you have him over a barrel time-wise, I bet you got one hell of a deal." Her voice was as cold as her eyes.

Her words were fancy, but the meaning was clear. She was calling me a whore.

"We're getting married because we love each other," I spat.

She looked at me like I was too dumb for words. "Nonsense, dear, you're just the flavor of the month. It's always about the money."

I couldn't take any more of this. I didn't have the courage to throw my tea in her face. Magnus might take offense. Instead, I jumped to my feet and spilled my glass as I did so. The tea rolled over the table and into her lap. I was already walking away by the time she yelped.

Dry clean that, Sheila, you old bitch.

I would have burned rubber out of the restaurant parking lot if my wimpy little car were capable of it. The further I got away from that evil woman, the better. My head throbbed. Now I could understand why Mr. Covington had banned her from calling the company.

My hands were shaking so badly I could barely hold my phone. I tried Bill's number. I had to talk to him. No answer. I left a message, begging him to call. It took two tries to get through to Judy.

"Judy, do you know where Bill is?"

My legs were shaking now too. I desperately needed to calm down. There was a Burger King up ahead. I pulled into the lot. I needed a shake *right now*.

"He went over to the Benson building, and I don't expect him back until later this afternoon. Can I give him a message?"

"No, thanks. I already left a voicemail. Please tell Karen to go ahead without me. I'm going to miss the advertising meeting."

I stumbled inside and ordered a chocolate shake. In college, that had been my ultimate comfort food. If I felt really bad, I could suck it down fast and give myself a brain freeze that was certain to take my mind off other things for at least a few minutes.

The brain freeze trick worked. The pain was so intense that I had to stop thinking about that awful lunch. I parked my butt at a table to think. I didn't want to try to walk with a brain freeze.

Nevertheless, on the way out to my car, I tripped and ended up sprawled on the cement, scraping my knee in the process. Just what I needed, a rip in my pants.

I settled myself back into the driver's seat, not yet ready to start the car. As confident as I was that Bill loved me, I couldn't shake the impression that Sheila was equally confident this was a ruse. I went over things again while sipping my shake. She thought Liam was plotting to take over the company. How much sense did that make? He hadn't even been in the building the last few weeks. He was newly married, though. That part was true. Bill had told me that.

I clutched the medallion Bill had given me. It warmed my heart. I had to trust Bill. I had been wrong about Barbie and him, and I had been wrong about him and sex-tape Kourtney.

I cringed. I had been wrong, wrong, wrong. I had to trust him. But I needed him to comfort and reassure me. *Bill, why aren't you here when I need you?*

I called his number again. This time, my message said I would wait for him at his condo. Before leaving Burger King, I ordered a second brain-freeze shake from the drive-thru.

Ollie was at his usual post when I walked into the Covington building and greeted me warmly. When I got upstairs, the condo in the sky was bright with sunlight, completely the opposite of my mood. That helped, and my second shake was still intact, so I put it in the freezer to keep for later, just in case. I rummaged through my purse to find my Advil supply. Three or four of those puppies were what I needed right now.

The couch beckoned, but first, I went to the bathroom and located Bill's first aid kit. It was so like him to have an organized kit in a little red tool box. Some Neosporin and a Band-Aid later, my knee felt better, and I was ready for the couch. I tried the TV, but it didn't drown her words out of my head.

The Bachelor re-runs held no interest. I switched to a *Survivor* re-run. No luck. I had fucking Sheila Lindroth on the brain. What was her game? Why would she be so cruel? What had I done to have her try to ruin my marriage before it began?

Maybe it wasn't me she was screwing with. Maybe she was trying to screw with Bill. No, it made more sense that she didn't think I was good enough for him. Who was she to pass judgment on me? We had never met before that night at the museum.

I had to get Sheila Lindroth out of my head. My brain hurt, and my stomach wasn't much better.

Maybe focusing on work for a few minutes was the answer. I went to Bill's office to check my email. I slid some file folders out of the way and fired up his computer. Luckily, I knew the password to log in. He told me he'd changed it to LaurenandBill4ever. *How sweet is that?* For a moment, my headache faded.

My email only held three routine messages.

As I pushed back from the desk, the title on the top file folder caught my eye—*COVINGTON INDUSTRIES FAMILY TRUST.*

Should I?

I was going to be his wife, so I might as well.

I trembled as I opened the folder and started reading. The third page contained a yellow highlighted section with a notation in the margin, *This is the problem – Garth.* As I read, the lump in my chest threatened to stop my heart. *The Trust will vote to install the HEIR as the replacement Chief Executive. The title HEIR shall fall to the oldest son of the previous HEIR, and if he be not married, to the oldest married son of the previous HEIR, and have he not sons, to the oldest married daughter of the previous HEIR, and have she no offspring..."*

I stopped reading. My vision blurred. Tears flowed. I slammed my fist on the desk. The lying sack of shit. He had to beat out his stepbrother. That was the reason for the rushed wedding. The Ice Queen had let the cat out of the bag. It was all about the money and power for him. Covingtons were so fucking competitive. He just couldn't let his stepbrother Liam beat him. I had been used again. But I was not going to be the doormat this time. *Fuck you, Two-a-Month Bill.*

I grabbed a Post-It from the stack, wrote *GOODBYE* on it, and stuck it on the open trust document. I took the ring off my finger and the condo key off my keychain and placed both of them on the Post-It. I grabbed my shake out of the freezer and went to the door. Turning the lever, I remembered Bill's medallion. I went back and added it to the pile on the desk. I didn't bother to lock the door on my way out.

Enjoy your life, you LSOS.

The tears kept my eyes so blurry I had trouble seeing the road clearly on the drive back to my apartment. I had to be strong. I could not be the doormat again. Once inside, the remnants of the shake in one hand and my purse in the other, I closed the door, fumbled for the light switch, and instantly tripped, falling on my injured knee again.

"Shit, Bandit!" I yelled at the cat as it scurried away. Crying, I curled up on the floor. "Why does my life always turn to crap?" I asked the empty room.

Bandit ventured toward me apologetically. He stayed cautiously just out of reach, purring softly.

I got up slowly, reaching to pet the cat as I did. Bandit backed away. Somehow, the lid had stayed on my precious chocolate shake. Sucking on the straw did not get me what I wanted though. It had gotten too warm to offer me the brain freeze I needed. I put it in the freezer.

I piled clothes into a suitcase and backpack. Stopping to tend to my knee, I replaced the blood-soaked Band-Aid with a fresh bigger one and cleaned up the blood dripping down my leg. I cleaned off my running mascara and wiped my face clean. Neither makeup nor work clothes would be going with me, just casual jeans, sweatshirts, and the like. I had just the place to go, where I could be alone to think, and nobody would know me.

I didn't want Bill to find me, so just like in the movies, I left my phone on the counter. *Off the grid,* they called it. I left Sandy a check for three months' rent and a note explaining that I didn't want to be followed. I took my favorite pillow and the bags down to the car.

Before I started out, I went back up one last time and called Brandon's rehab facility to see how he was. They assured me he was still there and he was on track. At least one thing wasn't fucked up today.

CHAPTER 35

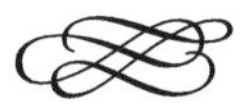

Lauren

My old neighbors, the Nelsons, had a place up in the mountains I'd gone to a few summers when I was young. I knew they didn't use it in the winter. I'd mail them a thank you and a check after this was all over, but I couldn't risk calling ahead and leaving a clue to my destination.

A quick stop at the bank netted me enough cash for a while. At least the bonus money from my promotion meant I could afford to disappear for a while and still pay Brandon's rehab. Another thing I'd learned from the movies——I wouldn't leave a credit card trail either. *Fuck you and your family trust fund, Bill Covington.*

The *low fuel* light blinked on as I pulled into a gas station in the valley. The young girl at the register with black lipstick, a nose ring, and silver skull earrings finally got off the phone to take my twenties. I went back out and started the pump, hurrying back in to buy a flashlight since I didn't have my iPhone with me anymore. It might get dark before I got there, and retrieving the spare key under the house was spooky enough in the daytime. There were now two people ahead of me in line, and Skull Girl was on the phone again, ignoring all of us. I laid a ten on the counter and walked back to my trusty little bucket of bolts.

There was a loud clank and scraping as I drove away, followed by screaming from Skull Girl as she came shooting out of the store, yelling at me.

What the hell? I gave her a ten for a five-dollar flashlight. Where's the crime in that? She kept yelling at me to stop, and I did, but I locked the doors and only lowered the passenger window a crack. I wasn't letting that teenage crazy get near me.

"You broke the fucking pump, you fucking asshole. Stop, you stupid shit, stop," she yelled into the car.

Oh shit.

The gas pump handle jutted out of the side of my car, and a section of hose lay trailing behind. I was in such a hurry I had gotten into the car without taking the nozzle out and putting it back on the pump.

It took five minutes to get Skull Girl to calm down. The sign on the pump said the minimum damage for driving off with the hose still attached was $500, which she demanded on the spot or she was going to call the cops and get them involved. I needed to conserve my cash for off-the-grid purchases, so I had to put this on a credit card. So much for leaving zero financial trail for Bill to follow, but at least I wasn't close to my destination yet.

BILL

LAUREN HADN'T RETURNED MY CALLS OR MY TEXTS. BUT HER FRANTIC messages had said she would meet me here. I turned the key, but the deadbolt wasn't locked. I never left it unlocked. The light was on in the kitchen. Maybe Lauren was here?

I called her name but got no answer. I searched every inch of the condo. It was empty.

She must have gone out for a walk or downstairs to the fitness center. Why hadn't she locked the door?

My computer was on, and as I went to turn it off, a glint of light caught my eye. It was her engagement ring, and beside it sat the condo key and the medallion I had given her, all three on top of a Post-It note.

GOODBYE, it read.

It lay atop the open family trust folder over the page that Uncle Garth had highlighted when he showed me the marriage clause we thought Liam was planning to use against me.

Shit.

I kicked the trashcan across the room. I threw the only thing I had in my hands, my keys, as hard as I could. They hit a picture on the wall, shattering the glass, sending shards to the floor.

What had I done? I should have made the time.

"Shit," I shouted. I paced around the desk.

Now Lauren must think I was hurrying our wedding because of the trust. That was partly true. The other part was that I couldn't wait to have her completely. She'd refused to move in with me until we were married, and I didn't want to be without her. It had become hard to live without her by my side.

I pocketed the ring, the medallion, and her condo key before retrieving my keys from the broken glass on the floor. I was going to fix this. She'd let me explain. She had to. I called her cell but got no answer.

That's probably good.

I needed to explain this in person. The trip to her place was interminable. I nearly ran a red light. I was so lost in thought, running through all the words I wanted to say to her. Bounding up the stairs two at a time, I composed myself and rapped lightly as I reached her door.

After getting no answer, I rang the bell and knocked more forcefully——still no answer and no sounds from within. A quick run downstairs and a check of the parking spaces told me her car was not here.

I drove to the flower shop on Pico Boulevard. The clerk thought I was nuts when I told her I wanted five dozen red roses and a vase big enough to hold them all. "Very lucky lady," she said as she rang me up.

"She's very special," I said. "I'm the lucky one."

Returning to the apartment, there was still no answer, so I slid down the wall and sat on the floor outside her door.

The first neighbor who happened upon me in the hall, an elderly lady, looked down at me with my roses and just laughed. She shook her head as she passed.

The second, a man, offered, "You musta screwed up real bad, huh?"

You have no idea, pal.

Finally Sandy came home and spied me from the end of the hall. "Hey, BD, what ya doing slumming down here?" Then she saw the roses by my side. "What, no candy?"

That girl had a satirical response for everything.

"Just waiting for Lauren."

"Better get up off the floor, BD. Ya know Mrs. Hiddlestone's poodle pees on the carpet out here." She laughed.

Great.

"Come on in. Maybe we can watch some *Bachelor* while we wait." She unlocked the door.

I hoisted the vase with the flowers, careful not to spill it, and followed her inside. "Thanks, Sandy."

I put the flowers down. My butt was sore, and the couch beckoned.

Sandy hadn't been kidding. She plopped down on the couch with me, clicked on the television, and navigated the DVR to *The Bachelor*.

"I've got just the episode for ya, BD. Candy goes topless in the pool to try to get the guy, and the other girls go nuts. In the end, she gets dumped. It's hilarious, but what do ya expect with a name like Candy?" She seemed completely engrossed in it as the show started.

I sat there working through my apology speech in my head, waiting for Lauren to walk in.

Sandy got up and offered me a beer on her way to the kitchen, which I declined.

"Oh shit," she exclaimed after a moment.

I looked over to see Sandy reading a piece of paper. The tortured look on her face did nothing to lift my spirits.

"What is it?" I moved toward her in the kitchen.

Sandy backed away, keeping the paper from me. "Bill, I'm so sorry" was all she said, but her face said volumes more. It was the first time she'd called me by my name instead of those initials.

The note had to be from Lauren. I snatched the paper with a quick lunge.

> Sandy-
>
> Bill lied to me. I have to leave for a while. Tell him not to bother looking for me.
>
> The check is for rent for the next three months.
>
> Love, Lauren

My heart dropped to my ankles. How could I have screwed up so badly?

Sandy stood in silence.

I fished my phone from my pocket and dialed Lauren's number again. I had to talk to her before this got even more out of hand. A ringtone sounded from Lauren's room. I rushed in, but the room was empty, and her phone was on the nightstand. She had left it. How was I going to find her?

Sandy joined me in Lauren's room. "Bill, she wants some time alone to think. Give her time. She'll come back and talk to you when she's ready." She paused and put her hand on my shoulder. "Bill, I've never seen her as happy as she's been with you. Give her time, and she'll come back."

I turned and took Sandy's hand. It was sweaty. "Sandy, where would she go?"

"You saw the note. She didn't tell me, and she's not stupid. She wouldn't go someplace I know about. She knows you would be over here asking questions. Trust me. She doesn't want to be found."

That was the last thing I wanted to hear, but Sandy was probably right. I thanked her and left.

Where to now? Without Lauren, I was rudderless. I sat in my car, unsure what to do next. My mind was frozen, but I had to figure out where she would go, where I could find her. She could be anywhere out there.

When I got back home, the enormity of the task of finding her hit me. How did I find a girl——scratch that, a woman——who didn't want to be found in a city of more than three million people, over fifteen million if you counted the surrounding cities? She didn't even have to be here. She could have gone up to San Francisco, or down to San Diego——or left the state, for that matter.

Those thoughts were not helpful, so I banished them for now. I had to make the task manageable, and I had to start before the trail got cold.

I started with family. That's who I would look to stay with or ask for help if I was in her position. Her mother had passed away, and she wasn't on speaking terms with her father——despised him was more like it. She'd said she didn't even know where he lived now, so the parents were out. Her only brother was in rehab. I had asked Sarah to make sure the company paid her enough in bonus money to pay off the rehab costs she'd incurred, and I also had Sarah locate a top-notch facility and arrange to have him moved there, but I couldn't remember the name of it.

A quick phone call to Judy remedied that. Sarah and Lauren had arranged to have Brandon moved to a facility in Malibu so he would be closer.

I finally reached someone who told me that yes, Brandon Zumwalt was still a patient after I told them the little white lie that I was his brother-in-law back from overseas. However, they wouldn't let me talk with him because his treatment regimen didn't allow for outside contact until three weeks from now. But, I could call back then.

So she wasn't hiding out with Brandon.

Four hours later, with no good answers, a bottle of scotch beckoned to me.

I fucked this up royally.

CHAPTER 36

LAUREN

IT WAS JUST AS I HAD REMEMBERED, ONLY COLDER. THE DOORMAT IN front of the door still read *Casa Nelson*. I grabbed my five-hundred-dollar-plus flashlight off the passenger seat. After a struggle with the cardboard and plastic it came wrapped in, I flicked on the light…and nothing. A quick check of the package told me what I should have known. I was a dumbshit. *Batteries not included.* I slammed my head into the steering wheel. What the hell else could go wrong today?

A trip to the local Rite-Aid garnered me batteries, and only wasted another half hour. I now had a working flashlight, and the key was where it had been those many years ago. Just with lots more cobwebs than I remembered.

As I let myself in, I turned on the lights to reveal a scene directly out of my childhood. It had hardly changed since my last visit, eight years ago. A quick adjustment to the thermostat, and I was ready to unpack and make this my temporary home.

This place held so many good memories. It was the perfect

place to dispel the disgust I felt with my current situation and the man who'd put me here.

But it wasn't just him. I had a part in it for falling for the story. I should have known there was no Cinderella ending in real life. Like they say, *If it seems too good to be true, it probably is.*

I SPENT THE NIGHT TOSSING AND TURNING. A LONG, HOT SHOWER IN the morning helped how I felt physically, but it didn't clear the darkness from my mind. How had I gotten into this mess?

Naturally, there wasn't anything in the cabin to eat beyond ketchup and mustard and some salad dressing that was way beyond its expiration date. But my money would go a long way at the grocery store up here. I didn't plan on wasting it at the local diner. First thing on my list this morning was a trip to the market.

I saw him walking toward me as I locked the front door behind me and went to my car.

"Hiya there. Ya musta come in late last night, huh?" He was an older man, bundled up against the cold, his thick glasses making his eyes seem larger than they were under his bushy white eyebrows.

He said his name was Patterson. He was one of the only year-round residents on this section of the lake and had appointed himself the local community watch.

I showed him that I had a key and recounted that I had stayed here often with the Nelsons during the summers, so he accepted me as a legitimate occupant of the house. He offered to come over if I needed help with anything. I neglected to tell him that the Nelsons had not *given* me the key.

I thanked him and drove off to the market.

An hour or so later, after a breakfast of microwaved oatmeal and instant coffee, I sat on the back deck of the cabin, watching the small waves lapping up against the sand and rocks of the shore not far from me. The gentle, rhythmic sound did its best to soothe me, but I was anything but content.

Bill had lied to me and used me to keep his precious job. I hadn't caught him cheating on me, but it almost felt worse. Instead of being the girlfriend who really wasn't, I had nearly become the wife who really wasn't. *Lucky me.*

Riley had been the one guy in college I'd thought was the real deal, right up until he broke my heart. All during summer vacation before my junior year, he had been connecting with his ex——coming to see me on weekends at the same time as he was screwing her during the week. At the beginning of the fall semester, he told me. I wanted to curl up and die, but that would've been letting him win, so I'd kicked him in the nuts instead. I spat on him as he crumpled. That was the last I saw of Riley.

He had turned out to be just like my dad. My father had been my idol until I was thirteen and came home early from school one day. The image of him with that tramp had burned itself into my brain. He had lied to Mom and me about her right to our faces. Mom had kicked him out the next day and never remarried.

Men suck.

The breeze chilled me. I hugged my knees closer to my chest. I should have brought warmer clothes. It had been quite warm here during the summers, and I hadn't anticipated the chill that could come with approaching winter at this altitude.

I closed my eyes, but I couldn't make Bill disappear, the latest one to break my heart. I missed his arms around me. I missed the sound of his chuckle and the sight of his dimples dancing as he laughed. He had treated me so well——that evening at Medieval Times, the lunches at his restaurant, the dinners at his condo, and that over-the-top night at the gala, the dresses, and the earrings. They all brought a warmth to my soul. He was so unlike any man I had met before.

But it had all been an act——hadn't it? What would our life together have been like? How long would it have taken me to learn the truth and have my heart broken? My mother thought she'd taught me men couldn't be trusted, but it was more accurate to say my father had taught me. Mom and I had both trusted him until that horrible day. If we couldn't see through the deceit of someone we knew so well, how had I thought I could trust someone I had comparatively just met?

I stood up and stretched. I needed to walk instead of just sitting here, wallowing in self-pity. I chose right and headed around the lake. How long would it take to walk the whole way? Three hours was my guess.

The gravel crunched beneath my feet and my mind turned as I went. Sheila had summarized it best. With the Covingtons, it was always about the money. They were so focused on winning that there was no room for anything else. Other people, acquaintances, and even friends became chess pieces to be manipulated in the game. Nothing was off-limits, nothing was sacrosanct. There were no rules except their version of the Golden Rule: he who has the gold makes the rules.

How could I have been so gullible? My own life should have taught me better than to trust a man I barely knew, no matter what he seemed to be. The thoughts made me nauseous.

CHAPTER 37

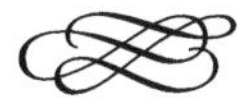

Bill

I SKIPPED MY WORKOUT THE NEXT MORNING AND WENT STRAIGHT TO work. I had essentially gotten no sleep, even with the alcohol. How could I sleep with my heart ripped out? A combination of Tylenol and Advil helped, but I still had a splitting headache.

Judy was her normal cheery self as I arrived, telling me a meeting with Uncle Garth was the first thing on my schedule.

I left the building to go to the Starbucks across the street. The normal office coffee was not going to be strong enough this morning. I ordered an extra-shot mocha and lugged it back to my waiting desk.

"You look like death warmed over," Uncle Garth announced as I returned.

I settled into my seat. "Good morning to you too."

He closed the door. "What is going on, William? You look like you have not slept."

How right he was.

"She left. Lauren left." Just saying the words made it more real, and the hurt I had tried to control magnified. Tears pricked my eyes. I pulled a tissue from the box in my side drawer.

He took a seat. "You mean Lauren has gone somewhere?"

"That's about the size of it."

"What brought this on? You two seemed so happy."

"She found out about the trust's marriage clause."

Garth pondered this silently.

I put down the tissue. "It was my fault. I meant to tell her, but we never found the right time."

"So, now she thinks you are marrying her to meet the trust clause?"

"Yup. She didn't even give me a chance to explain. She just left."

"Well, were you?"

"Was I what?" I shot back.

He shifted forward in his seat. "Marrying her to resolve the family trust issue?"

How could he think that? My blood boiled at the accusation. "Of course not. How could you even ask that?" I shouted.

He recoiled. "Calm down. You can see how, given your history, it could be a question."

He certainly had a point. What was it the tabloids had labeled me? Yeah, Two-at-a-Time-Bill, Two-A-Month-Bill, something like that. The night of my dad's crash, Lauren had found me with a bimbo in my bed, and judging by her reactions to the tabloid story on the accident with Kourtney——and the way her father treated her mother——she had obviously been primed to distrust me.

Looking up at the ceiling, I clasped my hands behind my neck, and tears welled in my eyes again. I rose and faced my uncle.

"I swear to you, that's not it. I love her. Since I've been around her, she brightens every day. She is strong enough to stand up to me and give me the unvarnished truth. She's smart and funny, with a zest for life. She's constantly reminding me to avoid living in a bubble of privilege. And, as demonstrated by today, she cared for me as me, not because of my family name or the money. She is the first truly honest girl I've known."

I knew all of this because I'd spent last night thinking about it as I dreaded life without her.

Uncle Garth was quiet for a moment, waiting for me to continue.

"I can't just wait for her to come back.

"Absolutely not," he said emphatically. "If she is the one for you, you go find her, and you tell her exactly how you feel. You tell her what you just told me. And do not give up. You fight to keep her."

"But right now I have to *find* her before I can tell her anything."

"You are smart. If she matters enough, you will figure it out. Remember, crisis reveals character. It is time to find out what you are made of." He left his chair and walked to the door. "Let me know if there is anything you need me to do." Turning, he opened the door and left.

I opened my drawer to get a pad of paper so I could make some notes and devise a plan. There, on top, was my grandfather's medal. Like Uncle Garth said, what was I made of? It was time for me to be as determined in the face of adversity as my grandfather had been. I put the medal in my pocket and grabbed my phone and briefcase.

I stopped at Judy's desk. "I have to go on a trip. I don't know when I'll be back. Garth is in charge while I'm gone. I won't be checking my email, and I don't want to get calls either."

"But——"

"Garth can handle anything that comes up."

"Is it Lauren?" she asked.

I sat in the chair next to her desk. "What have you heard?" I asked quietly.

Judy leaned in my direction to keep the conversation quiet. "She called HR yesterday and said she wasn't coming back."

"Thanks." I stood. "Get Sarah in HR for me, please."

I took the call in my office with the door closed. "Sarah, I want you to keep Miss Zumwalt on the payroll… I know what she told you. That was part of the cover story. Keep her auto-deposit going and add an immediate twenty-thousand-dollar bonus payment to it today. She's off-site on a special assignment for me until further notice… A secret assignment," I added. "And take care of any expenses that show up for her brother as well. Thanks."

Sarah agreed to take care of the paperwork, and knowing the way the company grapevine worked, the payroll clerks would see that everyone knew Lauren was on a special assignment by this time tomorrow.

I wrote a quick note to Judy detailing what I had just told HR and gave it to her. "Thanks, Judy."

She scanned the note. "Sure thing, boss, and good luck." She held up her hand with her fingers crossed.

Now to find my woman, my wife.

I RETURNED TO THE CONDO. OLIVER GREETED ME AT THE LOBBY DOOR. "I'll be sure to be there, Mr. Covington. Saturday afternoon is one of my regular shifts, but I got Carl lined up to cover for me."

The old man had me confused. "Huh?" I asked.

"The wedding, Mr. Covington. I wouldn't miss it."

"Thanks, Oliver. I'll let Miss Lauren know when I see her."

Naturally, Lauren had been thoughtful enough to invite Oliver. It wouldn't have occurred to me. I waved to the jovial old man as I entered the elevator to the twenty-second floor. I was going to have to deal with calling off or delaying the wedding if I didn't find her soon.

The sunlight blasted in the large south-facing window as I took in the expanse of the city.

Where are you, Lauren?

I needed professional help. I picked up the phone and dialed. Uncle Garth answered right away. "William, what can I do to help?"

"How good are those detectives you have keeping an eye on Sheila?"

"Hanson and his crew are top-notch, certainly the best I know of in the city and probably the best in the state. What kind of help do you need?"

I told him what I had in mind.

Brian Hanson called me back ten minutes later.

"I need some help finding a woman," I told him.

"Your uncle said as much, Mr. Covington. To do a good job, we're going to need some information and help from you. Getting started as quickly as possible is usually key in these kinds of cases. When and where can we meet?"

"I'm ready as soon as you are," I replied. I gave him the address.

"I'll bring two men with me. We can be there in twenty-five minutes."

Hanson arrived five minutes early, and he brought a man and a woman with him. He introduced himself, then Winston, a strapping ex-FBI agent who looked like he'd stepped right out of a recruiting poster for the Bureau, and Constance, an ex-Secret Service agent whose firm handshake undoubtedly came from being one of the few women in a predominately male profession.

We took seats around the dining table.

"Constance will be running this op," Hanson said.

She took over. "Mr. Covington, let's start with the logistics. Just like the other case we're handling for you, we have set up a Dropbox account for all the info and leads we collect." She handed me a piece of paper. "That's the account and login info for you, along with the cell number where you can text any information you gather. It is monitored twenty-four-seven and helps us all stay coordinated."

"Got it." I entered the phone number into my contacts.

"Send a test message to it now, and you'll get back contact info for everyone on the case."

I sent the text and got a near-instant reply with seven contacts. Each of my guests' phones also vibrated.

They asked about Lauren's family and any family real estate. I told them about her brother in rehab, her car, and everything else they asked. A quick call to the company got me the banking information they requested.

"We'll start surveillance on all this right away. It sounds pretty promising," Constance said. "We'll start watching the bank and the credit cards we get from her credit check for activity and see if we get a trail. What about close friends?"

"Her best friend is her roommate, but she is determined not to help."

As they prepared to leave, Hanson took me aside. "Mr. Covington, we'll start on this at once, but the hours can rack up pretty quickly. Do you have a budget in mind for this op?"

"No limit. I need to find her, and quickly," I answered.

"Understood," Hanson said as they departed.

I was lucky Uncle Garth had such good contacts, but now I was alone again.

Just me and my self-pity.

CHAPTER 38

Bill

It had been two weeks since Lauren left me, and my life seemed totally different than it had once been. I was surrounded in darkness, lost. The date we'd planned for our wedding had come and gone. Marco was now watching the restaurant *and* working the Farm Pod project for me, as I couldn't focus on anything. A few people from Covington had called, trying to get me to meet with them, but I wasn't interested in being consoled or interrogated.

I spent hour after hour of my days watching the entrance to Lauren and Sandy's apartment, hiding behind my laptop screen, hoping to see her return. The detectives were covering Brandon's rehab, and I figured this was the more logical place for her to come back to when she returned. If she wore a disguise, she might fool the detectives, but not me.

I watched from the coffee shop down the street. If I got here before seven in the morning, I could get the table with a line of sight to her building and an outlet so I could keep my laptop and phone charged. I pretended to be writing a book. I knew all the staff by name now. At first, the manager had tried to get me to move along. He didn't want me hogging one of his better tables for the whole day, but a Benjamin-a-day tip for him had stopped that. There were advantages to having a full wallet.

Constance and her crew had been busy early on, but not much had been showing up in the Dropbox folders recently. Lauren had made a five-hundred-dollar credit card purchase at a gas station in the valley the day she left. That maybe gave us an idea of the direction she was going, but otherwise, we were getting nowhere. Lauren hadn't come back for her phone. She hadn't tried to visit or call Brandon, which was our most promising possibility. She had withdrawn cash before leaving.

We did know she had *driven* away. There was no record of her purchasing a ticket with any airline, and the team had canvassed the airport, bus, and train parking lots for her car. It wasn't to be found. They told me it was just a matter of time before they got another transaction they could track.

I had gone over each of their reports multiple times, looking for a clue they might have missed, and so far, nothing.

I needed to do something, so why not try appealing to Sandy again? I had seen her leave for work an hour ago. I dialed her cell. She answered quickly.

"Sandy, have you heard from Lauren?"

"No, I haven't, but I think you know that because you've been watching my place every day for over a week now. I admit it's kind of cute, but it's time to stop, don't you think?"

I guess I wasn't as good at this surveillance stuff as I thought. She had seen me camped out at Peet's.

"I need your help finding her. It's been two weeks," I pleaded.

"Bill." The tone of her voice told me she was not an ally in this quest. "She's my best friend, and she doesn't want to be found, so I'm not going to fucking help you. But if you stop watching my place like some psycho, I promise to call you when she comes back." She hung up.

I dialed back and started talking before she could cut me off. "I just need the names of some friends you think I might check with."

Silence. "You're persistent, I'll give you that, but for a big boss dude, you sure are pretty fucking dumb. She doesn't want you to find her, so what part of *no* don't you understand? I said I'd call you, but only if I don't see your sorry ass in that corner window of Peet's tomorrow or any other day." She hung up again.

That girl was tough as nails, and there was no way I was going to change her mind now. I grabbed my stuff and packed up to leave. I dropped an extra Benjamin in the tip jar. There had to be another avenue to try.

Then it struck me. I put my stuff down again and called Uncle Garth. He understood what I needed, and he said he would arrange to have a man named James meet me there in an hour. I ordered a muffin and munched on it while I waited to leave to meet my next possibility.

~

I WALKED UP TO THE DOOR AND OFFERED MY HAND TO THE MOUNTAIN of a man who was waiting for me.

He had a tattoo of a heart with an arrow through it and the name *Rosie* on his wrist.

"Bond. James Bond," he said as we shook.

"You're kidding, right?" I chuckled, trying to be polite.

The barbed wire tattoo on his neck and his overall size told me not to mess with him. He was the kind of guy likely called "Tiny" or something equally absurd by the gang members or other ex-cons I imagined him hanging out with. These thoughts were best kept to myself right now.

"Doing this kind of thing, I tend to avoid my real name, and I always liked that line."

No names. I got it.

"Is this the one?" he asked.

"This is it, double-oh-seven. So do your thing."

He glanced both directions down the hall before he pulled out the kind of tools you see on the television cop shows, and in about ten seconds, we were past the door and inside Lauren's apartment.

I didn't feel comfortable having him watch what I was about to do. "Thanks, James, I've got it from here."

He just stood there. "I can't leave until you do." He put his hands in his pockets and leaned against the wall.

"Sure you can. I'll be all right."

"So you know how to use these to re-lock the door on your way out?" he whispered as he held up his tools.

I shook my head. He had a point about that. He was the pro here, and I was the amateur.

"I thought not, so make it quick." He crossed his massive arms and leaned against the wall.

I walked through the kitchen, which looked just as it had when I was here last. I opened the cabinets one by one. They all contained the glasses, dishware, and food that you would expect, but I needed to be thorough. I wasn't going to get another chance to check this apartment. The other drawers and cabinets in the living room yielded nothing.

Next, I opened the door to Lauren's bedroom.

Failure is not an option, dipshit.

If I were a journal, where would I hide? I looked through her bureau and found nothing but clothes. Her scent lingered on them. I got a lump in my throat, remembering what I would lose if I wasn't successful. I was careful to put things back just as they'd been. In the nightstand, I found underwear that brought my mind back to happier times. I gave myself a mental slap.

I needed to concentrate and stay on task, and as James had reminded me, time was of the essence. Sandy didn't keep a regular schedule, and I couldn't very well ask her when she would return.

I pocketed Lauren's phone from the nightstand. The closet was next on my list. On the upper shelf, I found a cardboard Nike shoebox with some old birthday cards people had sent her. This could be what I was hoping to find. I grabbed the box, checked behind the hanging clothes, and closed the closet doors the way they had been. I made one more quick pass of the room and was about to leave when I checked under the bed.

There were several short plastic cases with clothes in them.

Behind one full of sweaters, I saw some things that might help: two photo albums. I was hoping to find a journal, but no such luck.

I touched my pocket, confirming that I had her phone, gathered up the shoebox, put it on top of the photo albums, and carried the pile out of the room. I went back and took a pair of her yoga pants and a sweatshirt from the laundry basket, closing the door behind me to leave it as it had been when we came in.

"Got what you need?" James asked.

I was sweating now. "Not as much as I hoped to find, but it will have to do."

We left as quietly as we'd entered, being careful to turn off the lights as we shut and locked the door.

"Hope you find your girl with this stuff, man." His voice held genuine concern.

As we reached the street, he turned back to me. "Rosie left me once, and the guys were all saying 'let her go, she'll be back'. But chasing after her was the best thing I ever did in my life. Been married ten years now, with no regrets."

"Thanks, James. I'm trying."

In a high-pitched Yoda-like voice, he said, "Do, or do not. There is no try."

Then he burst out laughing, and I had to join in. There was a lot more to this guy than the big muscles and tattoos on the exterior.

The only Yoda quote I could think to answer him with was, "Judge me by my size, do you?" It sort of fit, given our relative weights.

"May the force be with you," he replied with a wave.

"And with you, double-oh-seven." I waved with my free hand as Master Yoda James Bond walked off.

Now I had to get this stuff back home and figure out the puzzle. At least I might have some more clues now.

~

Lauren

. . .

I WANDERED DOWN THE BEACH, KICKING ROCKS OUT OF MY PATH, smoothing the sand with the sole of my shoe. It had been weeks since I'd left home. It felt like an eternity. My wedding date had come and gone, and the Covington annual meeting was tomorrow.

How were Karen and my group doing at work? I made a vow to call Karen to catch up when I got settled in my new place. I had no idea yet when or where that might be, but I had to face the fact that they weren't my group anymore.

I had been walking for hours each day, needing the exercise, in an unsuccessful attempt to tire myself enough to sleep soundly at night. My days had been consumed with thinking about him. Bill. The Bill who cared for his employees at his restaurant so much that he had a profit-sharing plan for them. The Bill who spent his time working on his secret Farm Pod project to help inner-city families. The Bill who listened to my criticisms when any other boss would have fired me. The Bill who playfully bantered with Sandy. The gentle Bill. The sexy Bill. The funny Bill. My Bill.

Then I flashed back to lunch with the Ice Queen, Sheila. *"It's always about the money, dear."* She had been right. Hadn't she? I hadn't given Bill a chance to defend himself or explain things, but that's because there was no way he could. Or that's what I told myself. I was keeping my heart safe--not making the same mistakes over and over again anymore.

Bill had played me so expertly, I didn't even have a clue. He had probably taken acting classes. They probably had stupid rich kid classes at his prep school in how to lead girls on. I could kick myself for being so gullible. He was probably on to his next big-chested whore by now.

He had said he loved the way I made him feel, loved the way I looked, loved the way I did this or that. He had asked me to marry him, but he had never said he loved me. What would a rich guy like him see in a girl like me anyway? He needed me because of that trust document, but he didn't love me.

Then I would start the cycle again by thinking about the romantic Bill, the nice Bill, the caring Bill, the huggable Bill, the considerate Bill, my Bill, until I got back again to the cold, real world the Ice Queen had introduced me to.

I couldn't allow myself to love him. I couldn't trust that he wouldn't betray me again. I shivered. I had been just a means to an end.

I smiled. The Covington Industries' annual meeting was tomorrow. And he would lose. Covington would become Liam's company, and Bill's plan would have failed. The fucking weasel would lose the contest to his stepbrother. And I would be free of him. He couldn't use me anymore. By tomorrow I would no longer be a chess piece in his game of global domination.

Why don't I feel good about that?

~

Bill

The sun beamed through my window overlooking the city as I plopped myself down to look over the things I had found at Lauren's place. One locked iPhone, one box of old cards, and two photo albums. I tried the phone first. What would she use as the unlock code? I tried her birthday, the last four digits of her phone number, and the street address of her apartment building. No luck.

I knew the phone would erase itself after ten attempts, so I was down to seven tries. I tried my birthday, her mother's, and Brandon's after looking them up in the files. No luck. Four left. I remembered her referring to our first coffee date, but she didn't mean a real date. She'd meant the time I ran into her in the lobby and she spilled the coffee she was carrying for that horrible boss of hers. That was the moment I'd known she was different, special. Looking back, it was then she'd revealed herself as the one for me.

I went back to my calendar to find the day that had happened. It was the day my dad had called me in for the third time in a month to convince me to join the company, September tenth.

I had to wait for the timeout to finish before I could try again.

When it allowed me to, I tentatively typed the four digits 0-9-1-0… and the phone's home screen came up. It was a picture of the two of us from about a week after the gala. Warmth flooded me.

I went through Lauren's contacts and started calling the non-work ones, except for Sandy, of course. There were some who didn't answer, but nobody who answered had heard from her.

I gave the list to Constance so the team could follow up. Then I went through the phone's photo library, finding pictures there of the two of us, of Sandy, Sandy and her, Sandy and Bandit, and not much else. She wasn't into selfies.

The two albums of pictures beckoned, but the other thing calling was my stomach. I ordered a pizza. It would be a long night.

The pizza guy was at the door in less than an hour for the tenth day in a row. I started on the first album. I should have ordered something less greasy. I ate the pizza with a knife and fork to keep from messing up her pictures. I studied each one, taking them out of the book to check for writing on the back. Some had notes, but not all. I went over both books before packing it in for the night around two AM. I went to bed clutching the yoga pants and sweat-shirt I had taken from her apartment. I missed her so.

The next morning, I awoke with the conviction that I had missed something last night. My subconscious had figured it out and was nagging me to look at the pictures again and find what it had discovered.

I didn't bother showering before I grabbed the first stack of prints and started to cycle through them.

This wasn't working.

I put them down. Whenever I'd needed a fresh look at a problem in the past, I had gotten my best results after a long morning run to clear my head, followed by a no-carb breakfast of sausage and eggs. So I changed clothes and headed out.

The run made me feel better, and my shower afterward was quick. I was eager to get started. Scrambling eggs, I thought over the problem. Where could Lauren go that she would feel safe? She hadn't withdrawn a lot of cash on her way out of town, and she hadn't used credit cards. That ruled out hotel rooms. It had to be a place she felt safe, a place that would take her in——and it wasn't with family or current friends. I knew that much.

I added Tabasco to the eggs. After a few bites, it came to me. *The summer vacation home.* She'd told me how peaceful it had been by the lake in the summer, away from the smog and grit of the city. It was one of her favorite childhood memories, she had said.

What *exactly* had she said? She had gone with her neighbors until her father left. Now I knew what I was looking for: summer-time as a child with the neighbor girl by a lake in the mountains.

Not long after that, I hit pay dirt: a picture of a young Lauren and another girl with fishing poles on a dock. The back read *Laura and me fishing*. Now I had her name, Laura, and a face to go with it. I sorted through more pictures and found a dozen or so with Laura or Lauren in the woods or by the lake in a woodsy summer setting.

I sifted through the cards in the shoebox and found several from Laura as well, but none that looked recent. I searched Lauren's phone contacts again and found no Laura except one from work. An older lady.

What is Laura's last name, and where is she? Then it dawned on me that I didn't need Laura. I could find the lake and the house where they'd stayed.

A few of the pictures showed houses by the lake, and one picture, in particular, had been taken from the dock with Laura waving from the deck of a house just up from the shore. In that picture, I could see it was a two-story with wood siding painted gray. Another picture from a different angle showed that the house had a steep blue metal roof with a chimney near the front and a rooster weather vane on top of it. The windows were trimmed in red.

I came up empty searching the pictures for any street signs that might give me a clue. But now I had hope. All I had to do was find that house. I felt a glimmer in my soul for the first time in weeks.

Lauren, I'm coming for you.

CHAPTER 39

Bill

I FIRED UP THE COMPUTER AND STARTED WITH GOOGLE MAPS. THERE were a lot of lakes in the mountains around Los Angeles, and I wasn't even sure they hadn't traveled further upstate. I made a list: Lake Piru, Castaic, San Gabriel, Arrowhead, Big Bear... At least this was narrowing it down, considering I had started with the whole LA basin.

I started at the top of the list and went to the shoreline roads on Google Street View, navigating around the lake, looking at the houses on the lake side of the street. It was slow, but faster than trying to drive to every lake. I needed to find a gray house with a blue metal roof and a chimney near the front with a weather vane, and hopefully, red trim around some windows.

By lunchtime, I had navigated around the first lake with no luck. I ordered pizza again, the lunch of champions. Five Dr. Peppers and another pizza later, I took a break to stretch. Daylight had evaporated several hours ago under an overcast sky.

Where are you, Lauren? Am I getting close?

I was going blind looking at the screen for hours at a time, trying to go fast enough to get around the lake but slow enough to not miss a street and cover the whole lakefront without missing a house.

I thought of Lauren. What was she doing right now? Had she caught a trout for dinner, or was she cooking up a nice batch of spaghetti, sitting by the fire with a glass of wine? My bleary eyes were giving out on me. Not willing to risk making an error and missing the house, I grabbed her yoga pants and sweatshirt again and held them to me as I shut down the computer for the night and climbed into bed. Oh, how I missed that woman.

THE NEXT MORNING, TWO SLICES OF REHEATED PEPPERONI AND A DR. Pepper later, I was properly fueled for the task. I started back on my Google Street View search, slowly crawling around another lake.

Before lunch, the phone rang. It was Uncle Garth reminding me of the annual shareholders' meeting tomorrow morning.

"I'm still hunting for Lauren, and I have a lead, but it's going to take longer than this afternoon," I said.

"So, what do you want to do?"

"I'm going to keep looking until I find her. That's all I can do. Consider this my resignation from the company. It's up to you and Liam now. I'm going to find her. That's all that matters."

He didn't argue. He wished me luck and asked me to email my resignation, which I did right then and there. I ordered more pizza. I had to get back to the search.

At times, it felt like the Street View method was only a little faster than running the streets and alleys around each lake on foot, and it was just as tiring. I methodically checked the forward and back angles on each prospective cabin I came across. Then…

I FOUND IT.

A gray house with a weather vane on the chimney, located on Lake Isabella, at the far northern reach of my search. It would take me at least four hours to drive there.

I stuffed some clothes in a carry-on roller bag. My briefcase, suitcase, and backpack ready, I made myself take a shower, shave, and change. I needed to look my best for my fiancée.

I put on my tux for good luck. I was planning to re-propose to the woman of my dreams, and I had worn a tux the last time. And that time, she had said yes.

Rain had started, and the traffic was heavier than normal. Everyone joked that Los Angelinos didn't know how to drive in the rain because they saw it so rarely. They were right. Any bit of moisture on the roads mucked up the traffic monumentally. I wended my way slowly through the valley and up Interstate 5 toward Bakersfield. Passing Castaic, the traffic got worse. The sign ahead said chain controls were in effect over the summit.

Just great. Snow.

I had taken the BMW, not thinking there might be snow over the Grapevine this time of year. Goodbye to that four-hour estimate. This was going to be an all-day drive. With a little luck, they would lift the chain controls by the time I got there, as the rain was letting up here. The traffic inched along. Two hours later, I reached the chain control point. There were chain monkeys advertising their services for thirty dollars to put chains on for people who didn't want to get under the car themselves. My problem was I didn't have chains to put on.

The first guy I stopped at didn't have any to sell, and the same at the second and the third. I must have looked hilarious to the drivers in the four-wheel drives passing me by, scurrying around in the snow in a tux. Four was my lucky number today. The fourth guy, with the sign *Chuck-E-Chains,* said he would sell me chains and install them for a hundred and fifty. *Cheap at double the price* was my thinking for today. He completed the job in ten minutes.

I opened my wallet to pay the man. I hadn't been to the bank, and the pizza guy only took cash. All I had were three twenties and my credit cards.

Chuck-E was not very happy. He had already installed the chains, and no, thank you, he didn't take credit cards. Because he thought my Rolex looked fake, which it was not, he insisted on my sixty dollars *and* my watch. It was highway robbery, but that was nothing compared to getting my Lauren back.

This is what I get for not taking five minutes to think before jumping in the car. I had a perfectly good four-wheel-drive Land Rover back home.

With chains on, I crawled over the summit in a conga line of snow-spattered cars and trucks going single-file over the hill, unable to see the lane stripes on the road, each just following the taillights of the one ahead.

It was hours later when I finally reached the chain-removal area on the downhill slope. Another set of chain monkeys were advertising fifteen dollars for removal, but I didn't have even that much cash left after my encounter with Chuck-E-Chains. I was up shit creek again.

I'd better slow down and start making better decisions.

I pulled over near the end of the chain-removal area and squatted down in the slush to unhook the rubber tensioning band and disconnect the link in the chains. I tugged, but they were still connected on the inside of the wheel. I couldn't reach the latch without lying down in the slush. I pulled some shirts and pairs of jeans from my suitcase to put down on the road. The slush quickly soaked through after I lay on them to reach under and unhook the devilish chains.

I felt certain the cars passing by were filled with kids laughing and adults with their mouths agape at the idiot in the slush-stained tux doing his own chains.

Sure, laugh at me. Doesn't even matter. I'm on a mission.

The sun was going down as I closed in on the cabin. The rain had stopped, but the rock in my stomach grew heavier by the minute. Would I remember my speech? How would she react?

"Left turn ahead, then your destination is on the right," my phone announced.

I bit my lip and turned down the narrow street. There in front of me was the picture I had seen on the computer. I stopped the car and went up to the front door. I knocked, but there was no response from inside. I knocked harder.

After a minute I went around the side of the house to the back. Once there, I was able to see in the full-length windows that overlooked the lake. The shades were partly open. The house was empty and looked like it had not been occupied for a while. Everything was put away, the chairs up tight against the table that had a hint of dust on it. Not a cushion was out of place, no lights on, no pots or pans visible in the kitchen.

She wasn't here.

Fuck. Double fuck. Back to LA, you cold, wet, stupid loser.

She hadn't gone to her childhood mountain retreat. My shoulders slumped, feeling like a cat that had just dragged itself out of an ice-cold lake.

As I left the back deck, I turned around to take one last look, and it struck me: there was no red trim around the windows. I looked up at the chimney. The weather vane wasn't a rooster either.

I had jumped at the first house I saw that was close, and it was not a match to the pictures in Lauren's album.

Slow down, asshole.

I had been going way too fast today and getting everything wrong. It was time to refocus.

Remember, jerkwad, failure is not an option.

I got into my car, cranked up the heat, and took out my phone. I located a motel back in Bakersfield.

I hit the ATM followed by a quick drive through a McDonald's. I was back in business. I took a warm shower after checking in and changed into the only remaining dry clothes I had. I was ready to go.

Slow and steady.

By two in the morning, I had almost finished my search and located four more possible cabins at the lakes on my list. None of them were clear matches to the photos, but they were at least closer than the one I had already visited. I unpacked Lauren's clothes and climbed into bed with them like a kid takes a teddy bear.

As I tried to fall asleep, I saw Lauren in her gown at the gala, her face full of surprise and joy as she opened the box at the end of the evening that contained the ring I had given her, a ring she'd accepted, the ring that had made her mine.

Sleep eluded me for hours. I was too wound up. Would I find Lauren? How would she react? Should I change the speech I had memorized? What if she didn't believe me? How could I get her to believe me? Could she believe me?

~

THE NEXT MORNING I GOT UP AT FIRST LIGHT IN MY ONLY DRY CLOTHES and headed down to the buffet breakfast, laptop in hand. Some scrambled eggs, bacon, toast, and orange juice hit the spot. I didn't plan on stopping for lunch. I needed to be confident. Without hope of finding her, what else was there?

Today, I had a more thought-out plan, and I expected to have a better day than yesterday, although that was a pretty low hurdle. I checked that my phone and laptop were charged for the tenth time. I checked my wallet for the eleventh time as I loaded up the car and started down my route to the first lake on my list.

The first house I stopped at was as empty as yesterday's, but it was a closer match. The back deck facing the lake on this one was smaller than the deck on the house in the pictures, so I willed myself not to be disappointed that Lauren wasn't present.

Strike one.

The second cabin on my list was on another lake. I would have to backtrack some to get there.

Four hours later, a thin trail of smoke came from the chimney as I drove past and turned around to park on the opposite side of the street. My insides were in knots. I double-checked the house number from my notes. I walked up to the door. Sounds stirred from within, footsteps. I trembled with anticipation, afraid I would screw this up. I wasn't going to get a re-do on this. I had to get it right. I mentally rehearsed my opening line. I knocked.

The heavy wooden door creaked as it opened a crack. A teenage boy's face appeared. My heart dropped. A quick conversation with the boy and his mother confirmed that Lauren was not here, and the house was only ten years old, so it wasn't the one from her childhood.

The woman bade me good luck in my search as I started up the BMW and programmed the GPS for the next address on my list. These places were far apart, and the back roads were slow. It was getting late in the day.

Strike two.

A stop at a diner netted me a burger and fries as I studied the map. With two houses remaining, I chose the more eastern of the two lakes as my next destination.

Several hours later I rolled up in front of the third house on my list, I dreaded finding it empty as well. Evening would come soon, and there was still one house on my list after this. The rooster wind vane and the red trim on the windows were a better match than the last cabin, but there was no answer at the door.

Lauren's car wasn't out front, but this house had a small one-car garage, so it could've been inside. I swallowed hard as I knocked on the door. I silently recited my opening line. No answer. I knocked louder. Still no answer. I put my head against the door and listened. Silence.

Going around to the back, I peered in through the sliding glass door. A grocery bag sat on the counter, and a sweater lay over the back of a chair. There was a light on in the hallway. My heart raced. This house was occupied, and I hoped with all my being that I had found her. My legs were shaking as I knocked on the sliding glass door. I started my opening line in my head, waiting for an answer to my knocking.

The noise of a small outboard motor interrupted the evening silence. An old man steered his aluminum dinghy away from the shore a few houses down. The fisherman waved toward shore. Gulls made cawing sounds along the waterline as the wind whipped waves up against the sand and rocks. My eyes followed their noise.

CHAPTER 40

LAUREN

I AMBLED BACK TOWARD THE CABIN IN THE EVENING LIGHT AS SMALL waves lapped at the sand. A fish breached the surface a few yards from shore. Old man Patterson puttered out from his dock in a small dinghy, his fishing pole hanging off the side. This place was so much more peaceful than the city. That old man went out to fish this time every evening, his only care in the world outwitting a trout somewhere on the lake. I had talked to him a few times since I'd arrived. It felt reassuring to have a protector close by.

I shivered from the cold. This coat was thin, and I'd had enough of the lakeshore for one day.

An outraged gull dive-bombed me, objecting to my intrusion on his territory. A shout came across the water from the dinghy as Mr. Patterson waved to me and I waved back. I shuffled back to Casa Nelson.

I froze.

In the failing light, he stood on the deck, tall and imposing, hands in his pockets. His face was gaunt, his eyes piercing.

Bill.

~

Bill

Her form was unmistakable. Lauren hadn't seemed to notice me yet as she ducked an angry seagull. She looked thinner. She probably wasn't eating right. She kicked at the sand as she shuffled in my direction.

I trembled as I waited. I didn't want to scare her, and I couldn't risk her running away again without hearing me out. I wasn't going to get another chance to win her back. I willed my legs to stay still. I put my hands in my pockets.

Failure is not an option.

I kept my gaze fixed on her, trying unsuccessfully to read her mind in the distance, to gauge her mood, her fears, her feelings for me. My gut tightened. Would she be pissed at me or just disappointed with herself that I had found her?

She looked up, and I saw it, the spark of recognition. Her face was impassive. The smile I had hoped for, longed for, did not appear. She was shocked. She stopped, not moving toward me and not retreating.

I walked slowly toward her, and she came toward me until we were nearly touching. I forgot my memorized lines. I just smiled and looked into her eyes through her windblown hair. She had lost weight, and it wasn't just missing makeup; her face showed her lack of sleep.

She looked down. "You found me." She fidgeted with her coat.

I looked into her face, trying to decipher her feelings, but her eyes wouldn't meet mine. "No, that happened on September tenth."

She shifted her weight. Her eyes lifted momentarily. The fleeting hint of a smile appeared on her face as she brushed her hair behind one ear.

"I just *re*-found you." I put my hands on her shoulders. "Lauren, please listen to me."

She pulled back a bit but didn't break contact. Her face stayed impassive, her eyes down.

"I love you more than you could ever know. I meant to tell you about the family trust, but we kept putting it off. And, that is *not* why I asked you to marry me."

I had forgotten all the lines to my speech. I was lost, not knowing how to express myself.

She regarded me with a cold stare. "How did your company meeting go?"

I tilted her head up to look at me with a finger under her chin. "I don't know, and I don't care. I quit the company to come find you. You are ALL I care about."

Her expression turned quizzical as if what I had said violated the laws of physics. "Why don't you call, then, and find out?"

"I told you, I don't care. You're the only thing that matters to me," I said softly, trying in vain to hold her eyes, but she looked down.

She backed away. "Then give me the phone, and I'll call for you," she barked.

I balled my fists. "Like I said, not interested. I don't care about the company. I only care about you." I didn't know how to make her understand.

Her look told me she didn't believe me. It was like I was speaking in Martian or something.

What was so hard for her to understand? I took out my phone and showed it to her.

She moved to take it from me.

I heaved it as far as I could into the lake.

Startled, she jumped back. She threw her arms up. "What did you fucking do that for?" she screamed.

I yelled back, "Because I don't fucking care what they do. I told you I quit, and that's the truth. I just want to be with you. Let me show you, just you and me. Here. No Covington, no phones, just the two of us."

She was shivering. She paced back and forth like a caged

animal. She waved her hands dismissively. "Like I'm supposed to believe you now."

I held my hand out to her. "Let's get you inside. You look cold." I stood, waiting for a response.

She stopped pacing. For a moment, she didn't budge.

"Whatever," she replied.

She walked toward the cabin with me, looking down at the sand and rocks rather than into my face. She didn't take the hand I offered.

I sensed I had a small opening, but I had a long way to go. I had screwed up royally, and it had almost cost me everything—it still might. At the door, I guided her into the cabin with my hand at the small of her back. She didn't reject it.

A second chance is all I want.

~

LAUREN

I WAS SHIVERING AS MUCH FROM THE SHOCK AS THE COLD. I HAD never told Bill where this was. Sandy didn't even know about it, but he had found me just the same. Slowly, we walked back to the cabin. He was right that I was cold.

He had proclaimed that he loved me. How predictable. They always did that when you caught them lying. He claimed to not care about the company, his family's company, the one with his name on it. Then he surprised me by chucking his phone into the lake. Now that had not been in the script, I imagined.

Could he really mean he just wants to be with me?

He had remembered the date of our chance first meeting, September tenth, in the lobby where I had spilled the Witch's coffee on him. That surprised the hell out of me.

Old man Patterson was puttering his little metal fishing boat back toward his dock. It was probably too cold for him too.

We entered after I unlocked the back door. The warmth felt

good, almost as good as having Bill near me, though I fought with myself about admitting that. His heavy stubble said he hadn't shaved in several days. His hand on the small of my back as he guided me in the door brought back tingly memories. Our attraction was still magnetic. I needed to keep up my defenses and resist the urge to hug him. He was still an LSOS.

"Welcome to Casa Nelson."

"You must have had some great times here as a kid." His voice was kind and caring, his eyes soft as warm butter.

How did he know that? "Yeah, I sure did." *Good guess.*

"It's a wonderful view," he said, looking out over the back deck.

True enough. The air was crisp and clear, and the lake at sunset with the mountains all around was a beautiful sight, so unlike the asphalt jungle of Los Angeles and its constant smog.

He walked over to the fridge and opened it, followed by the pantry off the kitchen. "What have you got that I can cook for you?"

I hadn't bought much at the market. Food hadn't interested me since I'd landed here. Oatmeal, some Cheerios, some bread, peanut butter, strawberry jam, a can of tuna, but no mayonnaise to mix with it, and one Lean Cuisine. The cupboard was pretty bare.

His face said it all. The lack of contents surprised him. "How 'bout I round up some provisions at the market while you stay here and warm up?"

"Okay, but I want you gone tomorrow."

I could leave while he was out and be free of him, but he knew that and showed his faith in me by offering to go out alone. Since I'd agreed to stay put, I'd be the deceitful one if I left. I sat on the old leather couch.

I can't do that.

I also couldn't hold it in any more. "You lied to me, you bastard," I yelled. He was lucky I didn't have anything handy to throw at him.

He moved a bit closer, his face sullen.

"You needed to marry me before the meeting or lose your

precious company to your stepbrother. I can't trust a single thing you say. You used me. You had me sign a damned prenup so you could plan to leave me later after——"

"I never planned any such thing," he interrupted with infuriating calmness.

How dare he be so calm? "You did, and I spoiled your little plan for world domination or whatever because I found out your secret and now you're going to lose."

He hesitated.

"You're trapped by your own lies, Bill."

"Lauren, the only thing I care about losing is you. Can't you see that?"

"What I see is that you used me, and I'm done with that."

His eyes misted over. "I screwed up royally by not telling you about the trust earlier; I admit that. We put it off, and I shouldn't have allowed that."

"About time you admitted something, don't you think?"

"You are all that mattered to me before, and all that matters to me now. Just give me a week to prove it to you."

"I don't need a week to know a weasel when I smell one, and right now it stinks in here."

A knock came at the front door. He rose. "Expecting company?" he asked.

I shook my head and scampered over, but he answered the door before I got there.

Mr. Patterson was at the threshold, a stern look on his face, and the barrels of an old shotgun pointed down at Bill's feet.

"Everything all right, Miss Lauren?" he asked, looking at me. "I heard somethin' what sounded like yelling a-comin' from here."

He kept his grip on the shotgun and shifted his gaze between Bill and me. This was another difference from the big city. In my apartment building, you could shoot a gun or knock down a wall, and nobody would give it a second thought, much less come and check on you.

"Just fine, Mr. Patterson. This is my friend, Bill. I just yelled at him because he threw his phone in the water."

I smiled at the old man as I walked up to the door and put my arm around my ex-fiancé. I didn't want to marry Bill, but I sure didn't want him full of buckshot. The warmth of his body against mine was oddly soothing.

"Ya know there's a law against throwin' stuff in our lake up here." He lifted the shotgun ever so slightly in Bill's direction.

Bill shifted backward. "I'll swim out and get it tomorrow morning, promise."

The old man loosened his grip on the gun, lowered it, and chuckled. "Ya better be part polar bear then."

I smiled up at Bill and gripped him tighter. "He is." That seemed to convince Mr. Patterson I wasn't being abducted.

"I'm just down the road if ya need me."

He took his leave, and Bill closed the door.

I let go of Bill, walking slowly toward the couch and my waiting blanket, trying to control my impulse to yell at him some more.

"You sure have protective neighbors here. I think you just saved my life."

I faced away from him so he couldn't see my smile. "Just don't want to get a blood stain on the carpet. It's not my house." I wiped the smile off my face before I sat back down.

Bill grinned. "Whatever you say. I'll go get the food then." His eyes twinkled.

"Knock yourself out. I'll be here," I said as nonchalantly as I could manage. This time, I was sure I meant it.

While he was gone, I pulled on a sweatshirt and worked through what had just happened. Bill had somehow found me. He had come for me and told me he had forsaken his family company, which I didn't really believe. I had saved him from Mr. Patterson.

We had both taken steps toward each other, but did he mean it? Where would this lead? How could I know which was the real Bill? I brushed my hair and secured it back into a ponytail.

Forty-five minutes later, Bill returned with five bags of food that he loaded into the fridge and the pantry. He also brought in his luggage from the car. But he hadn't made any move toward fixing dinner yet.

He crumpled some newspaper and added layers of kindling in the fireplace. I watched the muscles flex beneath his shirt as he hefted logs from the wood pile and stacked them on top. Unable to find any matches in the kitchen, he lit a splinter of wood on the gas stove and used it to light the fire.

He handed me a glass of wine. "To new beginnings." He offered to clink glasses, but I demurred as the fire crackled to life. His eyes shone with sincerity.

He probably took acting classes.

He sat, and together, we watched the fire. The flames crackled and licked at the logs as the fire grew. Neither of us spoke. The firelight danced around the room as the daylight receded. I held my hands out toward the gentle heat as it grew in strength.

He jumped up. "Want some dinner? It looks ready to me." He had been watching the fire intently.

What the hell was ready? I was more confused than hungry. "Okay, but not much." I continued to watch the flames as he fumbled around in the kitchen. He hadn't turned on the lights, and that end of the giant room was dark.

He returned with a tray and knelt in front of the fire. "Come on. You've gotta help with this."

He waved me over. The tray held plates, hot dogs, buns, mustard, relish, and marshmallows.

"It's just like camping. We're having a weenie roast." He poked a metal skewer through a hot dog, offering it to me.

I climbed down from the couch. We huddled in front of the fire, cooking the dogs on our long skewers. The fire was so hot that I had to change hands occasionally. We got them done without burning anything, and we ate them sitting on the floor like little kids.

"I've never done this before," I admitted. "This tastes great."

"It's the fire. Hot dogs weren't meant to be boiled or cooked on hot rollers like at 7-Eleven."

He was right. These tasted better than any I had ever had, but maybe it was just the excitement. Maybe I was deluding myself again.

He fell silent as we worked on another batch. The corners of his mouth quivered and his eyes watered.

I took the last bite of my charred hot dog. "A penny for your thoughts."

He paused, pulled out his hot dog, inspected it, and returned it to the flames. His eyes misted over. "I was just remembering when my father taught me this."

"You miss him, don't you?"

"Yeah, I'm sorry I never really told him how much this meant to me, the camping trips and all." He sniffed. "The ghost stories around the campfire. The simple things like fishing in a stream or cooking over a campfire. I always thought I'd have more time to tell him."

I placed my hand on his. "I'm sure those times meant just as much to him." I wanted so much to hold him and comfort him, but I resisted the urge. I pulled my hand back.

He bit his lip. "Yeah, I just wish I'd told him."

Bill went on to tell me stories of his father taking him and his brothers and sister camping in Yosemite as we finished our second and third hot dog each. His stories were tender.

"Now for the dessert." He tore open the bag of giant marshmallows and stuck one on each of our skewers.

I lost the first one in the fire. It melted right off the end in seconds.

"You have to keep it out of the fire. Twist it so it gets browned all over, but not so soft that it falls off," he told me.

I squealed when the second one melted off the skewer as well. I couldn't get the hang of this. Bill pulled his second off and put it on my plate for me. I popped it in my mouth and spat it out just as rapidly. I shrieked. It had burned my tongue.

"You need to let them cool," he scolded me as he ran to the kitchen.

"Now you tell me," I yelled back. I swished some wine around in my mouth to quell the burn. That didn't do much.

Bill returned with an ice cube. "Quick, suck on this."

I did as he said, at least for as long as I could stand the cold. Then I spat the cube out.

He grabbed it and put it to my lips. "Keep it on the burned spot," he commanded. He pointed his finger at me sternly.

I took it back in my mouth and sucked on it some more, which felt worse than the burn it was supposed to soothe.

I hit him on the shoulder. "You should have warned me," I mumbled.

"You should be less impulsive," he retorted.

He made us two more marshmallows while I remained on ice-cube-sucking duty.

By the time the ice melted in my mouth, the burning sensation had gone. My knight had saved me again. Just having that thought told me I'd better not have any more to drink.

He cooked two more marshmallows, and we moved back to the couch to eat them after they'd cooled this time. I told him about the summers I spent here at the lake with my friend Laura and her family. We were sitting together now, and I was acutely aware of the warmth of his leg against mine. It was moving toward distracting as my defenses wilted. He asked to stay tomorrow, and I finally relented.

Bill added wood to the fire, and we talked on. The evening crept into night, the fire died down, and its light became dim. My attempt at exhausting myself during the day to make myself sleepy was paying dividends tonight for the first time as my eyelids drooped.

We still hadn't gotten back to discussing Bill's deceit, but it was time to call it a day. Bill asked which room he should take. I directed him to the room next to mine as he checked the outside locks and we said our goodnights.

You're still leaving after tomorrow.

CHAPTER 41

Lauren

I awoke the next morning to the sound of movement in the great room. I had slept soundly for the first time since coming to the lake. I didn't want Bill to know I had been using one of his USC shirts as my nightshirt, so I took it off and donned a bra, a UCLA sweatshirt, and sweatpants before venturing out of my room.

I found Bill busy in the kitchen. The smell of fresh coffee permeated the air.

"How about pancakes?" he asked as he saw me emerge.

He wore the same clothes as yesterday, very unlike him.

"Whatever the cook wants." I pulled my hair back into a ponytail.

The coffee smelled great, much better than the instant I had gotten at the market. He was percolating it. Who does that in these days of coffee machines?

"Percolator coffee?"

"Yeah, isn't that great? Just like camping. The coffee pot was in the cupboard. Hope you didn't expect French press."

He ladled some batter into the frying pan. He'd also sliced strawberries and a kiwi. He handed me a glass of orange juice.

"Here, you need your vitamins."

I drank up as instructed. "You've been busy."

"Couldn't wait to spend the day with you is all."

I rustled up plates and silverware for the meal, after which I indulged in a cup of his coffee as I watched him prepare a pile of pancakes. He placed some on a plate and decorated the top one with two strawberry-slice eyes and a whipped cream smile.

"Eat up. We have a big day ahead of us."

I carried my plate over to the table as he followed. "And just what do you have planned for us?"

I had resigned myself to letting him stay another day. It would be easier if I gave him a chance before telling him again to leave.

"Last night, you said you enjoyed hiking with Laura and her family when you were here, so I thought you could pick the trail you liked best and we would take a picnic lunch and enjoy the outdoors." He bounced in his seat like a little kid.

"I don't remember the names, except for the hot springs trail."

"Hot springs it is then."

He decorated two more pancakes for us——stick figures. Mine was a girl, and his was a boy.

"But first, I need to go swimming," he added.

"Are you nuts? The water is freezing."

He speared a bite of pancakes. "I promised the old man I would get my phone out of the lake."

"He was just kidding. It's too cold."

He finished chewing and smiled. "I promised I would, and I never lie. Besides, he's the one with the gun."

This was crazy. "Should I call the ambulance now or later?"

He didn't seem to appreciate the joke. I guess it impugned his manhood.

After breakfast, I helped him clean up and tried in vain to talk him out of freezing to death in the lake.

"Just bring lots of towels" was all he'd say.

When he came out in just jockey briefs, I was unprepared, and I ended up staring way too long. I brought a bathrobe and the towels as he requested and followed him down to the water. He ran in place and jumped up and down to warm up before plunging into the lake at the spot where he'd tossed his phone last night.

He stroked out quite a distance, then dove under. When he came back up, he went out a little farther and dove again, resurfacing with something in his hand. He started swimming back to shore, but not with the same vigor he'd had when swimming out. He slowed noticeably as he neared the shore and stumbled out. He lost his grip on the phone. I toweled him off quickly, grabbed the phone, and wrapped the robe around his quaking body.

We trudged back to the house as quickly as I could get him to move. If he fell, I wouldn't be able to carry him. He was turning white and shivering terribly. We made it inside and into my bathroom.

I turned on the shower and set it to warm but not hot.

His teeth chattered as he tried to say something. I got him in and turned him around. Then I joined him in the shower, with my clothes still on, hugging him and rubbing his muscles. The water streamed off his body cold, chilled by his frozen flesh.

The shivering grew worse as I upped the temperature a little and held him tightly, rotating him in the stream of hot water, sort of like we were slow dancing.

Over time, his arms and legs warmed from frigid to just plain cold, and his shivering subsided. He held me tightly as we rocked together, twisting around in the water. Good thing the cabin had a large water heater, as we stayed under the spray forever until he thawed.

He kissed the top of my head. "You were right. Bad idea."

"Ya think?"

We continued to hold each other in the hot water as his closeness melted my resolve. I disengaged myself and got out of the shower in my dripping wet clothes.

"Turn around," I instructed.

He dutifully turned toward the wall as I shed my clothes and placed them in the sink before wrapping my hair in a towel and leaving the bathroom to put on dry clothes. I went to his room to get him some dry clothes as well, but his suitcase was full of wet, soiled clothes, including formal wear. *His tux from the gala?*

I gathered up his clothes from breakfast and took them to him, retreating to the couch afterward. I didn't dare spend any more time watching his nearly naked body.

Emerging from my room——fully clothed, thank God——Bill turned up the thermostat before he came to sit on the couch with me.

I handed him the blanket. "That was a dumbass thing to do. Trying to be all macho and shit."

He smiled. "I told you, I keep my promises. The dumbass part was not getting a wetsuit first." He adjusted the blanket around his shoulders.

I had to chuckle at his logic. "I still call it having shit for brains. And by the way, how come you brought a suitcase full of wet, dirty clothes with you?"

He laughed as he pulled his legs up under him on the couch and wrapped himself more tightly in the blanket. "It's a long story, and it won't help your opinion of my brainpower."

That sounded intriguing. "I've got all day. My only walking shoes are soaking wet, so we'll have to cancel the hike you had planned."

The corners of his mouth curved up. "That sucks. I was so looking forward to walking behind you and admiring the scenery, so to speak."

I blushed. "Pervert." I threw a pillow at him. "I guess cold water shrinks your brain in addition to your other body parts."

"You peeked." He chuckled. "Now who's the pervert?" He threw the pillow back at me.

I rose from the couch. I didn't like where my mind was wandering. "I'm going to start a load of laundry."

I started a load as he built a fire. It would take two rounds of laundry with all the wet things I'd pulled out of his suitcase.

We stayed in for the day, and I slowly pulled the details of the wet formal clothes out of him. I would have paid to see him lose his watch to Chuck-E-Chains and crawl under his car to get the chains off dressed in his tux.

Getting him to fill me in on his search for me was more difficult. I was touched by the lengths he'd gone to and the effort he'd put in, including his run-in with James Bond. Bill was not only clever but much more determined to find me than I had given him credit for. My weeks of carefully constructed thoughts about him and his motivations now seemed wobbly at best. This didn't add up to a calculated business move, but I needed to be careful. My track record wasn't so great.

Bill asked about the five-hundred-dollar charge at the service station. We both laughed as I recounted my encounter with Skull Girl and the gas hose trailing behind my car.

Morning turned to afternoon as we talked, and talked, and talked——some parts laughing and some parts teary-eyed as we continued discussing our childhoods and families.

I told him several times that I hadn't changed my mind and I was done with him. Each time he just smiled, with infuriating puppy-dog eyes, and agreed that he had screwed up. He didn't even argue. He just let me vent.

He also avoided the elephant in the room all day, and I'd decided he had to be the one to address it. *He* had to be ready to talk about the family trust and why he hadn't told me before proposing.

As sunset loomed again, Bill started dinner. He had gotten the makings for chicken parmesan last night and busily worked on it for an hour. We had everything he needed except a mallet to pound the chicken flat, so he used the cast-iron frying pan instead. He hit the chicken so hard I was afraid he would break the counter.

When he was done, he turned off the lights. I had set the table, and we sat down to a candlelit Italian dinner complete with salad, linguine on the side, and red wine. He raised his glass.

"To happiness." We clinked glasses. "Smile, Lauren. Happiness looks good on you."

And smile I did, both outwardly and inwardly. I ate slowly, savoring the taste and smell of the food and the ambiance——Bill's face lit by candlelight and the flickering light of the fireplace on the walls.

He poured more wine. We drank and ate and drank some more as we cleared the dinner table together and moved to the couch, leaving the lights off. He added more wood to the dwindling fire as he told me how he'd met Marco in high school and how their friendship had remained solid while others came and went.

I caught myself concentrating on his eyes, kind eyes. The firelight highlighted the contours of his chin and the depth of his dimples. His dimples reminded me of our first lunch together, the day he'd saved me from my boss, promoted me, saved Sandy's cat, and rescued me financially——all in one day. That day had started out so shitty but ended so perfectly.

He was so handsome and dashing, my knight in shining armor. I couldn't resist him, and then he'd taken me to see real knights jousting on real horses. None of them had compared. The crowd that night had no idea that the real knight was not in the arena. He sat next to me the whole evening.

Bill had stopped speaking. He wore a questioning look.

"I said, how did you meet Sandy?" he repeated.

I had been lost in my daze. "Through a roommate posting, and we just hit it off. I admit she can be a little out there sometimes, but she always means well." I continued staring into those soft eyes, lost in the moment.

He moved over and put his arm around behind me.

I snuggled up next to him and laid my head on his shoulder. I started to trace figure-eights on his thigh as we sat watching the fire.

He kissed the top of my head. "I love you, Lauren Marie Zumwalt."

I couldn't say anything to that. I just couldn't. "You're just saying that because I saved your life twice in two days."

"How do you figure that?"

"If I hadn't sweet-talked Mr. Patterson, he would have filled you with lead last night, and if it weren't for me, you'd be a frozen popsicle out on that beach right now."

He laughed. "Objection, Your Honor. The geezer with the gun wouldn't have been here in the first place if you hadn't yelled your ass off out by the lake, and I wouldn't have had to promise him to do the polar bear swim in your lake either. So you almost *got* me killed twice."

"If you hadn't been fool enough to throw your phone in the lake, none of that would have happened, so it's still your fault."

We were having fun with this argument, just like old times.

He smiled. "If you'd believed me, I wouldn't have had to throw my phone," he said calmly.

"But you did, so it's still your fault."

"On that note, I will concede for tonight," he said as he stood and pulled me to my feet. He held my shoulders and kissed me on the forehead.

I wanted more, but he pulled away.

"Goodnight." He checked the front door deadbolt, and then the door to his room closed behind him.

Why did he shut me down and go to bed? Why had he thrown his phone in the lake, anyway? Was there something on it he didn't want me to see?

I lay awake in my room. The day had gone well——not the first part, where he nearly froze to death, but the rest of the day, up until now.

He'd shut me down, and we still hadn't talked about his deception. He couldn't just say he loved me, start joking about it, and leave it like that.

I heard noises in his room and listened intently. I got up to demand answers. I reached for the handle.

I chickened out.

I got back in bed.

He was infuriating.

It took forever to fall asleep.

CHAPTER 42

Lauren

The next morning, Bill was up early again, and the smell of fresh coffee tickled my nostrils as I opened my door. He had bowls of cut vegetables and grated cheese arranged on the counter.

"What would milady like in her omelet this fine morning? We have ham, bacon, a choice of Monterey jack, Swiss, or cheddar cheese, mushrooms, onion, bell pepper, and tomato."

Once again, he had outdone himself. I would have settled for a bowl of Cheerios with milk that wasn't out of date.

"I'll have whatever you're having," I replied meekly.

I didn't want to admit it, but I liked it when he called me milady. I came up behind him and laid my hand on his shoulder as he diced mushrooms.

"Careful there. If you distract me too much, I might slip and cut myself, and you would have to save me from bleeding to death."

I stepped back.

He put down the knife. "You know, I thought about you last night. It kept me up quite a while." He scooted sideways down the counter.

"Really?"

"What about you?"

I lied. "I just went right to sleep."

The moment passed. I had ruined it and probably hurt his feelings by not admitting the truth.

We still hadn't talked about why I'd left. As fun as this was, playing house and enjoying each other's company, it was just playing. It couldn't last. I had to confront his dishonesty, just not yet. He still had to be the one to bring it up or he wouldn't understand.

I went back to my room and dressed while he cooked. When I returned to eat, I found the breakfast up to Bill's standards, which meant great. He didn't say much beyond commenting on the weather and asking about going on a hike today. I still regretted ruining the moment earlier.

Looking out at the lake, I panicked for a moment. It must be after the first of the month. I had lost track of the days, and I needed to move money for Brandon's treatment.

"What's the date today?"

"Oops," he said as he looked at his wrist. "No watch, but I can check the laptop for you." He went to find it.

"Can I borrow your computer?" I asked. I would need computer access to move the money.

"Sure, what's up?" He called out from the other room.

"Nothing, I just have to check something."

He brought out the laptop and set it up on the small desk as I cleared the table. I felt like I wasn't keeping up my end of the chores. He had prepared every meal and done most of the cleanup since he'd arrived, shooing me away as I tried to help.

I powered up the laptop and checked the date in the lower right. I still had today to pay, but I would have been late if I hadn't thought to check. Relieved, I searched for the browser icon on the screen. There was a folder labeled *Zumwalt search*.

Bill had told me that was from the detectives helping him find me——help it turned out he didn't need. He'd found me all on his own, with a little help from James Bond.

I smiled as I remembered his story about that. The folder next to it was labeled *Lindroth surveillance*. My God, he'd been having them watch his stepmother. I opened the folder. The subfolders were labeled *Reports* and *Images*. I clicked on *Images*. There it was on the fourth row, a picture of me and Sheila at that sushi place, with Magnus in the background. Next to it was another picture of Sheila meeting with a woman who looked familiar, but I couldn't place her. I quickly closed the folders as Bill came up behind me.

"Where's the browser on this thing?" I asked.

He pointed to the lower left corner. "Right here. What do you need? Maybe I can help."

"No." I still didn't want to discuss Brandon with him.

He started to massage my shoulders. "Ready for your hike today?"

The shoulder rub felt good. "A little harder… Yeah, like that." The kinks I didn't know I'd had slowly relaxed. "What hike?"

"The hot springs, remember?"

"Oh, yeah." I shut the laptop, and he massaged a little lower, between my shoulder blades as I leaned forward. "That feels really good." I purred.

He kept up the pressure. "Is this good for you? Too hard?"

I moaned. "No, I like it hard."

"I've heard that about you girls."

I'd set myself up for that. "Pervert."

With a flick of his fingers, he undid my bra strap through my shirt and started rubbing lower, where the strap had been.

It felt relaxing and invigorating at the same time.

He continued with his magic fingers, lower down my back as I leaned even farther forward. He moved back up to my shoulders, leaned over, and whispered in my ear, "I give a wicked full-body massage."

The message was clear, but I couldn't go there. I straightened up and reopened the laptop lid.

"Stop, I have to do this. I have to move some money for my brother."

He took his hands off me and walked back to the couch. "I've already taken care of that."

"What?"

"I had HR take care of it before I left. The company is picking up the tab," he said, putting on his shoes.

"That can't be right. He's not covered in the health plan. I checked."

"I changed the policy. I didn't want you to worry."

He had taken care of Brandon to help me? "Just like that?"

He didn't want me to worry.

"HR told me I could make whatever rules I wanted. I am the boss, after all——make that I *was* the boss. But anyway, it's taken care of. You can check if you want."

That reminded me that he'd said he had quit the company. I closed the computer, re-hooked my bra, and joined him on the couch.

"How can I thank you?"

He stood. "You could agree to my invitation on a hike, and when we get back, we can give each other a real back rub."

I wasn't sure what a *real* back rub entailed, but I could guess that it might not include keeping my shirt on.

"Okay, I can handle that." I surprised myself by giving him a quick peck on the cheek before standing up.

"Or I'll make yours a front rub if you want." He chuckled.

He ducked the pillow I tossed at him. "Pervert. Keep that up and I'll have to give you a cold shower."

"Anything to get you in the shower with me again." He laughed as he went to the kitchen. "What do you want for your picnic lunch?"

CHAPTER 43

Lauren

The hike was a lot longer than I remembered, and it wasn't flat either. But I'd picked it, so I couldn't complain. My body didn't agree with my logic, though.

Bill had insisted that I lead the way while he was *admiring the scenery*, so I turned the tables on him, and he led the way back so I could watch his ass instead.

Once we returned to the cabin, I tried my hand at building the fire while Bill worked on dinner in the kitchen. He had planned chicken cordon bleu. I had never eaten so well as when he cooked. I was dirty from the trail dust, so I opted for a shower while he was preparing it for the oven.

He took his turn under the water while dinner was in the oven, then sauntered out, rubbing his hair dry with a towel.

I stroked his still unshaved partial beard with the back of my hand as he passed. "This looks good on you."

"If you like it, I'll keep it." He turned and smirked. "It might scratch a little though."

"In your dreams, cowboy." I had already had that dream. The

insides of my thighs tingled from the memory.

He opened the oven and added olive oil-coated asparagus and parmesan to the baking sheet with the chicken. "Dinner in fifteen. You ready?"

I poured the wine and finished setting the table. The dinner was simple yet elegant, just the chicken and parmesan-covered roasted asparagus, with pear slices on the side. We talked about the hike, the scenery, the hot springs——everything except what we needed to talk about.

The fire burned hot. I finished my second glass of wine. It should have been pleasant, but it was getting awkward. Bill had still avoided talking about what he had done.

He came up behind me as I was rinsing the plates in the sink. "Time for your back rub, milady."

I demurred. "Why don't we just sit and watch the fire?"

"I promised a back rub, and I keep my promises, that's why."

"We need to talk," I argued. We couldn't put it off another day.

He removed the back cushions to make space. "I agree. Now, on your stomach."

I gave in, took off my shoes and lay down.

He straddled me as he leaned over and worked my shoulders and upper arms, then down my back, kneading with his knuckles, followed by his palms, hard and rhythmic. I gave him soft moans of encouragement. He worked on my lower back for a while then moved up again. He again undid my bra strap through my shirt. He had a knack for doing that one-handed.

I pulled the straps to the side as he continued up my back to my shoulders and down again. I felt very relaxed. I whimpered as he kneaded harder.

"This your idea of talking?" I asked.

He kept working on my shoulders. "It's time we discussed you and me."

So now we get to it.

I tried to get up.

He pushed me down. "Stay put. I'm not done yet."

So this was how it was going to be? "Okay, let's talk."

He started back down along my spine. "I still want to marry you."

Fat chance. "I told you *no*."

He continued to kneed and rub. "Lift up." He pulled my shirt up to my shoulders and continued to work on the bare skin of my back.

The rubbing felt oh so good. The talk, not so much.

"You have to," he said.

"Yeah? Why is that?"

He moved down to my lower back. "Because I love you. You complete me, and I can't stand to be without you."

I couldn't see his face, but the words sounded sincere.

"I'm just the flavor of the month," I replied.

He dug his thumbs in hard along my lower back, seeming angry with my answer. "Lauren, I know I had a lot of girlfriends before, but you're the one for me, the only one. I've told you that, and I mean it."

I needed to look into his eyes to judge his words. I tried once again to turn over, but he held me down. I could hear the words, but he wouldn't let me see his eyes.

"Stay put. I'm not done yet."

I gave up struggling for the moment. "Why? Because I wouldn't drop my drawers on the first date?"

"It's hard for me to explain." He hiked my jeans down a few inches and started on my lower spine. "Since I met you, I haven't been the same. You helped me when I needed it the night of the accident."

I tried to turn toward him. He had my legs pinned.

He shoved me down again. "Don't be a brat. Behave yourself and listen. Ever since we met, you've been jumping to conclusions about me without listening. You need to stop that."

I gave up and settled into the cushions. It hurt to admit that I'd done exactly what he'd accused me of more than once.

"I was wrong to do that, but——"

"Never mind about that. You had the guts to say what I needed to hear at that first meeting after the accident, and later as well.

Nobody else had the honesty to do that. You were the only one strong enough to insist that we could salvage the Benson deal, and your persistence with old man Benson——showing him the Farm Pod project——is what got it done. You are smart, funny and courageous and loyal."

He shifted his weight down and started to work on my thighs. "I can't imagine what you had to go through with that miserable boss of yours so you could pay for your brother's treatment."

I couldn't take it any longer. I tried to roll over again. I needed to look into his face.

He shoved my shoulder down once more. "Mind your manners and stay put."

"No. I want to talk face to face," I complained.

"This is hard enough, Lauren. Just let me finish without being tempted to kiss you straight into next week."

I stayed face down. We needed to be verbal rather than physical. We needed to get this out into the open.

"You have never been like all the others."

There was that line again, just like at that first lunch. "What do you mean, *all the others*?" I asked.

He got off me and knelt by the side of the couch, starting on my calves. "They're all like Sheila, just some nicer than the others."

I shifted my head. I could see his face now that he wasn't on top of me. He clenched his jaw as he worked up and down my calves.

"She only married my father for his money. She's the one who showed me the downside of being rich——the way it can take over everything and distort relationships. She left a little while after Steven was born, and it devastated Dad. He never remarried, and he never even really dated after that. Sheila was always mean to us, and she never cared for Liam or Steven, even though they were her own children. When she left, they both stayed with us. She wasn't anything like my real mother."

It was sad to hear him talk about a childhood like that.

He blew out a breath. "In my experience, once a girl learned I was a Covington, she never saw me. All she could see was the name and the money. I even dated some actresses. I thought it would be different because they had fame and money of their own, but it was still the same. They only cared about the size of my bank account." He huffed as he continued on my calves.

"That's what she said about you."

"Who said?"

"Sheila. She said you only cared about the money, that you were only marrying me because of the trust."

He had paused, but he started kneading again. "It figures she would say that, projecting her priorities onto other people." He shifted to working on my thighs again. "That's not me."

"Then why keep it a secret? Why hide it from me until after the engagement?"

This was the only question that mattered.

He let out a long breath. "I told myself I was going to and I just hadn't found the right time. But the real answer is I was scared of losing you. This..." He waved his arm around the cabin. "This is what I was scared of. We were already dating when I found out about the trust, and I fucked up. I should have told you immediately, and I'm here to beg you to take me back."

"But the trust. You had to get married to keep your job and your company," I said. "That's why we had to rush the wedding."

"Rush yes, but it isn't why I wanted to marry *you*."

The words were nice, and he looked and sounded sincere, but how could I know if I could trust him?

"Look, if I just needed to get married, I could have made a deal with Cynthia. You met her. For the right price, she would have married me in a minute." His tone was angry and cold. His jaw clenched.

True. I had no doubt Miss Broadchest would do anything for the right price. "So she's a slut, and I was the cheaper option, is that it? Your stepmother thought I should have negotiated a better prenup."

He spanked me.

I yelped, more surprised than hurt.

"You are impossible, Lauren Zumwalt. You think I give a shit about the company and the money? If that's what you think, why didn't I just marry Cynthia after you left? Why did I quit the company to come find you?"

I didn't have answers to those questions.

"It's simple. The only thing that matters to me is you——not the job, not the company, none of it. The meeting's over by now, and the company is gone, and I'm here because of you. Only you."

He rose and stalked to his room.

I sat up and pulled down my shirt as he returned with his briefcase. The fury in his face scared me.

Anger clouded his eyes. He pulled out the medallion I had left at his condo. He put it in my hand and clasped his hands around mine.

"The day I gave you this, I said you were the only one for me, and that hasn't changed," he said.

His voice and his eyes conveyed the conviction I yearned for, but something still held me back.

"I'm sorry I didn't talk to you about the trust as soon as I found out. At first, I was scared of how you would react and didn't know how to do it, and later we didn't find the time. I don't care about the job. I quit the company. I don't care about the money. I just need you. I..."

His eyes misted. He let go of my hand and rifled through the briefcase. He pulled papers out.

"This is the prenup." He walked over and threw the papers in the fire. The flames flared as they consumed the document. "I don't care about the company. I don't care about the money." His eyes implored me. "You already have my heart, Lauren. Won't you please share my life with me?"

This was all more than I could handle. I started crying, my head in my hands.

He came and sat by me, his arm sliding around me to hold me close.

I sobbed. I hadn't believed him about Mall Barbie. I hadn't believed him about Kourtney, or the trust. I had believed the worst about him at every turn. I had ruined everything, and now he had given everything up for me.

For me.

What was I trying to protect my heart from? From happiness, it seemed…

I buried my face in his chest, sobbing and listening to the beat of his heart——the heart he'd pledged to me. His uncle Garth was right. Crisis reveals character, and with all I had put him through, the real Bill had been revealed to me.

"I'm sorry I put you through all this. It's just that after——"

"Shush, little one, it's all right. You can tell me later. I haven't done anything I didn't choose to do. Right now all I want is you by my side."

"But I cost you the company."

"I told you, if that's the price, I don't care. All that matters to me is having you. I love you, Lauren Marie Zumwalt."

"I love you too, but what if you resent me later for all of this?"

He clasped his hands around mine, holding the medallion once more. "Remember what I said. I promise that will never happen, and you know I always keep my promises."

I jabbed him in the ribs. "Yeah, even if it means turning into a popsicle."

"Not my smartest move, but a promise is a promise." He fished into his pocket and held out my engagement ring. "I want you to take this back… Please."

Silently I offered my ring finger.

He slid it back in place——where it belonged.

I wrapped my arms behind his neck and kissed him. Our lips melded together, our tongues stroking and dueling as each reacquainted itself with the other. His hair smelled of the strawberry shampoo in my shower, and he tasted salty from the tears, now both of our tears. He held me tight and then tighter. We sat like that, rocking back and forth for minutes, groping each other.

I eventually pulled loose and bit his earlobe playfully. "Your turn for a rubdown, BD. Lie down before I punish you."

He whipped off his polo and lay on the couch on his stomach.

"And after this, baby, I'm giving you your front rub."

I wiped away the tears. "Promises, promises," I said as I spanked him. "Now roll over on your back and stop complaining."

He rolled onto his back, a grin on his face.

I went to the kitchen and brought back a towel, and hidden inside it, the can of whipped cream.

"Put this under you." I gave him the towel and hid the whipped cream from sight. I took off my top and my bra.

He complied without a complaint.

I undid his belt and zipper and pulled down his pants and his boxer briefs, releasing his cock, which flopped heavily against his belly as his smile grew.

He had gone through so much for me, given up so much for me. I was going to give him back all that I could tonight.

I lifted his cock and kissed the tip. I gently sucked and started to take it into my mouth as he looked down at me. I put both hands on the shaft and moved them in unison with my mouth to groans from Bill that told me I was doing it right. I pulled the whipped cream can up from the floor.

His eyes bulged.

I squirted some over the length of his cock and proceeded to lick it off. I did this a few times more to moans from *my man*. I coated his balls and licked them too as I stroked his solid cock. I pulled and stroked faster and with a tighter grip, squeezing him just below the crown. I licked the tip as seductively as I could manage as I kept jerking him off.

"You need to get on, baby. I'm not going to last."

"What, a big guy like you, and you have no stamina?"

"You're killing me here, SP."

He had almost always made me come with his mouth or his fingers before he made love to me, giving me a track record of two orgasms to his one. Tonight, it was my turn to change the math.

"You need to come for me, BD. Then we're going to see how fast you can get hard again."

I hoped that was a challenge he would like.

The light in his eyes said it all. He fondled my breasts as I kept working his cock with my tongue and mouth and both hands until he arched his back and his legs went stiff, lifting his hips. I took him in my mouth as he lost it and shot his load of musky cum. I had never swallowed before, but *Cosmo* said guys thought that was hot. I looked up at his face as I swallowed it all and licked my lips.

His face told the story. A mixture of lust and love greeted me. *Cosmo* was right.

I pulled off my pants and straddled him. I slid my wet folds over his length and used my hand to guide him into me, taking all of him in one movement. I was so wet and so hungry for him. He wasn't as hard as before, but he was hard enough.

I did most of the work, riding him slowly at first, then faster, up and down and gliding forward and back, climbing my own hill of pleasure as he filled me again and again. I moved my hand around behind me to stroke his balls, careful to be gentle.

Slowly, he started to thrust with me and guide my hips with his hands as he got harder again. He put his thumb to my clit in his signature move for this position. The pressure on my nub each time I moved down on him started to send me over the edge.

I'd dreamed of this last night, I knew I had. The thought brought me quickly to my climax as my eyes squeezed shut, the starlights came, and the intense waves broke over me again and again. My core clamped down around him.

I had slowed down as I came, but I started moving again. I was going to make him come again. I knew I could do it. I could tell by his tension that he was getting closer. I grabbed the base of his cock and squeezed it with Sandy's ring hold as I rode him, following the guiding of his hands. I leaned over and brushed my breasts against his chest until he tensed and finally yelled out, pulling me fully down onto him as he found his release. I pressed my chest down on his, feeling the pulse of his cock in my pussy.

I was back with my man, and he was mine, all mine.

At two in the morning and then again at sunrise, he showed me the meaning of stamina. I had reached another triple. Whoever said makeup sex was the best didn't know the half of it.

CHAPTER 44

Bill

Lauren and I finished the week at the cabin, just the two of us —talking, walking, cooking, and sipping wine in front of the fire. I'd especially relished cooking meals with Lauren, a different recipe every time. She would pick them out, and we would shop together for the items we needed and share the cooking experience.

It was tricky at first. I had been independent for so long, but it was good to do this together, the two of us. She made me laugh. Occasionally, she threw food, and I would throw some back.

I hated for it to end, but she said we needed to go back to the real world. She wanted to stop in to see her brother now that his isolation period had ended. I arranged for a flatbed tow to take her car back, so she rode shotgun with me. The whole trip, I reveled in the random glints of sunlight off the diamond in her engagement ring, which she was wearing again. That ring made her mine. Again, and forever.

When we returned to my condo, I opened the door and walked

to the fridge. My place felt a bit alien after the rustic mountain cabin.

Lauren dropped her bags inside the door. "Did you arrange for somebody to feed your fish?"

"No, I didn't think of that. They would probably appreciate some." I pointed. "The food is over there on the counter."

She retrieved the can and shook a little into the top of the tank. The fish started feeding voraciously at the surface.

I pulled two beers from the fridge and popped the top on the first one. "Beer?"

"Sure." She peered into the tank. "Hey, how long are you going to keep these stupid phones in here?"

"Until I feel like I don't need to be reminded about the sharks out there anymore."

"You never really told me the story about the girl before Barbie."

I put my beer down and carried the other to her. "She came to the restaurant a few times, trying to pick me up, and I fell for it. When we got back here, she set her phone on the shelf in video mode, expecting that I wouldn't notice."

"You think she meant to blackmail you?"

"I assume that was the plan, but she didn't get the chance, luckily. I caught on before we did anything and kicked her out."

She took a drink of her beer. "You sure can pick 'em."

"Tell me about it." I hugged her and kissed the crown of her head. "Not a problem anymore, SP. I've got my girl."

She pulled back. "It's not fair to use that if you won't tell me what it means."

"Use what?"

"SP."

"If anyone asks, it means *snuggle pet*."

She smiled and hugged me again.

I kissed her forehead. "But between you and me, it means *sweet pussy*."

She pulled away and punched my shoulder. "Pervert."

"I prefer connoisseur," I responded.

She blushed and added more food to the fish tank.

"Do you want to borrow the car to go see Brandon?" I asked.

"No thanks. I think I'll wait until the morning. Visiting hours are almost over for the day." She picked her phone up off my desk, where it had stayed these several weeks, and turned it on.

I had gotten so used to not having a cell at the lake that I'd forgotten I needed to buy another until now.

"Twenty-three voicemails. You believe it?" she asked.

"You're a popular girl."

She scrolled through the list. "Fifteen from Sandy, one from Mr. Benson, and the rest I don't recognize."

She listened to them as I unpacked my things and got a load of laundry ready, as well as a bag for the dry cleaners. She was still listening when I got back.

"You know, Mr. Benson really is a sweetie," she said. "Catch this: he said I had to be dumber than a doorknob to not want to marry you, and if I needed him to explain why, I should give him a call."

"The old bird has a way with words, doesn't he? You want to call him and tell him problem solved?"

"Hey, you got some messages too, on the answering machine. Want me to play 'em?"

"Sure, I'll be right in."

The first few were routine. I had a prescription ready at the pharmacy. My dry cleaning had been waiting a week—did I want them to deliver it? My brothers and my sister had called to check in on me more than once.

"Your brothers are so nice. I wish Brandon was like that," Lauren said after listening to the second call from Stephen.

A next message was from Constance, saying they would keep trying, but they were still coming up empty on the search for Lauren. Did I want to continue the surveillance at Brandon's clinic?

She giggled. "I think maybe it's time to tell them you found me."

Then came the surprise. The next message was Constance's

boss, Brian Hanson. "Some very interesting information has turned up on the Lindroth surveillance. Look at images number 141 and 142 and the notes that go with them. Call me when you have had time to review them."

"Now that sounds intriguing," Lauren said as she went to my briefcase. "I wonder what she's been up to." She pulled the laptop from my bag.

I wasn't so interested. "I don't care anymore. I'm out of the company and done with her. She's Liam and Garth's problem now."

"Don't you want to see what they found on the Ice Queen? I do. Anyway, you can pass it on to your uncle, if it will help him."

She opened the machine and started it up. A minute later, we were perusing the folder and found the pictures Hanson had mentioned. Lauren expanded the first picture to full screen, then the second.

"I know those two," she shrieked. "That's Mall Barbie, and the other one—she's one of the Slut Sisters."

I didn't have a good recollection of that evening, but she could have been the girl I'd left behind the night of Dad's accident when Lauren had shown up. The other was for sure Katya from Pasadena who'd called herself Monica, the first to donate her phone to the fish tank.

"A what sister?" I asked. Sheila could be seen meeting with both of these sharks.

"The Slut Sisters are a pair of piranhas who prowl the Bucket every now and then, picking up guys, and Sandy and I always guessed they might be pros, if you know what I mean."

"The fish tank phones are from those two." My blood began to boil. Why had Sheila met with the phone sharks?

The notes attached to the photos said they had identified one of the women as Katya Droznik of Pasadena and had tracked a five-thousand-dollar payment to her from Sheila. They were still working to identify Barbie.

Sheila had been behind the blackmail attempts.

I could barely keep it together. "I don't know how, but I'm going to make her pay." The English language needed a new word for her, one a hell of a lot stronger than *bitch*.

CHAPTER 45

Lauren

After discovering his stepmother's attempts to trap him with those two whores, Bill was livid. It took him quite a while to cool down. Eventually he left for the phone store to replace the one that had gone swimming in the lake.

I perused some of the other information the detectives had gathered while watching the Ice Queen, and I continued going through the messages on Bill's answering machine, hoping for another tidbit.

Ten messages later, the voice on the machine was Uncle Garth's.

The message brought a smile to my lips, and I played it again before making the call.

~

Bill

. . .

UN-FUCKING-BELIEVABLE. SHEILA HAD USED THOSE GIRLS TO SET ME up, and I'd only escaped by luck.

At the phone store, they took my name when I walked in. The screen said I was fourth in line to be helped. I couldn't stand still, I was so mad.

The woman with a teenager trying out the new models against the wall shot me a concerned look.

I walked back over to the guy who'd taken my name by the door. "The name's Bill. I'll be right outside when you get to me."

He nodded, and I paced the sidewalk, trying to come up with a way to get back at Sheila. I couldn't think of anything that didn't involve physical violence.

An hour later, I had a replacement phone in my pocket, but no urge to use it. A little while after that I rode the elevator back up to the condo, only slightly less pissed off than when I'd left. Upstairs, I stopped in the hallway before opening my door.

My anger at Sheila clearly made me difficult to be around right now, and Lauren didn't deserve that. No, she deserved the better version of me. One, two, three large, calming breaths later, I let myself in.

Lauren rose from the couch with a glass of what looked like orange juice in her hand. "Connected to the world again?"

I nodded. "Yeah." It just wasn't a world I wanted to be connected to right now.

"Good," she said. "You're going to need it."

"All I need is a stiff drink—or three, or four, or five."

She put her hand on mine as I lifted the bottle of eighty-proof liquid pain eraser. "Not so fast, Mr. Covington. You have to have your wits about you."

I pulled my hand free and poured myself a double. "Maybe tomorrow."

She put her arms around me. "Before you drink that, you need to listen to something."

"I think we should go back to the mountains." I smelled the alluring aroma of the amber liquid before downing it. Everything else could wait. Tomorrow we could retreat back to the tranquility of the lake.

"Please," she said as she tightened her hug.

The word undid me. I'd promised her the world, and if it was important to her, I needed to fight through the anger and listen. "Anything for you." I put the glass down.

She dragged me to the other side of the room. "It's not over yet. Listen to this." She pressed play on my old-style answering machine.

Uncle Garth's voice came through the tiny speaker. "I fervently hope that when you receive this message you have been successful in convincing Lauren of your intentions."

I looked over and smiled at my fiancée.

"Since you were unable to attend the annual meeting, Steven and I agreed not to attend either. The result is that the meeting had to be postponed ten days for lack of a quorum. Sheila was, shall we say, unhappy. Please get in touch when you return. We must discuss your brother Liam."

I settled down into the desk chair. This was a shock.

She pointed her cell phone at me. "Liam hasn't won yet. You're still the CEO. You can save Covington."

"I promised to give it up for you, and I meant it." I didn't renege on promises, not ever.

She threw her leg over and straddled me.

Resisting the urge to cup the luscious breasts right in front of me, I put my hands on her hips.

"That was a marvelous gesture, but I still have things I want to accomplish at Covington," she said. "And I don't think you're done yet either."

"You mean?"

"I say we fight it, or did I agree to marry a wuss?" She cocked an eyebrow.

That gave me the out from my promise, and besides, calling me a wuss wasn't going to stand. "Liam isn't going to know what hit him." I held my hand out. "You're sitting on my phone."

She handed over her phone, and I dialed my uncle and put it on speaker.

"Lauren, I am so glad you called," he answered.

"Uncle Garth, it's Bill," I corrected him.

"William, I am glad to see that you are back. First off, were you successful?"

"She's sitting right here." I didn't need to add that she was on my lap. "And, along with letting me use her phone, she's wearing her engagement ring again."

"Hi, Uncle Garth," Lauren said.

"Hello, Lauren, and welcome to the family…again."

"Thank you," she said. "Bill and I just listened to your message."

"What is it about Liam that we should know?" I interjected. After I spoke, I realized I'd shifted to *we* instead of *I*, cementing Lauren and me as a team in my mind.

"It seems Sheila has taken advantage of him," he answered. "She managed to get his wife into a drug trial for her condition, and used that to extract some promises from your brother."

This was not good, because Liam would consider even a promise to Sheila as a commitment that couldn't be broken.

"Such as?" I asked.

"It seems your stepmother is in desperate need of a cash infusion."

"But what's-his-name owns, like, half of Sweden," Lauren pointed out.

"That may be," Uncle Garth said. "But he seems to have locked down her spending more than she cares for. The long and short of it is that Liam agreed to sell to Four Corners when he became CEO, so that Sheila could convert her shares to cash."

I figured that sealed it. "Then it's over."

"Not so fast, William. This is all dependent on Liam ascending to the CEO position at the next meeting, and Lauren and I have a suggestion."

I scrunched my face at my fiancée. "I'm listening."

Lauren shifted in my lap. "Uncle Garth and I were running

some numbers." My woman had been busy in my absence. "There are some ways we can affect the vote outcome..." She winked at me. "...so that you stay CEO, and the Ice Queen gets the screwing she deserves."

My eyes lit up. Sheila definitely deserved to be fucked over, and an hour later, we had a plan.

I made the call to Hanson, followed by one to Lloyd Benson.

CHAPTER 46

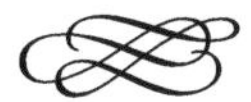

Bill

THE NEXT MORNING, LAUREN ENTERED THE COVINGTON BUILDING with me at a quarter to nine. Gus said good morning, as he always had. Not much had changed.

Except that we'd finalized our strategy last night.

A week ago, I'd thought I wouldn't be back here again—except for an exit interview. Instead, today was a day to reclaim my legacy, my family's legacy.

Upstairs, Judy greeted me as I emerged from the elevator. She gave me a quick, but emotional hug. "They're waiting for you in the conference room."

I pulled open the conference room door for Lauren.

Garth got up from his chair, and Lloyd Benson rounded the table faster than I thought possible for a man of his age.

"Well, the prodigal son returns," he said, shaking my hand. "I told you you'd made a good choice with this one, didn't I, Billy?" He gestured to Lauren.

"That you did, sir."

Uncle Garth shook my hand. "Welcome back. We have the papers ready."

"Let's get it done," I told them.

"You got quite the little filly here." Benson canted his head at Lauren. "If'n I wasn't already married, I'd steal her away from you."

I nodded, and Lauren smiled, but rolled her eyes. We all knew a good woman when we saw one. I signed the lines marked for me with little sticky arrows and exchanged my set with the ones Benson had finished.

A HALF HOUR LATER, I PULLED OPEN THE DOOR TO A DIFFERENT conference room.

Sheila's face shifted to surprise as Lauren and I entered, but she composed herself quickly, continuing her tirade against poor Uncle Garth.

"I am not going to put up with this a second time, Garth. You already made me cancel my trip to Prague by putting off the meeting last week. Now don't tell me you have another excuse to call off the shareholders' meeting."

She pivoted to me. "William, why, how wonderful to see you." She embraced me as if I actually mattered to her, which was a crock, for sure. "I was told you had left the company."

She didn't say a thing to Lauren, and she not very subtly checked our hands for wedding rings, which we did not have.

Garth continued as we took our seats across from her. "Sheila, I explained that I was called away at the last moment, and we could not convene the meeting last week without a quorum."

"In a rat's ass, Garth. You could have conferenced in," Sheila responded, her face red and her tone shrill.

Garth set her up for me. "Sheila, we are going to have the meeting in the boardroom in a few minutes, but first, you need to hear what William has to say."

That settled her for the moment.

"I'm listening," she said, her voice dripping with disdain.

"Sheila, we have some things for you to sign before the meeting." I slid the first papers I had brought across the table.

She hated it when I called her by her first name, and it showed in her brow. She read the top sheet and quickly slid the papers back to me. "I will not sign this. Now, let's get on with the meeting, Garth." She stood and pointed to Lauren. "And what is she doing here?"

"Sheila, only when William is finished, so just sit down" was Garth's firm response.

She huffed and took her seat.

"Sheila, I've talked with Liam, and he explained what you did to coerce him into marrying Roberta."

She interrupted me. "I just showed him the best way to get that poor girl into the drug trial for her condition."

My turn to surprise her again. "Yes, she needed insurance for the transplant and the trial, but I would have arranged that for them. He said you also told him you, and only you, could get her into the trial, and you wouldn't do that until he married her."

"Well, I am on very good terms with the doctor." She started to fidget in her chair.

I had her now. "I talked with Dr. Willhaven. His trial is still open to any patients wanting to participate. All they have to do is apply. It's less than half full so far. You didn't do a thing for Liam, and he knows that now."

"So? I tried to help my son. What does that have to do with this?" She tapped the paper she had refused to sign.

I extracted the enlargements of the two photos from my folder and slid them across to her. "Do you perhaps remember these meetings?"

A very brief look of concern crossed her face, quickly replaced by a smug smile. "No, I don't recall, but lots of people approach me. I can't be expected to remember them all."

I leaned forward. "Perhaps you remember paying these women five thousand dollars each?"

She remained smug. "I did no such thing." She huffed in exasperation.

Next I brought copies of the women's bank statements from the folder and slid them across the table . "Perhaps this will jog your memory."

"I don't recognize these."

"They're the bank statements from these two women, showing the deposits of your checks. Photocopies of the checks are attached, if you care to look at them."

She didn't look at the backup pages. We had her cornered. "I must have hired them to help me while I was in town. I hire lots of help. I don't remember."

I took out the last two items from my folder. "To refresh your memory, we have notarized affidavits signed by each of them." I slid them over.

The blood drained from her face as she started to read.

"Sheila, you have a choice to make here," I told her. "Garth has called a friend from the district attorney's office to join us. We can either show him how you conspired with these girls to blackmail me, or…" I paused. "Or you can sign the papers and never darken the doors of this building again, and Garth will instead tell his friend he just wanted a little free legal advice. We will rip up these documents. Now refresh me, Uncle Garth, what are the penalties involved here?"

Garth tapped the table. "Ten to fifteen on each count in state prison, and the federal charges on top of that for wire fraud—"

"Stop," Sheila interrupted. "Son," she pleaded to me.

I clenched my teeth. "I am not, and never have been, your son."

Her tone was contrite. "William, I was just trying to help Liam."

I still hadn't replaced my watch. "Lauren, please check your watch. Sheila, you have one minute to decide."

"Okay, okay, okay. I'll sign, but only if I have your word that those will be destroyed." She gestured to the other documents.

"You have it," I replied as I slid the paper back over to her.

She signed the top one and then the second. She stopped after she read the third. The top piece of paper retracted her objections to my father's will. The second was a power of attorney giving me the right to vote her shares as I saw fit in perpetuity, and saying she was to have no dealings with the company, its subsidiaries, or future parent corporations.

"This says I am gifting half of my shares in the company to Liam. You can't make me do that." She huffed.

I waited for her to calm down. I knew this would be the hard one because for *her*, it was always about the money.

"You said you wanted to help Liam." I paused. "Or you can always use the extra shares to buy spa treatments in prison."

"You asshole," she retorted as she signed the final paper and threw it in my direction. She stormed toward the door, but paused. "At least my Liam will be running the company." She slammed the door behind her.

Garth had a broad smile as he rose. "That went rather well."

"At least we didn't have any bloodshed," Lauren responded.

I was elated. I had to kiss my fiancée.

"You did a great job organizing this," I told her. "I can't thank you enough."

"One more meeting to go," she replied, squeezing my hand.

JUST A FEW MINUTES LATER, WE HAD SETTLED INTO THE BOARD ROOM. Sheila had left the building since I was casting her votes, and probably also because she'd been humiliated. Judy was keeping the minutes, and Uncle Garth called the shareholders' meeting to order.

"Let the minutes reflect that all the major shareholders are represented. Mr. William Covington is representing Mrs. Sheila Lindroth by duly witnessed power of attorney. Mr. Steven Covington is attending via telephone, and is also representing Miss Katherine Covington by duly witnessed power of attorney. Mr. Patrick Covington is attending via telephone. We have a quorum. The first order of business is the proposed sale of forty million shares to the Benson Group Incorporated. All those in favor?"

Uncle Garth personally, Liam, Patrick, Steven, and I all voted in favor, and Uncle Garth abstained on behalf of the family trust.

"All opposed?" Garth asked, but the answer was obvious since there was nobody else to vote. "Let the record reflect that the measure passed unanimously."

Judy scribbled away busily.

"Judy, would you please ask Mr. Benson to join us now? Thank you."

Lloyd Benson came in and shook hands all around the table, and he greeted those on speakerphone.

Uncle Garth continued. "The next item of business is the election of the chief executive officer. On behalf of the Covington Family Trust, I vote sixty-five million shares for Liam Quigley."

Liam was next. "I vote twenty-five million shares for William Covington."

Steven voted by phone ten million shares for me, and Patrick, Garth, and I voted another thirty million shares for me.

"Mr. Benson?" Garth asked.

Lloyd Benson scratched his chin for a moment. "I think Liam would make an excellent CEO." My heart stopped. "So, I'll vote my forty million shares…" He paused. "For Billy Covington." He laughed. "Gotcha again, son, didn't I?"

He sure had. I nearly had a heart attack. "No, sir," I lied. "Because if you had reneged on a deal with my fiancée, she'd kick your ass all the way to China."

He laughed so hard I was afraid we would end up calling the paramedics. "Ain't that the truth, Billy?"

"Bill," I corrected.

I was CEO again, and in a position to fulfill my promise to Dad, and it was all due to Lauren. She was the one who'd figured out that if we sold the shares to Benson as the first order of business, the trust shares wouldn't matter in the voting. And the added bonus of giving half of Sheila's shares to Liam had also been her idea.

Dad had been right. I went with my gut giving up the company to chase Lauren, and it had been the right thing to do. Money, power, control—none of it mattered when weighed against the love of a good woman. As I had told her, she completed me. Without her I was nothing.

I trusted her, and once I earned her trust, we became a team, a partnership in truest meaning of the term and ready to face our future together.

~

LAUREN (THREE WEEKS LATER)

"AHH, WILLIAM, DAAAAHLING. ARE YOU READY?" MISS BROADCHEST exclaimed as she exited the elevator and spied the four of us: Judy, Bill, Jason, and me. Today her nails were baby blue, once again matching her heels.

Jason picked up Bill's bag.

I gave my man a quick kiss. "Don't get into any trouble now."

"Be back as soon as I can," Bill told me. "And Judy, don't let Uncle Garth boss you around."

Judy merely nodded. There was not a chance in hell that she was taking any shit from his uncle.

In seconds, Miss Broadchest, Jason, and my Bill were in the elevator to start a trip Bill had refused to explain. "A secret project" was as much as I had been able to get out of him.

The elevator door closed, and Judy turned to me. "I don't like that woman."

I didn't see the point in responding.

"And he didn't tell you where they're going, or how long they'd be?" she asked for the third time this morning.

"Nope." It did sound silly to admit that. "He asked me to trust him, and I do."

Bill had shown me the value of trust, and so I did.

EPILOGUE

LOVE IS LIKE THE WIND, YOU CAN'T SEE IT BUT YOU CAN FEEL IT. -NICOLAS SPARKS

LAUREN

"...FROM THIS DAY FORWARD, FOR BETTER, FOR WORSE, FOR RICHER, FOR poorer, in sickness and health, to love and to cherish, until death do you part?"

I held my breath. I had dreamed of this moment since I was a little girl, and now it was coming true. A few months ago, I'd feared I might never hear these words.

It was a beautiful, sunny March day, bright and warm, with a sea breeze from the harbor.

"I do," Bill said.

Bill's loving eyes held my gaze as the reverend repeated the wedding vows for me, and I slid the ring on his finger.

"Yes, I do," I responded with a squeak.

I was so lost in the moment, I could barely wait for the next words. My hands shook as Bill clasped them inside his.

"By the powers vested in me by the great State of California and our Lord above, I now pronounce you man and wife. You may kiss the bride."

With that, Bill held me—not in one of his bear hugs, but gently

—as our lips met for the first time as husband and wife. He tasted of spearmint as his tongue sought mine. We held the kiss to the *oohs* and whistles of the crowd as he dipped me back farther and farther. I melted in his arms, those same strong arms that had hugged me so powerfully that first night at the hospital.

"I present to you Mr. and Mrs. William Covington," the reverend announced to the crowd assembled at the stern of the Queen Mary.

Our engagement had finally come to an end on a lovely spring day as we overlooked Long Beach Harbor. Bill hadn't wanted to wait this long, but this was the perfect location and the ideal weather. He'd relented when I told him I didn't want to chance the winter rains.

I put my hand momentarily to the huge sapphire necklace as we stepped down from the raised wedding platform.

The necklace had been Bill's present to me a mere hour before the ceremony started. It had belonged to the late Duchess of Westbrook. Bill said he couldn't resist the way it complemented my eyes.

I was going to have to stop calling Cynthia Powell Miss Broadchest. It had turned out that Cynthia had dated the Duke's son at some point, and Bill had only been able to procure the gorgeous necklace with her help. They'd arranged it on the mysterious trip they'd taken together months ago—the trip he hadn't been willing to discuss until today.

The Benson financing had ensured the financial stability of Covington Industries, allowing Bill to spend more time at his restaurant. The Farm Pod project was full speed ahead, and Bill had put me in charge until Liam got back from the East Coast. Juan, Paul, and the rest of the crew were great to work with, and Lloyd Benson's investment in the project had allowed us to pick up our development pace. We would launch nationwide two months from now.

As the sun moved closer to the horizon, the congratulations from friends and coworkers seemed like they might go on forever.

Liam shook Bill's hand vigorously. "Congrats, brother. You sure are one lucky guy."

Liam had joined us for a few days, but his wife, Roberta, was still in Boston in treatment and hadn't flown out, which was worrisome.

"Don't I know it." Bill squeezed me tight.

Liam smirked. "I just don't know that you deserve her is all." He laughed and punched Bill on the shoulder.

Bill laughed. "Well, shorty, some of us just get lucky."

Liam then gave me a hug and whispered in my ear, "Take good care of him. He's a good man."

"What did he say?" Bill asked as he leaned over in my direction.

"He said he's not short where it counts," I said softly.

Bill had filled me in on Liam's favorite comeback line at the cabin.

"I did not," Liam protested, his face turning bright red.

After Liam walked off, Bill tried again. "What did he say?"

"He told me he couldn't not help his mother, so he gave Sheila some money." It made sense. Liam was showing compassion, and no matter how evil I thought she was, she was still Liam's mother. Her plan to ruin Bill and cost ten thousand people their jobs in the process had been thwarted, and that's what counted.

My first dance with Bill was mesmerizing. Enveloped in his arms, I forgot everything else as the music slowed and the room evaporated. He and I were alone in the clouds. I pressed myself closer to him, fusing our bodies together as we swayed. His musky smell with a hint of spice filled my nostrils. I moved my right hip and leg forward, feeling the bulge in the crotch of his tux. My BD. The song was a long one, but I was still disappointed when it ended.

My father wasn't here, thank God. I didn't know if he was alive and didn't care. Old man Benson had walked me down the aisle and claimed the second dance. Bill kindly danced with Mrs. Benson.

Bill's uncle Garth joined us later and took us aside. "I thought you might be interested to know, Lauren, that the information you provided the police allowed them to run a sting on those women who were working your local bar."

"The Slut Sisters?"

"Yes, and they have got them dead to rights on several felony charges."

Today might have been a day for being magnanimous, but I wasn't feeling it where they were concerned. They deserved to have the book thrown at them for what they'd attempted with my husband.

Just then, Bill's youngest brother, Steven, approached. He was finishing his law degree at Columbia this year, and I hadn't met him or Bill's other brother, Patrick, before last night's rehearsal. He was just as tall as Bill, but leaner, with a baby face by comparison, clean-shaven and slighter in build than either Bill or Liam.

Bill greeted him with a hug and slap on the back. "You're looking a little pale there, Stevie. You ought to move back here where the sun shines when you finish up. We could use a Covington with a law degree out here."

"And work with my big brothers? No way. Three stooges are enough at one company."

Sandy arrived with Carlos in tow. She wore the strapless pink bridesmaid dress she'd helped pick out.

"How's it hangin', BD?" she asked.

Carlos towered over her because she had ditched her heels. It was unusual for Sandy to stay with any of her studs for this long, but she was clearly smitten. She liked to joke that he was the only model she knew who was smart enough to use a wristwatch with hands on it.

"Good to see you too, Sandra."

Sandy's smile only dimmed for a moment. She hated her full name.

"Bet you're looking forward to tonight, huh, girl?" She nudged me.

Sandy was an expert at making me blush.

"What bride wouldn't?" I squeezed Bill and looked up into his eyes.

"*B. D.*" She said slowly and with emphasis. "I think you got it covered."

She has no idea.

Then Sandy dragged Carlos off to the dance floor.

"Did you tell her what SP means?" Bill asked.

"No way. I'd never hear the end of it." I could feel my cheeks heat at the mention of his nickname for me.

"Would milady grace me with another dance?"

"Certainly, Sir Knight."

As we swayed to the music, I closed my eyes in the arms of my knight in shining armor, my everything.

"I love you, Mrs. Covington," he whispered in my ear.

"Love you more."

"Love you most."

As I closed my eyes again and pulled him tighter, I reveled in my good fortune. I'd survived Marissa, the boss from hell, to end up with the best boss in town, and the best husband I could have ever hoped for.

THE FOLLOWING PAGES START THE STORY OF BILL'S BROTHER STEVEN, and Emma, in **Chosen by the Billionaire**.

The youngest of the Covington clan, he avoided the family business to become a rarity, an honest lawyer.

She knows better than to trust a lawyer, any lawyer.

I HOPED YOUR ENJOYED READING ABOUT BILL AND LAUREN AS MUCH as I enjoyed writing about them.

SNEAK PEEK: CHOSEN BY THE BILLIONAIRE

Emma

"Just text me when you need to be rescued."

My heart fluttered.

That's all he said as he stood directly in my path and handed me his card. Piercing emerald green eyes appraised me with full, thick eyelashes, the kind that should be illegal for guys to have. Tall, dark, and handsome didn't begin to describe this hunk.

"Steven. Steven Carter, at your service." The words mesmerized me as I looked up to see them escape his kissable full lips that drew me like a magnet. I wasn't short, but he was well over six feet with shoulders broad enough to make Atlas envious and a chiseled jaw line to die for.

"From what?" I rasped, barely getting the words out. The dark-haired man blocking my way had me completely flustered. I had bumped into plenty of tall guys before, but right now, they all seemed like boys compared to this man. A real man. An eleven on the ten-point scale.

He nodded toward the dining area. "Your blind date, of course. You'll want to put that into your phone before you get back to your table, Miss...?"

I should have shouldered my way past him back to my table without a word, but I didn't have the willpower. I lied and used my favorite bar name. "Tiffany. Tiffany Case." All that awaited me at that table, after all, was boring Gordie.

In college, my girlfriends and I would use fake names when we went out so we wouldn't get stalked by the guys we met. I had tried a few Bond Girl names and settled on Tiffany Case. She was a redhead like me, and not as obvious as Pussy Galore. When I used my real name, Emma Watson, people didn't believe me anyway because they had seen *Harry Potter* and I looked nothing like her.

He licked his lips. "Tiffany. Lovely name. It suits you." Satisfied, he strode back into the dining area.

I had slipped up. Surprised by him, I had forgotten I was using Miranda Frost for my SuperSingles date tonight. I had to remember I was Miranda to Gordie and Tiffany to Steven.

Steven. I liked that name. The card was white with a gilded edge. Steven Carter and a phone number—nothing else. He had caught me on my second trip to the restroom. I couldn't stomach more than a half hour at a time with my date tonight. I lingered in the hallway for a moment as I fingered the card. Suddenly, tonight wasn't totally wasted. I added the stranger as a contact before stashing my phone back in my purse, along with the card. I pasted on a smile and made my way back to the table where Gordie was waiting anxiously to bore me to death on the topic of insurance.

"And the difference with whole life is…" I zoned out as he droned on, digging into my meal with the occasional nod.

Cardinelli's was an expensive place, and I was damned if I was going to leave without getting to finish my lasagna. I just had to tough out another half hour of how marvelous it was to sell insurance. Life, home, car, pet, mortuary, you name it, Gordie sold it. There was something to be said for getting into your work, but this was supposed to be a first date. I wasn't doing a second with Gordie.

From my seat, I could see my mysterious green-eyed rescuer over Gordie's shoulder, and he held up his phone with a questioning look. Gordie had no clue as I smiled at Steven. I took another bite of my lasagna. The quicker I got this date over with, the better.

My phone buzzed on the table with a text.

MEGAN: Home now

"If you need to answer that, I understand," Gordie said as I glanced at the message. That was sweet of him.

"It's just my sister telling me she got home okay."

Gordie smiled and put down his wine glass. "So is she checking to see if you need to be rescued from your date?"

Busted.

"No, we're good." He had guessed our code all right. If I didn't answer right away, she would call with an emergency that would give me an excuse to leave the restaurant. "She's just checking in." I texted her back.

ME: Ok

I put the phone down. "How's your Carbonara?" That settled Gordie down. I felt bad lying to him. He wasn't handsy, and he didn't seem like an axe murderer or anything, but he just couldn't help that he was less exciting than cold oatmeal. I flipped my ringer to silent mode and put the phone in my lap. Just one more thing to do.

At school, I had become an expert in texting under my desk without the teacher seeing, and now that was going to come in handy as I decided I felt more sorry for Gordie than anything else. I would amuse myself by texting the green-eyed hunk with the dark brown hair, even if he was sitting with that knock-dead gorgeous blonde.

ME: Not tonight thanks

He laughed with his date over Gordie's shoulder. And my

phone vibrated in my hand. Good thing it wasn't on the table anymore. Gordie kept rambling on as I nodded.

STEVEN CARTER: So you go for the low IQ type

When I chanced a peek, Steven was looking directly at me. I smiled at him over my date's shoulder as I typed my response. Gordie smiled back.

ME: Why say that?

STEVEN CARTER: Any guy who spends all night talking about himself without finding out what

Finding out what? Steven was right about talking all night. Gordie got that prize. A few seconds later, the answer appeared.

STEVEN CARTER: a beautiful woman like you has to say must have the brains of a mollusk

I giggled. Gordie smiled, happy that I'd found something he said amusing.

ME: It wouldn't be fair, and maybe I can learn something from him.

That was a stretch, more an outright lie. Maybe this was how Indian snake charmers did it. They talked to the cobras about insurance until they fell asleep. I called the waiter over and asked for some iced tea. *Need more caffeine, so I won't doze off.*

STEVEN CARTER: He's a moron - nothing else worth learning

"Don't you like the lasagna?" Gordie asked. He had noticed that I wasn't inhaling my food anymore.

I lied. "I was just letting it settle a bit. It's very good. There is just so much, and I need some tea to wash it down." I couldn't eat and text at the same time. I dropped my phone in my lap and started back attacking my meal.

A few minutes later, Gordie was filling me in on the intricacies of insuring homes against fire in the foothills when my phone vibrated again.

STEVEN CARTER: Tuesdays and Thursdays are the only days for a first date

I had chosen Tuesday evenings because my sister, Megan, made it her mission to come over on Monday nights to 'help me' go through the website candidates. She thought I needed help finding a suitable date. She was right about my needing help, but guys like Gordie were not the answer. There was a serious lack of candidates at the museum where I worked. Most of them were ancient enough to have sailed over on the *Mayflower*, except for Jonathon, and he was gay. I had finally agreed to try the SuperSingles website, and so far, the results had been pretty disappointing. Gordie was busy quoting automobile theft rate trends, so I had to entertain myself texting with Steven. Gordie had been talking so much that he hadn't gotten very far on his meal yet.

ME: Why?

STEVEN CARTER: Monday is no good - they only talk about the weekend games they watched

He had a point there.

STEVEN CARTER: Friday is out because they know you don't have work - they might expect a late-night treat

No argument from me. Megan and I had already ruled out weekend nights as not first date appropriate.

STEVEN CARTER: Wednesday, you will get some comment about wanting to hump you because it is hump day

I giggled because that had really happened to me once, and the guy actually thought it was funny. Gordie gave me a slightly puzzled look before he continued. He didn't think what he was saying was giggle-worthy. I guess loss ratios weren't meant to be funny.

STEVEN CARTER: Most important I'm here Tuesday and Thursday mostly

So the guy was here two nights a week. That would rack up some serious points on your credit card. I remembered seeing him here before. More than once, but he was always with that blonde knockout who was sitting with him again tonight. Some girls have all the luck. They have the looks, they get the good guys, and the rest of us are stuck with the Gordies of the world.

STEVEN CARTER: Better luck next time. Maybe number five is your lucky number

ME: What makes you think this is number four?

STEVEN CARTER: I can count

He was right. Gordie was my fourth SuperSingles date in as many weeks. I put my phone away and smiled at the implication.

He noticed me.

Gordie caught my smile and thought it was meant for him as he started to try to sell me on buying whole life insurance for myself. A half hour later, I passed on dessert and got out of the evening before I lost my sanity. Gordie was nice enough to pick up the check. He said it was deductible for him, but I thanked him sincerely nevertheless. Half of a big bill was still a lot for me.

Gordie gave the valet his ticket as we said goodbye and I walked toward my car. Valet parking was an extravagance I didn't need.

My mother always said, "You have to kiss a lot of frogs before you find your prince," but at least I got out of this evening without having to kiss this frog. On the way to my car, I took my phone out of my purse to call Megan and tell her I was heading home. It was still on silent, so I had missed the last text.

STEVEN CARTER: Have a nice evening Tiffany

I turned to look back at the valet stand, and he waved to me, his date standing at his side. I wondered what she thought of that. I waved back and dialed Megan.

Printed in Great Britain
by Amazon